SWORD OF

STONE

Sword of Stone

The Sword of Rhiannon

Melissa E. Beckwith

Cover design, book editing and formatting by
C.L. Cannon, www.fiction-atlas.com

Cover Art by Jackie Felix
https://jackiefelixart.deviantart.com/

Map by
Cornelia Yoder, www.corneliayoder.com

ISBN: 978-0-692-04794-1
10 9 8 7 6 5 4 3 2 1

Before you get lost in the enchanting world of *The Sword of Rhiannon*, pick up the spellbinding prequel to this thrilling epic fantasy series for FREE!

Click here to get Flight of the Raven for FREE:

http://eepurl.com/cOK495

CONTENTS

The lands and seas of
Ventra and Beaynid

To all my inspirationally talented cousins. You were my first playmates, my first best friends, and eternally all the best pieces of what makes me, me! I love you all.

CHAPTER ONE

A chill crept from the red waters
Boney fingers around dry throats
Blackness stopped the rhythmic beating
Morbid piles of death reached the sun
No one was safe
Those in wooden shacks or stone houses
Gave their last breath just the same

— Wasting Year; Rubi Jep

Clouds slithered over a full moon blocking the pale light, but he did not slow his horse. He pushed the animal harder as they careened down the road to Sona Tuath. The creature was lathered, and his breaths came in harsh grunts as sharp hooves cut through hardened dirt. The cold air turned to a soft mist, and then a lazy, May rain started to turn the road into mud. Rain dripped off his blond hair and down his neck, sending a shiver down his ridged spine.

Finally, the lights of Castle Sona Tuath came into view, and he pulled his horse to an abrupt stop at the rise of the hill. Giant torches burned across the battlements and he could see the shadowy figures of the Castle Guard as they stood at their posts in the rain. In the darkness, the castle looked like a monster that was tumbling from the womb of the mountain from which it had been carved. His horse sidestepped and pulled at the reins as the rain began to fall harder. He could not tell if it was the rain or the haunting vision of Sona Tuath that chilled his bones. It still was not home to him.

A flash of lightning tore through a black sky, illuminating the entire castle. He could see lights burning high up in the Tower of Roses—the Queen's Tower. He knew it was time to move on and quickly led his horse to the city's main gate. When the young guard saw that his king had returned, he promptly yelled for the gate to be opened. Flath galloped his mount through the slick cobbled streets of the city and up the long, curvy road to the castle gate. He was admitted without trouble, hurried to the courtyard and handed his mount to a stable boy. He entered through the back, startling a dozing servant and then rushed through the large kitchen. The cooks were busily starting to bake the morning's bread. His stomach growled at the wafting aroma, but he did not tarry. He raced through the long corridors of Castle Sona Tuath, water dripping from the hem of his coat only to be soaked up by the thick rugs under his muddy boots. The smell of grease hung in the air—this part of the castle housed the servant's quarters, where expensive, aromatic candles were not burned. Sputtering candlelight led him to a narrow stairwell which he quickly climbed, taking two or three stairs at a time.

Flath Basilias entered the queen's apartments to find it aglow with light. Unlike below, the scent of lavender and honey permeated the huge sitting area. The queen's ladies-in-waiting were standing near the mouth of the fireplace, their slight figures and frilly dresses casting monster-like shadows on the wall. They looked up when he entered, and for a few moments, the only sound in the room was the crackle of the fire.

One of the girls finally approached him, peering deep into his dark face as if assessing whether or not to let him enter. "Your Highness," she gasped and dipped into a deep curtsy which sent the others doing likewise as if they were all connected by an invisible string.

Flath took a deep breath, fighting exasperation. "You may all leave now. The Queen will not need you tonight." His voice was hoarse and colder than he intended.

However, he did not care what his wife's ladies-in-waiting thought of him. In a flurry of skirts and hushed words, the girls left the queen's chambers.

Flath opened the doors to Jocelyn's bedchamber and walked in slowly, not knowing what to expect and feeling more than a little apprehensive. The windows were closed tight, and an angry fire raged in a large fireplace. Candles and torches lit up every corner of the room, bathing it in reddish, glowing light. The heavy drapes on Jocelyn's bed stood open, and he could see the girl lying motionless amongst dozens of pillows. Flath removed his cloak and threw it onto an ornately carved wooden chair in the corner. Water still dripped from his hair onto his red and white overtunic.

Laura Felden looked up as he entered. "Sire, what took you so long to arrive?" she asked sternly.

He smiled at her. "The rain has made the roads treacherous, Surgeon Felden. One wrong step and my poor mount could have broken a leg ... or worse."

She shook her head and turned back to Jocelyn, who moaned softly. Laura mopped her brow with a cloth and pointed to a stack of clean linens, "Bring those to me, Janice," Her young assistant jumped to the task. Flath walked over to the fire and warmed his hands. He took a deep, breath and watched as the flames licked the blackened stone. Jocelyn cried out weakly, her thin voice drowning in the thick draperies of her bed.

He turned to Janice, "you may leave now," he said evenly. Laura looked up but held her tongue until the girl was gone.

"I need help, my lord. Unless you plan on helping me pull this babe from her royal womb!" she scolded.

Flath came closer and looked down at his wife as she lay naked and shivering. Her face was shiny with sweat and as pale as the moon. Pieces of her brown hair stuck to her cheek and neck. Her huge belly moved, and she groaned as if the child would tear itself from her body at any moment. Flath had a feeling of unease and resisted the impulse to step back. Laura looked up at Flath and leaned in closer. "She's too weak to birth this babe, and I do not think she will live through the night. I am sorry," she finished in almost a whisper. "The babe must live if it tosses and turns so much in her belly." It was a question as much as a statement.

"Aye, as much as I can tell." Flath looked back at Jocelyn and felt a stab of guilt. He had no love for the girl; their marriage had been one of diplomatic necessity. However, it pained him to see her suffer so. Her life would be over at ten and six—she had barely begun to live—yet he could not force himself to feel sorrow. He wished he could summon something more than fleeting guilt. He was disgusted with his lack of concern for his young wife.

He walked over to the window and opened the shutter to stare out into the night. He found his mind wandering to thoughts of Rhiannon Kossi—the dark-haired Empress of Ventra—a nation of fierce warriors far to the north. He wondered what she was doing at that moment.

"Your Majesty!" Laura exclaimed, and

Flath turned around. Jocelyn began to twitch, just a shiver at first, but then her limbs and head began to shake violently. The queen gasped for breath, and her eyes opened to show nothing but white. Flath ran to the bed, feeling utterly helpless. He knew the girl was dying. Suddenly the convulsions stopped, and Jocelyn lay motionless. "By the gods," Laura whispered, then quickly grabbed a small cutting tool. "Flath! Go to the cauldron and bring me the towels soaking in the water." The surgeon dropped his title and used his first name. He thought it was to get his attention. He had not realized he had frozen and was just staring at the dead girl. "Go on now," she gently prodded. "And wring them out first," she called after his retreating figure.

Flath plunged his hands into the hot water, dimly aware of the pain, suddenly overcome with fear for the infant's fate. Quickly he wrung out the towels and obediently brought them back to the surgeon. He gasped at the sight of the red flap of Jocelyn's belly lying open, blood soaking into bed linens. Laura gently cut through the glistening purple skin that cocooned the tiny child. Without taking her eyes from her work, she reached a hand out, and Flath gave her one of the towels, which she used to promptly dab the blood away from her long, straight slice. Quickly she dropped her cutting tool and parted the slimy blood-engorged skin to reveal a shriveled purple babe. Gently she lifted the infant from his mother's body. Laura turned the babe over then stuck her finger in the silent little mouth and dug out red mucus letting the child take its first breath. It whimpered but did not cry vigorously.

Sweat began to bead at Flath's brow and run down his back. He wanted to take a deep breath, but the air was heavy with blood and the dull smell of spilled innards, mixed with the heady aroma of the scented candles. Flath's stomach turned, and he fought not to vomit. He had seen so much worse on the battlefield, why was this thing so disturbing to him? He did not love this woman or her son, why should he care?

Laura took the rest of the towels Flath was

holding and gently wiped the child free from its birth fluids. The boy started to cry louder, and the surgeon wrapped him tightly in a small blanket, slowly rocking him in her arms until he quieted. Suddenly, Laura turned toward him, "King Basilias, may I present to you, your son, the High Prince of Sona Tuath." She handed the bundle to Flath and, not knowing what else to do, he took the child.

He refused to look at Jocelyn's son, but stood dumbly looking into Laura's plump face. "This child is not mine," he said coolly. Laura ignored him, turned back to Jocelyn's body and started to put her belly back in some semblance of normalcy, at least to the unobservant viewer.

"I am sorry for the loss of your queen, Your Highness." She finally said in an even voice, not turning from her task. Flath knew the surgeon did not like Jocelyn. However, she did sound sincere in an odd way. Perhaps, at a death, surgeons always felt a certain amount of regret or loss. Flath suddenly felt a pang of sympathy for the middle-aged woman.

Flath wiped the sweat from his brow still holding Jocelyn's son in his other arm. "This is not my son, and I will not keep him here." Flath raised his voice and tried to sound commanding and confident. His stomach tightened, and his mouth went painfully dry.

Laura finished with Jocelyn's body, then turned to Flath, wiping her hands and arms with the last remaining clean towel. "'Tis not my place to say, sire, but whose child is it then?" He did not mistake the sarcastic tone in her voice. She is going to be difficult, he thought.

"I have no clue, woman! The girl was pregnant when I took her to wife." Flath was indignant and quickly handed the sleeping child back to Laura.

"And you can prove this, your highness?" Laura narrowed her eyes at him. He suddenly felt squeamish then cursed himself.

"I cannot. However, it was not time for the child to come. Her time was still a month off." He was pleased with himself for presenting a good argument and almost smiled.

"The boy is tiny; very tiny. He could have been born early." Laura tried to reason with him. Again, he wanted to take a deep breath but could not because of the thick stink of the room.

"Jocelyn is tiny. She could not have had a large babe." He tried to keep the desperation from his voice. What if Laura would not take the child away? What would he do if she would not play her part? His fear gave way to anger. How could she refuse her king? Laura was silent. "Damn it, woman! I know this is not my son. You know it too. I have heard the rumors, though it has not been widespread, but a hushed word here, a sly knowing smile there. She was not a virgin when I bedded her on our wedding night!"

"Not being a virgin and being with child are two different things, sire," Laura said quietly. Her naturally happy face wore the effects of fatigue and sorrow.

He studied her face in the candlelight. She seemed to have more wrinkles around her eyes and mouth than she did when they

had first taken Sona Tuath. He had made her
First Surgeon in the castle when her husband
had died a month after the war was over. The
woman's wiry brown hair was more veined
with gray than it had been. She had lost the
rosy color in her cheeks, and she even looked
like she had lost some of her plumpness. He
hoped she was not ill. He had not spent that
much time in Sona Tuath, making every
excuse he could to get away from Jocelyn.
The wasting sickness had taken plenty of
people in Sona Tuath, and he knew she must
have cared for many that had died of the
illness. Suddenly he had the absurd feeling to
take the child away from her. Despite the
thickness of the air, he took a deep breath,
almost choking, telling himself he did not
care what happened to the child. It would be
easier if it did die. If he were a worse man, he
would just order the child killed, but he knew
he could never do such a thing and felt sick
that it even crossed his mind.

"Yes, I have heard the whispers," she
conceded. "But the Queen has been suffering
from the wasting disease for a month; this

could have caused her to have the babe early." She took a deep breath and let it out slowly. She did not seem to be bothered by the stench.

The infant started to squirm and squeak like a rat trapped in a sack of wheat. He turned and quickly walked over to one of the big windows, opening the thick, wavy panes of glass. The fire rose up, and a gust of cool air blew into the room. He sucked in the crisp, salty air as if he was just breaking the surface of a bottomless ocean. The sound of the angry waves of the great Carnaid Sea as they pounded the rocky beach below, spilled into the stuffy room. The smell of salt and fish replaced the scent of blood and feces. The cold wind dried the sweat on his face and ruffled the ends of his drying hair. The rain had passed, leaving the air cleansed as the eastern horizon shown a tinge of gray, the promise of a morning soon to come. He had to get this over with before the castle's inhabitants began to stir. The servants would be waking soon.

He turned to Laura and steeled himself.

"You must take the boy right away."

"Take him? Take him where?" She was incredulous.

"Give him to a friend or a family member; I care not. Makes sure he is far away!"

Your Highness, how can you suggest such a thing?" Her face had gone white. "He is but a babe! 'Tis not right for him to suffer for the sins of his mother, if sin she had."

Flath quickly walked up to Laura making her take a few steps back. "I will not claim this boy as my heir!" he roared. "Would you have me send him back to Yellow Island and chance another war that the Archigos will not aid us in this time?"

"Sire, what shall you have me do?" She hugged the child to her breast.

Flath was silent for a moment, then sighed deeply. Tenderly, he pushed stray hairs from her face. "Laura, you have always been a faithful servant to me, and the rebellion, your work during the war can never be fully repaid, I am always indebted to you. But I ask this one more thing of you."

Suddenly he could see the defeat in her eyes.

"What would my liege have me do?" she asked in a quiet voice.

Thank the gods! "Take the babe out of Sona Tuath and find him a home. Perhaps you have a family member that has just lost a child that would give the boy a good home? Take a wet nurse if you may, give her gold, or whatever she wants. Tell her he is the illegitimate son of a rich merchant or perhaps one of the newly appointed lords. Above all, use discretion and care, this must not become known. I will tell the people that the babe was stillborn and was so hideous that he could not be buried in our manner for he was ill-shapen to look upon."

Laura's eyes were glassy, and her face was still pale, but he could not discern what she was thinking. His heart was pounding in his chest, and even the roar of the waves outside was diminished by the sound of his blood rushing in his ears. His hands were clammy as he pushed a moment of doubt from his mind. This is the way it must be. "Will you again swear your fealty to the throne, First Surgeon of Castle Sona Tuath, Laura Felden?" He hoped his using her title would have a more dramatic effect.

"I swear my fealty to king and crown and country, Your Highness." She reached out and grabbed his hand, turned it over and placed her moist lips upon his father's signet ring...his signet ring. She let go of his hand, then went to an overstuffed chair by the large wooden door. Still holding the boy in one arm, she draped her cloak over her shoulders. "I will make up a story and leave the boy at my niece's house for a few days; her daughter is not yet weaned. That will give me enough time to find the boy a home."

Flath crossed the room and tenderly kissed her hand. "You are my friend Laura, and I thank you." She smiled up at him bleakly then covered the babe with her thick cloak. "I will be back soon after sunrise," she said and quickly left the room.

Flath walked over to Jocelyn's bed and looked down at the girl. Her face had gone lax, and the sheen of sweat had long dried. He noticed that her cheeks were sunken, and her head looked much bigger than it had when he last saw her. A dull pain of guilt washed over him again, and his throat began to tighten. He would not cry for such a heartless, conniving girl!

Timidly, he reached down and touched her cheek, almost jerking his hand away at the hard, cold flesh under his fingers. Her once small breasts had swollen in expectation of a child. They gave him no pleasure in life and sickened him to look upon now. Not knowing why, he lightly drew his finger down the swell of one almost expecting her to flinch. His hand strayed down to the long gash across her belly and found that even the grizzly wound had cooled. Carefully, he cupped her delicate hand, but it did not yield to his grasp. Finally, he let go of his wife's hand and covered her with the blood smeared linen, then walked across the room and sat down in a chair to await Laura's return.

***

Laura Felden ran down the long, narrow

corridor that led from the servant's quarters to one of the lesser used back doors. The child had not made a sound since she had left the queen's bedchamber and she feared he might be dead. That would make things easier for the king, she thought bitterly, then cursed herself. She had sworn fealty to King Basilias, and the way she was feeling was no less than treasonous. Still, what he did was thoughtless and immature. She thought he looked like a boy who got caught in the pie safe when he was scheming how to get rid of a babe that might or might not be the heir of Sona Tuath. She took in a deep breath of the cool, salt-laden air as she reached the door and quickly left the castle.

Laura did not stop at the stable to ask the attendants to ready her carriage. Instead, she hastened out of the castle gate with no more than a passing nod to the young guard on duty. Her dead husband's niece did not live far. Laura pulled her cloak tighter as a cold fog started to roll off the Carnaid Sea. The rhythmic pounding of the waves almost lulled her into complacency as she headed toward Sonja's cottage. How would she explain this infant and her need to leave it in her care for a few days? The woman was not stupid. She would probably have suspicions at the very least. Sonja was a shrewd woman and a might greedy, but she was the only woman she knew who was both nursing and would not refuse the surgeon. The young woman's family ties were not strong, and she had detested her uncle, but she remained kindly towards Laura after the old surgeon had died.

A muffled cry startled Laura and reminded her that she, in fact, was holding an infant barely come to this world. "Hush, hush," she soothed the babe in a soft voice. She worried that he did not cry out in a stronger voice and was not insistent towards her breast. She wondered if the child would even live to be taken out of the capital city of Sona Tuath. The sun had just started to peak over the dark horizon of the Carnaid Sea. She was thankful the storm had blown away. *It will soon be summer*, she thought distractedly as they hurried down the cobblestoned road still slick from the rain.

Laura traveled down the row of fabric and linen vendors and then turned down a broader street that held the food vendors and then a little further down was Trinket Row, as it was called. Every strange and magical thing in Beaynid could be found there. Oh, it was not as extensive as Tel 'Rhea's novelty market, but it was not as lacking as some markets she had seen. Finally, she reached Sonja's cottage on the fringe of Merchant Square. As she had hoped, no lamp burned inside—she did not want to interrupt business. Laura hesitated for a moment, then rapped loudly on the door. The babe stirred at the jarring motion and started to cry in earnest, maybe her worries about his health were unfounded. Finally, the heavy door opened. No candle burned within, so she could not see a face in the blackness.

"Aunt Laura, what brings you here at this time of the morning?" a low voice spoke from the dark.

"I am so sorry to wake you, dear, but I have a favor I must ask of you. May I come in?" The boy squawked in her arms.

"Of course," Sonja said as she opened the door wider to let her aunt enter. "I will make us some tea, Auntie."

"Thank you." Sonja was wearing a thin nightdress and her cottage smelled of incense and a sweet flower she could not identify. Laura took a seat next to the fire that Sonja began to kindle, and it did not take long before the fire built back up. The young woman quickly swung the kettle of water over the fire to boil. The infant gave a loud cry and Laura folded her cloak back to look at the boy.

"Oh! So, this is the favor you come to ask of me." Sonja smiled and kneeled to get a closer look at the babe. "'Tis so tiny!"

"Yes, yes. His mother was a slip of a girl. Very young." There, Laura was not lying, for, in fact, the queen was a small woman.

Sonja looked up into Laura's face. "What has become of the mother, then?" Her pale brow rose in question.

"His mother is dead." She could not bring herself to say any more. Sonja stood up and took the boy from her aunt. She smiled down at him and even from the weak light of the fire Laura saw the tenderness in her niece's eyes. "I have come to ask you to look after the boy for a few days."

Sonja looked at her aunt and tilted her head a bit. "Where is the father?" she asked warily.

"He, uh, well, he is one of the young nobles that the king has newly installed. You see, the mother was a servant in his home and..." Laura hoped her niece could not see the lie on her face.

"Ah, well." Sonja looked back to the infant and smiled. "So, you are a little bastard born, huh? We should get along just fine then." She sat down in the seat next to Laura, quickly opened the front of her gown and put the babe to one of her breasts. He sucked eagerly, and Laura let out a sigh of relief.

"I hope he will not disrupt business..."

"Oh no, my customers are used to seeing little Tiff around. Men usually do not take that long to finish. This little one will be fine." Laura blushed and was glad for the semi-darkness. Sonja had been a prostitute for years, but Laura still felt the sting of embarrassment at the mention of her profession. She wondered how the woman could talk so openly about it. She had never married, as those of her kind usually did not, and she had not shown any real aptitude for any honest work. She guessed whoring just came natural to her, if that sort of thing was natural. She worried for three-year-old Tiff, but Sonja provided well for the girl. She always had new dresses and toys, and though not one of the largest dwellings in Sona Tuath, Sonja's cottage was well built and furnished very comfortably. She had even hired a tutor for the little girl. If her niece knew who her daughter's father was, she never said, but Laura had come to realize that it really did not matter.

"The water is boiling, let me make the tea." Laura took a mitten and removed the kettle. She looked around the cupboards until she found tea and two cups, then carefully poured the water over the tea. "So, you do not mind if I leave him here for a few days?" she asked as she took the honey from the pantry then brought it and the tea to the table beside them.

"Oh no, I do not mind, in fact, I am grateful. Tiff is getting older now, too old for the breast. I feel lonely oft times. I know 'tis silly, Tiff is only three, and I certainly do not need another child around, but sometimes a woman just needs without reason." Sonja looked up from the nursing infant and smiled dreamily at her aunt. Laura was not quite convinced. She thought Sonja might also be lonely for some juicy gossip. "His father is a lord, you said?"

"Aye, from a town south of here, I did not ask just which one." Laura spooned honey into Sonja's tea and pushed the cup over to the woman who brushed a lock of her golden hair out of her face and took the cup.

"How did you come to know of this child's mother?"

Laura stared, feeling uneasy. "She worked in the kitchen in the castle. Apparently, this lord's wife threw her out when she found out that the girl was pregnant." Laura shrugged. "So, she came to find work in town." Laura tried to sound casual.

"It seems strange that the First Surgeon would attend such a low woman." Sonja smiled over her teacup and then took a sip.

"The other surgeons were with patients dying of the wasting disease. They did not want to leave their patients just to see to this, low woman, as you put it." Laura pushed herself to be bold. She knew Sonja was fishing for information.

"Oh, yes. Well, she was quite lucky to have you there."

"Not really, she did die," Laura said bluntly, almost remorsefully as she thought of the young queen who lay dead in her bedchamber.

"Poor girl." Sonja put her teacup back down and looked again at the infant at her breast. "Poor girl, indeed, to not have looked upon her beautiful child."

Laura smiled, this would work out just fine.

CHAPTER TWO

"The death of Queen Jocelyn Basilias during the Wasting Year was a shock at first but was quickly forgotten, for she was a capricious, petty ruler and all knew the oft-absent king abhorred his queen."
—*History of the Gypsy King; Thomas Ulln*

At dawn, the massive bells of the kirk tower rang out announcing the death of a royal. Citizens opened their doors and windows and gathered on the street, all asking, no doubt, what had come about in the night. Flath was standing on the balcony of what was once Jocelyn's study. He watched people sleepily emerging from their cottages and start to mill about in the streets, slowly starting to migrate toward the massive new kirk still being built for Ak, the One God of the Beaynidans.

One of the first things Flath did as reigning king was pull down the temple that Baobh had erected to worship Pom-Ni, the god of the Goyors. The worship of the pagan god never really caught on in Sona Tuath, but none challenged the foreign queen who had viciously taken the throne and disposed of the royal family. Disposed of everyone except me, Flath bitterly thought.

Now the carcass of a Beaynidan kirk, barely complete enough to hold ceremonies, called all the inhabitants of the capital city of Sona Tuath right to its front doors to hear the news of what had befallen one of their rulers. He wondered how many would secretly be relieved to hear it was Queen Jocelyn who had died. Almost immediately he wondered how many would have wished it had been him, instead.

After Laura returned, Flath quickly left to bathe and dress for what was sure to be a tiresome day. The first thing he did was order a bird be sent to Yellow Island to inform King Umar that his only daughter had died in childbirth. He found himself wishing he could send a bird north to Màrrach to tell Rhiannon also. The Archigos had posted quite a few messenger birds to use as a quick way to relay messages over the vast span of country that separated the two nations. Sona Tuath, in turn, sent their birds to Ventra. He laughed a humorless chuckle. What would he say to Rhiannon in any case?

He looked again out toward the kirk; the sun was breaking through the weakening fog that had poured into the city during the early, pre-dawn. The city, with its thousands of houses, businesses, inns, and taverns, all lay out below the castle like an unfolding blanket of humanity. Three wide, steep roads wound up the cliffs to different entrances to the inner wall circling the castle on three sides. The castle was built right into the white cliffs overlooking the Bay of the Gods and out to the Carnaid Sea to the east. To the south, the ever-growing city spilled out from the shorelines, docks, and wharves. West of the city, was cottages and farmlands as far as the eye could see and to the north, lay the edge of the Alba Forest.

Bells continued to toll into the crisp, salty air, bringing Flath's attention back to the present. The bell tower, the tallest structure in Sona Tuath besides the castle, was now glowing in the new sunlight. It's unfinished narrow shadow spread out across Merchant's Square like an accusing finger pointing at no one in particular. Flath straightened his rich blue jacket that had crisp white embroidery scrolling across cuff, hem, and pockets. He wore a white shirt that was fastened up to his throat with blue seashell buttons and lace that spilled from his cuffs. His pants were jet black, as were his shiny, knee-high boots. On the breast of this coat was sewn the Basilias crest: a gleaming white castle on rocky cliffs overlooking a scarlet sea, one tiny white gull floated on an invisible wind. He wondered why Baobh had not changed the crest when she took Sona Tuath. She had kept the Basilias crest but also adopted her own—a snarling purple dragon—that she flew under the white castle and red sea. Perhaps it might have been because she was of Basilias blood, after all. He still could not fathom that the bitter, vicious woman that had murdered his whole family had been his half-sister. When his head started to ache, he pushed the thought out of his mind.

He had shaved, and his hair was clean and plaited and tied with a black ribbon, and he wore the Beaynidan crown upon his yellow hair. The snake earring still dangled from his ear and his jeweled, panther-head sword still found its home on his hip.

His thoughts turned to the child he had sent from the castle only hours before. He had not thought of him until this very minute. He tried to determine what that meant about his character. The thought that the babe might actually be his was offending.

The little nymph was more than likely with child when they wed. Why should he even entertain the thought that the boy was his? After all, Jocelyn was not a virgin when he bedded her, and the child's arrival was too early.

No matter how many spirits he had drunk that night, he would never forget the frigidness of her body or the revulsion in her flat, green eyes. When he drunkenly questioned her about her lack of chastity she laughed at him and told him it was none of his business. He had been too drunk and disgusted to really care.

From the highest steeple the white flag of mourning was slowly raised, and right below it, the Queen's crest of a black falcon on a yellow background blew in the salty wind. Down below he could hear the faint sounds of mourning as some women of the castle spotted Jocelyn's crest atop the bell tower. He had not thought any in the castle would be much put out by her death, but mayhap he did not know his young wife as well as he thought he had. Rhiannon had always stood between them. Jocelyn knew that and even though she never loved him—for he knew that to be fact—she could not possess him, and it drove her mad with jealousy. He wondered how long it would take for word to leak into Ventra about the Queen of Beaynid's death. Would Rhiannon even care?

He pushed Rhiannon from his mind but strayed again to thoughts of Jocelyn's son. Laura had told him she had left him with a relative for a few days until she could get away and take the child out of Sona Tuath. He had not questioned her about his whereabouts but was disconcertingly curious. *Why do I care*, he asked himself. He folded his arms across his chest. He did not even know what the wench, Jocelyn, was going to name the child. It did not matter; whatever family he ended up with would want to pick a name for their new son. He was glad that Jocelyn did not live to give the child the Basilias surname. If the child could not be stillborn, then this was the next best situation.

Flath sighed and roughly sat down on a chair just off the balcony. His head was pounding, and his hands were clammy. He had not slept in two nights and was exhausted. It seemed colder and brighter than it had but a few moments before. He sighed again trying to clear his head. Jocelyn's body was now being preserved and prepared for the Mourning Procession and the ceremony and viewing afterward. Flath allowed Jocelyn's ladies-in-waiting to select her dress, hose, shoes, and jewelry that she would be presented in; he did not care as long as he did not have to look upon her again.

Later that morning Queen Jocelyn Basilias' ladies-in-waiting walked in front of the funeral procession as it finally made its way through the castle gates at noon. They were dressed in long gowns of plain white cloth with veils and head coverings to match and silently dropped flower petals to the cobbled street. Jocelyn was dressed in her most elegant gown of scarlet and cloth-of-gold, gold torques encrusted with diamonds circled her neck and ears, and her graceful, bejeweled Beaynidan crown sat atop her perfectly groomed hair, oiled so that it shone in the spring sunshine. Clear glass encapsulated the ornate coffin as it was carried down the steep road from the castle and onto one of the wide city streets toward the kirk in the middle of town.

Behind the wagon Flath ambled along, attempting to look stricken. He tried to concentrate on putting one foot in front of the other and forced his mind to think upon what was happening. He was glad that the pace was mercifully slow for in his exhausted state he could not walk any faster, in fact, he was praying to Ak that he would make it to the kirk. Even though the day was warm, he felt chilled, and cold sweat beaded on his forehead and trickled down his back. He pulled his jacket tighter and fought off a shiver.

Behind Flath, Teo and the rest of the King's Counsel walked, and behind them a few newly titled Lords and Ladies that had happened to be at court. Adam was not present, and the messenger that Flath had sent to Bell with the news of Jocelyn's death wouldn't reach him for days.

People poured into the street and followed the Queen's procession as it slowly made its way to the chimes of the kirk. The bells would ring from sun up to sun down for the next nine days, as was the custom in Beaynid. Flath did not know how he would stand the thrum of the enormous bells for the rest of the day let alone more than a week. As the procession finally reached the stone kirk, six attendants stepped out of the shadows cast by the enormous shell of a building, whose completion still lay years ahead, and took Jocelyn's casket inside. She was placed upon the altar, and Flath escorted to the High Seat in the balcony.

"Ye alright?" Teo whispered into his ear as Flath sat down.

"Fine," he said shortly. He was annoyed with no one in particular, except Jocelyn maybe, his head was pounding, and he was suddenly so very thirsty.

"I am sorry Teo, I am just too weary to be burdened with this." His old friend placed his thick hand upon Flath's shoulder.

"'Tis alright, laddie, 'tis to be expected."

Finally, the Priest of Ak took his place on the altar. His billowing white robes were ornately embroidered with gold and scarlet thread, tiny gems had been sewn into the robe and winked in the sunlight that streamed in through the large windows. His headdress stood up erect, coming to point, and the gems encrusted within shown bright like tiny stars. He held a golden scepter with a rounded chunk of clear amber at the top. Jocelyn had brought him over from her homeland, Yellow Island. He was quite showy and very pompous as he looked down on everyone packed into the kirk. Flath could not stand the man, but grudgingly attended service when he was in Sona Tuath—which was not often of late. He was not brought up to worship Ak, or any other god. Leading the life of a gypsy did not lend itself to acts of religious devotion. Sure, he believed there were gods, and his family did mention one or two occasionally, but as far as showing loyal reverence, they never did.

The priest went on and on about the sanctity and greatness of the One God, Ak and then about his fiery wrath that was to be the fate of all nonbelievers. He praised the queen as a woman of kindness and righteousness and told of how she looked down on them now from the realm beyond the stars where she ruled with other kings and queens that had passed beyond before her. The priest's jowly, accented words started running together as Flath's eyes grew heavy and he slumped in his seat.

Finally, the priest stopped talking, and suddenly the kirk was drowning in a powerful chorus of voices and instruments. The otherworldly music would stir the heart of anyone listening, but Flath had no ear for music today. Slowly he got up from his seat, and he and his counsel descended from the balcony and took up a feather and a lit candle.

They placed the soft, white feathers atop
Jocelyn's coffin to help her spirit ascend to
the other world beyond the stars and placed
the candle upon the opulent silver candle
holders placed around her body.

Flath said no word to the priest, but
quietly walked from the church and slowly
climbed into the waiting carriage. Teo
jumped in a few moments later, and the
carriage started its trip back up to the castle.

"Yer sure yer okay, lad, ya look terrible?"

"Just a bit worn-out, I had a long night."

Teo was quiet for a moment, then, "I'm
sorry fer yer wee barin."

Flath looked over at the stout, red-haired
man not comprehending what he was talking
about and then remembered the infant he
had sent away. "Thank you, old friend." Flath
was far too exhausted to try and explain to
Teo what he had done; he knew the older
man would not approve. What was he
supposed to have done? Raise the child as his
own—his heir? No, he would not let that
happen. He reasoned that the boy would be

safe and happy in his new home, wherever Laura decided to leave him. The child would never know of his origin, and Flath would not have to wonder every day for the rest of his life if the boy was really his or not. Tis much better this way, he reasoned.

In time the bells halted their relentless cries over the city, and everyone went back to their regular duties. The King and Queen of Yellow Island had arrived five days after the bird was sent—their yellow and black standard blowing in the harsh wind. They were ill-prepared for the journey and in their haste to leave, they barely brought enough supplies for the trip to Sona Tuath let alone the sail home. They stayed for three more days—the queen sobbing as her only daughter was carried to the mausoleum. After the ship was restocked with provisions, the King and Queen boarded the North Star for home. The North Star was a small, shallow-hulled ship that was able to cut through even rough seas quickly. It had tall masts and what seemed like endless mountains of billowing white canvas.

Flath stood on the balcony that was off of his living quarters in the Tower of the King— the apartments that Baobh once inhabited. His headache had gotten worse, and he had to fight to keep his knees from buckling, but still, he watched the North Star dissolve into the shimmering red sea and finally disappear over the horizon. He looked out over the choppy waters and wondered if Baobh's bones still lay on the rocky bottom of the sea. He hoped her body had been quickly consumed by the large, silver sharks that frequented the Bay of Gods. He shivered and pulled his coat tighter and remembered how, in the white-hot light of a bolt of lightning, he had seen her body fall into the sea and he could still hear the wailing of her abandoned son. He closed his eyes and pictured Rhiannon as she was that night. Her short hair was plastered to her face from the rain, her eyes fixed in disbelief that Baobh was finally dead as the tip of her great Venturien sword, smeared with blood, rested on the stone floor. She was the very image of an Archigos Warrioress and, even more: their empress.

Teo walked up beside Flath. "Ya need ta get some rest, lad. Ye don't look sa good."

Flath looked over at his friend and saw concern in his eyes. "I am fine, 'tis been a long week." As he said the words, he knew it was not true. He had been feeling increasingly weak and cold over the last week. His head pounded and made it difficult to see through the bright sunlight.

"Aye, it has, but ye look haggard and pale. I think I will call Laura ta have a look see."

Flath shook his head, which sent the room spinning. "Laura has left to stay with family in the country for a while. She needed time to recover from caring for Jocelyn for so long."

"Then I will bring another healer. Ye look bad." The worry was quite apparent in his voice now.

Flath left the balcony and threw himself on a chair. "It might just be the start of a cold.

I will be fine." But as the words left this mouth, he knew they were a lie. He did not feel well at all.

Teo did not look convinced and took a seat next to him. "The wasting sickness still prowls through the city looking fer more ta devour. Look, even the Queen has fallen prey ta the sickness. Ye need ta let a healer look at ye."

He looked over at Teo, and suddenly his vision blurred, and his friend's voice echoed as if Flath were standing at the bottom of a well looking up at the red man. And then his world went black.

***

Flath crumpled to the carpeted floor like an abandoned marionette. Teo jumped up and took his friend's face into his wide, calloused hands. As he had feared, Flath was burning with fever. He gave a loud curse as he dragged Flath into his sleeping chamber and hoisted the taller man into bed. Quickly he ran out of the room and flung open the wooden doors. A frightened valet looked up, startled at Teo's sudden appearance.

"Get Ian up here now...and a healer!" Teo roared.

"Yes, my lord." The boy turned and ran, disappearing down the long hallway.

It seemed to take Ian a moon's journey to arrive, but the young man suddenly appeared at Teo's side as he gasped for breath—it was a long run up all those stairs.

"My lord," he breathed. "What has befallen the King?"

Teo turned and grabbed Ian's arms, forcing the young man to look at him. Reluctantly Ian pulled his eyes from his king and gave Teo his attention.

"Listen ta me, lad. Ye must get down ta the mews and send birds with a message ta Rhiannon ta come quick wi her wee necklace." Teo pushed Ian toward the door.

"Will the king die?"

"Not if she hurries."

CHAPTER THREE

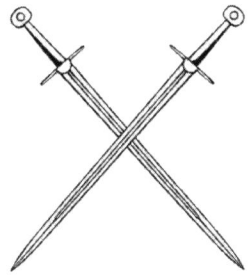

"A woman's heart is unknowable and predictable all the same. Her love is both a burning sun and cold ocean. However, within this deep place of paradoxy lies a certainty that she will always choose love over anything else."
—Code of the Feminine; author unknown

"Here, drink this, my dear." Tess carefully handed Rhiannon a steaming cup of tea. The sweet liquid ran down her throat and immediately shot through her arms and legs as if it were whiskey. It warmed her and immediately made her feel relaxed.

The Empress of Ventra looked at her grandmother and smiled. "I don't think this is working."

"Oh, it will. It will, or we'll have a problem as you have no other siblings." Tess's withered face wrinkled into a smile. Rhiannon remembered the story of her great aunts who, despite giving birth to seventeen children between them, produced no females—therefore no heir. Her cousin Shankee, the former proxy empress, was born of one such male. She had cousins aplenty—most she had not even met thus far. Shankee was not the oldest but chosen to rule in Rhiannon's stead because of her authoritative attitude and the advisors' presumption of her aptitude for war.

Maybe Shih' Ni is not meant to be the father of my heir, she thought, but quickly pushed the thought out of her mind. "I will not dismiss him," she said with conviction.

Tess nodded, "I thought you might say that, but you might think differently in a few years if you still have not conceived."

"Then someone else will have to. Maybe Kyia, she's a Kossi. Or one of Shankee's children." Rhiannon narrowed her eyes at her grandmother in defiance.

"Who knows Verna's will? I have used every fertility secret I know, and still, you have not conceived, my dear."

"Grandma, it's only been four months!"

"Yes, yes, I keep forgetting. Really, that isn't that long at all." The old woman smiled again.

"Okay, let's stop talking about this. I came to visit, remember?"

"Well, drink your tea dear, maybe you'll have something to tell me when you next come to visit." Tess chuckled.

Shih 'Ni had left three days before to inspect the North Fort. It was a military fort that protected the coast. Because of the rocky shore and only one place a ship could anchor and send boats to shore, the fort was not manned as well as the one in the east. Still, there were a hundred warriors and their families stationed at the North Fort, so they would be able to defend the shore against a good sized troop, and if many more than that swarmed the beach, it was only two days from Màrrach and the reinforcements that could defeat almost any army. He was not expected back for another week. When he returned, Rhiannon would accompany him to the East Fort. She was listless and wanted to leave Màrrach, if only for a few weeks. She was disappointed not to have gone with the trading party that had left last month but could not leave on an extended trip with Shih 'Ni's inspection tour planned, leavening Màrrach with no leader. However, Rhiannon knew Shankee could easily handle anything that came up while she and Shih 'Ni were away, even though she would not have liked it.

Rhiannon was excited to see the growth of East Fort. With the construction of three large docks and several storehouses, East Fort was growing from just a military base to be more of a shipping port. She had employed hundreds of builders and dozens of shipwrights who were busily building three quick, shallow-hulled, warships to patrol the cost. There was not a sailor among the Archigos, but Rhiannon had hired agents to find the best sailors to man her ships and to teach her younger warriors to sail.

She also commissioned the construction of a large cargo ship. With new trade alliances with Sona Tuath, Yellow Island and, even Assuria off to the northeast, she expected much growth in Ventra. Her advisors were in disagreement of these changes, however, but Rhiannon would not be dissuaded. She argued that the warships would make the coasts easier to defend and the cargo ship would make it easier to do business with Tel 'Rhia and places even farther away, bringing further prosperity to Ventra.

They, however, remained very wary at best. The Archigos had done things the same for a thousand years, and they were secure in their wealth so saw no reason to change. But perhaps because Rhiannon had grown up in a capitalist society, so vastly different from Ventra, she felt the progress would be healthy for her people. After all, Turr 'ah had her own trading vessels, and though Màrrach did receive a percent of all goods traded in Turr 'ah, Rhiannon knew they could make much more having their own ships. It was up to her to convince her advisors that change was good for Ventra.

Suddenly Rhiannon's big silver she-wolf, Luna, jumped up from the warm hearth and darted for the front door bringing the Empress of Ventra out of her thoughts. Etâhpe'o-poeso, a massive winged cat, looked up from where she had been sleeping on one of the beds in Tess's empty infirmary, but then closed her eyes and went back to sleep. Her cubs from last year had all grown and flown away, and now she was back to being a lazy feline. Perhaps she would have more cubs this season.

Rhiannon got up and opened the door to see Kyia slide off her horse. An Oread groom took the reins and led the horse away. "This came for you," she breathed and handed her the tiny scroll that had obviously come from a messenger bird.

"The king is sick, come right away. Bring necklace. Ian," Rhiannon read the note aloud then looked up at Kyia. "When did this come?"

"Thirty minutes ago. I pushed my horse as fast as she could go."

"Ready my horse!" she yelled at a groom standing in the stable doorway. She turned to Tess, "I must go."

The old woman nodded. "I know."

It did not take long before Rhiannon was thundering into the courtyard of the Grand Palace of Màrrach, the biggest glass-domed marble living structure of the Archigos. She jumped from the back of her sleek, black horse, Zellan, before he even came to a stop. "I must go right away. Tend to him and pack some oats and grain. I'm going on a long trip," she ordered as the slight, fair-haired Oread took the dangling reins and led Zellan away. She wished one of those ships were already finished; it would have been a much shorter trip to Sona Tuath.

Once inside the building, she ran into Xev. She looked at him, and for the first time noticed that he was no longer a boy, but a young man now a few inches taller than her. If she had had time, she would have commented on how proud Tim would have been if his best friend had he survived the War of the Gypsy King—so the Beaynidans now called the mêlée that took the throne of Beaynid from Baobh and placed a legitimate Basilias once again in Castle Sona Tuath. A hard stab of pain jolted her at the memory of the boy so wise beyond his years the boy that she had adopted as her brother.

"Xev," she choked out. "Please, go to the kitchen and tell them to prepare travel rations for several weeks." Xev continued to stare at her like a big owl, his expression blank. "Quickly!" she called over her shoulder as she ran up the staircase to her rooms.

Rhiannon stuffed clothes fit for travel into her large leather pack along with a few grooming items. A trip that normally took about a month to complete would have to take her half the time. She had no one to slow her down, and Zellan was trained and conditioned and should be able to keep pace. She knew Luna would come but doubted the wolf could keep up though she would be able to track her with little effort. She hurried to a large cabinet that held her weapons, strapped a leather harness across her chest, hung her small throwing axes, fastened her sword and scabbard over her shoulder and slung her bow and quiver over the other shoulder. Knives and daggers were strapped to calves and arms finishing the deadly ensemble. She touched the cool stones at her neck and took a deep breath. Don't fail me, Mother. She tied her shoulder-length hair back in a leather thong and turned to leave to find Kyia standing in the doorway.

"I have to go; you know that."

"I know, and I'm going with you." She could see the grip of her sword poking up from her left shoulder, the tip of her bow over her right.

"No, this is something I must do on my own." Rhiannon shook her head and started for the door. Kyia blocked her way.

"You can't risk yourself by going alone."

"I'll travel faster alone. You know Kalouaii can't keep up with Zellan." Rhiannon pushed her aside and quickly left the room.

"I'll follow you!" She heard Kyia call as Rhiannon left her chambers and ran down the hall—Rhiannon knew her cousin would follow.

It was full dark when Rhiannon rode out of Màrrach and through Laoch Valley toward the steep, jagged peaks of the Vel' Kur mountains. They had left Màrrach swiftly, fleeing into the blackness with only the silver shine of Luna's thick coat as a witness to their passing. Zellan's black hooves cut into the hard dirt of the road as he sliced through the night like a dark bolt of lightning. She could not see her but sensed the big, tawny cat flying above. As they reached the gentle foothills of the mountain, Rhiannon slowed him into a steady trot. The half moon provided just enough light to start ascending the mountain.

A few hours before dawn, Rhiannon stopped to rest awhile before resuming their scramble up to the spine of Vel' Kur. On the third day, they reached the other side and, with Luna at her side, she once again urged Zellan into a gallop and disappeared into the green, summer meadows. Every morning, a few hours before dawn, Rhiannon would stop, unsaddle, and bridle Zellan, then turn him lose to sleep or feed. She would put the sack of grain or oats out for him, roll out her bedding and fall into unconsciousness. In the morning she would wake to find Luna sleeping beside her and Etâhpe'o-poeso resting not far away.

On their long, swift journey through Beaynid, Rhiannon would spot Peso flying high on a warm current through the clouds. The June days were hot and sticky, and she was surprised at how grateful she was for the afternoon storms that brought rain to cool the land. She had become acclimated to the northern climate and missed the cold air and pure, sparkling spring snow. She found herself missing Màrrach even though she so recently had wanted to get away for a while.

The road out of the Vel' Kur Mountains

was not traveled too often, mostly by the trading parties that left in the spring and fall of each year heading to Bell and then off to Tel 'Rhia. Màrrach did not have many visitors, but occasionally rich merchants from Turr 'ah, or even farther away, and nobles from surrounding countries would be guests of the Archigos. However, they arrived by ship via the busy docks of Turr ' ah. Not too many travelers wanted to pass over the sheer cliffs and rocky passes of Vel' Kur.

Rhiannon was surprised at how well the road looked for being so unused. Someone, decades or perhaps even centuries before, had lined both sides of the road with good sized rocks now dull and covered with patches of rust-colored lichen. She supposed that on their twice annual trips into Beaynid her warriors repaired any parts of the road that had been disturbed or ill-used due to weather. Once her ships were finished, this road would probably go unused and reclaimed by the land once again.

Rhiannon heard that Flath had started

paving the busy road from Sona Tuath west across the whole of Beaynid to the bustling port city of Tel 'Rhia. It would take him years to widen and pave the route, which had now been officially named King Basilias Road. He had employed a considerable amount of men from the more impoverished villages, and they worked tirelessly toward their goal. Their women and older children were left to tend their farms. The Oread that had decided to stay behind in Beaynid worked alongside the women and children and were of tremendous help to the villages they now called home. The warriors that Rhiannon had left in Beaynid patrolled the land and kept peace and, much to her relief, were treated hospitably.

The rough seas of the Carnaid were not as easily traversed as the calmer waters of the Western Sea and gentle winds of Mermaid Bay where Tel 'Rhia sprawled. The wide, well patrolled King Basilias Road would make trade much more manageable, so Beaynid was eagerly anticipating the completion of the thoroughfare that would pull them from the ashes of a land suffering from the aftershocks of war.

The thought of Flath made Rhiannon's heart ache. She was overcome with sorrow and longing and a dark fear that she might not be in time to save him. She gripped Zellan's reins tighter and resisted the urge to push him into a gallop. He had been swift on their journey so far, but she knew he could not hold the pace forever and did not want to drive him to injury.

On the sixteenth night of her journey, she crested a grassy hill, and the lights of Castle Sona Tuath came into view. She gasped at the forgotten sight of its great white walls glowing in the light of a full moon. It had been nearly a year since she left the castle and Flath behind. The roar of the agitated waves broke upon the shore battering the cliffs and shattering what would have been a quiet night. The smell of fish and salt penetrated the crisp air and floated away on an eastern wind.

She kneed Zellan into a run, and they careened down the hill toward the outer wall.

As they approached, she could see guards gathering on the wall near the massive front gate looking down at them and pointing as they approached.

"Halt!" a guard ordered as she slid Zellan to a stop a few feet from the older man. "What business do you have in Sona Tuath?" he demanded harshly.

"I am Empress Rhiannon Kossi of the Archigos, and I am here to see your king," she replied in Ska. As if he were waiting for her, he bobbed his head then ordered the gate to be opened. They raced up the steep cobbled street that took them to the castle, and when she got to the gate at the inner wall, she was let in again without a challenge. Zellan was breathing in gasps, his black coat white with foam as she slipped from his back and handed the reins to a waiting groom. She dashed past four guards and slammed the door to the castle open where she found four more guards. Paying no heed to their cries of alarm, she sprinted out of the entry hall and toward the stairway. Taking two stairs at a time she reached the top and headed for the second grand staircase. At the top, she turned down the well-lit hall that would lead her to the last set of stairs that would bring her to the Tower of the King. She knew this part of the castle for she had been here before, though it seemed a lifetime ago. Behind her, she could hear the shouting of guards, but she kept running. Her lungs burned, and she could not get enough air. Her legs threatened to fall out from under her, but still, she kept running.

At last, she reached the large, ornately carved double doors that led to the King's chambers. She announced herself and the two guards that were stationed there quickly opened the doors to let her in. Taking huge breaths of air heavy with the scent of candles, she sprinted to Flath's bedchamber. Teo looked up and jumped to his feet.

"Hurry, lass!" His eyes shown with tears and wet tracks disappearing into his red beard, worry creased his tired face.

Rhiannon unfastened her necklace, and, with great trepidation, she moved toward

Flath. She gasped when she saw his pale skin that had taken on a slight greenish tint. Dark smudges hung under his eyes in a macabre smile. "He's so thin...so thin!" she cried.

Quickly she flung herself on the bed beside him and placed the Necklace of Verna on his bare chest. It seemed the room was devoid of air and sound and life as she breathlessly started to sing. The words were no longer foreign to her, for she understood every one. They told of the world as it was before man when time and universe was ruled by capricious gods. Then the song turned to Verna and the creation of her children. It told of the migration of the people that would become the Archigos and Verna's love for her children. The stones glowed brighter as she sung the story of Verna's gift to the Archigos and about its powers to heal—and also to hurt. Instead of the words of protection, however, she sang the sweet words of comfort and healing. Finally, the ancient words came to an end, and the stones slowly dimmed and cooled.

Teo took the necklace from her trembling hand and gently brushed the sweat streaked hair from her shoulder and returned the Necklace of Verna to her neck. It was warm on her throat. Weakly she crawled into Flath's bed, took his slack hand in hers and laid her head next to his. She listened to his breathing as it turned from a ragged gasp into the deep, rhythmic motion of a man in restful sleep. Her eyes grew heavy, and she finally gave in to the blackness of sleep.

She awoke to a gentle touch on her cheek. Flath was looking at her; his cracked, dry lips curled into a lazy smile. "My beautiful Greannmhor," he whispered.

"You need to sleep," she said affectionately and ran her fingers over his bearded face.

"Am I dreaming?" he innocently asked.

She thought for a moment. "Yes, you're dreaming," she answered, knowing she would leave immediately. It was better if he thought she was just an apparition. She had no doubt that Teo would tell him she had come, but for now, she wanted to just be a dream. Perhaps it would be easier to leave him, she tried to reason with herself, but the thought still pained her deeply. "Sleep now, my love," she crooned and stroked his cheek until his swollen lids closed, and he once again slumbered peacefully.

When she was sure he was sleeping soundly, she carefully got up from the warm bed. Her bones creaked and protested as she stood and stretched. "Will ya be leav'n now, Rhiannon?" She turned to see Teo sitting in a chair on the edge of the sputtering shadows.

"Yes."

He nodded his head knowingly and looked over at the flames in the fire pit as they stabbed into the darkness of the chimney. She walked over to him and could see the darkness under his eyes and how his clothes looked stale and his bright, red hair unkempt. She kneeled down and looked into his tired face. He turned his green eyes to her. "You know I must go. I have responsibilities in Ventra. Not to mention a husband." He shook his head again. She squeezed his knee and slowly stood upright again. "How long did I sleep.

"Ye've been sleep'n a whole day and half the night." He finally smiled.

"That long?" she said in alarm.

"Oh, aye! Ya even slept through the boy's rambl'n and when I gave him wee sips of water."

She smiled affectionately at Teo. "I've missed you."

"I've missed ya too, lass." Teo stood and took her into his arms. "'Tis sa good ta see ya."

She kissed his forehead and stepped out of his arms, and then, as if she had just remembered something, she asked, "Where is the Queen? Why isn't she attending her husband?" Suddenly she was very angry, her voice accusatory. She wanted nothing more than to throttle the girl.

Teo took a deep breath as if trying carefully to formulate his answer. "I'll be guess'n ye haven't heard," he stated warily. When Rhiannon did not answer, he went on. "Jocelyn died over a month ago of the waist'n sickness."

Rhiannon gasped. "The baby?"

"The barin was stillborn," he answered sadly.

Rhiannon's stomach clenched as waves of conflicting emotions washed over her. Jocelyn's young, snide face and protruding belly hung in her memory like a canker. "Why was word not sent to Ventra?" she finally asked in a meek, almost fearful voice.

"Flath didn't want word sent, but I was sure the news would ha made its way ta ya by now."

"Why would he not want me to know?"

"I dinna kin, lass." Teo shrugged his broad shoulders.

Rhiannon suddenly felt supremely out of place and urgently wanted to get back to Ventra. "I've got to go now," she said softly, "May the sun shine down upon you."

Teo nodded his head in resignation as she turned to leave. When she reached the doors, he called out, "He never stopped love'n ya." She stopped but did not turn around. After a moment she pulled the heavy doors open and left.

CHAPTER FOUR

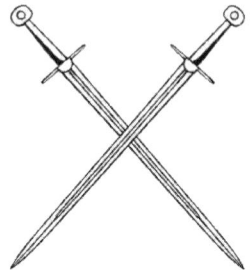

"The Race of Forest Folk known as Goyors live in the Alba Forest in northern Beaynid. They have powers of the earth and are Guardians of the Forest. At one time it was rumored that thousands of Goyors lived amid all the forests of Beaynid. No one knows why there are only a few now who live in the small hidden village of Ghroc."
—The Forest Folk: Goyor; Sarah Unell

Fuzzy, red squirrels scampered up rough-barked trees and bravely leapt from branches high up in the canopy. From the treetops, a chaotic, yet somehow harmonious, chorus of bird-song serenaded Rhiannon as she and Zellan plodded along the road. Fingers of bright sunshine poked through the canopy and slashed across the road. The brief warmth felt good on Rhiannon's skin as she passed through the beams of golden light. Luna had slunk off into the forest to hunt, and she was sure Etâhpe'o-poeso silently floated on the wind above her. It was a long journey back home, but she decided she would enjoy the quiet time to herself. She knew Shih 'Ni would already be on his way to find his errant wife, but at that moment, with the gentle, forgiving sunshine on her face, she did not care.

Rhiannon's journey home was at a much more languid pace and a week out of Sona Tuath she turned off the well-traveled road that eventually forked into smaller paths leading to villages and farms in northern Beaynid. One of the less traveled roads, the one that she would take, lazily followed alongside the serpentine Tangue River and eventually led to Ventra.

But for now, she left the road and traveled west along what was not much more than a deer path farther up into the thick trees. She knew the path well, and it soon brought her deeper into the Alba Forest. Off to her left, she could hear the roar of Huntsman's River as it flowed west and eventually dumped into the Western Sea. As Luna silently appeared as if from nowhere, Rhiannon slid from Zellan's back and led him into a terrible thicket that melted away as they passed through. She felt a tingling where the Emissary Beads touched her skin at her throat alongside her mother's necklace. Eerily, seemingly impassible gnarls of thorny vegetation dissolved right in front of her as she followed a once invisible path. Soon the familiar village of Ghroc appeared all around her.

Meandering paths paved with grey stones and lined with blooming flowers lead to thatched roof cottages that looked as if they grew right up from the forest floor. Blossoming vines with brightly colored flowers of every hue imaginable covered lamp posts and trellises and ornately carved benches placed in gardens and along the water. A forest brook bubbled over rocks and happily flowed through the middle of the village. Vine covered bridges arched over the water at regular intervals linking both sides of the village together.

"Empress! Empress!" A group of children called as she stooped down and little Singing Brook flung herself into Rhiannon's arms.

Her younger brother, Fox, ran up and wrapped his arms around Rhiannon's neck. "You've come back!" he said and buried his face in her hair.

"I've missed you, Empress," Singing Brook said sweetly. Just like the first time Rhiannon had met the girl, she closed her little hand tight then opened a chubby fist to reveal a beautiful red flower that the girl quickly fastened to one of the thin braids in Rhiannon's hair.

As all Goyor children, Singing Brook was

perfect in appearance. Their dark skin was never marred by pox or too much sun or even slight blemishes. Singing Brook's brown eyes were ringed with thick dark lashes, her curly hair was pinned up with tiny, sparkling combs and little white flowers were sprinkled throughout her hair. Her delicate ears were pointed at the tips, and small gold hoops hung from each earlobe. Beads and bits of shiny things were sewn into her olive green dress that was as soft as velvet against Rhiannon's skin. Her little brother was dressed much the same way in a dark green tunic and trousers. A wreath of small yellow leaves hung around his neck.

"Where's Master Shih 'Ni?" a little boy of about four asked, peering hard into the brush behind her.

"He didn't come this time, Bear Paw, I'm sorry," Rhiannon answered turning toward the plump little boy.

"Why didn't he come?" Fox asked.

"He had to stay behind and take care of Ventra for me."

Fox seemed satisfied with that answer. However, Bear Paw stuck out his bottom lip, folded his arms and flopped down on the ground. After a few moments, he moodily started to scratch behind Luna's ear. Rhiannon had to stifle a laugh.

When Rhiannon looked back up, she saw Journey-Of-The-Moon and another man walking toward her. "Hello!" she called and stood up.

"Greetings, Empress Rhiannon." Journey-Of-The-Moon smiled. "Your visit is unexpected, but very welcome none the less."

"I was passing by and thought I'd stop for a day or two. I need a change of scenery." Rhiannon shrugged.

"Rhiannon, I'd like you to meet Fire-Caller, he is caring for Kaat."

Rhiannon was still not sure of the customs in Ghroc, so she gave a slight, awkward bow. "It's nice to meet you, Fire-Caller." He was a tallish man with dark skin who was wearing a long white robe. A wreath of green Temmer Tree leaves circled his head, and an Emissary

Bead necklace hung at his throat. His black eyes were big and kind and his smile very warm. He had a familiar look to him, but Rhiannon could not place it.

"How is the little guy?" Rhiannon looked at the child in his arms. He would soon be a year old. Kaat looked up at Rhiannon and smiled. For a moment her heart stopped. She recalled how hard it was to hand him over to Journey-Of-The-Moon and how she had coveted the infant. She reached out and ran her fingers over the smooth curve of one chubby dark cheek. "He's beautiful," she breathed. She sorrowfully wondered if she would ever have her own children.

Fire-Caller put Kaat down, and the small child walked over to Rhiannon and hugged her legs. "He is doing well, empress," the man answered.

Rhiannon bent down and scooped up the boy. "I can't believe how much he's grown. He's walking so well now!"

Journey-Of-The-Moon laughed. "Goyor children learn quickly, for they have much to accomplish in the forest."

Rhiannon felt a tap on her thigh and looked down. "He's my brother and my cousin," Bear Paw announced proudly. Rhiannon looked back up at Journey-Of-The-Moon, and her brows rose inviting an explanation.

"Fire-Caller is Bear Paw's father..." She hesitated for only a moment. "He's also Baobh's uncle."

"Baobh's mother, Raven, was my sister," he explained.

"Oh, well, it's good that Kaat has some family then." Now that she knew that Fire-Caller was related, she could clearly see a resemblance between him and Baobh. Rhiannon felt awkward. She had killed his niece, as the ancient Goyor prophecy dictated. However, she still felt like she owed Fire-Caller some kind of apology.

Sensing her discomfort Journey-Of-The-Moon took Rhiannon's elbow "Come, Rhiannon, let us share a meal and I will have a room made ready for you. Please stay as long as you wish," she offered and led her down the shaded path toward the middle of the village. Zellan slowly followed as Luna ran off ahead with six little children trailing after her. She knew Etâhpe'o-poeso would not be far behind.

Rhiannon stayed in Ghroc for two days then left the Forest Folk village to continue her journey home. The day after leaving Ghroc, Rhiannon was back on the road toward Ventra when she heard horses approaching around a corner immediately ahead of her. She had passed many travelers on the road, for the weather was warm, and the people were of good cheer. Most of the travelers she passed were kind to her, waving and greeting her merrily, a few even recognized her as the Empress of Ventra and were happy to see her, however, some were wary or even rude. She paid their ill will no heed but smiled sweetly at them and continued on her way.

However, the sounds of these travelers were not from noisy, lighthearted Beaynidans leisurely traveling through the countryside. She heard the soft thump of steel-shod hooves and the almost noiseless movement of an Archigos war party. Leather made up most of the warhorses tack, and the warriors themselves wore no mail or loud armor. It allowed them great stealth and also granted them greater agility in battle.

Rhiannon pulled Zellan to a stop and waited for them to round the corner. The air was hot and humid, and she could smell rain in the distance. She took a deep breath, and her stomach tightened with sudden anxiety. Flath would live, Beaynid would keep their king, but Shih 'Ni would be livid and her warriors affronted at their empress's sudden flight to be at Flath's side. She had left quickly, and only Kyia and Tess knew why, but word of Flath's illness had most surely reached Ventra by now, and they would have realized where their empress had run off to. Even worse, she also knew that word of Jocelyn's death would probably have reached Màrrach by now, and she did not want to consider the implications of that bit of news.

Kyia was the first to come around the

corner, Luna padding along beside Kalouaii. She had expected her cousin to smile and be happy to see her, but Kyia wore a somber, unreadable expression. Rhiannon hated it when she did that. For all Kyia's good qualities—and there were many—she could be silently judgmental, making one feel staggeringly guilty with just a minuscule expression on her face. Others might not realize it, for she was quiet by nature, but Rhiannon knew her best friend well and knew the difference between her reserved personality and the silent treatment—she was definitely getting the silent treatment.

Kyia rode up to Rhiannon and stopped. "Hail, Empress," she said and a very faint smile formed on her lips then almost instantly faded. Maybe it was not as bad as she thought...

"Hello, Cousin." Rhiannon did smile. Etâhpe'o-poeso walked over and rubbed against the belly of Kyia's paint mare, Kalouaii, who looked down at the cat in shock and offense and quickly moved away.

Then Shih 'Ni rounded the corner and

stopped. He rode atop his tall, dappled grey warhorse, Santu. His face was hard, and she could see the hurt in his dark eyes. His usually clean-shaven face was stubbled with dark whiskers, and his hair lay down his back unbound except for two skinny side lock braids woven with multicolored beads and two small brown feathers. Suddenly she realized how much she had missed him and a wide smile spread across her face as she urged Zellan to approach her husband. When she stopped beside him, she found no words but kept looking at her sleek, powerful warrior and Ventra's tjaty.

"How fares the King?" he asked in a tight voice.

The smile on her face faded, and she felt hurt that he had not greeted her before asking about Flath. "He'll live," she said nonchalantly.

Zellan nudged Santu, and the grey gave a low warning that almost sounded like a growl. Zellan threw his head back and whickered as if laughing and nudged Santu again. Santu was a very serious and disciplined horse, and his training would not allow him to be baited into a confrontation. Zellan, lacking the lifetime of training as an Archigos Warhorse, and being the arrogant creature that he was, took great pleasure in taunting Santu whenever he could.

Shih 'Ni looked at her a few moments longer then turned his horse around and started back the way he had come. The three warriors that had been waiting behind him also turned and followed him back down the road.

"I guess he's pretty mad," Rhiannon commented as Kyia came up beside her.

"Wouldn't you be?" she replied coolly.

Rhiannon looked over at her cousin. "I guess I would be if I were him, but what's your problem?" she asked, just as levelly.

Kyia was silent as she watched the warriors disappear down the path mottled with uneven shade. "Did you really have to go?" she finally asked.

"He would have died."

Kyia looked back over to Rhiannon, her face was hard, and her eyes were cold. "Would that have been such a bad thing for Ventra?"

Rhiannon's eyes widened, and she tightened her grip on her reins. "How can you even ask me that?" Her voice rose in anger.

"You're killing Shih 'Ni with your unfaithfulness. You save a man's life at the cost of your mate's. You need to decide whose life is more important."

"I have not been unfaithful!" Rhiannon roared. "Is saving a man's life equal to being unfaithful to my husband?" she demanded.

"Saving that man's life, yes."

"Kyia, why are you treating me this way?" Zellan stomped the ground as if wanting to end the fight.

"I know the Queen, and her baby, are dead. Shih 'Ni knows also."

Rhiannon took a deep breath; she knew that was coming. When she stayed silent, Kyia continued. "You are aware I care deeply for Shih 'Ni, and I can't stand to see him continually injured!" the smaller woman snapped.

"You also know I loved Flath very much.

Shih 'Ni knows that too. He knew going into this marriage that I loved another man, yet he accepted that." Rhiannon finished her sentence quietly as her anger dissipated in defeat.

"You loved him? So you no longer love the Suen?"

Rhiannon thought about seeing Flath wasted away in the throes of death and then remembered how it felt to wake up next to him, seeing his tender smile and warm, mismatched eyes. Then she thought of her husband sitting tall and proud on his mount, his sleek black hair stirring in the wind, the hilt of his mighty Venturien sword sticking up over the hard curve of his shoulder, his dark, penetrating eyes watching her approach. "I want to go home," she finally said and kneed Zellan on toward Ventra.

CHAPTER FIVE

*"During the first years of Empress Rhiannon
Kossi's reign Ventra went through some drastic
changes that were a radical departure from the
way the Archigos had done things for many
generations. Empress Rhiannon was credited for
the shipping port in western Ventra, the creation of
the Venturian Navy, and the ambitious project of
building the third massive glass-domed housing
structure in Màrrach."*
—*Ventra, Land of Ice and Warriors; G. P. Love*

The weather stayed warm over the next two weeks, even up into Ventra. Shih 'Ni continued to be in a foul mood and said very little to Rhiannon. Kyia was distant, and the one warrior and two warrioress' that came with them did not have much to say to her either. Rhiannon was being chastised, she knew it. She could clearly see their side of the situation, but at the same time, she knew that nothing on earth could have kept her from healing Flath. She was too weary and more than a bit chagrined to try and lighten the mood, so she stayed quiet and brooding as well. The last week of their journey, as they approached the Vel' Kur Mountains and then passed over them, a cool, slow-moving storm blew up from the east, and they rode in a constant drizzle. By the time they reached Màrrach, they were soaked and miserable.

As soon a Rhiannon bathed and dressed in dry, clean clothes she made her way out of the palace and to the sacred place where the altars to their gods and goddess' burned continually, even in the worst of weather. The drizzle had finally abated, and a shy sun was making a short-lived appearance as it hung just above the spine of the mountains. The air had grown chill, and the ground was damp. Methodically she made offerings to Tek' Ju, the god of safe journeys and good luck. She also threw meat and spices on the burning altars of Khepera, the god of new beginnings. Finally, Rhiannon offered grain and fruit to the altars of Selqet the goddess of love and marriage and to Aubo, Baubo, and Min, the goddesses of fertility and childbirth. To Verna she placed a handful of the bitter smelling Velk leaves onto the fire, their waxy golden fronds taking the flame immediately. She had felt awkward and almost hypocritical when she first started making offerings to the gods and goddesses but knew, as their empress, she must conform to the often mysterious, pagan rituals and worship of the Archigos religion, even if she did not fully believe in them herself.

Rosa, a maid in the Foster estate, went to mass every Sunday without fail and would talk of Jesus and Mary and some of the saints when

Rhiannon would sit in the large kitchen and watch her bake. This is how she learned of particular Bible stories. They were somewhat interesting, but she never gave them much creed.

Over the time she had spent in Ventra learning the ways of her people she became more comfortable in her worship of the myriads of gods and goddess the Archigos followed. Despite the strange things that had happened during her Fiann she was still not quite convinced of the reality of the gods, but being the Empress, she had to try at least to believe.

Since the day she came through the Tree of Jur, her belief system had been completely wiped clean. Things she knew to be true just two and a half years earlier seemed nothing but fairy tales now. Her life growing up on the ranch, all of her friends and acquaintances and her relationship with Matthew were unreal now in this world, so harsh and immediate. She wondered how Matthew and Daniel faired and if they missed her and her father, Peter.

Like she had hundreds of times before she imagined how the headlines of local and even national news must have announced she and her father's disappearance. She suddenly wondered if Daniel or Matthew could have been blamed for their vanishing. She sincerely hoped not and wished she could have told them goodbye.

She took a deep breath; the air smelled of smoke, incense, and even burnt carrion. She looked past the smudge of grey smoke toward the east. Green hills just starting to brown under the summer sun gently rose up out of the valley, and the horizon disappeared into a grey, afternoon sky.

Rhiannon had just finished and turned to leave when Shih 'Ni walked up to her. "Interesting choice of gods to honor upon your return home." His voice was flat but did not hold the hostility that it had over the last two weeks. He had bathed and shaved, and his clothes were impeccably clean, as always. His glossy, black hair hung down his back in one thick braid. The golden torque at his neck and simple circlet on his dark head that were symbols of his position as tjaty gleamed even in the weak sunlight.

"Why do you say that?" Rhiannon playfully raised an eyebrow, hoping to lighten the mood.

"Luck, new beginnings, and fertility?"

"We have both been making fertility sacrifices since we were married. Why's it so strange?" They walked side by side, not looking at each other.

"I thought that maybe things had changed," he said hesitantly—very uncharacteristic for him.

Rhiannon took a deep breath then smiled up at him. "Nothing has changed. We must still give Ventra her heir." Timidly she took his hand. He accepted it and even squeezed her hand slightly.

"You know I had to go, Shih 'Ni."

He was silent for a long while. They slowed their walk, almost to a stop. "I know," he finally replied.

"The necklace was the only thing that

could have saved his life. But it doesn't change anything." Rhiannon was trying to convince herself as much as Shih Ni.

"The Queen and her spawn have conveniently died, and you say nothing has changed?" His voice was thick.

Rhiannon stopped and looked up at her husband. A cool breeze stirred his dark hair, as his hard, black eyes watched her. "I don't regret my decision, Shih 'Ni. You are the one I chose, and you are the one I still choose." Rhiannon's throat was tight; it hurt to swallow. She was overcome with emotion and was angry at herself for being so weak. "Must we go through this again?"

Shih 'Ni let Rhiannon's hand slip from his. "Have you no idea of the lack of confidence you have created in me as tjaty? I am your mate, I am tjaty, yet I can't leave Ventra without you sneaking off to see him!"

"I didn't announce my departure, but I certainly did not sneak away like some child running away from home! And I didn't go off to see him. I went to save the life of the King of Beaynid. There's a quote from my world that says 'With great power comes great responsibility.' How could I have purposely let him die when I have the power to save him?"

"You oversimplify the situation, Rhiannon." His voice was steady and his gaze as sharp as his sword. "You are trying to justify your actions, but I can see the guilt in your eyes."

He was right, she did feel guilty, but why should she? She saved a man's life! She looked away from him in defeat. If the situation were to happen again, she would make the same decision. She knew she had made the right choice, so why did she feel so guilty?

"I came home, didn't I? I am here with you, aren't I?" She took both of his calloused hands in hers. "I am committed to you, Shih 'Ni. I am determined to give Ventra her heir; to give you an heir." She smiled up at her husband and was relieved when she saw his eyes soften.

He took her into his arms. "I love you, Rhiannon," he whispered.

The next day Rhiannon called for a

meeting with her advisors, and after dinner, they met in her large meeting hall. Just like the rest of the Grand Palace (or Verna's Palace, as it was sometimes called) and the palaces of Tec 'Lo and Nei 'Rum, it was made of amber, coral, pink and rusty brown colored marble with fingers of wispy, white veins feathering along the sleek walls. Long, honey-colored beams lined the ceiling, and thick, gold-colored drapes covered massive windows and pooled on the carpeted floor.

A large fire burned in the fireplace along the wall, each end was framed by ornately carved marble pillars encrusted with small gems that sparkled in the firelight. Golden statues of different gods and goddesses stood around the room as if to oversee the running of their people. The ivory planters dispersed throughout the room were overflowing with broadleaved trees of the deepest green and smaller bushes and vines gently flowing over their heavily carved beds. The atmosphere was calm and homey, but Rhiannon felt anything but.

Her advisors sat around a solid, round, mahogany table that was so polished that it shined in the sun that had come out that afternoon and now lit up the room through the huge windows. Shih 'Ni was sitting at her right, Kyia at her left, then the rest of the advisors sat, not so patiently, around the arc of the table. Shankee was there, along with another warrioress named Forlia Domis.

Forlia was perhaps five or six years older than Shankee, in her late forties. Her reddish-brown skin was very smooth and without a crease. Her long, hair was still as black as the day she was born. She trained in the yard every morning and could easily ride down warrioress' much younger than she. To say she was beautiful would be an understatement. However, under all that lethal beauty was an arrogance supremely Archigos. She was also very intelligent, and that attribute kept a lot of what was truly in her mind from rolling off her tongue and ultimately offending a lot of people. She was the most outspoken about the changes Rhiannon was making in Ventra.

Forlia thought it was sacrilegious for the Archigos to learn to become sailors and hated the idea of Venturien ships.

Next to Forlia sat Javuil Nys, an uncharacteristically happy Archigos Warrior. He was in his late sixties and had also served as an advisor to Rhiannon's mother, Sernia. His counsel was always sound and well thought out. His jovial attitude might have made it seem he was unconcerned, but he was always studious and his wealth of experience shown in this practical advice. His long hair was mostly grey now, but he kept it in a long warrior's braid with beads and little brown feathers. He did not train anymore and had gotten a little plump, which was very uncommon amongst the Archigos, but his warm, carefree personality kept anyone from commenting about his saggy physique.

Ykellen Gunn was another of Rhiannon's advisors. He was a little older than Javuil and an avid historian of not only Archigos history but world history as well. He was looked to for advice about dealing with other peoples or on new policy that might concern Archigos history or religion. His hair was completely white, and he kept it at shoulder length, as was the custom of older male Archigos who were no longer considered warriors. His snowy hair was thinning, and his braid was more like a mouse's tail than an actual braid of hair. He had served on Shankee's Advisory as well as Empress Tammrah's Advisory before her. His skin was leathery, and his nose was slightly hooked. His hooded eyes were kindly though, and despite his years, he'd shown a sharpness that Rhiannon trusted.

Gen 'Lon Xultrm was the newest Advisor to the Empress. He was only thirty-one, a few years younger than Rhiannon, but Shih 'Ni argued that he would give her the perspective of her younger warriors. He was also Shih 'Ni's cousin. He was as tall as Shih 'Ni and just as good of a warrior. He wasn't quite as somber as his cousin, but she could tell he took his position as one of Ventra's Warriors very seriously and felt privileged to serve as one of Rhiannon's Advisors. His reddish-brown skin was taut with muscles, and the blue scroll of his warrior tattoos lay smoothly across his chest and arms. He wore the customary undyed leather with beaded fringe, and his shiny black hair fell in a thick braid down his back with multiple colored beads and two small brown feathers attached. He watched her close now with his dark, almond-shaped eyes. He had taken a mate right after returning from the War of the Gypsy King and was about to become a father. After returning home from war so many warrioress' became pregnant that it seemed Màrrach was going to be overrun by babies.

Rhiannon took a sip of her tea then cleared her throat. "As everyone here knows, I made an unscheduled trip to Sona Tuath. King Basilias was very close to death, and I used The Necklace to cure him. He will live." Rhiannon looked around the table at her advisors. None were smiling, not even Javuil. She continued, "I apologize for not notifying the council and for leaving Ventra without a tjaty or declaring a proxy while I was away." Rhiannon took a deep breath. "I had no time to make the appropriate arrangements; King Basilias was taking his last breaths when I arrived in Sona Tuath so delaying my trip would have proven fatal."

"Is this something that we can expect to happen regularly; there is a wasting illness in Beaynid, is there not?" Ykellen asked, not unkindly.

"No. It's a sad fate, but the life of a king is more important than that of his subjects, and since he's the only royalty left in the kingdom..."

"Then we can expect you to abandon Ventra every time King Basilias has a problem?" Forlia's fist was clenched, and her gaze was sharp.

Rhiannon sighed; she knew this was coming. "No, of course not. This was an extraordinary circumstance." Rhiannon cleared her throat again and took a deep breath. "I decided that the stability of a bordering kingdom was important to Ventra and so I went to render aid to their dying king.

That's all." Rhiannon clenched her teeth and gave all her advisors a sharp look, ending at Forlia's uncompromising face. Anger started to simmer at the base of her spine. How dare they question her. She was their empress!

"I think we are spending far too many resources, both in the warriors and in the tons of food we've sent south so far. What business do we have even being in Beaynid?" Forlia was not going to let this go.

"Empress Rhiannon is opening up new channels of trade and cooperation with Beaynid, Advisor Domis." Shih 'Ni's deep, soothing voice was welcome to Rhiannon's ears. She had not been sure he was even going to attend today's advisory meeting. "We should be giving her our support; she's making Ventra stronger."

"What she is doing is making us weak! Weak in the eyes of her warriors and to those impotent, sniveling Beaynidans she's trying so hard to coddle, they melt like snowflakes at every hardship!"

"Hold your tongue, Forlia, you speak to

your empress!" This warning was from Shankee. Rhiannon was pleasantly surprised at her cousin's backing.

Rhiannon took another deep breath and let it out slowly. "Thank you, Shankee." She smiled at her cousin and was happy when Shankee returned the smile. Then she turned to Forlia. "Advisor Domis, I know you do not approve of the work I am doing in Beaynid, or in the building of our new ships, for that matter. You are a traditionalist and wish things to stay the way they always have been in Ventra. I understand that, and that is one reason why I asked you to join the Advisory Board. You bring another perspective to our group, and I value your opinion.

"However, I have made my decision with regards to opening up trade and communication with Beaynid, Yellow Island, and even Assuria." She looked around at each of her advisors again. "This will change things here in Ventra, and it's my opinion that it will change things for the better."

Rhiannon took another deep breath and

pushed on, "Before I was called away, Shih 'Ni and I had been discussing the possibility of constructing another residential building." Javuil and Ykellen both smiled, and Gen nodded his head in agreement. Rhiannon immediately felt relieved. "Over half of our warrioress' have become pregnant since our return from the war, and it seems we will be in need of some extra room."

"The Empress is indeed correct!" Javuil said in a sing-song voice, "I am to be a grandfather thrice over! Both my daughters and my son's mate are all going to be blessing Verna with little ones." The old man smiled and looked at everyone at the table.

Ykellen patted him on the back. "I have you beat old friend. I am to be a great-grandfather!"

Rhiannon looked at Shankee who, despite herself, could not hide a smile from usually cynical lips. She knew her cousin was to be a first-time grandmother herself, as Li was to give birth any day. "So we are all in agreement?"

"Yes, Empress!" Ykellen acknowledged. "However, this massive construction project would require more miners and a large number of builders. The Oread have not been blessed by their gods as we have and their numbers have not increased in great enough quantities to supply us enough workers."

"Especially since the Oread we sent to Beaynid to help the villagers have decided to stay there," Shankee said.

"You're right." Rhiannon sighed. "Tess has said that Assuria has great mines and many miners..."

"We are already employing many foreigners at the East Fort," Forlia protested.

"Yes, we are, but our needs at this point are very great. And after their work on state projects are complete, if these foreigners and their families decide to stay in Ventra and continue to work or even farm, we will be able to collect taxes on all the goods and services they produce. Ventra's resources can be put to greater use. Look at the wealth that our land has already produced for us. Our gems, minerals and horses are highly prized throughout the world."

"Is it good for Ventra to grow so large?" the older woman questioned. "Surely we don't want Ventra overrun with foreigners!"

"We must fully investigate this issue. There has been many a civilization that has grown great and powerful only to fall because of their arrogance and complicity...not to mention their greed." Ykellen's words were pointed and caused Rhiannon pause.

"Very true, Advisor Gunn. Perhaps I am getting ahead of myself. However, the fact still remains that we are running out of room and a new residential building must be started soon. It will take years to complete, and if we want to get this thing done before your grandchildren or great-grandchildren are ready for the training yard, we need to make some decisions now. Shall I send agents to Assuria requesting miners?"

"I don't see any other way. My wife and I are already sharing my mother's chambers," Gen 'Lon said glumly.

"There is precedent," said Ykellen. "It's been almost a hundred years now since Ventra opened up trade with Tel 'Rhia."

"That's right! And things have only improved since then," Rhiannon quickly stated. Javuil's happy face was beaming once again. Forlia sat heavily back in her chair and looked defeated. Javuil turned his bright smile on her, and she lost a bit of her sharpness.

"I know this will take a bit of getting used to, but I did take three economics classes at the university, so I have a basic knowledge of how things work, and I will gain even more knowledge as things progress." She was not sure if they understood what a university was, but she was really hoping she sounded confident. She looked down at Shih 'Ni who was looking up at her with a broad smile of encouragement on his handsome face. She touched his shoulder tenderly.

Forlia looked defiant, Shankee wore a resigned expression, Javuil and Ykellen both nodded in hesitant agreement, and Rhiannon knew Kyia and Shih 'Ni would go along with almost anything she requested. "Then it's decided. I shall send out a group of ambassadors to Assuria!"

Later that night Rhiannon slowly walked across her bedchamber to stand next to Shih 'Ni. "Are you coming to bed?" Rhiannon thought she sounded needy and pathetic, like some timid new bride on her wedding night. When Shih 'Ni did not answer, she became nervous. Perhaps he did not plan on ever sharing her bed again. That would prove fatal to her attempts at producing an heir. But she would not put him aside; she knew that. He could not stay mad at her forever.

"Our bed has been cold lately," she said jokingly. His stoic face remained hard. "C'mon Shih 'Ni, it's been a week, and I've barely seen you!"

"A man has his pride, Rhiannon." Shih 'Ni sounded weary, and she knew he was tired of keeping up the illusion of being cross with her when they were alone. He had been very supportive of her in the Advisory Meeting, and for that she was grateful.

"Yes, a man is prideful, and I can understand that," she sighed, "but this has gone on long enough." Her attempt at keeping the mood light was failing miserably.

His face hardened as his dark eyes searched hers. "I know I told you that I would accept the fact that you loved another man when you agreed to take me as your mate, but it turns out that I'm not all right with it." His voice was deep and calm.

Rhiannon's chest tightened, and she found it hard to swallow. A warm tear trailed down her cheek as she looked at the pain on her husband's face. "Oh, Shin 'Ni, what have I done to you?" she whispered and took him into her arms. Tears streamed down her face as he wrapped his solid arms around her. His body was warm next to hers, and he smelled like soap and the smoke from the sacrificial fires burning in the valley.

"Rhiannon, I love you. I have loved you since we were children. You are everything to me. Please let me be your husband. Let me love you," he breathed into her hair. He pulled her away from him and looked down into her wet eyes. The skin of his bare arms were both hard and soft under her touch. "I would gladly lay down my life for you and not because you are my empress but because you are my wife. Let go of this man you can't have and see the man that's standing before you. The man that will help you rule, help you defend Ventra and will eventually grow old with you."

Rhiannon smiled up at him, and his face softened. At that moment Flath seemed so far away; like a past that never happened. At that moment she knew she loved Shih 'Ni. Her heart broke for Flath, a dream never realized. She painfully swallowed past the stubborn lump in her throat and realized she had to move on. She took a deep breath and closed her eyes and said a silent goodbye to the man that had haunted her dreams and held her heart so tightly.

When she opened her eyes another man stood before her. He was fully opened to her, his eyes pleading with her, his full lips curled into a smile that was barely there. This man was the man of her future. This man was the man of her heart. "Let's make a baby, Shih 'Ni," She whispered and brought her lips up to meet his.

CHAPTER SIX

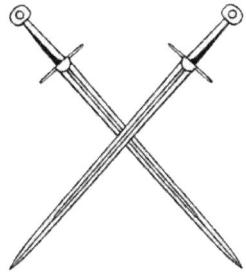

Dark Warrior an answer he did seek
Upon a horned horse, he reached the peak

He stood in Verna's golden light
Biting wind carried his plight

With her tongue, she tore his heart
His world was ripped apart

Sorrow in her azure eyes
She heard his plaintive cries

Her soft whisper was in his ear
A new prophecy he did hear

—*Warrior's Lament; Kyia Kossi—Gods and Goddesses of the Archigos; Ykellen Gunn*

S ummer passed over the land of Ventra in a long stretch of warm, sunny days. A few architects had just arrived from Assuria and were busy surveying and drawing up plans for the new residential building. Some of Rhiannon's agents were still in Assuria gathering miners, masons, craftsmen, and builders. She expected them to be gone for a while.

Warriors and those few warrioresses who were not heavy with child practiced on the hard-packed earth of the training fields and the Oread worked just as hard in the lush green fields of crops that always produced to abundance. Soon all would be busy with the harvest. It seemed the wombs of Ventra where fruitful...except for Rhiannon's.

An arrowhead of geese slowly winged across an azure sky and lazily called out to each other as they floated by. The summer hues of browns and tans had slowly turned to reds, oranges, and yellows as fall crept closer to settling into the northern kingdom of Ventra. Shih 'Ni watched Màrrach disappear behind a stand of trees as he sat atop Santu who was gently meandering down a well-worn path. Rhiannon had left that morning to visit the old healer woman in the woods, Tess, so she would not be back to Màrrach for a few days. He was in no hurry, for he was in fear of what the Ceremony Keeper might tell him. The last time he had gone on the spiritual journey the Archigos called a Niju was when Rhiannon suddenly showed up in Màrrach that cool day two years earlier. It was then that he was assured Rhiannon would be his mate one day.

He laughed bitterly at himself. "Yet the gods have denied us an heir," he said to no one in particular. Santu's ears flickered at the sudden noise, but he kept plodding down the track. The gods certainly had a depraved sense of humor, he thought. Why would they give him Rhiannon but refuse to bless Ventra with an heir? This Niju would answer his questions, he was sure of it!

He finally reached the Ceremony Keeper's home in the woods not too far from Màrrach. The structure where she lived with her four great-granddaughters, several times over, was made of a patchwork of different building material. Some of their house was built of wood, but some of it was made from metal, dented and settled into a soft patina from the harsh northern winters. Still, other parts were made from thick glass of different colors, full of waves and bubbles. The Oread were excellent craftspeople and artisans, but this place looked haphazard and purposeless like a young Oread was just practicing his or her craft. Shih 'Ni supposed it matched the old lady's personality, though.

He tied up Santu's reins on a post and knocked on the door. One of the Ceremony Keeper's great-granddaughters slowly opened up the door then upon seeing who was standing before her, opened it wider to let him in.

"Our tjaty! What disharmony blows you to my door on this day?" the old lady crooned.

"I seek a Niju," he quietly replied, almost embarrassed. She nodded as if she expected him. Who knows, maybe she did know he was coming. Being blessed by the gods, the old woman had a bit of mysterious power surrounding her; the fact that she claimed to be over 180-years-old, notwithstanding. "Come closer, tjaty, and let us dulcify those troubled thoughts!" She waved him closer with her bony arm, the dark wrinkled skin swaying with her movements.

The Ceremony Keeper's white hair fell in two long braids down her chest. She wore a thick strip of beaded leather dyed purple around her head. An elaborate network of blue and purple beads was strung across her neck and wrists and hung from her sagging earlobes. Shih 'Ni could hear the beads banging together whenever she moved. Heavily creased black eyes pierced Shih 'Ni through the heart. He knew what she was thinking; Ventra's tjaty could not provide an heir. He clenched his jaw, lifted his chin and looked down at the old woman, his Archigos pride suddenly bolstering him. He hoped this new-found courage would last through the Niju.

Finally, the old woman turned her heavily wrinkled face to her four great-granddaughters, nodding her head, and the girls immediately went to work setting up for the spirit journey ceremony. A fire was already crackling in the hearth warming the cottage. One apprentice grabbed two small glass bottles from a worn cupboard; another one gently lay a thick blanket on the floor while the last two made a cup of some awful smelling tea. The aroma reminded Shih 'Ni of when he was in the cottage last, on the day Rhiannon returned to Ventra. He was filled with confusion and such intense emotions he was afraid his mind and soul would be lost to Lacti, the dark place those who have fallen into disfavor with the gods are sent. But his mind and soul were soothed by the Niju last time, and he hoped that this time would be the same.

Shih 'Ni sat down on the blanket, already warmed by the fire. At the Ceremony Keeper's urging he took an old ceramic cup from her withered, reddish-brown hands and gulped down the hot tea she handed him. It burned his throat going down and tasted like mold. One of the dark-headed young apprentices threw a handful of something powdered into the fire. It immediately sizzled, and a purple smoke started to hang in the warm air. It smelled familiar, for he had smelled it before, but he still wasn't ready for the acrid taste of the smoke as it burned his mouth and nose. He off-handedly wondered what plant could make such a caustic smell. He coughed but took in huge breaths knowing the bitter smoke would help him on his journey.

He lay back on the blanket, feeling exposed and vulnerable as he clenched his fist and nervously stared at the sloping metal ceiling. Finally, he closed his eyes, taking long, deep breaths quieting his pounding heart. He could hear the old woman begin to chant over his prone body quietly. It seemed like a song but had no tune, and every word was different, not to be repeated. He recognized the words to be a form of ancient Venn, but their meaning was lost to time long ago. The room was becoming overpoweringly warm, and he started to sweat. He could hear the beads on the old woman's wrists as her hands passed over his body sprinkling some kind of ceremonial water on him. The droplets of water were cool on his hot skin. Soon her raspy rhythmic voice became soft and soothing as he felt himself start to fall asleep...

Shih 'Ni gradually became aware of the feel of a harsh wind blowing across his cooling skin. It rushed by his ears deafening him to his surroundings. What was once a soft, warm blanket meeting his back, was now cold, hard rock. He lay there with his eyes closed for several long moments gently stroking the dry dirt under his long fingers. Through the frenzied rush of wind, he could feel the slight warmth of the sun. He strained to hear anything past the wind but still could hear nothing but the wind's forlorn wail.

Gathering his courage, he slowly opened his eyes. It must have been early evening since the sun was setting in a pool of orange and red that painted the sky. Feeling stiff and sore he sat up and looked around. He was sitting on a rocky outcropping overlooking the vast Laoch Valley, Màrrach was way off in the distance; its glass domes sparkling like jewels in the sunset. Immediately he felt homesick. Màrrach was the most beautiful city in the world, he was sure of it. He had traveled all over Ventra and Beaynid, spent time on the peninsula in the coastal town of Turr' ah; in the sprawling, bustling shipping town of Tel `Rhia on the western coast of Beaynid; and he even spent a little time in the eastern castle city of Sona Tuath. However, nothing could ever compare to the mystique and majesty of the home of the mighty Archigos: Màrrach.

Slowly Shih 'Ni became aware of another presence. A slight warming of the air and a disturbance in the way the wind toyed at his hair. He looked to his right and saw a magnificent horned horse serenely lying on the ground next to him; her long, strong legs tucked up under her. Her coat was so shiny black; it was almost blue. Her mane flowed out from her in long dark ribbons on the wind. Her large black eyes stared at him, inviting him closer.

Shih 'Ni recalled the story Rhiannon told him of what happened to her during the Fiann and recognized the horned horse to be Rhiannon's mother, Sernia. The horned horse stood up, all the while keeping her deep eyes upon him. Shih 'Ni slowly stood and hesitantly walked closer to her. He was unsure of what Sernia wanted of him. She nuzzled him to her back, and he climbed on.

She turned and started ascending a rocky trail that led up into the darkening clouds. He gripped her mane and tightened his legs around the horned equine. They climbed higher and higher as the sky darkened and the wind whipped past Shih 'Ni's ears. They rose so high up that Shih 'Ni could swear he could taste salt in the air from the Carnaid Sea many miles away to the east. Finally, they stopped upon a ledge that was thrust out from the mountain like a stony finger pointing into the sky. Shih 'Ni slid off the back of the horse and walked toward the edge. When he looked back, the horned horse was gone and in front of him stood a woman. It was indeed Rhiannon's mother.

Sernia stood tall looking seriously at Shih 'Ni. She appeared just as she had when they were children. Her raven hair blew out in long fingers upon the wind. Dark eyes assessed him under arched brows. Reddish-brown arms came together as her long, elegant fingers clasped each other in front of her. She wore a brown, leather, sleeveless jerkin with matching trousers and brown, beaded slippers. Her top was cut low, and he could see the red diamond-shaped birthmark above her heart, along with the scrolling blue imperial tattoos that disappeared under the leather. Even without the jewel-encrusted crown upon her dark head and the Necklace of Ventra around her elegant neck, she was still very much an

Empress of Ventra.

Her pink lips curled into a smile and her eyes softened. "Shih 'Ni, you have grown into a good-looking man."

"My Empress," he breathed and bowed.

"No more your empress, my dear, but still the mother of your mate. You have treated her well Shih 'Ni, and for that, we are all grateful to you."

Getting right to the point, he held out his big hands and pleaded, "Sernia, we cannot produce an heir. What am I to do?" Suddenly she looked past him. Shih 'Ni turned around as a huge eagle flew up and landed right on the edge of the cliff. He stared at its golden plumage and bright sky-blue eyes. Abruptly it raised its head and screeched into the night. Bumps rose along Shih 'Ni's arms as he felt as much as heard the great bird's cry. His stomach clenched, and he stepped back. The moonless sky was black now, but miraculously he could see perfectly, and it only slightly registered to him how strange that was.

Before his eyes, the giant eagle started to

blur into something else, its plaintive keening lost in the whipping wind. Its golden feathers melted into pale skin until what stood before him was a woman. Her golden hair whipped in the wind as she stared down at him with piercing bright blue eyes. Shih 'Ni's heart slammed in his chest, and he gasped as he fell to the ground and bowed his head low. "My Goddess, Verna," he breathed, not sure at all she could hear him over the howl of the wind.

"Rise, tjaty," she commanded in a voice that fantastically did not waver on the wild wind that blew past them. He did as she bade him and forced himself to look into her blue eyes. He saw compassion there and perhaps sadness. He wondered what cause a goddess would have for sadness. "You are a blameless man, virtuous to a fault. You are zealous in your devotion and protection of Ventra." Shih 'Ni beamed at her words of praise. She raised a graceful arm and gently touched his cheek. "You are a favored son of Ventra, Shih 'Ni." But then her lips turned down slightly, and he was filled with trepidation.

"Thank you," he whispered reverently, aware that her next words would bite.

"However, you are not the tjaty who will produce Ventra's new heir." Her words were softly spoken as if she knew how it would tear at Shih 'Ni's heart. With effort, his dark eyes held hers as he silently pleaded with her to take back her words. "I am sorry, Great Warrior, for I know you deeply love the Empress, however, events have already been written into the Tome of Life. Neither you nor I can change that. I am here only to tell you that you must move on and to soothe your soul, if it is possible."

He opened his mouth to beg for another chance and to plead with her not to make him leave Rhiannon and Màrrach, (for he knew he would have to leave as Rhiannon would never set him aside) but he shut his lips knowing it would do no good to argue with a goddess. He took a deep breath and started again, "Your words make me bleed, My Lady, but I will do as you ask and leave Màrrach immediately." Despite his feigned bravery, his words sounded small and broken in his ears.

Verna clasped her delicate hands then opened them, and in one hand she held a shining golden feather about the length of Shih 'Ni's hand with a thin, leather thong attached at the top. She stretched out her arm and quickly tied it to his dark hair. "You will not leave Màrrach with nothing, though it is not much. I will always be with you, Great Warrior." And then she leaned close to him; he could smell a sharp, smoky aroma: the leaves from the Velk tree. She whispered into his ear and hung on every warm breath she bestowed upon him. His eyes widened at what she prophesied. It was almost too much to believe, especially since his position as tjaty was being taken away from him and he was being thrown out of Màrrach, but he obediently stored her words away in his heart. When her warm breath left his ear, he immediately felt a loss so great he wanted to weep.

"My Goddess," he whispered with emotion and reverence and went into a deep bow. When he straightened up, she was smiling at him. A huge, beaming smile brightened her unbelievably beautiful face; her eyes were so blue he could almost see right through them. Her whole body began to glow, and he could feel the radiance coming from her form. She became too bright to look at, and he shielded his eyes.

"It is time for you to sleep now, Great Warrior," she said, and then softly touched his forehead. Immediately he melted to the ground, and as he lay there, he caught a glimpse of Verna's pale form turning back into the golden eagle and flying away before sleep took him and he was lost to the blackness.

In the darkness, he flew over the three massive, glass-domed, marble structures that made up Màrrach and watched as Archigos and Oread alike were busy at their work. Sacrificial smoke smudged the air over the huge concrete bowls holding the sacred fires. All of their torches burned off the darkness, giving Màrrach a golden glow. Children played, warriors trained, great War Horses grazed in vast meadows. This was his home, and he knew this would be the last time he would lay eyes upon her splendor and beauty. Emptiness lay hold of him.

He then flew into the forest and over Tess's house. He saw Rhiannon talking and laughing with the old woman. His heart broke at the sight. He wept bitterly, sobbing and shaking and his stomach and bowels felt like they wanted to empty. He shook with emotion as he watched the only woman he had ever loved, knowing it would be for the last time. He turned away, unable to look at her any longer. He was grateful to Verna for giving him one last look, but he could not help the bitterness from creeping into his wounded heart. Suddenly he was black inside and knew life would not be worth living if he could not be at Rhiannon's side, but, too, he recalled Verna's promise.

Eventually, he noticed the wind had stopped. His skin felt warm and clammy. Where there had once been vastness, now there was closeness: he was in a structure. Gradually he remembered he had gone to the

Ceremony Keeper's residence to seek her help with a Niju. He took a deep breath and smelled the spicy potion the apprentice had thrown in the fire. He felt the softness of the blanket he lay on and wished he could stay there forever. Then he remembered he had been banished from Màrrach. All over again he experienced the emptiness of having no home and the overwhelming pain of losing Rhiannon.

"Up you go, tjaty!" the old woman croaked. "Your Niju is over, my son, and it is time you go. Up, up, up!" His eyes flew open at the abruptness of her dry voice.

Slowly he sat up and rubbed his aching head. "Thank you, Ceremony Keeper," he said weakly and stood on wobbly legs that would barely hold him.

"I see the Goddess gave you a token!" she said with pride like she had been a part of the whole ordeal, which, he concluded, she had, really. He suddenly remembered the feather Verna had given him, and his hand went up to gently touch it as it hung in his loose hair. It felt heavy and substantial, though he could barely feel it in his hair. He wondered if it held any power, then the bleakness of his future roared in on him, and all he wanted to do was get out of the Ceremony Keeper's dwelling.

Without answering the ancient woman, he nodded to her while vaguely wondering where her four apprentices had gone off to, then hobbled to the door and let himself out. Taking a few deep breaths, he climbed onto Santu's back and rode back down the path he had come from earlier. However, when he got to the place on the road that would take him back to Màrrach, he led his horse in the opposite direction. Santu hesitated for a second in confusion but quickly followed Shih 'Ni's urging toward Turr 'ah. He turned his back on Màrrach, the place of his birth, the kingdom he was helping to rule, and slowly rode away.

CHAPTER SEVEN

*"Within the waters of the Western and Desert seas
dwells a curious race of people known as Selkies.
They are said to have been created by the Ocean
Goddess, Clyphia. There have been many reports
from shipwrecked sailors of the heroic acts of the
Selkies dragging the drowning sailors to safety. It
is said they are led by a mighty Selkie Queen both
powerful in magic and beautiful to look upon."*

—*Field Guide of Beaynid; Myrin Zantroc*

R hiannon looked at her grandmother
as she stood in a shaft of late summer

sunlight. The old woman's hair was twisted up into a loose bun, its color more grey than red now. Her plump cheeks and thin lips were scrunched into a smile as she was bent over a plant, harvesting its leaves for some medicine or another. Rhiannon could not help but smile as she watched her work. She had wanted family her whole life, and now, even though she had lost her father, she was still surrounded by family.

Her grandmother's face was weathered now, but she could see where Tess had been beautiful once and knew what her grandfather, Lu 'Oun, must have seen in her. She wondered what Tess must have looked like as a young girl of the River Clan in far-off Assuria. Lu 'Oun must have been struck when he first saw her pale skin, bright red hair and deep green eyes, so different from the dark people of Ventra.

Come here, Rhiannon, and help me pick these," Tess called out.

"Okay, grandma!" Rhiannon answered, but then turned around when she heard the quick thumping of someone's feet on the soft, mossy ground. Usually, Luna or Etâhpe'o-poeso would have warned her if someone was approaching, but they were both back at Màrrach with their brand-new cubs. Som 'Kel, Shankee's second oldest child, now a young man, ran up to her out of breath.

"Empress," the young man huffed. Clearly, he had been running quite a while.

"Tjaty Shih 'Ni is missing!"

Rhiannon's brows shot up, and her eyes widened. "Are you sure?"

"Yes, my Empress! He told Gen 'Lon he was going to the Ceremony Keeper seeking a Niju and he never returned." Som 'Kel sucked in huge breaths and looked quite worried.

"How long has he been gone?"

"Three days, Empress. He left Màrrach right after you did."

Rhiannon's stomach clenched. Suddenly she felt very uneasy. "Has someone talked to the Ceremony Keeper?"

"Yes. She told Kyia that he left her dwelling days ago!" Som 'Kel was clearly panicked, and

Rhiannon wondered what was going on in Màrrach. "Kyia is readying a party to go look for him and requests your presence immediately."

Tess had walked up to them. "Looks like you have to rush out of here again." She patted Rhiannon on the arm. "Go find your man, daughter."

They pushed their horses and a half an hour later Rhiannon, and Som 'Kel rode into Màrrach, and she could see horses being readied and a group of warriors was gathered in a staging area outside of the Royal Palace, or Verna's Palace as it was sometimes called. They were checking their bags or cleaning their weapons while the small, white-haired Oread scrambled around fulfilling requests from the Archigos Warriors. They looked like they were readying themselves for battle! Rhiannon's mood turned grave. Kyia was nothing if not eternally composed so for her to take such drastic measures was quite unnerving. She began to think Shih 'Ni's supposed disappearance might be a problem.

She looked around, and Som 'Kel was gone, so Rhiannon shrugged her shoulders, rode up to the staging area, and jumped off the back of her horse. She handed her reins to a waiting groom, "Please see to Zellan, and I think we'll be leaving again shortly." The small, Oread groom bowed and led Zellan away.

Finally, she saw Kyia melting out of the group of warriors. She was dressed in a tan long-sleeved tunic and trousers. Her long, dark hair was twisted into two plaits; all beaded decoration was missing. Her sword was already strapped to her back. She quickly walked up to Rhiannon, her brow crinkled in concern.

"We're going after him," she stated without preamble.

Rhiannon looked out over the group of warriors that surely numbered about two hundred. "Do you need so many?" she asked, almost hesitantly.

"Empress, your tjaty is missing."

"Are we sure he's missing? Maybe he just

went into the forest to be by himself for a while."

Kyia shifted, clearly impatient to be away. "I spoke to the Ceremony Keeper. She said she was sure he conversed with the gods, and then he was quick to leave."

Rhiannon sighed, that did sound ominous. "Okay. Where do you think he went?"

Kyia looked to the west, the mid-afternoon sun shining on her rounded face with her small, flat nose; her diamond nose stud winked in the light. "Turr 'ah. It would be quicker to seek passage from there than to go over the Vel 'Kur Mountains. If we are lucky, he will have to wait to book passage, and we can catch up with him there if we make the trip with haste."

When Rhiannon did not respond Kyia looked up at her. "What makes you so sure he has completely left Ventra?" Rhiannon hesitantly asked.

The younger woman's eyes, several shades lighter brown than most Archigos, were severe and clouded with worry. "He spoke to me over his concern about not being able to produce an heir."

Rhiannon let out a gush of air and looked down shaking her head. "Not that again."

Kyia reached out and grabbed her cousin's arms. Rhiannon looked back up at her. "Yes, that. He's intensely worried."

"What is there to be worried about? It's only been seven months since the Nikah, and he knows I won't set him aside and chose another tjaty."

"Does he really know that, Rhiannon?" She knew her cousin must be serious because she dropped the incessant title she usually used.

"Of course he does...doesn't he?" Rhiannon started to become alarmed. It suddenly dawned on her that perhaps she did not know Shih 'Ni as well as she thought she did.

"He told me he was going to seek a Niju and he would ask the gods and goddesses once and for all if he was the rightful tjaty." Kyia stuck out her chin slightly, and accusingly looked up at the taller woman.

Rhiannon's stomach sank, and she was overcome with helplessness. "Oh no," she whispered as her brows drew together in concern and her jaw clenched. Finally, she conceded, "We must leave at once." Her words were desperate and thick with emotion.

As suddenly as he had disappeared earlier, Som 'Kel was standing at Rhiannon's shoulder holding out a packed bag for his empress and standing next to him was Xev carrying Rhiannon's assortment of weaponry. They were both also packed to leave. A young Oread woman handed Rhiannon the crown of Ventra and Rhiannon bent down so the smaller woman could put it upon her head. If she could not find Shih 'Ni before he left Ventra, it would do no good for a head of state to appear without her crown in a foreign territory, Rhiannon abstractedly thought. She took a deep breath, Shih 'Ni was really missing!

Gen 'Lon, one of her advisors, and Shih 'Ni's cousin walked up to Rhiannon. "The council has been advised, and your warriors are ready to leave, Empress." He was clearly also coming along. Rhiannon was not surprised. He was close to his cousin.

"Very well." She took another deep breath and looked out at her warriors who were all now looking at her. "Let's go!" she called out, and everyone started toward their horses which were all waiting in a group, their fair-haired Oread grooms silently standing by their equine charges.

The ride to Turr 'ah was a blur to Rhiannon. She barely ate or slept, and she and Kyia both were mostly silent on the trip. Finally, after a little over a week, they rode into the medium-sized port city of Turr 'ah. Most of the western part of Ventra was settled by the Turr who lived in small villages throughout the countryside. They were "ruled" by the governor who in turn paid tribute and taxes to the Archigos who allowed them their relative anonymity. The governor, who was an elected official (Rhiannon thought that quite democratic of them), lived in the capital town of Turr 'ah which was located halfway down the small peninsula on the western coast.

The smell of fish and salt hung heavy in the late summer air. It was much warmer here then it had been in Ventra and Rhiannon could feel a sheen of moisture on her skin. She was hoping to get a bath tonight. She was also desperately hoping they would find Shih 'Ni here.

She looked off to the south toward Tel 'Rhia and could see the angry grey of storm clouds billowing high up into the sky. If that storm was heading their way, they would have a hard time booking passage. She hoped again that Shih 'Ni had not had time yet to leave. She became anxious to get to the dock and inquire of Shih 'Ni's whereabouts.

People turned to stare as their party of two hundred Archigos Warriors ambled down the sandy, cobbled roads toward the dock. Modest, little single-story houses lined both sides of the streets. The houses here were mainly whitewashed, though peeling paint was evident on most of the homes due to the harsh, salty wind continually peppering them with fine sand. An unrelenting sun-bleached old wooden roof shingles that barely clung to several of the houses. Every house, though, had a brightly colored, freshly painted door and flower boxes that, even at this time of year, overflowed with a multitude of flowers. The explosion of color was quite unexpected.

Rhiannon knew the governor had to know they were in town by now and expected him to show up at any time. She had met him and his wife at her Fiann, and he seemed like a nice, if not a little nervous, man. With no sign of him, they kept up their pace down toward the ocean.

As they crept closer to the docks, the houses turned into shops. All were immaculately kept, even the more modest ones further away from the market. As they approached the market, the shops got bigger and more ornate. Several gem shops looked quite prosperous, and all had two or three men standing guard outside. This is where most of the jewels pulled out of the Del 'Norte Mines ended up. Most of Ventra's enormous wealth came from precious stones.

As the sun set lower in the horizon, they made it to the crowded Turr 'ah market. Rows upon rows of noisy vendors lined many blocks. Rhiannon's senses were overwhelmed by the sea of humanity. The smell of roasting meat filled the air trying to overcome the smell of salt. Hawkers called out loudly from their booths, selling everything from cloth, to trinkets, to food, to buttons, to shoes, to weapons. Anything anyone would ever need or want was here. Rhiannon sighed wondering how they would ever find her husband in this mess.

Four of Rhiannon's warriors went ahead of her and started parting the crowd to make a path for their party. Children darted in and out of the group followed by a mangy looking dog here and there. Parents did not seem to mind their children wandering away. The crush of the crowd hesitantly started to part way. The noise of the market was oppressive after the week they had spent traveling in mostly silence. Rhiannon looked to the south, and it seemed the sky was growing darker, but the clear sky above the market was painted a brilliant orange and red. She watched long-winged gulls float overhead making their way inland—a storm was coming. Tendrils of perfume and spices wafted through the air. Rhiannon sighed and squeezed her knees tight around Zellan, and they started to move into the crowd.

As they painstakingly made their way through the streets, she saw a few city guards wearing their bright green and white uniforms in the crowd but as soon as they spotted the warriors, they melted back into the sea of bodies. They passed a booth selling liquor and Rhiannon suddenly desperately wanted a drink and then felt guilty; they were here to find Shih 'Ni, nothing else.

Rhiannon looked over at Kyia who was riding right beside her. The younger woman was riding straight-backed, staring ahead, focused on her target—the docks-not letting herself be distracted by the noise and activity. She knew Kyia cared very deeply for Shih 'Ni and wondered, not for the first time, why they chose not to marry. Neither would talk about it.

The sun was setting as they finally arrived at the docks. There were two smallish cargo ships docked at the wharf and one larger one floating out in the bay. Rhiannon slid from Zellan's back and looked around for the Harbor Master's office. She was sore and tired, and she twisted, stretching her back a bit. When she straightened up, she saw an older man walking toward them at a clip, his red robes flowing behind him. A ring of light-colored hair grew around a large bald spot on top of his head, and he had a white beard worn short as was the purview of Turr men. He wore a thick robe, an ornately embroidered shirt, matching trousers, and a pair of red slippers that hardly looked like they should be so near water. A sandy-haired young man holding a ledger trotted along behind him, his sandaled feet scissored down the dock after his master.

"My Empress," the older man breathed and dipped into a bow. "I am the Harbor Master. How can I be of assistance to you?"

"Has there been an Archigos Warrior here in the last few days seeking passage?" Kyia and

Gen 'Lon walked up and stood beside Rhiannon.

"Yes, Empress, he was quite insistent about booking passage to Tel 'Rhia as soon as possible."

"So, he hasn't left yet?" Rhiannon asked hopefully.

"He left this morning, your Highness on The King's Rest." The Harbor Master wrung his pudgy hands suddenly looking very nervous. "He was very clear that he must leave right away. Something about state business, or something...," he trailed off.

Rhiannon's heart sunk. "We need a ship right away, then."

The Harbor Master's shiny brow wrinkled in concern. "I'm sorry, you need a what?"

"I need a ship to take my warriors and me to Tel 'Rhia immediately."

"Well, um....um...," he stuttered, clearly at a loss. "Empress, I beg your forgiveness, but we have no passenger ships in dock at the moment."

Rhiannon looked at the two ships tied up

to the wharf that were currently being unloaded. They were both too small to accommodate two hundred warriors and their horses. Then her eyes drifted to a much larger ship anchored in the bay as it bobbed on the choppy waters of the ocean. Her eyes lifted to the storm that she could now tell was rolling toward them.

She lifted her arm and pointed to the ship in the bay. "That one. We'll take that one."

The Harbor Master looked from her to the ship, then back to Rhiannon. "But, Your Highness, that ship is not unloaded yet, and I am not even sure the captain would agree to take on passengers." He shifted from one bright slippered foot to the other still wringing his liver-spotted hands. His young assistant grabbed his ledger more tightly and cast his eyes down to his feet.

Rhiannon stepped closer to the shorter man and leaned in, her black eyes piercing him. "Unload that ship now, and we are taking it immediately. Is that clear?" Her voice was low and steady; deadly.

"Empress...I, um..." The Harbor Master's face reddened making the ring of his white hair stand out even more on his mottled, bald head now covered in a sheen of nervous sweat.

"Pegg, do as the empress commands. Get that ship docked and unloaded now," a deep voice ordered from behind Rhiannon.

"Yes, sir, Governor Brun." Harbor Master Pegg twirled around and in a flash of red robes marched off down the docks, his young assistant at his heels.

Rhiannon turned around to face Trevin Brun, Governor of Turr 'ah as he bowed and smiled at Rhiannon. She was taken aback at how handsome the man was. She had met him briefly at her Fiann but was so distracted at the time she hardly remembered him.

"Governor Brun, thank you for your assistance." Rhiannon smiled, genuinely relieved.

"Unfortunately, I am afraid, Empress Kossi, that even if we can get the ship unloaded tonight, that storm on the horizon will prevent you from leaving until it passes by." His green eyes held sympathy for Rhiannon. As if to make his point for him, a sudden gust of wind blew up tugging at his dark brown hair.

She sighed. She had been afraid of the possibility that the storm would impede their departure. She looked back out toward the south. The dark, angry storm was building; she smelled rain on the blowing wind. She felt a moment of sympathy; it was going to be a miserable night for those deck hands unloading that ship during the storm. She turned back toward Trevin. "Perhaps you'd be so kind as to find us accommodations for tonight?

Trevin smiled again, dimples barely showing through his dark, closely cropped beard. "Of course, Your Highness. Follow me."

Governor Brun had placed her warriors in the best rooms at all of the most luxurious inns Turr 'ah had to offer. Rhiannon, Kyia, Som 'Kel, and Gen 'Lon were invited to stay at the governor and his wife's manor situated on a bluff overlooking the bay. Travin's wife, Mela, was even more stunning than he was.

She was tall and willowy with shiny chestnut colored hair that fell to her knees. Her large, almond-shaped eyes were the brightest azure blue she had ever seen and were ringed by long, dark lashes. Her flawless skin was just kissed enough by the sun to give it color but not to prematurely wrinkle. She wore a low-cut red dress, heavily beaded and embroidered with full skirts that fell to the ground. The diamond and ruby drop earrings and matching necklace she wore across her delicate neck surely came from Ventra's Del' Norte mines.

While the storm started to howl outside, they were treated to dinner with succulent fish roasted in herbs Rhiannon could not identify. There was steamed asparagus, buttered sprouts, creamed kale, loves of fluffy, hot bread thick with seeds, and rich, chocolate pudding. Rhiannon ate as fast as she could, drinking several glasses of wine, all the while listening to the storm rage outside. She wondered if the ship had been unloaded yet and if Shih 'Ni were safe aboard his vessel sailing south toward Tel 'Rhia. She tried to follow the dinner conversation but knew she was utterly distracted. Though Trevin's deep tones and Mela's soft, soothing voice along with the help of the wine eased Rhiannon's anxiety a bit.

Not soon enough it was finally time to retire for the night and she and Kyia were shown to their shared room on the third floor of the mansion. Rhiannon pulled off her clothes and left them in a heap on the floor and climbed into her huge feather bed. The room was dark and smelled of honey wax candles and lavender oil. Sheets of rain pelted the large windows cloaked by thick draperies. An excited fire roared in the hearth warming the room and casting long shadows that danced with the rhythm of the wind.

As exhausted as she was, Rhiannon could not fall asleep so easily. She heard Kyia moving around and knew her cousin was not asleep either. "Do you think he's alright?" Her voice was small and scared. She hated her weakness.

Kyia did not answer for what seemed like a long time. Finally, she spoke up, "I have had a bad feeling since we left Màrrach. I cannot shake it no matter how hard I pray to Verna. I do not think he is safe, no."

Her voice was almost accusatory, something Rhiannon had come to expect from her on this journey. "He will be alright. We will find him and bring him home." Her words sounded hollow and false even to her. She sighed and shut her eyes, forcing herself to get some rest as the wicked wind howled and beat against the windows.

***

In the morning, the storm had cleared, and a sunny blue sky greeted them all as they started to board the massive Sea Falcon. It seemed to take an interminable amount of time for the ship to get loaded with supplies and to secure the cargo and the horses, however by mid-morning they were sailing out of the Bay. Rhiannon was restless with worry as she traversed the ship from bow to stern, over and over, willing the ship to gain speed across the miles of ocean they had yet to cross, but, despite its name, the Sea Falcon was a lumbering beast.

She walked up to Kyia who stood at the bow of the ship, her long, unbound hair blowing in the wind. She looked like the proud figurehead of some ancient vessel. She wanted to say something to lighten her mood but could not bring herself to say anything for her own mood was morose, so she just stood next to her and stared out over the dark water.

"What will you say to him to make him come back with us?" Kyia finally spoke.

Rhiannon had not thought that far ahead. Her stomach clenched at the thought that they might find him, and he would refuse to return with them. "Do you think he wouldn't come back with us?"

"I know when he sets his mind to something you won't be able to talk him out of it."

"I could order him to come back. I am his Empress."

Kyia's lips curled into a humorless smile.

"You could try."

Rhiannon sighed again, feeling defeated. Shih 'Ni was stubborn and if he truly felt that Ventra's best interests were being met by him leaving he would not return. "What can I tell him to change his mind about leaving?"

Kyia looked over at her pinning her with a sharp look. "You shouldn't have gone to Sona Tuath last spring."

Rhiannon could feel her face growing hot. She did not expect to be attacked again on this subject by her closest confidant. "I did what I thought was right." She lifted her chin in defiance.

"You pierced him and took his confidence." Kyia would not be intimidated; her face was dark.

Rhiannon bit off a retort that his confidence should not be governed by her actions. She looked back out over the water and suddenly felt crippled at the thought that she had irrevocably damaged her marriage and wounded Shih 'Ni so greatly that he would leave the only life he's ever known. Tears started to slip down Rhiannon's cheeks as she realized that perhaps there was no hope, even if they did find him. "I did this to him," she whispered. Kyia placed her warm hand on top of Rhiannon's as it rested on the smooth wooden rail. She squeezed it, trying to comfort her cousin and then walked away.

The next morning Rhiannon was awoken by loud horns being blown and many voices shouting. She jumped out of her bunk, stuffed her feet into her boots and ran up to the deck. Sailors were running about while her warriors all stood on the port side of the ship looking toward the coastline that they had been following all night. Bumps formed down her arms, and her stomach tightened as fear washed over her. She spotted Kyia and ran over to her. The younger woman was looking out over the water with horror.

Hesitantly Rhiannon slowly turned to face a scene of carnage. Angry, jagged chunks of wood that had once been part of a ship were floating haphazardly upon the water. Wooden crates that were once full of supplies were now bobbing along the ocean currents. Further, toward land, the enormous curved hull of a ship rose up above the water like a giant monolith, its intricately carved figurehead staring sightlessly into the heavens. The salty wind blew the smell of carrion onto the deck and Rhiannon grabbed the rail of the ship until her knuckles turned white. Her heart was pounding in her chest, and she took her breaths in small, fast gulps. She was frozen and could not move or utter a word.

Someone off to her right yelled out and pointed to the swath of brown sandy beach where many bodies lie baking under an unusually warm morning, for it would soon be fall. A whimper slipped from Rhiannon's parted lips, and she could see from the corner of her eye Kyia looking up at her with concern in her eyes. Rhiannon started to shake, and her knees buckled. She slid to the deck turning away from the morbid scene.

Kyia crouched beside her and took her hand. "You will be all right, Rhiannon." Her cousin's words echoed in her ears as if she were far away.

The captain started shouting out orders, and the lifeboats were filled and dropped into the water. Rhiannon climbed into one of the rickety little boats with Kyia and Gen 'Lon, and the sailors rowed steadily to shore. As they made their way through the debris field, Rhiannon noticed flashes of black gliding just under the surface of the grey water. She looked a little farther out and saw sleek black bodies lithely sliding through the waves circling what was left of the doomed ship.

Rhiannon looked down and sucked in her breath when she saw two huge black eyes staring up at her. The animal's round, dark-furred head slipped from the surface, all the while holding Rhiannon's gaze. She was sure it was trying to communicate with her, but she had no clue what the animal was trying to tell her. Finally, the creature barked twice, quite loudly, and disappeared under the cold water. Gen 'Lon leaned in toward Rhiannon and whispered, "selkies." His dark eyes darted toward the animals that were now headed for the shore.

The lifeboat smacked the sandbar with a thud sending Rhiannon into Kyia. The younger woman looked up at her cousin with fear and sorrow in her eyes. Rhiannon nodded to her and jumped from the boat. There were men's bodies lying everywhere upon the sandy beach. Rhiannon's warriors spread out trying to make identification of those lost.

Rhiannon stood amid the carnage not knowing what she should be doing. She felt useless and confused. The sun was shining in her eyes giving her a headache. She tried to make decisions but was paralyzed. Her warriors went about their business without her command. Rhiannon took deep breaths trying to calm herself, telling herself that perhaps this boat was not the one Shih 'Ni had booked passage on. However, as if on cue, two of her warriors brought over a large chunk of the boat's hull. Carved into its side and painted a cheerful bright yellow was the name The King's Rest. Rhiannon's hands went to her mouth, and she bit her lip to keep from crying out. "Keep searching for your tjaty," she finally said in between deep breaths.

Distraught and at a complete loss Rhiannon looked a little farther down the beach and was shocked when recognition set in. She screamed and ran down the beach, her unbound hair blowing out behind her. Her boots found it hard to find purchase in the shifting sand, but she pushed on as fast as she could. Finally, she fell to her knees at the grey, bloated body of Santu. Rhiannon turned her face up to the sky and wailed a long, forlorn sound. She gently stroked Santu's body and cried hysterically. All hope was now lost.

After a while, Rhiannon became aware of a hand on her shoulder. She wiped the tears from her eyes and looked at the hand that rested there, long, slender, delicate webbed fingers with curved black nails. Dumfounded Rhiannon twisted her head up to see who was standing behind her, but the sun was in her eyes, so she slowly stood.

A naked woman stood before her, her body still dripping from the ocean. Long tendrils of shiny black hair fell to her waist. Round, black, pupilless eyes stared back at her and Rhiannon immediately recognized them to be the same ones she had seen on that creature swimming by the boat earlier. "Selkie," Rhiannon whispered in awe.

"Aye, milady, I am Astrid, Queen of the Selkie." Her face looked human, yet not quite. Her skin was dark and shiny and had bright bioluminescent blue dots around her forehead, outside of her wide, dark eyes and down her sleek arms and legs. She was quite captivating.

Rhiannon bowed. "I am Rhiannon Kossi, Empress of Ventra. Do you know of any survivors from this shipwreck?"

In turn, Queen Astrid bowed to Rhiannon. "I do not, Empress. We only came upon this scene this morning. The storm forced us out further into the depths of the ocean. I wish we could have been here to help." It was then that Rhiannon noticed several naked men and women standing behind their queen. The looks on their faces were both curiosity and sympathy. Behind them were her warriors and the sailors from Sea Falcon. "I am sorry, sister. Perhaps this will ease your pain and worry a bit."

She handed Rhiannon a small shell. It was white on the outside and pink on the inside. It did not look very special, but immediately Rhiannon's mind started to clear, and she began seeing what must be done. Rhiannon smiled brightly at the woman who smiled back. They hugged, and Rhiannon walked over to her warriors. "Bury all these bodies. Santu's first." When she turned back around all the Selkie were gone from the beach, but she could see their little heads bobbing up and down watching them from the water.

It was an arduous job burying two dozen men and one warhorse, but as the sun set, the lifeboats full of exhausted warriors and sailors rowed back to the Sea Falcon. Too tired and suffering too much grief to eat, Rhiannon went straight to her bunk and fell asleep. She dreamed of Shih 'Ni, his rare laughter, his stern instruction with the sword, and even to what he looked like first thing in the morning: mussed hair, dark stubble and sleepy, black eyes staring at Rhiannon with love. She woke in the middle of the night sobbing into her pillow. She knew Kyia, who shared the space with her, heard her cries of anguish, but she did not care.

Her life would never be the same without Shih 'Ni, and she only had herself to blame for his death. She was not sure how she could go on without him. Not being able to sleep, she threw off her blanket and marched up to the deck. The cool air blew through her hair and dried her tear stained face. She could not understand how this could be happening to her. She had not been completely sure of how much she loved Shih 'Ni until she saw his dead War Horse lying on that lonely beach. Her feelings ran deeper than she had first thought, and she felt an enormous hole in her chest when she pondered her life without him now. There would be no children. There would be no growing old together. Rhiannon crumpled onto the deck and started sobbing again. She shook and tightened up her muscles until she felt like she would explode.

Finally, she remembered the shell that Astrid had given her and carefully took it out of her pocket. Once again, a feeling of calm came over her. She spread her legs out upon the deck and took in deep breaths of moist, salty air. She laid her head back against the rail reveling in the sway of the ship. Tears ran down her cheeks as she concentrated on just breathing. After a while, she became aware of someone sitting next to her. She did not have to open her eyes to know it was Kyia. Again, Kyia's warm hand found Rhiannon's. Nothing was said. Nothing had to be said. Life would not be the same, but it had to go on. Somewhere out in the darkness, Rhiannon heard the plaintive barking of the Selkie Queen.

CHAPTER EIGHT

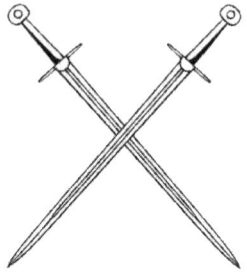

*The tears of the Empress of Ventra wet land and
sea
Her tjaty was gone and could not hear her plea
The words of his Goddess caused him to flee*

*Goodbye Warrior from the land of Ice and Blood;
your empress weeps a never-ending flood*

*His body lies in a watery grave
His land; his people; he will no more save
Drowning in sorrow, for her husband she does
crave*

Goodbye Warrior from the land of Ice and Blood;

your empress weeps a never-ending flood

Tjaty Shih 'Ni Master of Ventra a mighty man of
war
His stories will be etched in lore
Though he will walk his beloved land no more

Goodbye Warrior from the land of Ice and Blood;
your empress weeps a never-ending flood

—*Goodbye Warrior; Ju 'Blm*

The days rolled by, one into the other as they bobbed along down the Beaynidan coast. Rhiannon numbly stared out over the undulating grey water of the Western Sea—her mind was blank, and she was barely aware of the feel of the smooth shell she constantly gipped in her hand. She stood at the bow of the ship, the dark fringe of her unbound hair, now half-way down her back blew out behind her. It had been almost a year and a half since the Fiann rituals during which her hair had been shorn off. So much had happened since then it was hard for Rhiannon to fathom.

Though she did not look at her, Rhiannon was acutely aware of the Selkie Queen and her court as they escorted the Sea Falcon further south. There was a connection between she and Astrid that Rhiannon could not understand, perhaps it was through the shell? It was as if their minds brushed up against each other—the Selkie Queen giving her support. The feeling was alien yet comforting. It was hard for Rhiannon to form a thought as she stared out over the vastness of the sea. She knew the only reason that grief had not swallowed her whole yet was because of Astrid's gift. Rhiannon had no idea how it worked, nor did she care. She cared about nothing, in fact.

The deck of the Sea Falcon rose and fell in lazy arcs that Rhiannon was hardly aware of anymore. The air was salty and filled with the call of seabirds, but Rhiannon did not notice. Kyia hovered around constantly yet only approached to beg her to take a little food and water, which she occasionally did, but everyone else stayed a safe distance away.

Rhiannon thought she might be broken beyond repair. It was as if she could not feel anything, not even the wind across her chapped skin. She could not bring herself to cry, or shout, or to curse Verna for her husband's fate. Her mind felt as if it were wrapped in gauze and her body was floating above the Sea Falcon as it cut through the foamy swells. The only connection she felt at all to this world was the tentative link between her and the Selkie Queen.

Finally, on the sixth day, the fog in her mind started to recede, and she became aware of the sailors scurrying across the deck, busy at their chores. She noticed the jagged coast getting nearer as the Sea Falcon headed into Bay of The Mermaids and into Tel 'Rhia. Like a phantom, Kyia was suddenly standing beside her and Rhiannon jumped when she heard the woman speak. "Your warriors are readying to disembark, my Empress. Will we wait for another passenger ship to take us back to Turr 'ah?" Rhiannon looked down at her cousin trying to understand her words. The smaller woman looked around at the activity going on. "I know the captain and crew will be glad to be rid of us. We make them nervous."

Finally, the puzzle pieces of Kyia's words came together. "No, I think we'll ride back to Ventra. I need some time off this ship, or any other, for that matter."

Kyia looked at her keenly, worry spread across her face. "All right, I'll tell the others to be ready to ride." Rhiannon watched her cousin walk away, her steps measured as if she wanted to turn around and say something else. She knew Kyia blamed Shih 'Ni's death on her even though she dare not speak it aloud. She knew all her warriors blamed her—and they should, it was her fault! Rhiannon balled up her fists, feeling the feather-light weight of the shell in her right hand, and looked at the approaching bay. She wanted to scream or cry or lash out, but she could not get up the will to do anything beyond take another breath.

Within the hour the large gangplank was lowered, and they started to disembark. As Rhiannon lead Zellan over the wooden ramp from ship to shore, she glanced down into the dark water and was not surprised at all to see the seal face of Astrid looking up at her with those oily, black eyes. The shell still gripped in her hand, almost seemed to hum lightly as she felt Astrid's gentle touch in her mind. The Selkie Queen offered love and sympathy— feelings that threatened to overwhelm Rhiannon. Rhiannon stopped to look at her, and not for the first time, wondered why this fantastical creature would even care about her. She smiled, trying to send her gratitude to the Selkie Queen. With a last bright spark of love, Astrid barked then slipped beneath the dark waters of the bay.

Rhiannon and her warriors made their way from the bustling docks into the busy city shivering with activity. Tel 'Rhia was the largest and most populated city in both Beaynid and Ventra. Docks spread out in both directions across the gentle curve of Bay of The Mermaids. Enormous wooden warehouses crowded the area and blocked her view of her immediate surroundings. There were huge houses built right into the towering hills circling the bay and disappearing off into the distance. Rhiannon had never seen such a densely populated place since coming to this world.

Gen 'Lon and a few other warriors went out ahead of Rhiannon and cleared a path through the humanity. If Turr 'ah was busy, Tel 'Rhia was utterly teeming with people and animals of all sorts! Even though there were city workers aplenty, it was hard not to step in animal waste. Bodies pressed together as they tried to move through the city. The cacophony of voices—all kinds of different languages— grated against her skull and sent her head throbbing. Her warriors enveloped her to keep the crowd away, but still, the stench of body odor, cooking meat, and animal feces made her gag. Her pulse quickened as they slowly made their way through the crowded street and were suddenly in the middle of a vast market square. Rhiannon had no desire to look at the wares being offered, all she could see were her warrior's backs anyway. Her eyes were laser focused on the leather tunic stretched across Xev's broad back. The hot autumn sun blazed down on her head making her break out in a sweat. Her mouth went dry, and she swallowed down the bile threatening to come up. She started to shake and squeezed the shell still in her hand, surprised it had not shattered already.

Slowly a feeling of calm overcame Rhiannon. Her pulse slowed, and her shaking subsided. Astrid's shell was hot in her hand as her mind mellowed and settled into a comfortable numbness. Detached she watched the activity around her, like so many ants busy at their work. The noise died down to meaningless words that seemed to be spoken in slow motion. She took slow, deep breaths not even aware of the thick stench any longer.

After a long time, they finally came to the other side of the market square. Her warriors spread out, and Rhiannon was able to see more of her surroundings. They were still in the market district. Shops lined the precisely laid-out streets, all neatly cobbled and cleaner than the streets by the docks. Inns and taverns were everywhere. Rhiannon wondered if they should seek rooms here but then desperately just wanted to get out of Tel 'Rhia.

As they turned the corner onto one of the wide streets that climbed up the hills surrounding the bay, Rhiannon saw a small boy sitting outside a tavern. She suddenly had a staggering pain in her heart when she thought of Tim and how much she missed him. She was not sure why he haunted her memories just now, for this boy was much younger and had a shock of dark hair. He peered up at her with defiant brown eyes. The boy looked nothing like Tim. Beside him, in a cage, was a small golden colored monkey. It shrieked at her when she bent down to look at it and shrunk away from her as far as it could get. She could clearly feel fear radiating off the small creature. Her heart broke for the monkey, and she could think of nothing else except taking it with her.

Rhiannon looked over at the boy who was studying her with his wary black eyes. His skin was dark, but grime made it even darker. His hands were small and calloused, and his nails were caked with dirt. His filthy clothes hung on his thin frame in tatters. His feet were bare.

"How much to buy the monkey?" Rhiannon asked quietly. Her voice sounded strange to her; like it was not hers.

The boy looked up at the crown she had forgotten she was even wearing. "'Tis not for sale. She is my pet." His voice was a little deeper than she had expected. He was older than he looked, just malnourished.

"Is that so? She doesn't seem too happy to be in that cage."

The boy looked over at his monkey. "She bit me, so she has to stay in there."

"Maybe she was hungry?' Rhiannon offered.

The boy let out a funny sound between surprisingly straight teeth. "No more than I am!"

"Well, I'd be glad to give you coin for your monkey. She's mean anyway, why would you want to keep her?"

The boy looked like he was contemplating something. "She was my brother's, but he died a few weeks ago. It does not seem right to sell her."

Rhiannon knew the boy was weaving a sad story for her. "Well, if you were going to sell her, how much would you think would be a fair price?"

The boy scratched his head and thought for a moment; his eyes kept sliding up to her jewel-encrusted crown. "I'd say ten silver pieces," the boy replied, seemingly making up his mind.

Rhiannon nodded her head. "All right," she said as she stood up.

Suddenly Xev put his hand on her arm. "Empress this street urchin seeks to rob you. That monkey is half starved, and even if it were healthy, it wouldn't be worth three silver pieces.

"That's not true!" The boy howled. "This monkey is rare! 'Tis from Dar 'Ven, far across the Desert Sea."

"Psh, he tries to rob you, Empress!" Xev

exclaimed.

"That might be so. However, I think this poor boy has suffered enough. Give him twenty-five gold pieces, Kyia." She heard a few indrawn breaths from her warriors but paid no mind. "Are you in agreement to that offer?" she asked the boy who was now on his feet staring at her as if she were in shock.

"Aye, your excellency!" he exclaimed in shock.

"Good." Rhiannon smiled and turned away as Kyia counted out the boy's new wealth. "Xev will you be kind enough to gather my monkey?"

"As you wish, Empress."

***

It was late. The golden sun had slipped into the Western Sea by the time they made their way out of Tel 'Rhia. Rhiannon felt raw and exhausted as they left the farms and crofts outside the enormous city and headed out into the gently rolling hills of western Beaynid. Before it got too dark, they made camp amongst a stand of trees. They made a fire for light and warmth as the night cooled but ate from the supplies they had brought. Tomorrow they would have to hunt if they wanted fresh meat.

Rhiannon sat on a boulder and watched as camp was set up. A few of the younger warriors took the War Horses, removed their saddles and bridles, and let them graze, knowing they would not go far. A few of the horses went down to a busy stream and drank their fill. Kyia carefully laid out their bedrolls and packs. She felt thankful for her cousin's friendship and loyalty. She knew Kyia was also grieving Shih 'Ni's death, but she did so silently.

Several warriors sent up a perimeter and started patrolling vigilantly. No one would dare attack an Archigos War Party. However, one never knew the lengths a group of stupid men might go to achieve a legendary reputation, which was assured of anyone who could take a group of Archigos.

She looked over to the cage that housed her new monkey. They had fed the thing bread, fruit, and even cheese until Rhiannon was sure the poor thing would be sick, but it just wanted more food. When they got home, she would pick out a perfect name for her and let her out to roam and play in the solarium. Rhiannon knew Dar 'Venn was a long way away; the poor girl must have gone through a lot only to end up with a bunch of Archigos Warriors heading to Ventra. She sighed and squeezed the shell in her hand. Rhiannon was not at all sure she was ready to face her people with the sad story of the loss of their tjaty. Anxiety spread through her as she pictured the faces of her council members with the news. She knew they would blame her. In fact, all of Ventra would blame her!

***

The sky grew darker as the cold sparkles of stars appeared overhead. Rhiannon lay upon her nest of blankets, covered up tightly. She still held the shell in her hand as her thoughts drifted to her husband. She agonized about his last minutes in the cold water, being battered by storm-swept waves. She wondered if he had thought of her as he drowned. She sobbed quietly as tears soaked her face and hair. As the others slept, she lay feeling as if a chasm opened in her chest, exposing her heart, and making her wish she were dead.

Like a dam had broken, emotions rolled from her like the churning waves that took her husband's life. She forced herself to lie still, but sobs silently wracked her body. She tried to be silent for she did not want to wake her warriors and make them witness to her weakness. Tears spilled down her cheeks as the glowing moon tracked across an inky sky filled with millions of twinkling stars. She feared she would never be whole again.

In the morning Rhiannon sat atop the same boulder and watched as her warriors broke camp. The overwhelming sadness from the night before had subsided into resigned numbness once again. She was thankful that apparently none had observed her breakdown. In fact, none had shown much reaction to Shih 'Ni's death. Even Gen 'Lon, usually stoic anyway, held his sorrow in check. The Archigos were nothing if not emotionally reserved.

"We're ready to leave now, Empress." Kyia walked up to Rhiannon holding the reins of both Kalouaii and Zellan.

Rhiannon stood up, took a deep breath and hopped up on Zellan's back. "I am going on alone. You all will return to Màrrach as quickly as you can and advise the council of what has happened." Kyia, Gen 'Lon, and several of her warriors all started contesting at once. She had expected the uproar but was still surprised at their adamancy. "I will hear not another word. I need some time alone and cannot return to Màrrach just now."

"Empress, you will not be safe traveling alone!" Gen 'Lon approached her with a beseeching look on his face. "Shih Ni would kill me if he knew I let you wander Beaynid alone!"

"Shih 'Ni is no longer here, and I am your Empress, I will hear no more arguments on the matter." Rhiannon pulled on Zellan's to the right to leave, but an older warrioress grabbed her reins and stopped him in his track.

"I cannot let you leave, my Empress." Her dark eyes, just starting to show age, bored into Rhiannon. She could almost hear the woman's accusations that this predicament was all her fault. It was all her fault!

Rhiannon's anger started to simmer as she yanked her reins out of the warrioress' hands. "I am your Empress, and you shall obey me." She looked back up at all her warriors who stood stunned. "You shall return to Màrrach immediately!" Rhiannon kicked Zellan into a cantor and left them standing in shock, the monkey's plaintive chirps being carried away on the breeze.

Rhiannon traveled east through the Plains of Ak and turned a little north skirting Bell. She could not face Tim's father, even now. She cursed herself for being such a coward. In the distance, off to the right, she saw a large stone manor being built. It was almost complete. She knew that to be the home of Adam Pem; the newly install Duke of the district of Bell. Because of his loyalty and dedication to the rebellion, he had been awarded a title, a large swath of land, and a little money to build his keep.

Because Flath had divided Beaynid into four districts and given over the rule of those districts to men who had fought with him in the rebellion, (or in the case of Tel 'Rhia and Cargh, monetary support) lawlessness had decreased and the need of her warriors as peacekeepers had been steadily declining. Her warriors and their families had slowly been trickling back into Màrrach, glad to be home. The Oread that she had left with farmers, though, seemed to like it in Beaynid and not many had returned. She guessed it was because of the milder winters.

Rhiannon continued on northeast into the Alba Forest. She hunted almost every night since her travel provisions had run out the week before. She wondered if her warriors had gone back to Tel 'Rhia and took a ship back north or if they had continued by horseback. If they had stuck to land and made haste, they would be at the Pass of Koslyn by now. Rhiannon had been in no hurry as she traveled the past few weeks. She had much to think about and was grateful for the quiet time to herself. She did miss Luna and Peso, however. They had both given birth within weeks of each other, six cubs for each mother. Rhiannon smiled when she thought of the solarium at home full of pax and wolf cubs.

Rhiannon continued on her journey down narrow trails in the Alba forest. She found a shallow place to cross Huntsman's River, but still, Zellan had to swim when they reached the center of the crossing. It had not rained in over a week, so the rivers and streams were still passable; luckily, since there were no bridges in this part of the country.

Without even knowing her destination when she had left her warriors dumbfounded in that meadow just outside of Tel 'Rhia three weeks earlier, Rhiannon finally stopped. The sun had set, and now the large clearing was growing dark. Weary from travel, Rhiannon slid from Zellan's back. She took a deep breath and removed the shell from her pocket squeezing it tightly in her palm. A feeling of calm started to wash over her as she carefully studied what had brought her hundreds of miles northeast and separated her from her warriors. Had she known all along she was going to end up here? Even Rhiannon did not know the answer to that question. Letting Zellan's reins drop to the grassy floor she slowly approached. Was it sheer luck that she arrived just in time, for tomorrow would be the fall equinox.

Time seemed to stand still here in this primeval clearing located in this ancient forest. The birds were quiet as if to show reverence to the King of the Forest that stood in front of her like a magical beacon. It lay dormant now, innocent and blameless, though Rhiannon knew that was a lie. The shell's smooth surface warmed Rhiannon's hand as her mind fought disquieting thoughts.

Through the dim, dwindling light Rhiannon peered at where her long, sad odyssey had first begun two and a half years earlier: she now stood before the Tree of Jur. Its huge, gnarled trunk held up massive branches still full of dark leaves, shimmering in a dry breeze that dared to blow through the forest clearing. She edged a little closer, mesmerized by the gaping opening in the tree, its inky darkness so deep the brightest light would not penetrate it. She could feel its draw on her soul calling her home.

She peered up at the living monolith standing before her. Hundreds of human bones hung eerily from the dark branches of the tree gently swaying in the breeze in a macabre dance of death. Flashes of white drew her eyes and gave the tree of bone and mist an otherworldly appearance. The Priests of Jur had hung the bones of their dead upon the tree many years ago in the act of reverence and worship. What they left was a ghoulish spectacle which most people avoided. But Rhiannon had been drawn to the tree's sheltering arms and promise of home.

Rhiannon stopped before the tree and hesitantly held out her hand. The bark was rough and warm under her fingers. It would still be hours before the tree's portal opened, but she could feel a current running through the tree and the air as if it siphoned power from the forest in preparation. She mindlessly rubbed the rough bark wondering how it would be to walk back into her life in Montana. Matthew and Daniel would be shocked, but she knew she would still be welcome. Could she do it? Could she leave Màrrach for good? She edged closer as she counted everything she had lost since coming through the tree: her father, Tim, Flath and now Shih 'Ni. The loss was too great to bear—she could stand to lose no more.

Unaware of time passing, Rhiannon stood before the Tree of Jur as the full moon traveled across a black sky. She felt no hunger or thirst or even a need to rest. She was not aware of Zellan as he grazed and every so often looked up at her to make sure she was still all right. Her ears were deaf to the night insects or the hoot of a nearby owl. Enthralled by the tree, she stood by its side all night like a sentry at her post. Finally, the moon dipped behind tall pines, and the cold stars gave up their twinkling as night turned to dawn and then the sun started to rise turning the sky from pink to blue.

Rhiannon felt the humming of the tree before she heard it. Under her caress, the already warm bark turned hot, and she pulled her hand away. A thick mist started to pour from the tree and roll across the clearing. The smell of pine was replaced by the aroma of dirt and blood, and the tree started to glow an amber color. This was it. This was her chance to right the wrong that had been done her when she was brought here. The pull of the tree was hard to resist and then she wondered why she was resisting at all. She moved closer to the opening that was now aglow in light.

Slowly something started to eat away at her haunted thoughts. A nagging that became louder and could not be ignored any longer. She was being watched! Her pulse quickened as she squeezed the shell in one hand and pulled her sword free with the other. Slowly she turned around ready to face what she was sure was an attack.

Peering through the mist, though, was not the face of an enemy at all. "Rhiannon, don't," Kyia pleaded, tears running down her cheeks—Rhiannon dropped her sword to the ground, and the amber mist swallowed it whole.

Rhiannon looked at her cousin, and anger started to burn deep within her. How dare she disobey her direct order to return to Màrrach with the rest of the warriors! The pull of the tree was great, however, and Rhiannon turned back around to face it.

"Rhiannon, no!" Kyia pleaded again. "We need you. We need our empress." Kyia's voice sounded thin and insubstantial compared to the loud humming from the tree.

As she peered into the opening of the tree, Rhiannon tried to remember what her life was like in Montana. She had loved Matthew once. They were to be married. Daniel was like her second father, more attentive and affectionate than her own father, Peter, had been. Her life had been full on the cattle ranch.

Or had it? She began to recall the

nightmares she had been plagued with and the feeling that her life was meaningless and that there was something more she needed to be doing.

She remembered seeing Flath's face in those dreams, and her heart ached to see him again. Then she pictured the face of her dead husband and was brought low by feelings of guilt. All the events of the past two and a half years played out across her mind, and she saw every moment like she was watching a movie. A sick, twisted movie that did not have a happy ending. Why was she brought here to end up like this? Why did she have to suffer all this loss?

And then she remembered the shell she held in her hand. She pictured her beautiful, shining city of Màrrach, the enormous glass domes sparkling under the Venturian sun. She saw Luna and Etâhpe'o-poeso playing in the lush solarium, and she longed to run her hands through their fur and see their faces. She thought of Tess, Shankee and Xev and all those she had met since coming to Màrrach. She thought of the woman that stood behind her: a cousin that had become her best friend.

She pondered over all the strangeness of this world: her mother's necklace, the Goyor, the pax, the sochair and even Astrid, the Selkie Queen—especially Astrid. How could she leave this land only to go back to a mundane existence that meant nothing? How could she leave Flath, even after what he had done to her?

Slowly she turned around and looked at Kyia. Her dark eyes were red with pain and worry; huge tears streaked down her round face. She held out her arms and once again pleaded with Rhiannon to come away from the Tree of Jur. Suddenly, the pull was no longer there. The humming still floated on the autumn breeze, and the mist still swallowed the clearing floor, but its song did not call to her soul any longer. Rhiannon took a deep breath, retrieved her sword and walked away from what could have been her escape.

CHAPTER NINE

*Long ago when the world was new, and dragons
ruled the earth and sky
People were afraid to walk in the woods or climb a
mountain high
Fair maidens were carried off and brave knights a
'plenty did die*

*Could anyone save the land and its people?
Was there a man who could slay the dragons so
evil?*

*The king put out a proclamation, clear
Any man who rids the land of dragons could have
his daughter, dear
Many a man wanted the princess, but from the*

dragons, they quaked with fear

Could anyone save the land and its people?
Was there a man who could slay the dragons so
evil?

Finally, one man was bold enough to answer the
call
His name was Garr, and even in his helmet and
armor he wasn't very tall
The princess worried he was hideous and didn't
like him at all

Could anyone save the land and its people?
Was there a man who could slay the dragons so
evil?

The king was desperate though and sent the man
on his quest
His sword was sharp for the first ten dragons were
barely a test
'Twas no time before he had killed all the rest

Could anyone save the land and its people?
Was there a man who could slay the dragons so
evil?

On the fateful day, the land was clear the man
returned to the king
The king cried out in joy, and the kingdom did
sing
Birds were calling, and flowers blooming for it
was still spring

Could anyone save the land and its people?
Was there a man who could slay the dragons so
evil?

At last, the king brought his daughter out
Her pretty face held a pout
And then Garr removed his helmet, and everyone
let out a shout

Could anyone save the land and its people?
Was there a man who could slay the dragons so
evil?

The princess laughed, and the king grew pale
For Garr was a woman and not a male
Now listen all because this is a cautionary tale

Could anyone save the land and its people?
Was there a man who could slay the dragons so
evil?

Men may be big and strong
But when it comes to bravery, they oft have it
wrong
For this is a heroic woman's song

There was someone to save the land and its people!
There was a woman, in fact, who could slay the
dragons so evil!

—Garr the Dragon Slayer; G. L. Niv

A mild November sun shone down upon Flath as he sat on a worn bench in a quiet corner of the Royal Garden. A dark pond spread out before him; lily pads lazily floated across its chilly surface while frogs sat atop them sunning themselves in the weak fall sun. It was rumored that his father and Baobh's mother, Raven, met here to have their trysts. Flath almost laughed out loud. What a mess that had created. I guess he could forgive his father that mistake, Ak knew Flath had made so many himself. Jocelyn being the biggest one.

The castle had gotten over their queen's death rather quickly. Rubi, the wizened crone that was the head cook in Castle Sona Tuath, who also fancied herself a poet, and her aged assistant, April, had sat upon their stools and barked out orders, as they did every day. Their apprentices had made quite a feast for the King and Queen of Yellow Island when they had come to attend their daughter's funeral. It had been six months, and he had heard nothing from King Umar. They still sent their aid every month, though it had been getting less and less. That did not bother him. Ventra was still a major contributor to Beaynid both monetarily and militarily with their warriors keeping the peace and their little servants, the Oread, helping the country's farmers.

Over the summer, Beaynid's stability had grown. Flath had divided Beynid into four districts and gave over their day to day rule to two dukes and two earls. One earl—the Earl of Tel 'Rhia—was a woman. She scoffed at the title of Countess. She said that if she was expected to do the duties of a man, she better well get the title as well. Flath smiled when he thought of Jade McVail. She was a tough, shrewd woman who kept that huge city running smoothly and he was glad that she was on his side.

Each had their own group of men who kept the peace and swore fealty to both their district leaders and their king. Things seemed to be running smoothly. So smoothly, in fact, that Flath wanted to leave Sona Tuath for a while. He had not been out of Sona Tuath since the night Jocelyn died. Up until then, he had grown used to spending long periods of time away from the castle. He was becoming restless. It had not yet turned bitter cold this winter, so it would be easy just to ride away ...or would it?

A bluebird flew up onto the lamp post beside the bench where Flath sat, cocked its brilliant azure head and looked down at him. Flath mindlessly studied its bright feathers and dark eyes. The bird chirped at him a few times and then flew away. Flath was struck at how alone he suddenly felt. He sighed and thought of Rhiannon but quickly pushed her out of his memories. Not one letter or message had come from her since the day she rode out of Sona Tuath after saving him from the wasting sickness four months earlier. He ran his hand through his hair and aimlessly looked back over at the pond.

Teo was back in Perth with his family, Adam was busy building his little castle in Bell and looking for a wife. Ian was ever occupied with commanding the Sona Tuath Castle

Guard; even Laura seemed always to have something to do and could not spare much time to talk with him since he had sent her on that heinous errand six months ago to banish Jocelyn's infant.

He had often thought of the tiny babe despite his desperate attempts to put the child far from his mind. Last month he had finally broken down and asked Laura what had become of the child. He recalled the shock on her usually pleasant face. Hesitantly, she told him that she had left the boy with her nephew, Hurr Kemp and his wife Tonnah, in Misty Peaks, and the child was well. She had left a wet nurse with the babe that they had named Alex. With a mischievous smile on her face, Laura had told him yesterday that the nurse had recently returned to Sona Tuath for a visit and told her the once tiny, sickly boy had grown strong. Blast that woman; she knew Flath's interest had been piqued.

Suddenly, he was struck by a thought so profound that it almost knocked him off the bench. He would go visit Misty Peaks and see how the boy faired with his own eyes! He would put months of worry to rest by making sure himself that the child was doing well. Why had he not thought of this earlier? He was about to jump up and start making preparations for his trip when he realized how suspicious it would look for the King of Beaynid to suddenly show up in the tiny town inquiring about a babe that supposedly was the unwanted bastard child of some castle worker. A babe born so close to the time when the queen had given birth to a still-born that had hastily and quite suspiciously been buried in the middle of the night without any proper burial or official mourning time (rumors were still circulating the city about that bit of news).

Defeated, Flath took a deep breath and let it out in a noisy gush. How could he get in and out of Misty Peaks without being noticed? Suddenly the bluebird came back and now sat on the scrolling iron arm of the bench. It looked up at Flath almost like it wanted to say something to him. Flath blinked a few times thinking he was going mad. Then the bluebird started to sing! A long, complicated, utterly beautiful song that Flath had never heard come from a bird before. All at once Flath was hit with another idea: he would disguise himself as a traveling minstrel! He could sing! He loved to sing, and in fact, he had done it for a living as a boy.

"Thank you, little beasty for the perfect idea!" Flath announced and then jumped up and headed for the castle to pack for the journey. The bird cocked its head and gave him a knowing look and would have smiled if it could. Flath did not notice.

***

Flath slipped out of Sona Tuath that afternoon. He hastily told his most senior advisor, Viceroy Penn Hodge, that he would be away for a few weeks. Of course, Penn tried to talk him out of leaving, he even outright forbade Flath to leave Sona Tuath without a regiment of guards, but Flath had quietly slipped away before the man could mount a defense. Once outside the city he changed his clothes, stuffing his expensive royal garb into his shabby pack and put on something more like a traveling bard would wear. Flath stabled his fine royal steed at a village at the foot of the Elk Mountains and bought a rather questionable looking piebald mare to continue on his journey.

She turned out to be good-natured and did not mind carrying him up the steep, rocky roads snaking up into the Elk Mountains. Because of her spots, he named her Peighinneach, Peig for short. Her coat was bright white with irregular splotches of black and brown. Her mane had been shorn, so it stood up like the bristles of a multi-colored brush. She had one bright, blue eye, the other being dark. He felt an instant kinship with the horse with mismatched eyes. He could tell she was an intelligent animal by the way she sized him up when he first saw her. She had been the stable master's son's horse. At first, the boy did not want to part with the creature. That was until Flath gave him a few pieces of gold, however, then the boy happily even saddled the horse up for him.

Two days later Flath made his way down the well-worn road into Misty Peaks. Flath went over his story again in his head. Absentmindedly, his hand went to the lute strapped to Peig's back. He was now Taylor the traveling minstrel just returning from Tel 'Rhia on his way to Sona Tuath and deciding to stop at Misty Peaks. He knew they would want any news of things going on in the huge port city. As king, Flath got reports all the time about what was going in his kingdom. So he had some news, but he could make up the more interesting and juicy stuff as well. He smiled to himself as he slipped into his new persona. It was almost like the old days traveling around with his family. His excitement grew.

He put Sona Tuath and the throne behind him as he stopped at a stable near the only inn in town. The days had grown cold, and Flath pulled his cloak tighter around his neck. Finally, a fair-haired boy of about eight came out and took Peig's reins. He had a splash of freckles across his fine-boned face, and he turned his bright blue eyes up at Flath, assessing the stranger. "See that she has a good washing and brushing and some extra oats, too." Flath smiled at the boy and mussed his hair as he handed him a few coins.

"Yes, sir!" The boy was enthusiastic as he opened a chubby hand and counted his coins. Flath removed his bag and lute and a long burlap bag which hid his panther-headed sword and scabbard from Peig's back. "Are you a bard, or a poet?" the boy asked excitedly.

"I am Taylor, the traveling minstrel." Flath bent in an elegant bow. "At your service."

"Will you be performing tonight?" The boy could hardly contain his excitement.

"I will be."

"Do you know Garr the Dragon Slayer?" The little boy looked up at Flath with so much hope he had to laugh.

"Of course I do! Any minstrel worth his salt knows that song."

The boy dropped Peig's reins, danced around and clapped his hands. Peig took a step back and looked at him with annoyance but was obviously used to children. "I will be there for sure!" the boy announced when he finally quit dancing and took up Peig's reins again.

"All right, I will be looking for you," Flath called out as the boy started to lead the spotted horse into the stable.

"My name is Bryan, by the way!" the boy hollered over his shoulder as he disappeared into the building.

Flath took a moment to look around. In all his years of travel, he had never actually been to Misty Peaks. It was not really on the way to anywhere. The broad and well-maintained King's Road that ran from Sona Tuath west over the Elk Mountains and eventually to Tel 'Rhia was miles to the south where the mountain was easier to traverse. Misty Peaks was out of the way, but a gem to anyone who found it. From the wide, pine needle-strewn dirt road he could see a small butcher shop, a bakery, and a tiny store that probably sold flour, sugar and other staples. There was also a smithy, a cobbler, and a few other small storefronts. A little farther down the path, he could see many A-framed houses peeking out from under the tall pines. They were all well-kept and had large flower gardens out front that now lay dormant except for a few brave late year blooms. There had not been a snowfall yet this season.

Finally, he turned to the inn. It stood in the center of town. Its three-story bulk towered over all the smaller buildings and did not look like the rest of the modest town. It was the only structure with a gently pitched roof. It was painted a sort of rusty muted red color with a wide front porch filled with chairs and a few swings and even a large stone hearth in the center. This was definitely where the town gathered. If it had been built on the King's Road, it would no doubt be filled every night. As it was, Flath was glad for its seclusion. This would be the place he would stay for the next few weeks. This is where he would finally see Jocelyn's son.

Wanting to get out of the cold, Flath bounded up three wide stairs and across the porch and into the inn. The interior was massive, too massive for the few hundred people who called Misty Peaks their home. He wondered where the owner had gotten so much coin to build such an impressive place so far off the busy roads. The inn was clearly not that old. Huge polished iron candelabras hung from the tall ceilings, and oil burning sconces were placed every few feet all around the great room. In the center of the room was an enormous stone hearth, open on both sides, its chimney disappearing into the ceiling. A roaring fire leapt inside the hearth, warming the room from the chilly day outside. Dozens of large wooden tables and chairs were neatly positioned across the room. The floor was swept clean of any crumbs or debris. Off to the left four wide steps lead to a large stage area. This is where he would perform.

"Greetings, traveler!" a friendly voiced called out. "Welcome to the Sudsy Dog Inn!"

Flath looked up to see a young man walk out of the kitchen. He was wiping his hands on a crisp apron hanging from his narrow hips.

"Greetings," Flath offered back, thinking that was the strangest name for an inn he had ever heard.

"Are you in search of a room? Or a hot meal?" The man walked up to him and smiled.

"I am looking for a place to stay for a few weeks as I am a traveling minstrel."

The man's brown eyes widened as if he suddenly noticed Flath was carrying his lute. "You are most welcome and, in fact, if you would agree to perform every night, your stay and meals will be on the house."

"Most generous of you, innkeeper. How could I turn down an offer of that magnitude?" Flath smiled, put down his bags, and clasped the man's hand in a vigorous shake. "My name is Taylor."

"'Tis nice to make your acquaintance, Taylor. I am Xavier McVail, owner of this establishment." Suddenly, Flath got anxious— he wondered if Lady Jade was a relation of his. If so, they were from one of the richest merchant families in the port town. He wondered how this young man had ended up in Misty Peaks.

"Half-owner!" a woman's voice called out. A young, dark-haired woman waddled out from the kitchen; her hand placed on her belly swollen with child.

"Forgive me," Xavier laughed. "Allow me to introduce you to my wife, Lady Kih of Caltrona."

Flath bowed, "Milady, I am at your service." He stood up and smiled. She looked him up and down, her large grey eyes stopping on his face. "You look familiar."

Flath grew nervous. Had his rouse been discovered already? "I do travel a lot, milady. Perhaps you have seen me perform."

"Perhaps," she said slowly as if she did not believe him. "I could have sworn I have seen you in Tel 'Rhia."

"I am there quite often, milady. I am sure our paths have crossed at one time or another." Her pretty face scrunched up as if she were trying to recall something. His dread grew. If this man was, in fact, the younger brother of Lady Jade McVail, he had most likely been to the massive celebration that had been held after Jade had received her title. A celebration that both he and Jocelyn had attended as King and Queen of Beaynid.

"I am sure you are tired from you travel. Dear, can you fix our resident bard a meal while I show him up to his room?"

Flath felt relieved when Lady Kih smiled up at him. "Of course!" She turned and waddled back into the kitchen. Disaster avoided, at least for now.

Word had spread and by the time Flath had taken his place upon the stage later that night, the inn was packed. It seemed almost everyone in town was there, including Bryan, along with a dozen other little children that now sat eagerly on the floor waiting for him to begin. Flath winked at Bryan and started to sing Garr the Dragon Slayer. His smooth baritone voice was swiftly carried through the rafters and melted down to the pleased audience.

By the time he started his third song he had observed everyone in the room and to his consternation, there were no couples there with a child as young as Alex. He was disappointed for he was sure they would be there tonight with everyone else. Finally, halfway through The Sprite of Loch Mór, the heavy wooden door of the inn swung open and a couple walked in from the cold night holding a bundle that Flath hoped was a young child. His eyes followed the couple as he steadily made his way through the song. By the time the song had ended the couple was sitting on top of a table in the back of the crowded room. He took a deep drink from a mug of ale to ease his dry throat and watched as the woman unwrapped the child. There, sitting upon the woman's lap was a chubby brown haired little boy. For certain this must be Alex!

By the time he was done singing that night, it was very late, and the couple had gone. Over the next week they did come and see him perform several more times, but each time they left before he could get a chance to talk with them. Sometimes they had the young wet nurse and her child with them when they came. Every chance Flath got, he studied the young boy's face. He had hoped no one had noticed how he had stared at the couple.

Lady Kih had seemed to forget that she had seen Flath somewhere before and never brought it up again. The McVail's were excellent hosts, and Flath happily settled into his masquerade, rather wishing he would not have to go back to Sona Tuath at all. He liked having no responsibilities beyond entertaining people for his room and meals.

He had found out that Xavier was indeed the youngest brother of Earl Jade McVail of Tel 'Rhia. It seemed he was bored of being a merchant and of the teeming populace of the huge city and wanted a quieter life. He had taken his new Caltronian bride, his sizable inheritance, and they decided to stay in Misty Peaks. When construction first started on the inn, people laughed at him for wanting to build such a huge structure so far away from the busy road, but when construction had completed, almost a year later, the inn soon became the hub of all the town's activities.

Even the aged Alderman quit using his house for town meetings and moved them over to the new inn.

Finally, on his last night in Misty Peaks, Flath had finished his performance for the night, and the couple was still sitting at their table. Flath took a long swig of his ale, put his lute down and tried not to hurry over to the couple who were now engaged in conversation. As he walked up, the couple turned to him and smiled. Flath fought not to look at the boy sitting on his father's lap.

"How is it that I have met everyone in town except for you and your family?" Flath asked the young man.

The man clasped Flath's hand and laughed. "Our son seems to get quite cranky in the evenings. I am Hur Kemp, and this is my wife, Tonnah. This little one is our son, Alex." Hur bounced the tiny boy on his knee.

"As I am sure you have heard, my name is Taylor." Flath's eyes slipped to the boy who had left infancy and was growing quickly into a child. Now that he was closer to him he could clearly see Jocelyn in the boy. Drool wet his chin as he busily gummed his father's finger.

"Oh aye! You are famous in Misty Peaks," Hur said, but Flath paid him no mind. Flath knelt down and looked into the boy's big, guileless eyes. Was there a spark of recognition? How could that be, the boy was hardly from Jocelyn's womb the last time he had laid eyes on him. Flath felt a chill come over him and he fought the urge to turn and run from the building. He suddenly felt empty and sad. Sadness that threatened to overtake him! He stood back up and looked at the couple who were almost on the edge of alarm, or at least confusion.

"'Tis a braw young boy you have there. He will grow up to be a fine young man." Flath could see the looks of relief on the Hurr's faces.

"He really is a good baby," Tonnah said proudly as she reached over and smoothed Alex's mop of chestnut hair. "Do you have any children of your own, Taylor?"

"I, uh, I...no, good wife. I have no children," Flath's words stumbled out of his mouth as if to accuse himself.

***

Over the winter Flath braved the cold weather and deep snow and made many trips back up to Misty Peaks. Viceroy Hodge had increasingly gotten used to the King of Beaynid disappearing for weeks at a time and did a good job of keeping the castle running while Flath was away. Through all his bluster, Flath was sure the older man was enjoying his position of power. Flath did not care as long as he was able to slip out of Sona Tuath when he wanted to, and the man was doing his job. The reign of a kingdom was heavy, and Flath cared not for the responsibility.

Finally, winter started to fade from land, even way up in the Elk Mountains. Spring covered Beaynid in wildflowers, and the scent of passionflower hung in the air like honey. Flath had arrived in town the night before and now sat in the inn finishing up his noon meal with the Alderman and a few others. The door opened, and Flath turned to see Hurr walk in holding Alex. Flath stood up and went to him.

"'Tis nice to see you, Hurr. I did not expect to see you until tonight."

"I needed a break from working in my fields, as small as they are, and Tonnah needed a break from little Alex, so I thought I would come down and share a drink with you." The young man smiled at him, but Flath could only see Alex's face. He was growing fast and would be a year old in a fortnight. His face still bore a heavy resemblance to Jocelyn, but it was slowly changing as babyhood faded away. "Let me show you something!" Hurr proudly announced as he backed away from Flath. Hurr set Alex down on his chubby little legs. "Go ahead, walk to Taylor," Hurr encouraged his son. Alex looked up to Flath and smiled. Then a determined looked crossed his pudgy face, and he started to toddle over to him. Flath was struck with such pride it took his breath away. As if he were in a trance he bent down and opened his arms as Alex stumbled into them. He laughed and fought not to cry. He was filled with such emotion that he was stunned.

"Well done, Alex! You are such a big boy now!" Flath cried out, and then realized he was being over enthusiastic. He looked at Hurr who was smiling but clearly had a confused look in his eyes. Hurr walked up to Flath and held out his arms to take his son. All of a sudden, Flath did not want to give Alex up, and he had to fight with himself to hand the boy back to his adopted father. Flath laughed nervously as he handed Alex back to Hurr. He felt the stab of emptiness as Alex left his arms.

"Taylor, you need to find a good woman and settle down. Have a couple babes of your own." A look of empathy crossed Hurr's face, tanned from working in his field. "There is many a good woman in Beaynid." Hurr winked. "I have had a few. 'Course, do not tell Tonnah." He smiled up at Flath in a conspiratorial manner. Flath laughed but suddenly felt sorry for Hurr's young wife. She was pretty bland to look at, but more importantly, she was a good mother to Alex.

Over the next two weeks, Hurr and Tonnah brought Alex in to see him sing every night. Flath took great pleasure in seeing Alex every day, watching him carefully waddle across the wide, wooden planks of the Inn, becoming a better walker every day. Flath was not even aware of how attached he was becoming to the boy; he was just lost in the simple pleasure of having Alex near.

Since Hurr had first mentioned it, and even probably before then, if Flath would have admitted it, he had been thinking about taking another wife. It was past the obligatory period of mourning, and Beaynid did need another queen. However, only one woman would do for him. He would not make the same mistake again.

Over the winter, word had trickled into Sona Tuath of Shih 'Ni's death. He wanted to sail up to Màrrach right away to offer Rhiannon his comfort, but he recognized she needed time to grieve. Now, however, he felt he could put it off no longer. He would leave for Ventra as soon as he returned from Misty Peaks. Viceroy Hodge would not like it, but he could call it an official state visit to Ventra. He was not sure of how Rhiannon would receive him, but he had to try and win her back no matter the cost.

A soft, late May rain started to fall as Flath left Misty Peaks on Alex's name day. He had brought the boy a present from Sona Tuath. Nothing too extravagant, for someone like Taylor could not afford anything too expensive, but it was a small toy carved out of oak. Flath felt torn leaving Alex for what was sure to be a long period since he did not know how long he would be in Màrrach. At the same time, he was almost giddy with the thought of seeing Rhiannon again after so very long.

The rain started to fall a little harder, and Flath pulled up the hood of his cloak and rode down the path that was quickly turning to mud. Lost in his tumultuous thoughts of Alex and of Rhiannon, Flath was suddenly overwhelmed with a feeling that he was being watched. His hand reflexively went to the dagger he wore on his belt, his sword was hidden in a bag behind him. Carefully, he peered into the darkness between the heavy tree cover and kneed Peig into a trot. He could pick nothing out, but the feeling was intense, and he was sure someone looked out from the trees as he passed. He kicked Peig into a gallop and disappeared around a bend in the path once again thinking about Rhiannon.

CHAPTER TEN

"On the eastern side of Beaynid and Ventra rages the Carnaid Sea. This sea is unique from all other known bodies of water in that it is a bright red color. Its seas are rough for most of the year and not safe to sail upon during the winter. A cold and scouring wind almost constantly blows off of its ruddy horizon. However, that is not the strangest thing about this sea. For reasons unknown to modern science any mammals that spend anything but the briefest amount of time in the waters will be bleached white! Fish do not seem to be affected by this uncanny phenomenon and the white dolphins and small whales that navigate the sea do not seem harmed by their pale coloring."

—Field Guide of Beaynid; Myrin Zantroc

Baobh watched as Flath nervously looked around the forest, she would have laughed if it were possible in the bird form she now wore. He could feel her watching him, but he would never see her hidden up within the dark branches through the gathering mist. She fought the urge to change into a ferocious creature and tear out the usurper's heart. She sighed, she had a plan, and she needed to stick to it. Patience had never been one of her virtues, though.

After Flath had galloped away like a coward, disappearing into the rain, Baobh flew a short distance away from where she had hidden her mule-drawn wagon. She landed on the ground and silently melted back into her natural form. The grey mule sidestepped and looked over at her with his huge black eyes but settled down quickly.

Natural form, ha! She laughed bitterly, the only sound in the forest beside the splatter of rain. She would never see her natural form again. Her once flawless, creamy, cocoa-colored skin and dark hair were now as pale as the moon. Even her eyes were white, though they were still as sharp as any Goyor's. The caustic waters of the Carnaid Sea had burned away all her beautiful color! She was disgusted with herself every time she caught a glimpse of her hands or a lock of her long, blond hair. One thing the sea could not wash away, though, was her unrivaled beauty. This was what she was counting on to make her plan work.

The rain was still falling when she rode her carriage into Misty Peaks. She pulled up in front of the inn and jumped down. There was no one around in this weather. She tied her mule's reins up to a post, climbed the stairs, and entered the cavernous room. A lively fire burned in the pit in the middle of the room keeping the temperature warm.

Four men sat around a table nearest the fire. As soon as she entered, one man jumped up and approached her with a smile. "Hail, traveler!" Baobh already knew from her reconnaissance that this was the inn's owner,

Xavier McVail. She dropped her hood and saw Xavier's eyes widen, and then quickly his face became friendly again. What a diplomat, she thought. "You are welcome to the Sudsy Dog Inn. My name is Xavier McVail." He gave a slight bow of his dark head.

"I am Danja Quil." She had practiced saying that name over and over again so many times she almost thought it really was her name.

"Would you like a hot meal or a room?" He sounded intrigued. "'Tis not often—or, ever, actually—that we have had the pleasure of accommodating one of the Forest Folk. Though you do not look as if you are from Beaynid." Was that a question? She had to try hard not to laugh at his curiosity. But she had had a long time to perfect her story.

Baobh smiled sweetly up at him. "You are correct in that I am not from this land, but I hail from a place far across the Southern Sea called Dar 'Ven." She looked deeply into his brown eyes and could see he was satisfied with that answer. "I have been traveling a long time.

I am looking for a place to settle, actually." At hearing that, another man that had been at the table with Xavier looked up. "I am an herbalist and am looking for a place to live and ply my trade." Xavier turned as the older man got up and ambled over to them. "This is Alderman Kind. He is the one that can help you get settled in Misty Peaks. Can I offer you some tea while you talk business?"

"Do you have anything stronger, Inn Keep McVail?" She winked and smiled up at him. She took pleasure in his nervousness.

Baobh and Alderman Kind sat at a corner table and sipped tea while she regaled the old man with her made up stories of her life in Keyll, a Forest Folk city in Dar 'Ven and then traveling around Beaynid with her carriage, selling her cures. She smiled a lot and pretended to care about him and his little mountain village. She had planned for this for a long time, so it felt natural—though beneath her.

Alderman Kind fell easily under Baobh's charms, and after he was convinced that Danja

Quil was a bona fide herbalist, he welcomed her to Misty Peaks. They went out into the cold spring morning, and Alderman Kind showed her to an abandoned A-framed cabin tucked into the woods but not far from her real target—Hurr Kemp.

"Unfortunately, our village healer and herbalist disappeared over the summer. This was her cabin. I am sure she will not return, so you're welcome to it," he said proudly as he opened the heavy wooden door for her. Baobh knew the herbalist was not coming back because she had made sure of it. The poor woman had met her demise by the sharp claws of a bear one afternoon when she had been collecting herbs in the forest. No one would ever find her body, which was surely nothing but bones, by now.

"This will work perfectly," Baobh breathed, and a smile crept across her face as she looked around the dusty cabin.

"There's a small stable out back for you to keep a horse and even a hot spring for bathing. You got lucky, Miss, with this cabin!" Ha, luck had nothing to do with it, you fool, she thought. "Your nearest neighbors are Hurr and Tonnah Kemp." He pointed vaguely off to the right. "Nice couple. They have a little boy named Alex. They will help you with anything you need."

Baobh faced Alderman Kind and turned her unnaturally light eyes up at him and smiled. He was captivated, she could tell. "Thank you, Alderman. You are the sweetest man." She placed a hand on his arm. He blushed and almost choked.

"Well, let me know if you need anything," he called as he quickly left the cabin. "I'll have someone bring your carriage down for you!"

"Thank you, Alderman!" She waved at him from her front porch. This is going to be so easy, she thought.

She spent the cool weeks of early summer getting settled into her new cabin. It was a far cry from castle Sona Tuath or even Lord Rull's desert compound at the Sangron Oasis in the middle of Katlom Desert. However, she was making due. As frequently as she could, she took the form of a little bird and watched the Kemp family. The weather was warming up, so Hurr spent most of his time in his field. Tonnah would get bored (and probably lonely since her wet nurse had left to go back to Sona Tuath the week before now that Alex was weaned) and would take Alex out for walks or out to Hurr in the fields. Alex always seemed to have a little-carved toy gripped in his chubby little hand.

At least a couple times a week the family would go down to the inn for dinner and socializing. A local girl was learning how to play the harp, and the town dutifully listened to her play most nights. Baobh had yet to make an appearance at the inn, however. Since she had lost her throne and her appearance had changed so drastically she had become self-conscious. Her confidence had been shaken to the core, and she felt her once legendary dark beauty had been stripped away from her. Oh, she knew she was still attractive to men, but her birthright—the flawless darkness of her skin, hair, and eyes—had been ripped away from her forever. She was fortunate though to still have the powers of her people, the Goyor.

She watched now as the little family left their cottage and made their way to the inn. She could hear the liquid notes of the harp floating out into the evening as they opened the door and went in. She needed to move to the next step in her plan. She needed to get Herr alone!

She flew quickly back to the Kemp's cottage that now stood dark and empty. Silently, she melted back into her natural form. Suddenly, she felt exposed, her heart hammered in her chest. She looked around, but there was no one to see her. She had been living in the middle of the desert in relative solitude with nothing much to do for over a year and a half. She was rusty at subterfuge and felt deficient. She sighed as she gripped the doorknob and slipped into the house.

It was dark inside, but her Goyor eyes were as sharp as ever. She made her way to the kitchen and found their jar of tea. She took some dried herbs from her pocket that looked and smelled just like tea and sprinkled them in with the Kemp's dried tea leaves. These were leaves from the Zern bush found deep in the forest. For reasons even she did not know, their poison only affected women of breeding years. This tiny amount would do nothing but make Tonnah sick, but she had once used it in much larger doses and wiped out an entire generation of women in Bell. Two years ago she would have laughed out loud and felt accomplishment at her revenge. But now she just felt petty and numb. Was she getting soft? She still had much work to do, now was not the time for compassion! Baobh shook the jar, mixing the potent Zern leaves with the innocent tea leaves and then replaced it in the cupboard.

She was about to leave when her sensitive Goyor ears heard someone running down the path to the cottage! She froze. Someone turned the doorknob, and the door swung open. She backed up and pushed herself against the kitchen counter. She knew it was too dark to see her, but her heart was pounding in her ears just the same. Hurr Kemp walked into the room; his pale hair shone in the moonlight coming from the windows. He was looking around for something but then stopped, stood up straight and looked right at her. She sucked in a breath suddenly unsure of the cover the darkness gave her. "Hello!" he called out. She was sure he saw her, but then he slowly turned his head peering into the rest of the cottage. He walked over to a lamp and struck a match. She was sure to be seen now! Without a thought, she melted into the form of a small grey cat.

Suddenly able to see now, Hurr picked up the little wooden toy that Alex had left behind. Then his blue eyes settled on Baobh. "Well, how did you get in here?" He walked over to her and ran a calloused hand down her fuzzy back. She meowed up at him, and he smiled. "Come on now; you must leave before Tonnah finds you and has a fit." He gently picked Baobh up, blew out the lamp and set her outside. "Go on home!" He called over his shoulder as he jogged back down the path to the inn. Her mission had worked. As long as they drank the tea in the morning, Hurr was bound to come and see the town's only healer.

That morning Baobh woke in a good mood. She and Lord Rull had laid these plans so long ago, and she had been so patient, but now was the time to make her move. She bathed in the hot springs behind her house taking time to go over her plans yet again as she relaxed in the hot waters. She took extra time plating her hair and tucking golden beads into their folds. She picked out a luxurious blood-red dress with a low-cut neckline. She hung rubies in her ears but left her neck bare as not to distract. She still had not gotten used to her paleness, but it was something she could work with. She had bought the most expensive and alluring perfume she could find in Tel 'Rhia when she was preparing for her journey to Misty Peaks. Goyors did not use perfume but understood humans were quite fond of its aroma. She hoped Hurr found it favorable.

Just as she had planned, by noon Hurr

knocked on her door. Baobh looked at herself quickly in a large mirror that hung in her bedroom, and then rushed to let him in. When she opened the door, she swore she heard his indrawn breath. He stood looking at her with those bright blue eyes not saying a word. She smiled up at him, "Greetings," she said cheerfully.

"Greetings," he said slowly, as if unsure. "You are the healer?"

"A Master Herbalist, but yes, a healer too. My name is Danja Quil. You must be from the village?" She smiled again and put her hand on his arm.

"Y—yes. My name is Hurr Kemp. I am your neighbor to the south. Not really far away, at all."

"Wonderful! You are well met, Hurr." She squeezed his arm, and she could feel him tense under her touch. This was going to be so easy, she thought. "Please come in and tell me what ails you." Completely unable to resist, Hurr followed Baobh into her cottage. She led him over to her work area, neatly stuffed with bottles and jars of different herbs and powders. "What seems to be your trouble, Hurr?"

"'Tis not me, ma'am, 'tis my—wife." Did he hesitate? She smiled brightly at him and took his hand. It was warm and calloused, and he shook slightly.

"Tell me what is wrong with her." She pierced him with those white eyes of hers, and she could see him come under her power.

"She has been sick all morning. Vomiting and feverish." He spoke in a low voice almost as if he did not want to intrude in the trance he was under.

Baobh pretended to think for a moment, then turned and took a glass jar from her cupboard. She opened it and put a few scoops of the dried herbs in a folded paper. "Make a tea out of this and give it to her. Make sure she drinks all of it. This should make her well quickly." She smiled up at him again, and she found he was grinning at her dumbly.

"Thank you, Miss Quil." He fished in his pocket and put a silver coin on her counter.

Too much for what she gave him, but she was pleased he seemed to be completely under her charm now.

"Please, call me Danja."

"All right, Danja. Thank you, again."

With apparent difficulty, he turned to leave. Baobh touched his arm again, stopping him in his tracks. "You probably know I have a hot spring behind my cottage. Hot springs are renowned for restoring health. You should bring your wife for a bath; perhaps the water would make her feel herself again." She laughed a dainty, feminine sound. "I soak in the hot waters every single night, and I am the picture of health." She slowly drew her petite hand across her pale chest and watched as Hurr's eyes trailed after her elegant fingers. She smiled and gave him a long, pointed look when he was able to pull his eyes away from the low-cut neckline of her crimson dress. Did he get the hint, she wondered?

"I will certainly try to get her down here, ma'am. H-have a good day!" he shuddered and ran out the door. Baobh laughed after she shut the door. That was easy!

It was not until three days later that she felt him watching her bathe. She was beginning to wonder if her charms had not been enough after all. But now she stood naked under a full moon, up to her thighs in the hot water. She slowly ran soap over her body knowing he watched her every move. It took effort, for she was putting on a show, but she took extra time to wash her hair then dunk under the water. She came up from the hot springs like some kind of enchanted water nymph, focused on her prey. She began to sing as she used her long fingers to comb through her hair, the color of moonbeams. Night jasmine bloomed and filled the air with its honey-sweet aroma. Insects chirped and sung along with Baobh's clear, lilting voice as it was carried upon the spring breeze to Hurr as he hid in the shadows captivated by Baobh's beauty.

This went on every night for a fortnight. She knew he was weakening. During the day she watched him leave his wife early in the morning and not come home until night.

Tonnah and Alex stopped visiting with his mid-day meal in his fields. Almost as soon as he arrived home at night, he would start on his way to Baobh's private pond. She had to quickly fly back to the hot springs and undress before he got there.

Finally, one night after she had finished a particularly enchanting song she stood up, water slowly trailing down her naked body, and she looked directly at Hurr as he stood hidden in the darkness. "You can come out, my dear Hurr," she called out playfully.

It took a long minute, but he finally emerged into the moonlight. "How did you know I was watching you?" He was genuinely surprised.

She giggled. "I have known since the very first time you came to watch me bathe." He walked up to her and quickly pulled off his boots. She studied his face; he was neither embarrassed nor apologetic. His eyes were dark with a burning, wild passion that was on the edge of consuming him. She walked up closer to him to the edge of the water and laid her hand upon his chest and felt him stiffen. "I am of the Forest Folk, we can see in the shadows where humans cannot. Tell me, Hurr, do you like what you see?" she asked playfully as she slowly turned around, her bare skin glistening in the moonlight.

He said nothing, just took a few steps into the water and took her in his arms. At first, she was almost shocked, but was this not what she had been planning the whole time? He took her face in his rough hands and softly bent her head up to his, taking her mouth. Gentle at first, but then his passion became unrestrained as his hands hungrily traveled over her wet skin. As he urgently kissed her neck, Baobh unbuttoned his shirt and threw it to the ground, then did the same for his trousers smiling up at him as he stepped out of them and let them float away in the water. She laughed and tugged him deeper into the pond, knowing she had him now.

***

Every evening Hurr would meet Baobh in

the steaming waters of the hot springs. If
Tonnah grew suspicious, Baobh knew not, for
Hurr never spoke of her. In fact, they did
almost no speaking at all. She was careful to
take the right herbs to prevent a pregnancy;
that did not play into her plans for the future.
As the long weeks stretched by, Hurr's passion
did not wane. He worshiped Baobh as if she
were some ancient fertility goddess filling him
with virility and passion. She knew it was time
to further her plan.

In the afternoons, while Alex napped,
Tonnah would work in her small kitchen
garden, sometimes venturing into the woods
for wild herbs. It was one of these
unseasonably warm afternoons that Baobh
quietly followed Tonnah into the woods.
Baobh looked to the heavens and said a quick
prayer to Pom-Ni before she slipped into the
form of a great, brown bear. It was not until the
deed was done, and Tonnah's bright red blood
was dripping from her muzzle, that she
realized she had prayed for forgiveness for
what she was about to do. She ran from the

savaged ruin that had been Tonnah Kemp's body wondering why she felt so guilty. What had happened to the strong, ruthless Queen of Beaynid?

After she had washed Tonnah Kemp's blood from her body in a nearby stream, Baobh went back to the Kemp's cottage, took the form of that little grey cat and slipped into an open window. She curled up next to Alex and watched him sleep. This pale little boy with unruly nut-brown hair was most likely her nephew. Here, basking in the warmth of this little boy's body, Baobh let herself mourn the loss of her own son, now over two summers old. She recalled his flawless dark skin, huge black eyes, and perfect chubby, little face. She could not cry in her form as a cat, but inside, her tears flowed like an endless ocean. She hardly got to suckle her own son before that vengeful barbarian came to take her throne, her mate, and her son away from her. Baobh would have her revenge in the end, though, for Lord Rull had promised.

After a while Alex started to stir—he would

awaken soon, and she knew Hurr would not be back from the fields for a long while still. Leaving the warmth of Alex's body, Baobh slipped out of the cottage and then took the form of a bird. She located Hurr hard at work in his fields, but now she needed to get his attention. She floated down into the forest and retook the form of a bear. She ran through the woods roaring and growling as loud as she could. She went near several cottages huffing and grunting and generally making a ruckus, riling up the inhabitants of Misty Peaks.

After she wrestled enough people away from their chores making them concerned enough to check on neighbors and sending Hurr home to make sure his family was safe, Baobh slipped into the unassuming form of a little bird and watched the drama unfold. Upon finding Alex alone Hurr and the rest of the town went into the woods, armed with swords and clubs, for they had all heard the bear, and the loss of their original herbalist was still in their minds. They anxiously searched for Hurr's young wife.

Overcome with remorse and hating herself for being so weak, she did not want to be near when Hurr found the torn body of his wife, so she nervously flitted from tree to tree some distance away. When she finally heard Herr's anguished cry as it echoed through the forest, she felt she would break in two. *What have I done?* Suddenly she felt exposed as if all the trees in the wood were looking at her and accusing her of murder. She flew away home, her heart pounding in her chest.

Hurr did not come to her that night, nor the next night, but on the third night he knocked on her door, and she let him in. Everyone in town had heard what had become of Tonnah Kemp, so it would only be natural she would know of what happened. She looked up into his blue eyes, almost as if to apologize. She saw sorrow on his face and certainly guilt. But he was unable to wash the passion and need from his eyes. He had no words, he just effortlessly picked Baobh up and carried her to her bed.

Sure, the town's people would talk of their

affair when it became known, but Hurr was a young man, and it was not beyond belief that he would take another wife soon. Yes, decorum would dictate they wait a while, but she knew Hurr would not wait long. Her plan was coming to fruition. She would someday have the throne back—if only through her step-son, the rightful King of Beaynid—but she would also see that usurper, Flath and his greedy lover, the Empress of Ventra dead, and the prophecy finally put to rest, unfulfilled...eventually.

CHAPTER ELEVEN

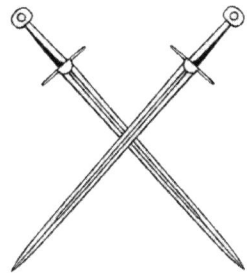

"Though the empress has not been the same since she returned from her travels in Beaynid without our tjaty, she has been unusually restless since receiving word that the King of Beaynid would soon be visiting Ventra. Her moods range from morose to outright panic. I worry for her."

—*Unpublished diary of servants; Tyla O' Vumm, personal servant of Empress Rhiannon Kossi*

Rhiannon sat on the grass in the solarium. Luna laid her head on her lap, and she mindfully stroked her soft fur. Etâhpe'o-poeso was stretched out in the sun, her coarse purring reverberating through the area. She had had two matching diamond-encrusted collars made for both Luna and Poeso. At first, they were a little annoyed at having to wear them but quickly got used to them, and Rhiannon thought they were gorgeous, if a little extravagant. But she was an empress, so why not?

The little golden monkey that Rhiannon had named Jo Jo was never far from her side since she and Kyia had returned to Màrrach. Rhiannon had made a collar for Jo Jo as well, but she would not tolerate it, of course. Rhiannon took a deep breath, it was July, still a little cool outside this far north, but in the ever spring-like setting under the huge glass domes in Màrrach, the temperature was always perfect.

A couple of black swans floated on the glassy surface of the pond, not even giving her a glance as they paddled by. Birds sang from high up in the treetops. It was peaceful in the solarium, though a storm raged inside Rhiannon's head. She looked down at the missive again. It had come a month earlier and read like a party invitation—though Flath was the one inviting himself and his new nobles to Màrrach! Did his gall and outrageousness know no bounds? She was sure word of Shih 'Ni's death ten months earlier had made it to Sona Tuath by now, but she had not planned on this kind of presumptuous reaction from the southern kingdom.

Rhiannon set the missive down next to her, and she unconsciously gripped the smooth seashell in her hand. She had had a delicate golden loop and chain fashioned into the top of the shell she so could wear it as a bracelet, and it would be easy to hold at all times. Rhiannon's anxiety had grown steadily worse over the long months since Shih 'Ni had died and sometimes Astrid's gift was all that could calm her. She wondered if she would ever see the Selkie Queen again. She hoped so, though she did not know how since Rhiannon felt she could never leave Ventra again. The world seemed so large, and chaotic. She was content to live out the rest of her life here in the solarium. She had accepted the fact that she would not be giving Ventra her heir and her advisors had said nothing about it since she and Kyia had returned seven months ago.

As a matter of fact, now that she thought about it, most people gave her a wide berth. She figured they were afraid to say the wrong thing. When she and Kyia had returned to Ventra, Rhiannon had gone straight to Tess's house and stayed there for almost six weeks. Reluctantly, she returned to Màrrach. By that time, she had been away from the palace for almost four months. She knew Shankee was loathed to once again accept the duty to rule for so long.

And now she was faced with this mess. The governor and his wife, Trevin & Mela Brun had arrived yesterday at the invitation of Rhiannon's council. Apparently, it would have been the height of rudeness if they had been snubbed from this huge celebration... feast... banquet? She was not sure what it was being called—nor did she care. They were extremely nice and were not demanding of her time at all. She was incredibly thankful for their thoughtfulness. She sighed heavily, and Luna lifted her head and looked up at her. She gently licked Rhiannon's hand, as if offering comfort, then laid her head back down upon her lap and continued with her nap. Rhiannon thought again about just disappearing out to her grandmother's house but knew she could not. Duty demanded she be here to receive the Beaynid delegation...that included their king.

Kyia walked up to Rhiannon and sat next to her. Rhiannon turned and gave her cousin a smile. She had been the only thing that had kept Rhiannon from returning to Montana. Rhiannon still did not know if it had been the right decision, but when she thought about it more, she knew she could not have left her responsibilities and her family here.

"A scout has just arrived and said the party should be here within the hour."

"They made good time, then. They just arrived at Eastern Fort four days ago. I would have thought it would have taken that huge of a party at least a week."

Kyia snorted—very unlike her. "When have you ever known the king to delay?"

Rhiannon looked over at her cousin and best friend. The younger woman was looking out over the large pond. She knew Kyia did not want Flath in Màrrach.

"I admit it isn't ideal that he be here just now, but we must at least try and make him welcome."

Kyia did look over at Rhiannon then. She studied Rhiannon with those cinnamon colored eyes. "You really don't want to see him, do you?"

"No." Rhiannon did not even have to think about her answer. Her emotions were still raw from losing Shih 'Ni only ten months ago. She did not need the complication of Flath right now.

"What do you think he's after?'

"I'm not quite sure. I think it would be in

bad taste for him to expect anything so soon after Shin 'Ni...' her words trailed off. She squeezed the shell, and it warmed in the palm of her hand. Immediately she felt the calming effect wash over her body and quiet her mind.

After a while, Kyia spoke again. "But he will. You know that."

Rhiannon nodded her head. "Probably. What is the Council saying?" she asked but was not sure she wanted the answer.

"They're uneasy. They think you'll fall right into his arms again."

Suddenly Rhiannon was furious! She did not even really know why. "Do they—do you—really think Shih 'Ni meant so little to me that I'd run right back to Flath? Or do they think I'm so weak a woman that I would forgive his betrayal so quickly? Or is it that they just want to control me?" Rhiannon almost expected Kyia to be surprised at her outburst, but Kyia was as level as ever and just stared at Rhiannon waiting for her tantrum to be over.

"They're concerned, that's all," she finally

said.

Rhiannon turned and looked out over the water again. "So their opinion is still to never accept Flath as an equal, as an ally, or a man." It was a statement rather than a question.

"We are a stubborn people, Rhiannon. They might never accept him." Since that emotional morning, Kyia had found Rhiannon ready to step through the Tree of Jurr they had grown closer, and Kyia had finally left off calling her 'Empress'—at least when it was just the two of them.

Rhiannon gently nudged Luna's large head off of her lap and stood. She brushed off pieces of grass from her leggings. "Well, I guess I better go make myself presentable for this mob." At that Kyia did laugh. "How're the preparations going?"

"All the rooms and refreshments are ready and the feast for tonight is almost done. The musicians and entertainers that Governor Brun brought with him have been practicing all day. I'm actually quite annoyed at their constant caterwauling. Silence definitely has its virtues."

Rhiannon laughed. "Well, time to make ready for the King of Beaynid's arrival."

An hour and a half later Flath's large party rode into Màrrach. Rhiannon had quickly bathed, and her personal servants had styled her dark hair into long, tiny braids then pined them up into an intricate pattern all over her head, placing small sapphires and diamonds within the braids. The jewel-encrusted crown of Ventra sat upon her decorated head. The necklace of Ventra and the emissary beads were strung across her long neck. She wore a deep blue colored chole studded with tiny diamonds and hemmed with silver thread and miniature silver bells. The top was low cut to show her diamond-shaped birthmark, and the bottom came to just under her breasts; the tiny bells chimed whenever she moved. A large sapphire was placed in her navel, and a matching blue skirt called a lehanga hung tightly across her hips and fell to her slippered feet. Silver ropes of tiny bells were wrapped around each ankle.

The summer sun was just setting over the western hills as her guests arrived. Despite the strict talk she had given herself earlier, her breath was still stolen when she caught sight of Flath riding atop his sorrel gelding. Gone was the thin, pale man so close to death as he was when Rhiannon last saw him so long ago. The strong, powerful man she knew during The War of the Gypsy King (as it was now known) had returned. But this time he wore the crown of Beaynid and a golden signet ring on his long finger. All weakness had been banished, and he looked like he rode forth to conquer. But conquer what, Rhiannon did not know—or perhaps she did, but would not admit it.

The day was warm but cooling quickly as the clear sky turned from blue to pink then a vivid red. A soft breeze ruffled Flath's blond hair as he climbed the pink sandstone stairs towards the immense marble doors meticulously carved into a scene of the Venturian countryside. Rhiannon stood just outside of the huge doors with her council members: Kyia, Shankee, Forlia, Javuil,

Ykellen, and Gen 'Lon. All wore a stern, yet aloof expressions on their brown-skinned faces. An expression mastered by all Archigos but Rhiannon, it seemed. As soon as Flath stood before her, she broke into a huge smile, despite herself. She knew Shih 'Ni would not have approved. "Well met, King Basilias." She bent into a bow.

"Greetings, Empress Kossi." If he was taken aback by her formal greeting, he did not show it.

"How was your journey?" Rhiannon stood straight; her hands gripped in front of her, the shell held tightly in her left hand.

"The sail up here on Siren's Bane was relatively smooth, for the Carnaid, and the ride from Eastern Fort was quite enjoyable. Your country is beautiful, Greannmhor!" She flinched at his use of that term of endearment. It had been so long since she had heard it. She had hoped he had not seen her reaction but when she saw the corner of his eyes tighten she knew he had.

"Lassie, ya sure are a sight fur sore eyes!"

Teo ran up the stairs and wrapped his burly arms around Rhiannon in a bear hug. She half expected a warrior or two to tackle him, but when she glanced over her shoulder, everyone looked rather amused.

She put her arms around the older man and laughed. "Teo, it's so good to see you again." She hugged him tightly, her apprehension suddenly melting away. She had missed him.

Ian and Adam walked up to her and bowed. "Empress, you look like a jewel!" Ian exclaimed.

Thank you, Ian," she laughed. She had missed all of them! Feelings and memories rolled like an angry ocean, and she could not stop the tears from falling.

"Ach, weel have no of that, milady!" Teo wiped a tear from her cheek. "'Tis someone I want ye ta meet, finally." Teo turned and motioned for a woman to climb up the stairs. A plump middle-aged woman in a fine dress and bright red shoes walked up to Rhiannon and curtsied low. She straightened back up, clasped her hands in front of her and kept her eyes on the floor. "Lassie, 'tis my wife, Lady Shawna, the Duchess of Perth."

Rhiannon walked forward and clasped Shawna's hands in hers. "It's so nice to finally meet you, Duchess. I've heard so much about you from your adoring husband." Rhiannon could tell the woman was not yet used to her new title.

She turned her grey eyes up at Rhiannon and smiled. "'Tis me honor fur sure, Empress." Her face was pleasant and just starting to show a little age. Rhiannon was surprised about that, figuring birthing and raising five children would age a woman quickly!

"Please, call me Rhiannon. We're all family." Rhiannon smiled warmly at the woman. "Your husband found me lost in the forest and started this whole adventure for me."

"Aye! He tells the story all the time…ta anyone who weel listen," she laughed looking over at Teo who had the good grace to look abashed.

Rhiannon stood back and looked over the crowd. There were a hundred other people in various dress—even veiled—plus about fifty Sona Tuathian Royal Guardsmen and about the same number of warriors from the desert territory of Cargh—the southernmost point of Beaynid. "Welcome to Ventra!" Her voice was strong and clear, and she spread out her arms in greeting. "I'm sure you all are exhausted from your journey. Please let us show you to your rooms. Our feast will begin in a few hours." At that, a small army of Oread poured out of the palace and started to help the royal Beaynidian delegation to their chambers.

***

Later that night the banquet hall was packed. It was a large room anyway since all the Archigos who lived in the royal palace ate dinner there at night, but tonight, with hosting so many visitors, it was unusually busy. The Turr' ahian musicians that Trevin and Mela Brun had brought with them played a lively tune just loud enough not to interfere with conversation but was actually quite pleasant despite what Kyia had said about them earlier. Rhiannon thought she just might employ some permanent musicians for Màrrach, or perhaps have some Oread professionally trained as musicians.

The huge iron candelabras flickered with thousands of candles and wall sconces burned in earnest giving the hall plenty of light. The enormous fireplace lay sleeping on this summer night, for it was already warm in the room with all these bodies. Women's elaborate dresses and expensive jewelry sparkled in the wavering light. The tables were covered with platters of roasted wild boar, pheasants and venison. Huge brightly painted bowls were filled with potatoes, carrots, broccoli and leafy greens. Later would be deserts of cakes, sweet dumplings, poached fruit, and some fancy chocolate candy imported from Tel 'Rhia by way of Turr' ah.

Seated next to Rhiannon was Flath—as diplomacy dictated—and on her other side was Earl Ryman Toliver and his colorful daughter, Abla. Apparently, they were very important people in Cargh. She guessed that was why Flath had given the man a title when he clearly did not need one—his family's wealth was old (or so she had been told). She avoided talking to Flath on her right who looked like he was just enjoying the food and music, and she struck up a conversation with Ryman. "How are you finding the festivities so far, Earl Ryman?"

"Earl, ha, indeed! In my country, I am a king!" His double chins wagged at his outburst. He had been imbibing the expensive liquor from Turr' ah all evening, and his words were slightly slurred. In light of that, Rhiannon felt it would have been highly inappropriate to point out that the Katlom Desert was, in fact, part of Beaynid, and therefore under the rule of the king.

"How do you like the music?" Rhiannon asked, trying to change the subject.

"In our country, we have divine poets that speak eloquent words of great importance to music so beautiful it would turn your ears to gold!" Rhiannon sighed. What could one say to that? Ryman stuffed a chunk of meat in his mouth and then licked his fingers, shiny with grease.

Rhiannon decided to try again, but with Ryman's daughter instead. The alternative was talking to Flath—she was not ready for that. She leaned forward and caught the woman's eye. "How was your journey, Lady Abla?"

She smiled coolly, her striking green eyes twinkling with mischief. "It was not as arduous as I thought it would be, however, your weather up here is much too cold for my liking." Her accent, like her father's, was thick, but not unpleasant.

"Yes, it takes some getting used to," Rhiannon agreed. "How do you like these musicians from Turr' ah?"

"They are acceptable, but if you're willing, I would like to show you music from our country." Again, Rhiannon wondered why Ryman and his daughter felt they lived in a foreign country? She had never seen the Katlom Desert but now wondered about its vastness.

"I would love to hear your music! Did you bring musicians?"

"All Buni people are musicians of some sort, Empress Kossi." Suddenly she pushed herself back from the table whispered something to her four veiled ladies standing behind her, and then at the three men standing behind her father. They all followed her to the stage where she quietly spoke to the Turr' ahian musicians who ceded the stage to the Buni.

Rhiannon had not noticed, but the men had been carrying their instruments under their cloaks. They whipped them out and started tuning them and tightening up reeds. Rhiannon was shocked when the ladies, Lady Abla included, deftly removed their scarf's and the light cloaks they were wearing. Lady Abla, of course, went unveiled, but her attendants left their gauzy pastel colored face veils covering everything under their eyes. Under the loose flowing garments, they wore tight halter tops sparkling in the fire-light with tiny jewels and low cut, loose long fitting pants made out of the same gauzy material as their veils. All the women slipped tiny finger cymbals on their forefingers and thumbs. Around their waists were tied thick golden belts of some sort with hundreds of tiny round disks that caught the light and shimmered across their hips. They were quite a spectacle. Everyone grew quiet. Ryman laughed, and Rhiannon looked over at him. He had a wide smile on his pudgy face, and he eased back in his chair and clasped his hands across his enormous belly.

Rhiannon's attention was taken back to the musicians and dancers when the music started. It was like nothing she had ever heard. There were two flute-like instruments, both held straight out in front of the musicians. One was straight and long the other was a bit shorter, but the end was flared out. The stringed instrument was like a guitar, but pear-shaped and had thirteen strings. It had a tinny sound.

The women all raised their hands above their dark heads and posed there for a moment. At some unseen cue, they clashed their little symbols and started to dance. Their hips shook inhumanly fast as they all moved in perfect time. Their long, slender arms swayed with the music telling a story all their own. Their lithe bodies rolled and moved like the ocean following the alien notes of the music. Rhiannon could not rip her eyes from the dancing, shimmering women as they gyrated, spun, and shook. Finally, she took a minute to look around at the dining hall. Every eye was on the performers. Everyone had stopped eating and talking and was just staring, mesmerized by the sparkling, vibrating women and the hypnotic music as it was flowing out into the hall. Rhiannon gave a side glance to Flath who was watching with wide eyes. She wondered if the gypsies he grew up with ever had any dances like that!

Rhiannon finally turned her eyes back to Lady Abla and her women. They shimmied and dipped and did impossible to follow moves as they slowly made their way to each table. Rhiannon was impressed with their stamina, grace, and talent.

Finally, the exotic dance and haunting music ended. Everyone jumped to their feet (even Ryman, albeit slowly) and clapped thunderously. There were shouts and whistles, Rhiannon had never heard such ruckus in the dining hall before. The women replaced all their scarves and loosely fitting attire and followed Lady Abla back to her seat at the table.

"That was amazing, Lady Abla!" Rhiannon said, almost as breathless as Abla was.

"Aye! Very well done!" Flath said from behind Rhiannon. She caught her breath at the sound of his voice, so close to her. Her mutinous memory recalled all the times he used to sing to her in his deep, smooth baritone and she wanted to melt into a puddle and disappear. Suddenly she just wanted to get as far away from here as possible.

"Thank you," Abla said as she tried to catch her breath. "That dance is called Calu'chu Maba in the old tongue." The Earl's daughter smiled proudly, her olive-toned skin shimmering in the candlelight from a light sheen of sweat.

"What is it called in Venn?" Flath asked.

She laughed and pierced him with her emerald-green eyes. "Lovers Consummation is as close as I can translate it." She winked at him suggestively, and Rhiannon had to fight the urge to throttle the woman. She took a deep breath, gripped the shell in her hand, and smiled warmly at Lady Abla and took her seat at the table once again. This is going to be a long night, Rhiannon thought. Again, she wondered how long everyone was planning on staying.

Eventually, the meal was over; dessert had been served and eaten, people had drunk their fill and started to make their way up to their rooms. Rhiannon had avoided talking to Flath all night, but as everyone else cleared away, she felt uncomfortable avoiding him. Finally, Rhiannon turned to Flath. He was staring at her. "Do you find your rooms acceptable?" The question sounded lame even to her.

Flath leaned back in his chair and smiled, never taking his eyes from her. After a while, he nodded his head. "Aye, Rhiannon, I find my rooms acceptable."

Rhiannon sighed; this was not going to be easy. "How are you getting on in Sona Tuath? Getting used to ruling a country yet?"

"I guess perhaps as much as you are."

Was that a smirk? Was he making fun of her? Suddenly she felt the burning spark of anger. "Why are you here, Flath?" His irritating smile faltered, and she claimed a small victory.

"What kind of welcome is that? If you treat all your guests in this manner, Greannmhor, I'm not surprised if your hospitality earns a reputation."

She smiled realizing she was being hostile. "I'm sorry, Flath, I've had a rough year."

His expression turned serious, and he leaned forward in his chair. After a moment of hesitation, he reached out and rested his warm hand on her knee. "I am sorry about Shih 'Ni. I wanted to send a letter with my condolences, but I did not know what to say."

He looked genuinely sorry for her, but she wished he would remove his hand. She squirmed under his touch; she felt like Shih 'Ni were somehow watching them. Her breath was taken away at how much she yearned for the feel of his touch, but her need repulsed her.

"Thank you," she murmured when she was able. Heat began to rise in her face, and despite the death-grip she had on the shell, she was still finding it hard to breathe. "I'm sorry, I am so tired...I must lie down." She jumped from the chair and ran past startled servants and guards and left the hall as quickly as she could.

When she reached her rooms, she tugged the pins from her hair and threw the jewels onto her dressing table. She left a trail of clothes leading to her bed and crawled under her blankets. She started sobbing, huge tears running down her face. She did not know why she was crying, but she could not hold it back. Her throat was painfully stiff, and her stomach was clenched. A pain so deep burst from her chest and cried out with sorrow. She cried deep into the night, even Astrid's gift could not soothe her. Luna and Jo Jo sat on her bed, helpless at the depth of Rhiannon's anguish.

Finally, when the night was at its deepest and most lonely, the Empress of Ventra drifted off into a fitful slumber.

CHAPTER TWELVE

*An eastern wind blew him into Màrrach one
summer
His peculiar eyes twinkled when he saw the
empress
She colored, but would not look away
He professed his love
But she ran him through anyway
Through the winter he stayed
Her heels he always followed
At last, her heart started listening to his song
Will he be the first Tjaty King?*

*—The Tjaty King; author unknown—Tales of the
Ancients; Burnk Lau*

The next day Rhiannon kept to her rooms. Kyia came up to check on her twice, but she assured her she just needed some rest. Kyia had looked at her swollen eyes suspiciously but did not question her further.

Rhiannon sat on her balcony and watched the sun slowly travel across the cloudless sky. Etâhpe'o-poeso lay napping in the warm summer sun. Luna and Jo Jo had both grown restless at Rhiannon's glum mood and had left to run in the solarium. She still had the giant cat for companionship at least.

As she listened to Poeso's rough purring, her thoughts turned to Shin 'Ni and how much she missed talking with him. She wished she could have spoken to him before he decided to flee. Her chest hurt when she thought about how he must have felt in his last moments in that turbulent sea.

Then she thought about Flath and how much she wished he had not shown up in

Màrrach. She was overcome with guilt as she admitted she was, after everything, still in love with him. Yes, she loved Shih 'Ni, but it was a different kind of love. She felt hopeless and lost and did not know how she was supposed to handle the situation she now found herself in. She had no one to talk to about it. Kyia certainly would not understand. Tess, her grandmother, would, but she did not live in the palace, and it would be unacceptable for her to leave her guests to disappear into the woods.

As the sun set, exhausted, Rhiannon drug herself to bed in the hope that she could get rest. Poeso had gone off to hunt, and Luna and Jo Jo had followed her to her massive bed and sat watching her try to fall asleep. All she could think of was Flath's touch on her knee. She resisted the urge to cry again and after a long while she finally fell into a deep sleep.

The next evening she went down for dinner, she knew she could hide no longer. She sat through dinner avoiding talking to Flath and only speaking to others when spoken to. She hoped her morose mood did not show on her face; she kept Astrid's gift tightly gripped in her palm.

The week slowly crept by. After a while her esteemed guests started to depart, they rode out over the green hills of Ventra, trailing away like ants under the warm summer sun. Finally, after six weeks, only Flath and his guardsmen were still at Màrrach, and then two weeks later, he released them to return to Sona Tuath and their families.

And then it was just Flath and the Archigos at dinner every night. She had traded pleasantries with him but nothing further and avoided being alone with him. Rhiannon noticed most of her council looking at him with unabashed suspicion and, in Gen 'Lon's case, open hostility. She knew they would call a meeting soon and demand to know what his plans were. She had no answers.

It had been almost two months since she walked through the lush solarium which had been a daily event before Flath showed up. In fact, she had not been outside of the palace since the day he and his group arrived seven weeks earlier. Zellan was probably wondering where she was. Feeling angry at herself for hiding in her rooms, she marched down to the solarium with Luna, Jo Jo and Poeso trailing behind her like a ribbon of fur and feathers. She sat near the edge of the northern pond and watched the swans gracefully glide across the dark water. Birds sung from the treetops and crickets and frogs called out to each other. It was not yet twilight, so Poeso was content to playfully rub her huge head up and down Rhiannon's arm and back as she watched Jo Jo scamper up a tree following an angry squirrel. Luna laid on her other side offering her silent support as she had for years.

Rhiannon contemplated what she was going to do about Flath, if anything. He was a visiting royal from the neighboring kingdom. It would be the height of impropriety to ask him to leave, let alone throw him out! She ran her fingers through the cool grass trying to come up with a diplomatic solution.

"Hello, Greannmhor." Rhiannon jumped

and turned around to see Flath sitting next to her. Her voice was stolen from her, and she could not move under his gaze. "I apologize if you wanted to be alone, but I have just not had the opportunity to talk with you."

"Did you think that might have been deliberate?" Rhiannon found her voice, and her anger blazed.

Flath chuckled. "Ah, you have not changed a bit, Greannmhor."

"Stop calling me that," Rhiannon ordered and looked back over the pond as a few fat ducks waddled by.

"Of course, great and wise ruler of Ventra." Her anger dissipated, and she had to try hard not to laugh as she gave him a sideways glance.

They did not speak for a long moment and then she asked, "Why didn't you leave with your men?"

He had been looking out over the vastness of the solarium but then turned to her. "I had not gotten an opportunity to speak with you."

"So, you'll leave now?"

He laughed again and smiled his wide,

lopsided smile. He was sitting close enough that she could see his mismatched eyes as they held hers. Damn him; she thought as heat crept up through her chest and over her face. "Always the diplomat, Greannmhor."

"Tell me why you're here, Flath."

He let out a long breath, and with the sigh, she could hear his anxiety and exhaustion. She immediately felt sorry for him, and then cursed herself. "I have missed you, Rhiannon. This is not how things were supposed to end up for us."

"And whose fault is that?"

"Aye, 'tis mine, for sure. But can we put it past us now?"

"You married another woman! Put it past me?" Rhiannon's voice was shrill, her throat ached, and she could feel the tears well in her eyes.

"I did what I thought was best for my kingdom. 'Twas an awful decision and a horrible thing to do to you, I apologize, Rhiannon. I will regret my decision until the day I die."

"Not good enough." She turned away from him and pretended to watch the swans.

After a while, he said quietly, "I will not leave until I have won you back, Rhiannon."

Rhiannon stood and looked down at him. "Winter comes early in Ventra. The Pass of Koslyn will be impassable, and the Carnaid Sea is dangerous in the winter."

He looked up at her and smiled again. "Then I shall be stuck here until spring."

She shook her head and walked away. When she got a little further away, she passed Shankee as she stood with her arms folded watching Flath sit on the grass. "Beware, Cousin; he is your weakness." Rhiannon walked away knowing she spoke the truth.

The next morning Rhiannon grabbed her sword and went out to the practice grounds to try and work out some of her aggression. It had been a while since she had practiced with the sword. As she got closer, she noticed a ring of warriors watching something, a match she assumed since she could hear the clash of the swords. When she was close enough, she was surprised the see Flath in a heated battle with a warrior. Both men were shirtless under the warm mid-summer sun, a sheen of sweat making their skin shiny—one light, one dark.

The warrior, Lumah Ki, took Shih Ni's position of Master at Arms after he had died. He was a little older, in his late thirties or early forties, Rhiannon guessed, but he was very experienced and one of their best warriors. The man also had an ego. She hoped Flath would realize this and choose his actions accordingly. After about ten more minutes, Flath missed a move that Rhiannon had seen him do a hundred times before and the match was won by Lumah.

Smiling proudly, he grasped Flath by his forearm in respect and Flath congratulated the older man on his victory. Rhiannon wanted to laugh because she knew Flath had purposely let Lumah win, but it was the right move. A few of the younger warriors even patted Flath on the back. They seemed to be more than just tolerating him. Rhiannon was surprised.

When Flath noticed Rhiannon standing in

the crowd, he yelled over to her, "How about a match, Empress?" Rhiannon felt pinned under his gaze as everyone turned to look at her. She smiled slightly and just shook her head. "Oh, come on. You cannot be intimidated by me, Empress Kossi. Monarch to monarch; let us duel!"

She sighed; her sword seemed too heavy in her hand as she slowly moved out of the crowd to face him. "All right, Your Majesty, let's fight," she challenged as she held her sword aloft, silver blade gleaming in the summer sun.

The first clash jarred her arms and shoulders, and she cursed herself for slacking on her training. He was fast, and he was granting her no breaks; however, he was fatigued from his first match, so it should have been easier. Over and over again she blocked his swipes forcing her back with each blow. A rage started to simmer in her, and she fought hard to control it. Finally, he got under her blade and twisted it with his, trying to pry it from her hands. His blade slid down hers, making an almost musical sound as he leaned in close. "If I win you must marry me," he whispered, his breath warm over her already heated face.

Suddenly, her seething rage boiled over— her sight was tinged with red as the voices of her ancestors called her—and she answered. She shoved him away with more strength than she knew she had. He stumbled backward but recovered quickly parrying a vicious swipe as she brought her sword down on him. Like lighting, she thrust and swiped at him backing him further away. The crowd melted from her awareness, and it was just her and him, their blades clashing across the practice grounds.

Fatigue was eating away at his defenses, and she worked harder, pushing him to get sloppy with his moves and slowing him down. Her bloodlust could not be sated. Finally, Flath grew too slow and left an opening, and she took her opportunity and brought her Venturian blade down upon his abdomen. He grunted under the impact of her sharp blade. He dropped his sword, and his hand went to his side as blood started to gush through his fingers and pool in the dirt at his feet. He looked up at Rhiannon with shock and sorrow. She was having trouble processing the scene as she looked at his startled face to the quickly flowing blood making a growing pool on the ground.

Her anger had been dowsed, and the call of the ancients had faded into silence. She watched Flath's face pale, his eyes roll back, and his body fall to the ground in his own blood. There were gasps as she slowly looked around at her warriors who all wore a look of horror. She was not quite sure what was happening. Suddenly Lumah ran up to Flath's lifeless body and held his tunic to the younger man's gaping wound. Even Gen 'Lon ran over to assist the King of Beaynid as he lay dying from Rhiannon's own had.

"Empress!" Lumah called to her several times before she realized that buzzing noise was her being called. Finally, she looked down at him. "Empress, your necklace, quickly," he beseeched her.

Finally, she realized what she had done. "Oh god, Flath!" she screamed as she knelt down in his blood and fumbled at the clasp of the Necklace of Verna. As Lumah pulled his tunic away, she gasped at the ugly, gaping wound. Black blood poured from his body. She quickly placed the stones on the wound and started to sing as the stones warmed and started to glow. She sang loudly as huge tears rolled down her face. Her song floated out over the practice grounds and was carried away on a warm wind over the green hills of Ventra.

When the song was through, and the stones cooled once again, she pulled them away from Flath's wound and found it had already started to heal. She looked up at a group of Oread that had gathered in anticipation of being needed. "Please, get a wagon ready and bring it and my horse here, quickly!" She turned to Lumah. "We must get him to my grandmother."

"Yes, Empress," he replied warily. Was he afraid of her? God, what has she done?

The sun was still high in the bright sky when they reached Tess's woodland infirmary. Rhiannon had a warrior ride ahead and alert Tess that they were coming with the king. She was standing outside waiting for them, her hands tightly clasped in front of her. She was shifting her weight from side to side and Rhiannon could see the tightness in her jaw. She looked worried, which made Rhiannon even more panicked. She wondered if there was a limit to the stone's power. Perhaps Flath was too far gone. She knew the black blood had meant she had struck an organ which most certainly would have been fatal had she not had the Necklace of Verna.

Her warriors carefully took Flath from the wagon and transferred him to an open bed— the same one, she noticed, that she had recovered in after Baobh's attack which seemed so long ago. She thought about Tim and tears started to trail down her cheeks. She missed him every day. She wondered what he would have thought of the predicament she currently found herself in. She could have used his kind words and pragmatic outlook.

It was not until four days later that Flath finally awoke. Rhiannon had not left his side. Both Shankee and Kyia had come twice to inquire about the King of Beaynid's health and ask whether a bird should be sent to Sona Tuath informing Viceroy Hodge of what happened. She told them to wait, for she was sure Flath would soon wake. And thus, he did, to find Rhiannon's fearful face looking back at him.

"Hello, Greannmhor. Are you here to finish the job?" His voice was weak, but his lopsided smile was warm.

She laughed and scrubbed away the tears on her cheeks. "You're not worth the effort to kill." He chuckled then gasped, tenderly touching his side. "Oh, Flath, I am so sorry. I don't know what happened."

He looked back up at her with is mismatched eyes. "'Tis all right, Greannmhor, I was being cheeky. I suppose I will have to find another way to trick you into marrying me now."

Rhiannon gently lowered a cup to his lips and let him drink his fill and then she tenderly wiped the drips from his stubbled chin. "Flath, it's been less than a year since I lost my husband. I don't want to talk about this now."

"He was a good man. A fierce warrior and Ventra will be diminished because of losing him. But you did not love him. Not in the way you love me, Greannmhor." He sounded sure of himself, and even though he was right, she resented him for saying it out loud.

Rhiannon looked away, fighting the tears again. She was glad Tess had taken the morning to gather herbs in the woods and was not there to see her caving. Finally, she looked back over at Flath who was studying her. "You hurt me, Flath." Her voice wavered as she lost her battle with her tears as they spilled down her face again. "You gave me a wound far deeper than the one I gave you."

He reached out and took her hand in his. It was warm and calloused and so full of life. She was surprised to see tears running down his face, so full of remorse. "Rhiannon, I can never make up for the hurt I have caused you. I can only try and explain that I thought I was doing what I must for the good of Beaynid."

"And what's changed now? Has Beaynid lost their hate of me and my people?" Her voice was sharp and full of emotion.

"Aye! My people, many of them anyway, realize they owe their lives to the Archigos. There are some who still hold on to their prejudices, but I see now that people can change. There is hope!"

Rhiannon sighed and shook her head. "Even if our people could accept one another, I don't think I could ever forgive you, Flath." She used her words as a weapon and knew she struck his heart when she saw his countenance fall. She had won. She got up and walked to the door as Tess came in. "It seems the King of Beaynid will live. He's awake," she said to her grandmother and walked out of the cabin.

Assured that Flath would now live, she took Zellan back to Màrrach and resumed her life. She knew it would take Flath a while to recuperate and she felt relieved of the pressure of his relentless pursuit. The day after she returned to the palace, however, the council called a meeting.

She now sat at the massive mahogany table so highly polished it reflected light back into the room from the huge windows that went from floor to soaring ceiling in the council chambers. "I think we need to send the King home as soon as he is well enough for travel. We cannot allow him to stay any longer!" Forlia Domis was standing, pounding her fist on the table. Her voice was shrill, and there was fire in her eyes. Rhiannon sighed. They had been in here for twenty minutes discussing Flath, and she was at the end of her patience.

"Hold on, Forlia, we cannot simply kick a foreign monarch out of our kingdom. That would be very imprudent," Ykellen Gunn tried calming the flustered warrioress down.

"Ykellen is right, Forlia. We have to be cautious in this regard." Javuil Nys was reclining in his chair; his spatulate hands were resting on his protruding belly. He smiled warmly at Forlia trying to ease her mood, but Forlia was having none of it.

"Since when are we so weak as to coddle this gypsy king?" she spat. Rhiannon disliked the woman. She had fought Rhiannon since she took the throne. Rhiannon found her uncompromising and rigid in the old ways and was sorry she had asked her to join her council. "What say you, Shankee? You have no love for the Suen."

Shankee had been trying to stay out of the debate up until then, and Rhiannon turned to her legitimately interested in what she thought. After a long pause, she spoke. "I believe the men are correct; we need a diplomatic solution to this problem." Forlia dramatically threw her arms in the air and made a rude noise and Rhiannon could see Shankee's jaw clench. She was growing tired of this meeting as well.

"I also think we should escort the Suen out of Màrrach as soon as he returns from the healer." Rhiannon was not surprised to hear Gen 'Lon wanted Flath gone. He was still mourning Shih 'Ni's death and was threatened by Flath's perceived nearness to replacing his cousin. He wanted Flath gone before Rhiannon could make a terrible mistake. She was not sure she could disagree with the young man. "Kyia, you haven't said anything on the matter. How do you feel about the Suen taking up residence in Màrrach?"

Kyia was sitting next to Rhiannon, and she could hear the younger woman expel a breath. "I agree that he needs to go as soon as possible. However, I don't think we should kick him out. Beaynid is our ally now; we must be careful of how we react to this problem." She then turned to Rhiannon. "It must be our empress that makes it clear to him that there will be no future joining of our kingdoms by marriage and that he must leave immediately!" Rhiannon almost flinched at Kyia's angry words. She could not believe it. Her best friend and cousin had just thrown her under the bus, as was the expression in the land where she grew up.

Rhiannon grew irate and was finished with

this council meeting. She took a deep breath and stood up slowly, placing her hands on the smooth, cool surface of the table. "I appreciate all of your council and sharing all of your opinions. However, you all serve at my pleasure and while I can decide to accept your advice—I can also disregard it completely." Rhiannon gave Forlia a sharp look, and the older woman sat down quickly. "It is my decision to not make a decision at this time." She heard a few angry sighs, but she continued on, "When the King of Beaynid returns from my grandmother's house, then I will decide how and when he should leave. Thank you for your time," she said, and turned and walked out of the silent room.

It was not until a week later that Flath rode back into Màrrach on his sorrel gelding that he had requested to be brought out to him. One of the warrioresses that Rhiannon had left at Tess's to guard the king had arrived earlier and announced the king was returning. For decorum's sake, she stood out on the sandstone steps of the royal palace, just as she had ten weeks earlier. She studied him as he slowly got down from his horse and handed the reins to a waiting Oread. Clearly, his wound was still tender. He approached the grand stairs with an ever so slight limp from an old leg wound and climbed the stairs as quickly as he could. He bowed low, and Rhiannon knew it must have cost him pain to do so. "Empress, I have returned to you and your gracious people's hospitality." She had to suppress a laugh at the grand announcement, but she knew she must not have hidden the amusement on her face because Flath gave her a little smile as if he were sharing some secret that was just between the two of them.

Suddenly, it was just the two of them. She was aware of how the warm breeze pulled at his hair as it brushed across his broad shoulders and the way his golden snake earring sparkled in the sunlight. She admitted to herself that she had missed him, deeply.

She searched his mismatched eyes trying to discern if she could ever trust him again. He reached out and took both of her hands in his.

"Take a walk with me, Greannmhor." Flath dropped one of her hands but kept the other one, and they strolled into the solarium. They found a bench near a small waterfall and sat in silence looking over the giant park. A plethora of flowers was always blooming filling the air in the solarium with perfume. Birds darted around and sung from high up in the treetops. Frogs and crickets added to the ambiance.

Finally, Flath looked over to Rhiannon and spoke. "By my count, you have saved my sorry arse three times. I owe you a lot."

Rhiannon snorted. "To be fair, I almost killed you once, so that last time really doesn't count."

He laughed. "That might be so, but I would still be just as dead if you had not used your necklace to heal me." He squeezed her hand. "Some of your people might have been content had you let me die."

"That would be true. Especially Shih 'Ni's cousin, Gen 'Lon...and maybe my cousin, Kyia," her voice trailed off sadly.

He took a deep breath and let it out slowly,

holding her with his eyes. She could clearly see one of his eyes was slightly greener than his blue eye, something most people would not notice until they were close enough. Rhiannon felt panic start to rise and gripped the shell in her free hand; Flath still had hold of the other one.

He finally started to speak. "Rhiannon, when I was in Sona Tuath my life was bereft of any happiness. When you left, you left with my heart. These past years I have been but a shell of a man." Rhiannon tried to look down, but he gently guided her face back up to meet his. "Greannmhor, my life is meaningless and empty without you. I will not leave here without you as my wife." His voice was soft, but his words were forceful.

The shell had melted the panic away, but it was replaced with a dull anger that warred with the love that still burned inside of Rhiannon for Flath. "I can't just forget your betrayal with Jocelyn." She meant her words to be filled with venom, but they were almost apologetic, and she cursed herself for being weak.

"I know 'twill take time for you to trust me again, Greannmhor. I told Viceroy Hodges that I would not return to Sona Tuath for a time. I also asked Teo to stay in Sona Tuath and give aid to the Viceroy until I return—with you."

"You assume much, Flath. What if I never get over what you did to me?" That time she saw that her words did sting him.

"I know we can rebuild what we once had. I have to believe that, for not having you is the only thing in this world that will completely destroy and unman me." His voice was full of emotion, and she could see the truth in his eyes.

His flowery words started to thaw the ice around her heart that she had fought so hard to keep cold and hard. She did not want to forgive him, and she certainly did not want to love him again. But did she have a choice, really?

She thought of Shin 'Ni and fought not to cry. Her stomach clenched, and her heart ached. She had loved him, but in a different way than she loved Flath. Shih 'Ni knew that. He was even convinced that Verna had not blessed their pairing because she had not produced an heir. So, he left. Left to make room for Flath. At that realization, she did start crying. Tears streamed down her face, and Flath took her in his arms. She laid her head on his wide chest and relaxed in the protection of his strong arms as she let her tears silently wet his tunic.

Summer faded into fall, and then winter was quickly upon the land. Flath received birds regularly with messages on how Sona Tuath was fairing without their king. Flath and Rhiannon spent their days together talking and laughing as they walked through the solarium and often took their dinners together in the private dining room. Rhiannon's warriors were slowly becoming accustomed to Flath walking the halls of Màrrach and courting their empress. It seemed even Kyia and Gen 'Lon were reluctantly accepting the inevitable.

One frigid morning, after a blanket of snow lay on the ground shimmering under the winter sun, they went out to visit Tess and to sit under the ribbon-like branches of the Tree of Everlasting Spring. Upon the lush, green grass under the long fingers of the tree, Rhiannon agreed to marry Flath. She looked out over the winter forest that ringed this special tree remembering when she decided to marry Shih 'Ni in this very spot, and she suffered a stab of pain and guilt alongside her joy. They stayed at Tess's for a week and made their plans for the future with the blessing of Rhiannon's grandmother.

When they returned to Màrrach, Rhiannon announced amid gasps there was to be a nikah on the winter solstice a few days away. The Oread jumped into action, and the Ceremony Keeper and her apprentices were told to make ready, and her warriors tried to accept they would have a Suen tjaty. After she made the announcement, she called a council meeting and took questions and concerns from her council members. Her mind was made up, and their complaints broke into little pieces upon her solid will. She felt strong and sure of herself and would not back down. Forlia and Gen 'Lon still fumed in anger. However, Kyia seemed resigned to the idea of having Ventra and Beaynid finally allied by marriage.

On a bitterly cold afternoon on the shortest day of the year, Rhiannon once again stood on the sandstone steps of the royal palace looking out over her people on the day of the nikah. It had only been two years since she stood in the very spot just before she married Shih 'Ni. Guilt ate away at her like a million little ants on a piece of forgotten food. *Shih 'Ni left me! Left me so that I would marry Flath. What do I have to feel guilty about?* She tried to push away the acrid feeling of guilt, but it was her constant companion.

When the drums stopped, she slowly made her way down the stairs and to the line of waiting warriors. Four of Ventra's best, unmarried warriors and Flath stood before her. Naked except for deep green loincloths, all wore a covering of goosebumps in the brisk winter air. Flath's pale skin stood out next to the Archigos' darker tones. Flath's chest was the only one that was as of yet unmarked by tattoos, though soon after the nikah he would receive his markings as tjaty. He would hold no official military rank, so his markings would not be as elaborate, but at least he would have his tjaty tattoos.

She smiled up at him after she fastened a rope of gold around his waist and he hung the shriveled, brown length of umbilical cord around hers. He beamed at her under the smear of herbal paste the Ceremony Keeper's apprentices carefully applied to his face. Solemnly they walked down the line of marble altars and set each ablaze. She wondered how Flath felt honoring the many gods and goddess' of the Archigos being raised to believe in the One God. Though his face was serious—as required by the occasion—he smiled at her with his eyes. His dedication to the One God did not seem to hinder his taking part in Archigos ritual. Perhaps gypsies did not worship Ak.

Finally, they made it to the ancient Ceremony Keeper in her long white robe and ever-present pipe. When it was time, Rhiannon produced the palm of her left hand and could see the tiny white lines that were already there from oaths she had taken before: one to Tim and one to Shih 'Ni—both gone from her life forever. Sadness tugged at her heart, but Shih 'Ni orchestrated this moment when he had left her and Ventra, and Tim would have heartily approved of this union.

That evening darkness fell early across Ventra, and despite the fact that some of the Archigos were reluctant to accept a Suen as their tjaty, they celebrated just the same. Wine, ale, and expensive imported liquor flowed like the waters from The Tree of Eternal Spring. Some celebrated a union that they hoped would finally give Ventra an heir, some drown their sorrows, but all knew change was coming to the land of the Northern Warriors.

CHAPTER THIRTEEN

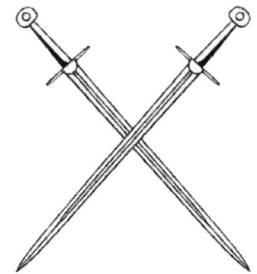

"The Empress of Ventra sailed into Sona Tuath one spring standing tall next to our king. He would marry her the next day, and she would be coronated as our next Queen of Beaynid. The events that followed were heinous and hard, even for the law abiding Suens of the capital city. Events that would not soon be forgotten."

—*History of the Gypsy King; Tomas Ulln*

Rhiannon looked down at the red waters of the Carnaid Sea as the foamy water broke over the bow of the Siren's Bane. The scouring wind lifted the heavy braids of Rhiannon's hair and threatened to knock the crown of Ventra from her head. It was spring, but the fabled wind of the Carnaid was still icy cold. She pulled her cloak tighter around her body causing Jo Jo to shift her position as she sat quietly on Rhiannon's shoulder. Luna and Etâhpe'o-poeso sat on each side of her as if to lend her strength.

The ship slowly made its way across the Bay of the Gods and into port. Thousands of people were gathered on the docks and up into the surrounding streets. She was overwhelmed, and they had not even gotten off the ship yet! The shell was tightly clasped in her warm palm. Her other hand went protectively to her swollen belly. It had only been four months since the nikah, but her pregnancy was quite obvious. She was worried the baby was going to be huge since her belly had grown so large so quickly, but Tess had assured her that she and the baby would be just fine. Ventra was overjoyed they would soon have their long-awaited heir, assuming it was a girl. Beaynid did not know yet—she would be sure to keep herself wrapped in her cloak.

She was wondering where Kyia was when Flath walked up to her and tenderly put his arms around her. Jo Jo gave a squeak of annoyance and jumped down. "How is my son doing?"

Rhiannon laughed. "How do you know it's a boy?"

"I just have a feeling."

Rhiannon sighed. "I surely hope not. Ventra needs her heir before they throw me out!"

Flath slipped his hand into her cloak and gently rubbed her belly. "If it 'tis a girl then Beaynid will have to wait until the next one for their heir."

"I don't know if I want to do this again." The sickness she suffered the first few months had finally passed, but she did not like the feeling of sharing her body with another being.

"Ah, 'tis what women do, Greannmhor. You will change your mind."

She socked him playfully. "Really? I am a warrioress, that doesn't really fit with pregnancy very well."

"Your attitude will change when first you lay eyes on that babe. Or so that 'tis what Tess told me."

"Oh really? What other wisdom has my grandmother shared with you?"

"A lot, Greannmhor, you should listen to everything your granny tells you."

"Ha, that's just because she's such a big fan of yours."

He looked at her with confusion. "What is a fan?" Rhiannon tipped her head back and laughed loudly feeling the anxiety drain from her body. After her coronation tomorrow, she would be the Queen of Beaynid just like the siochair, deep in the Shash-nah forest, had predicted so long ago. If the people of Sona Tuath did not approve, well they would just have to get over it like the Archigos eventually did. When Rhiannon did not answer his question, he kissed her on the forehead, took her hand and led her to the disembarking area with Luna and Poeso following closely. Jo Jo, full of excitement at the crowd's noise, jumped back onto her shoulder, clinging to Rhiannon in desperation.

When they left the ship, there were cheers but much to her dismay, if not surprise, many people wore scowls and even shouted jeers at the warriors that accompanied her. Her heart slammed in her chest as she realized these people still hated her and her warriors. Even after all the work they had done in Beaynid and all the charity she had given them, they still bathed in their prejudice! Anger simmered in her spine as she glared at the people—her people now.

Flath led her to the waiting carriages, and she and her party made their way up the steep cobbled road to the white castle of Sona Tuath. Their ride was silent, and Rhiannon knew Flath could tell something was wrong. She was sure he saw the hostility on his people's faces as they walked by. She squeezed his hand, and he leaned in and kissed her brow.

That evening Flath met with his advisors, and the meeting went late into the night. She was lying in their massive bed stroking Luna's fur, lost in dark thoughts when Flath finally returned. His face was serious, and she grew worried. "What is it?" she asked with trepidation.

He stood in front of her and took a deep breath. "The Advisory Board has strongly suggested that we have an official wedding in the kirk. They are worried that the people will not accept our union without the blessings of the priest."

Rhiannon laughed. "That's what you're worried about? You know I'm not particularly religious—even about the beliefs of my own people. If they want me to stand in front of a priest and say some silly vows, so be it." She could see that Flath was both relieved at her agreement and at the same time alarmed at her lackadaisical attitude toward religion—

though he had told her after the nikah that as a gypsy he was not beholden to the One God either.

"All right," he said slowly. "Then the wedding and the coronation will take place at the same time tomorrow afternoon."

Rhiannon gently pushed Luna from the bed, laid back and pulled the heavy feather comforter from her naked body. "Come to bed, husband. We will worry about it tomorrow."

In the morning a group of lady's servants arrived to assist Rhiannon. Kyia folded her arms in front of her and gave them a skeptical look. Her personal servants that she had brought with her from Ventra were unaccustomed to Beaynidian tradition (as was Rhiannon) so they hung around the corners of the chambers and watched Rhiannon get ready for both her wedding and her coronation.

Like in Màrrach, she was thoroughly bathed, but of course, no consideration was given to the fickle gods and goddesses of childbirth and fertility. At the sight of her swollen belly, her lady's maids slipped each other disapproving looks. Rhiannon guessed that the whole of Beaynid would know she was pregnant by the end of the day. She hoped Flath had already informed The Advisory Board. Otherwise, they were going to get a surprise.

When she was dried off and put into a soft robe, she was sat next to the fire, and a strange apparatus was used on her that took the warm air from the fire and blew it onto her drying hair. Her hair was dry in no time, then oiled and twisted into an elaborate design complete with golden hairpins.

A shockingly extravagant crimson and cloth-of-gold dress was carefully carted in by three servants. "Oh, my!" Kyia laughed. The servants turned their eyes down, and Rhiannon could tell they were offended.

"It's…beautiful! Isn't it, Kyia?" She grabbed her cousin's arm and pulled her close. "When in Rome, do as the Romans do," she whispered in Kyia's ear.

"What's a Roman?" The younger woman looked up at her with one dark brow arched.

"I'm just saying we need to adjust to how things are done here." Rhiannon noticed that Jo Jo, who had been watching the proceedings from the bed with Luna and Poeso, was now hiding on top of one of the massive wardrobes. I guess she doesn't care for the dress either, Rhiannon thought.

"You really want to wear that monstrosity?" As an official of the Venturian Government, Kyia was not dressed as a warrior for this important event. She wore the traditional Archigos chole and matching lehanga in her favorite deep green color, embroidered with silver thread and hemmed with tiny silver bells. She wore a silver and emerald necklace and belt around her bare waist. Emeralds at her ears, and around both wrists, sparkled in the sunlight coming from the large windows in the room. Rhiannon had made a shiny silver circlet with an emerald in the center, crafted just for Kyia to wear in Sona Tuath. Of course, Kyia thought it would draw too much attention to her, but Rhiannon insisted she wear it anyway. She looked at her cousin now and beamed at her beauty and grace. She hoped her best friend would soon find a man she could love and spend the rest of her life with.

Then Rhiannon sighed and gave her a sideways glance which made Kyia giggle. "Okay, let's get this thing on!" she announced and walked over to the nervous looking servants who then started on the laborious task of getting a six-foot-tall Archigos Warrioress into the flamboyant dress. When the corset was tightened (and carefully maneuvered above her swollen belly), the stays were buckled, the sleeves were tied on, and the dress was fluffed to maximum volume, Rhiannon and Kyia stood in front of a huge mirror surrounded by intricately carved wood darkened with age.

Who she saw staring back at her overwhelmed her. She had just become settled as the Empress of Ventra. Now she was also the Queen of Beaynid—a wholly different creature. Rhiannon fought the urge to grab the shell, telling herself that she had become too dependent on its use. An older servant woman came forward to powder her face, and Rhiannon shooed her away. "Well, what do you think?" She turned to Kyia.

Kyia looked back up at her and smiled. "I'm surprised the dress actually fit!"

Rhiannon laughed. "What are you trying to say, I'm fat?" Rhiannon put her hands on the swell of her belly, not even noticeable under the voluptuous deep red skirts of her dress.

Kyia plucked at the heavily embroidered dress. "It's long enough to fit even your height."

"That is surprising." Another servant brought in a shiny pair of red shoes and slipped them on her feet. Again, another perfect fit. "People must have been up all night making these," Rhiannon wondered aloud.

"Aye, Your Grace. Two cobblers and ten seamstresses worked all night to finish on time." Was her tone accusatory? Rhiannon thought she was just being overly sensitive.

"Well, I will have to be extra generous to them. Please see that I get a list of their names." The servant looked taken aback but nodded her head. The next two women came up and fastened ruby earrings on to her earlobes. Rhiannon was pleased with how well they matched the Necklace of Verna. Her fingers brushed across the brown emissary beads still stung around her neck. She wondered if she'd ever use them again. And then she wondered how Kaat was growing. The infant they had found in this very room...

"Your Majesty, 'tis time to go," an official-looking woman announced, and Rhiannon was brought out of her dark musings. She turned to follow the woman out of the Tower of The King and down to a waiting carriage that would take her to the kirk. Kyia took Jo Jo, (it would have been inappropriate for a queen to be married and coroneted with a monkey on her shoulder) and Luna and Poeso both jumped off the bed to complete the menagerie.

As Flath and Rhiannon made their way

down the steep roads toward the kirk, she could not help noticing how eerily empty and quiet the streets were. She studied Flath as he swayed with the motion of the carriage as it bumped down the cobbled roads. She wondered if he noticed the calm of his streets and hoped it was not an indication of ill things to come.

When they finally reached the kirk that was still under construction and probably would be for many more years to come, a footman opened the carriage door and let Flath out then Flath turned to help Rhiannon extricate herself amongst all the frills and heavy skirts. Luna and Poeso jumped out after Rhiannon. They looked a bit anxious, but both were intent on her. Rhiannon knew that between the two war parties she brought with her to Sona Tuath and her furry companions that followed her everywhere, she was safe. She noticed Flath's gloved hand was resting on the panther-headed pommel of his sword hanging at his waist. He, too, was uneasy it seemed.

There was a crowd standing outside the kirk and Rhiannon wondered why more people had not attended the affair to see their king at such an important event. The majority of the citizens looked happy or at least interested; some even cheered—a few, though, wore those hostile expressions as the people on the docks from the day before. A nagging feeling that something was not right started to wash over her, but she pushed it away trying to concentrate on what was expected of her in these ceremonies. As Flath and Rhiannon started walking into the kirk, Kyia, still holding Jo Jo, got out of her carriage and followed them in.

When they entered the kirk and started walking down the long, carpeted aisle to the dais, Rhiannon could hear people gasp. Nervously she glanced up at the balcony. People filled both sides of the giant stone cathedral. Their faces and bright clothing blended into one. On each side of the aisle stood stony-faced Royal Guardsmen, and behind them stood even more spectators;

their dress not as fine as the people upstairs. She noticed some pointing to something behind her. She figured it must be her animals. The Sona Tuathians were not yet used to seeing a wolf and a pax roaming freely, not to mention a squeaky little monkey. Rhiannon took a deep breath, gripped her shell tight, and kept walking down the aisle. When they got closer to the dais, Ian was standing there proudly in his crisp uniform as Head of the Sona Tuathian Royal Guard. She smiled at him bashfully answering his I told you so grin.

When they reached the dais, Rhiannon and Flath silently climbed the eight stairs to the top. Kyia and the animals drifted off to the side where all of her armed warriors stood. Flath looked over at her and smiled encouragingly as they stood in front of the priest. The man was painfully thin and had a wrinkly, concaved face. He stared at her with hollow eyes; a large conical hat stood erect on his snow-white hair. He wore heavy chains of gold and jeweled rings on every finger. His bright red robes completely swallowed his small frame.

Finally, he started to speak in a language she did not understand. His eyes were closed, and Rhiannon wondered if he were praying. Suddenly his eyes sprung open, and his voice boomed out over the crowd, reverberating in the graceful stone arches above. He started speaking in Ska now. He reached over and picked up a thick, ancient looking tome, opened to a specific page and started reading. After what seemed like an excruciatingly long time the priest returned the book to its place on the table next to him. Next, he stuck one boney finger in a golden chalice and drew a circle on both Rhiannon and Flath's foreheads, leaving a shiny, oily substance behind. Flath then removed a small signet ring from his pocket and placed it on the forefinger of her right hand. "This was my mother's," he whispered to her proudly. She had to stifle a laugh at his childish exuberance.

Finally, the priest joined Flath and Rhiannon's hands and wrapped a surprisingly fragrant green vine around their clasped hands; the shell swinging forgotten on Rhiannon's wrist as she looked into Flath's mismatched eyes and smiled up at him. She figured that after two weddings there was no changing her mind now—not that she wanted to. Also, one of their kingdoms would have an heir at the end of summer. Rhiannon's hand went to her belly, hiding under so much fabric. She felt tears pricking the backs of her eyes when she thought about having Flath's child.

The marriage ceremony now complete, Flath squeezed Rhiannon's hand then left the dais to stand next to Kyia. Four burly assistants now carried a large, ornate throne onto the dais and placed it in the center. Rhiannon was motioned to sit, and on shaky legs, she walked over and did as she was asked. The priest stood in front of her and once again spoke loudly in a different tongue; she wondered what he was saying, another prayer, perhaps? Again, he picked up his thick tome and started reading in Ska from a different page. He stated that monarchs are chosen by the One God, Ak, and anointed by the priestly class to rule over their kingdoms, and any who would fight against that would receive everlasting destruction. Rhiannon thought that was a bit harsh and wondered where Baobh's soul was now.

Rhiannon took a deep breath and let it out slowly when the priest put a long (and surprisingly heavy) golden scepter in one hand and her gleaming Venturian sword in the other. He droned on with more foreign words and sprinkled water on her. Drips ran down her face, and it took all her will not to scratch at the powerful itch they left in their shiny trails.

Finally, the skinny, old priest took up the large, jewel-encrusted Beaynidian Queen's Crown (that Flath had commissioned before he even left for Màrrach the summer before) and carefully set it on her head. Suddenly she felt the weight of the world fall upon her, and she wondered if she had made the right choice. The hall was reverently silent as she looked up at the people in the balconies. She saw Teo and Shawna up there, and they both smiled warmly at her. Adam was standing next to them and on this left was Jade McVail, who seemed bored.

From the corner, Luna started to growl. Just as Rhiannon began to wonder why, something shattered several of the enormous stained-glass windows sending a shower of sparkling shards down on the guests and guardsmen alike. As the projectiles hit the tiled and carpeted floor they burst into flames. People started screaming and running in every direction to get out of the way of the fire as it ate up the carpet and anything else flammable. Rhiannon watched as the priest disappeared behind a huge red curtain at the back of the dais and as she turned back around Flath and Kyia were at her side. Flath grabbed the sword from her hand, and Kyia pulled her up from the throne. Her mind was slow to react to what was actually happening.

Jo Jo scampered around the floor screeching, Poeso took to the air and flew out of one of the windows. Snarling, Luna bolted out of the door, and in the back of her mind, Rhiannon almost felt sorry for whoever the wolf and pax were after. Flath and Kyia escorted her from the dais and around the growing flames. She looked back to see the dais start to burn and she felt a feeling of loss knowing that ancient tome would soon be gone. Rhiannon looked up at the balcony to see if she could spot her friends but could not pick them out in the frantic crowd trying to escape down a narrow stairway.

As they passed Ian who was barking orders, she yelled out "Find Teo and Adam! Get them out!" her voice mingled with the screams echoing in the cathedral, but he nodded and looked up searching for them, and then they were gone, toward the door that was already crammed with people trying to escape. She was encircled by her warriors and they none to gently shoved people out of the way. When they reached the door, they quickly exited the kirk and headed to their awaiting carriages. Before she would get in, she turned to one of her War Party Leaders, "Take your warriors and go back in and make sure the dukes and the earl get out," The woman nodded and called to her warriors, and they went back into the burning kirk.

Flath helped Rhiannon into the carriage, and Jo Jo darted in right after her, then Flath quickly climbed in. Rhiannon looked through the small window and saw Kyia climbing into her carriage, and then her view was cut off by warriors climbing on top of the carriage and running alongside, their swords drawn. As reality set in Rhiannon turned to Flath, tears streaming down her face. "What have we done?"

The carriage bounced up the road, her warriors hanging on for dear life, others trying their hardest to keep up but falling behind. When they made it up to the castle, Rhiannon's warriors jumped down and escorted her up to the King's Tower. Flath stayed below giving orders to his guardsman to protect the castle at all cost.

As soon as she entered the chambers that she and Flath shared she yelled out for her Oread servants. Both Oread and Suen servants came running. "Help me out of this confounded dress!" she ordered as she ripped the Queen's Crown from her head and tossed it on the expansive dressing table. The Suen servant's eyes grew wide as they watched the priceless state symbol roll and almost hit the floor.

"What happened, Empress?" Tyla, her senior personal Oread servant, asked.

"Someone attacked us and set the kirk on fire." Her young Suen servants gasped, and Rhiannon looked over at them as their faces grew even paler. "It will be all right. We'll catch whoever did this." Rhiannon tried to reassure them, but she was not sure she succeeded for both the young women looked at each other and then turned their eyes down. For a fleeting moment, Rhiannon wondered if they had anything to do with it.

It took forever, but finally, the elaborate dress with its sleeves, corsets, and petticoats all lay in a heavily embroidered heap on the carpeted floors. Rhiannon kicked off her perfectly fitting shoes and threw on her leather tunic, pulled on her breeches and laced up her boots. She strapped her small throwing axes across her chest and her large dagger to her right thigh. She looked around for her sword but then remembered Flath had it. She wondered if he had left it in the carriage. She spotted Jo Jo peeking out at her from the top of a huge wardrobe and felt sorry that she did not have the time to comfort the poor creature who was clearly frightened. She sighed, she would deal with Jo Jo later.

Just as she turned to leave, Flath walked in the room. He looked at his wife, ready for battle, with surprise on his face. He then looked to the servants who stood in the middle of the room not knowing what to do. "Leave us." Oread and Suen alike darted out of the room.

As they left the room, Rhiannon reached out and gently grabbed Tyla's sleeve, "Could you check on Kyia, for me. Bring her up here?"

"Yes, my Empress," the older woman bowed her head then silently left the room.

Rhiannon looked up at Flath noticing he had an apprehensive look on his face and then she noticed he was holding something in his hand. He held it up for her to see. Her hands went up to her mouth, Astrid's shell, attached to her wrist, swayed with the motion. Flath held Kyia's silver and emerald circlet. She snatched it out of his hand. "Where did you get this?"

He placed both of his hands on her arms and looked into her black eyes. "Some guardsmen brought it up. Her carriage was attacked, and she was taken." She started to quake, and Flath's jaw grew tight; she knew he realized what was coming.

"Where is my sword?" Her voice was barely above a whisper.

He took a deep breath, already defeated. "May I remind you that you are carrying our child?" He gave her arms one last squeeze then let them go and moved out of the way. "Your sword is lying on the couch in the next room."

Taking deep breaths, Rhiannon gently placed Kyia's circlet on the bed and left the room, took up her sword and ran down to the courtyard. She turned to the first guardsman she saw. "Have the gates shut. No one leaves."

"Your Highness, the King has already ordered us to shut the gates."

"Good. I want every guardsman who is not helping at the kirk here, now.

"Yes, Your Highness." He bowed and ran off. Soon a bell started to peal out through Sona Tuath; Rhiannon figured it called the guardsmen to arms.

By then the war party she had left at the kirk where returning. They looked tired from jogging all the way up the steep road to the castle. Their faces were black with soot and smudged with sweat. They walked over to join the other war party standing in front of Rhiannon. "Were you able to get them out?" Rhiannon asked the War Party Leader, hoping for the best.

"Yes, Empress. Everyone is out of the Kirk including the dukes and the earl."

Rhiannon took a deep breath, but worry for Kyia clouded her thoughts. She looked out over her warriors and the guardsmen that had started to gather with them. She heard Flath walk up and he stood beside her. Rhiannon looked up at the blue sky. The scouring wind off the Carnaid Sea left the sky bereft of any clouds. The bright sun was just overhead. They had plenty of time to find Kyia before it got dark. The castle city of Sona Tuath was large, but her warriors were fast and deadly and would find her.

When all the guardsmen who were not otherwise on duty somewhere else finally gathered in the courtyard, Rhiannon called out to all that stood before her. "Today a cowardly attack took place putting many lives at risk. They have even gone as far as kidnapping a member of the Venturian Royal Family. They have taken my cousin!" Rhiannon could hear the gasps from the war party who had just returned from the kirk. "We will split into groups of four and search every single house and business in this city. Is that clear?"

All of her warriors shouted out in agreement, but the guardsmen stayed silent, looking to Flath. "You heard your queen! You follow her instructions exactly!" His voice was strong and commanding and left no room for interpretation.

Because she did not want to take the time and effort to fight with reluctant guardsmen, she took her war parties, and Flath took his guardsmen, and they went out into the city. In small groups, they started at the docks, and then the poorer areas then started working their way up the hill to the more affluent houses. At the commotion, most of the people were already outside of their houses, but a few of the houses had their doors shut tight. She ordered her warriors to kick the doors in. Families huddled in the corners with such vitriol on their faces it almost took Rhiannon's breath away. She would not let that deter her, however. She would find Kyia.

They searched for hours as the sun traveled across the sky and finally set over the purple shadow of the Elk Mountains. Somewhere along the way Luna found her and sniffed around every house and business they searched. Torches were brought, and they searched on as night covered the city. The wind finally died down, and clouds slithered across a full moon. The night was unusually warm and sticky. They had just left searching a house when a yell went up, and guardsmen called to them. Rhiannon, her sword gripped in her hand, ran toward the commotion.

She and her small group of warriors ran uphill toward a more well-off section of the city. They stopped in front of a medium sized manor house. There were flower boxes under each window overflowing with fragrant, bright flowers. The house was freshly painted and had ornately carved shutters on all the huge windows. Hardly a house of someone who dealt in nefarious actions. Luna lifted her fuzzy head and sniffed the air. Just as Rhiannon was wondering what she was about she whimpered and ran into the house.

"Your Highness, we have found Lady Kossi," a young guardsman stated.

Rhiannon's heart started to pound in her ears. "Is she alive?" She was almost too afraid to ask.

"Aye, my Queen, she lives." He led her into the house. They went through a receiving room where a fat, well-dressed man stood in the corner with warring expressions of defiance and terror. The guardsman led her and her warriors into a back room that had a small hidden door in one of the plastered walls. She could see a torch burning inside. The guardsman looked extremely nervous. "S—she is in there, Your Excellency," he stammered and pointed to the opening in the wall.

Quickly she rushed into the room and gasped. Kyia was sitting in the corner, swaying slightly. Luna was gently licking her face. There was a gag wrapped around her mouth, blood dribbled from her nose onto her filthy, torn choli, exposing her breasts. Her hands were tied behind her back, and both of her eyes were purple and swollen shut, and there were tiny burns on her bare arms and legs. Her lehanga was torn almost in half and barely hung to her waist. Rhiannon ran to her, dropping her sword with a clang, and gently removed the filthy, blood-soaked gag from her cousin's mouth and quickly untied her hands, fighting back tears of pure rage. Kyia collapsed in her arms. "It's all right, Kyia, I'm here. You're going to be all right," she whispered into Kyia's matted hair, and Kyia began to cry.

As Kyia's body was wracked with sobs, Rhiannon's heart broke into a million pieces, and she began to shake with white-hot wrath that threatened to destroy all of Sona Tuath. "Your Highness, Lady Kossi's carriage has arrived." Rhiannon was beyond thankful that someone had the forethought to have sent for a carriage.

"I need something to cover her," she said, and someone handed her a blanket that she draped over her battered cousin. Two of her warriors helped Kyia to her feet, and when she could not walk, one of them gently picked her up and carried her out of the manor.

Rhiannon slowly picked up her sword and walked up to the four people who were standing in the shadows. "Who are these people?" she asked the guardsman who stood next to them, not taking her eyes from her victims.

"They were found in this room, Your Highness, during the search."

"Did you do this to my cousin?" she asked the first man. Rhiannon spoke in Ska so there would be no mistaking her question. Her words were smooth and low as she smirked at him hoping he would say yes. Her heart thumped in her chest as the familiar feeling called to her, and her vision took on a red tinge. The three men and one woman all wore the same obstinate, defiant look on their ugly faces. "I guess that's my answer then." She smiled wickedly at them and saw the fear finally register in their blue eyes.

She ran the first one through with her sword, his blood pooling on the stone floor. She heard the guardsman gasp, and two of her warriors stepped closer in case he was inclined to intervene. The second man went down just like the first. When she got to the woman, she spat at Rhiannon's booted feet. "Archigos whore!" The woman's voice was shrill and broke on the walls of the tiny room like so many shards of glass. "May the men of this city use you as vilely as they used your whore cousin!"

Rhiannon flinched, and a deep wound was opened when she thought of what Kyia had endured. Rhiannon lifted her head and let out a thundering war cry that would reverberate through the city—a foreign eerie sound— letting them know just who their new queen really was. She held her bloodied sword high and cut the woman's hateful head from her shoulders. It rolled away, almost trying to escape. The last man met with same fate. She heard the young guardsman run from the room and empty his stomach. Three more guardsmen were crowding the door, looking in with shocked faces. "Hang their bodies in the market square."

"M-my Queen?" one of them asked.

"Hang their vile, dirty bodies in the square! Now!" She screamed, gripping her sword ready to use it if they did not comply. Wisely one of the men turned and started ordering the bodies to be hung in the marketplace. Rhiannon and her warriors left the room and went back to the man who was in the receiving room. Luna was staring at him growling menacingly. By this time anxiety was clear on his face and he started to shake when he saw Rhiannon and her warrior's approach. "Who are you?" she demanded in a voice barely under control. The pudgy older man clamped his thin lips shut in defiance and at least tried to look brave.

"He is a merchant. He owns a small warehouse at the docks." Flath's voice was tired and sad, brittle as a dry leaf.

Rhiannon smiled at the merchant coldly, her eyes burning with revenge. "Not anymore." His eyes grew wide with shock just before she buried her sword in his fat gut. He fell to the floor with a wet sounding thud. She wiped her blade clean on the man's expensive tunic and sheathed her sword. "Hang this fat one with the others," she ordered a guardsman who was standing next to his king. Knowing better than to question his queen, he and two others drug the lifeless, hulking body from his house and out to a waiting wagon. When they all walked out of the house, Rhiannon turned to Flath and asked, "where's his wife?"

"She died of the wasting sickness a few years ago."

"Pity." Rhiannon grabbed two torches from the hands of guardsmen who were nervously milling about and threw them in the house. She was surprised at how fast the house started to burn. About that time Ian rode up on a horse and jumped down. She could see a moment of shock, but it was quickly hidden. "Ian, see that this wretched place burns to the ground, please. But make sure the neighborhood doesn't burn down with it."

He bowed. "Yes, Queen Basilias." She had but a moment to wonder at her new name and was not altogether sure she liked it.

"Ian, may I borrow your horse, so I can go check on my cousin?"

"Aye, of course, Your Highness." Wearily Rhiannon went to his horse and took up the reins.

Suddenly Flath was beside her. He took her in his arms and kissed the crown of her head. "You did good," he whispered and let her go. She smiled up at him and even as exhausted as she was, she jumped into the saddle of Ian's horse and, with Luna at her side, kicked the beast into a run-up to the castle to see how her beloved cousin faired. The future would bring a bloodbath for sure. She would hunt down every single person who had anything to do with what happened at the kirk and most especially, to Kyia. Sona Tuath would feel the wrath of Ventra!

CHAPTER FOURTEEN

Grabby hands that hurt and bruise
Red vision and burning flesh
Fists unyielding to yielding skin
Eyes swollen, sharp coppery bite on my tongue
Violation needy and persistent
My soul is dark, never the same
The sun will always be black

—Black; Kyia Kossi

Rhiannon stayed at Kyia's side over the long weeks that her cousin recuperated from her physical injuries. Laura and her assistant Janice worked tirelessly to mend Kyia's broken, bruised and burned skin. Her rooms constantly held the smell of the stinky salve the First Surgeon used on Kyia's damaged skin. Thankfully none of her bones were broken, though everyone knew it was her emotional scars that would take the longest to heal, if ever. Rhiannon's necklace could do nothing to heal that kind of wound.

As the spring air, heady with the scent of passion flower, warmed into summer, Kyia started venturing from her rooms out to the Royal Garden where she would spend hours quietly looking out over the trees, bushes, and flowers. Rhiannon, her belly growing more rotund every day, was always nervously hovering around her wounded best friend. Luna or Poeso, or both, were Kyia's constant companions. Rhiannon's warriors kept a respectful distance but could always be spotted amongst the trees.

Flath deployed his Royal Guardsmen out into the city to find all who had anything to do with the attack on the kirk or on Kyia. Rhiannon was not surprised, but she could see Flath was taken aback by the numbers of people who were being brought forth as agitators or outright seditionists. Each new day would bring more buildings painted with black X's which supposedly was a symbol of an Anti-Archigos Movement in Sona Tuath. As the summer progressed the seditionists, who adopted the moniker—AAM Warriors— started attacking fellow Suens who did not support their radical views. Homes and businesses were burned to the ground; some people had even lost their lives.

Flath asked Teo and Adam to send men from their duchies who would be willing to work with the Royal Guard for a while until the insurrection could be squelched. Men and their families from Beaynid started to arrive and soon guards filled the streets of Sona Tuath all day and night. The burnings stopped altogether. Eventually, the black Xs disappeared, and arrests were down. Rhiannon knew Flath felt like he was winning the uprising, but she had her doubts.

As summer started to fade and the days gradually grew shorter, Rhiannon felt an increasing restlessness. It was not safe for her to venture into the city and even the enormous Royal Garden grew too small for her. Her belly was so enormous she was uncomfortable all the time and even walking was a chore for her. She continued to worry over Kyia's recovery, for the younger woman was still quiet and withdrawn. Darkness shadowed her face, and purple wedges hung under her cinnamon colored eyes. Rhiannon wanted to take her home.

As fall slowly crept across Beaynid to the shores of the great Carnaid Sea, Rhiannon and Kyia sat on a bench quietly studying one of the many statues in the Royal Garden. Rhiannon watched as Jo Jo scampered up a nearby tree. They were sitting in front of a statue called The Changing of Rylee. It depicted a young

Goyor woman shifting from her natural form into that of something that looked like it had goat legs. The artist was very talented and descriptive in the ripples of the woman's clothing, the texture of her skin, even the pained expression on her face. She wondered if shape shifting did hurt a Goyor or if it was just the artist's speculation. Then she wondered what Baobh had thought of the statue. She had not had it removed, so I guess that said something.

Lost in her thoughts of Baobh and her memories of the war, Rhiannon almost jumped when Kyia took her hand. Rhiannon squeezed her hand but did not say anything. She felt awkward and did not even know what to say to her cousin, so she kept silently pretending to study the sculpture. "Thank you, Rhiannon." Kyia finally spoke, her voice soft and hesitant.

"For what?" Rhiannon turned toward Kyia.

"Thank you for finding me." Kyia looked over at her cousin.

Rhiannon swallowed past the lump in her

throat. "Well, it wasn't actually me that found you."

Kyia's lips curved into a sad smile. "But you avenged me." That she did. The five bodies—now nothing more than shiny-boned skeletons—still hung in the Market Square.

Tears started to run down Rhiannon's cheeks to splatter on her huge belly. "You should never have been riding in that carriage alone." Concerned, Luna, who was sitting at Rhiannon's feet, looked up at her and licked her hand in support.

Kyia squeezed her hand. "It wasn't your fault." But Rhiannon could hear the weakness in Kyia's argument.

"It was my fault. You should never have been here in the first place." Rhiannon looked away over the garden. "None of us should be here," she said quietly. Poeso came wandering up, her massive wings folded tightly upon her back, and collapsed in a shaft of warm sunlight beside Kyia and started to purr.

"Are you having second thoughts about your marriage?" Kyia arched a dark brow in question.

"Not about my relationship with Flath, no. But I doubt now that we can ever bring Ventra and Beaynid together." Rhiannon sighed and rubbed her belly. "And now I am possibly going to bring Beaynid's heir into this mess."

Rhiannon looked back over at Kyia who was smiling encouragingly at her. Rhiannon's heart broke that after everything her cousin had been through, she was still thinking of Rhiannon first. "It will probably be a girl, anyway," Kyia offered then turned her eyes upward to follow a bird as it lazily floated across the blue sky. It was peaceful in the garden. Rhiannon was sure that was why Kyia spent so much time here. The leaves of the trees shivered in a salty breeze, and she could hear water off in the distance. Jo Jo was squeaking at something up in the tree— probably a squirrel. Soon the leaves would start turning red, pink, orange and yellow as the land cooled off.

After a while, Kyia spoke again, "I want to go home, Rhiannon." Her words were quiet but determined. She lowered her eyes back to Rhiannon. "I am going home. Before the Pass of Koslyn becomes impassable during the winter." Tears welled in her brown eyes and fell down her rounded cheeks. "I don't want to leave you, but I cannot stay here any longer."

Rhiannon dropped Kyia's hand and leaned over and hugged her cousin, pressing her belly against the younger woman. She felt Kyia's warm tears on her arm and knew she could not let her go alone. "I will come with you. We'll take the Siren's Bane back to Ventra and pick another ship for the horses. It will be much quicker."

Kyia sat up and pinned her with a sharp look. "You are too close to your time. You can't travel." She was incredulous.

"I still have several weeks left, and the voyage will be quick. It's the ride from Eastern Fort to Màrrach that I'm worried about. But I'll have you there to deliver the baby...just in case." Rhiannon laughed, but it was true, she could deliver on the road home. The thought terrified her, but women have been doing it forever!

There was no humor in Kyia's eyes. "I don't think it's advisable for you to take on this journey right now."

"I am an Archigos Warrioress and the Empress of Ventra; I can deliver a baby on the trail! Besides, Verna will protect me when we're back on Ventra's soil." Kyia gave her a smirk; she knew Rhiannon did not hold too closely to the Archigos' religious beliefs.

"How do you think Flath will take the news of his wife, so heavy with child, leaving on such a long journey?"

Her stomach clenched when she thought of telling Flath, and she felt an overwhelming sense of sadness at the thought of leaving him. She knew he could not leave Sona Tuath with the city in turmoil and after being gone courting her in Ventra for so long. "He will undoubtedly be very upset."

"Don't you think he'll want to be present at the birth of your child?" Kyia tenderly put her hand on Rhiannon's belly.

Flath was keenly looking forward to the

birth of their child—much more than Rhiannon herself was. She was doing her duty by giving Ventra an heir (hopefully), but she did not rejoice over the child as she felt she should—like other mothers did. For that, she felt supremely guilty. "We'll send a bird announcing the birth as soon as it's born. And when things calm down here, he can come up and join us. But I've wanted to go home for a long time now." She smiled apologetically at Kyia. "I didn't say anything to you because...well, I guess I just didn't know how to talk to you."

The haunted expression returned to Kyia's face, and Rhiannon instantly regretted bringing up her recovery. Kyia's physical wounds had long since healed, leaving some minor scaring but her mind was slow to put the torture behind her. From what that evil woman had said to Rhiannon on that sickening night, Rhiannon knew Kyia had been raped, but she had never asked her about it or even mentioned it. She did not know how. Suddenly Kyia's sad smile returned. "Then we shall leave this horrid place together."

Rhiannon gave Kyia another hug then, with effort, stood. "I will tell Viceroy Hodge to ready the ships, and we'll leave tomorrow." Always in fear of being left behind, Jo Jo quickly climbed down the tree and jumped on her shoulder, wrapping her fuzzy golden tail around Rhiannon's neck.

Rhiannon had the viceroy sent for as she sat uncomfortably on a couch and oversaw the packing of her things. Tyla was busy packing Rhiannon's more valuable things and instructing Rhiannon's other servants when Viceroy Hodge hesitantly approached. Rhiannon asked him to ready the Siren's Bane and another ship capable of carrying all of their horses to leave in the morning. He was concerned at her traveling so close to giving birth, but Rhiannon would not back down, and eventually, he left to follow her orders.

A short time later she became aware of someone watching her. She looked over and saw Flath leaning in the doorway, arms crossed, studying her. Her heart dropped.

There was no anger on his handsome face, only worry, and loss. She hoisted herself up off the couch and went to him, and he took her in his solid arms. She laid her head on his broad chest, listening to the rhythmic thumping of his heart and started to cry. She cursed her erratic hormones. She would miss him deeply.

"I must go, Flath. Kyia is not healing like she should."

He took a deep breath and sighed. "I know, Greannmhor. This place has not been kind to her—or any of you."

She looked up into his mismatched eyes. "I will miss you."

He smiled tenderly at her. "I will miss you more. And I will follow as soon as I am able. In a few weeks, things could look much different, and I will sail up as soon as I can."

"The waters of the Carnaid are near impassable during the winter. I don't want you to chance the crossing." Even though it had not been in the Carnaid, memories of finding Shih Ni's shipwreck came into her mind, and she grew cold with fear. "Please don't try it in the winter." She looked up into his eyes pleading with him.

"I will leave well before winter, Greannmhor, but if I am delayed, I promise that I will take a ship out of Tel 'Rhia if the season grows too late." He smiled at her and kissed her tenderly. The thought of their separation cut her to the bone. He gently rubbed her belly. "I will follow you as soon as I may," he breathed into her hair.

The next morning the sun seemed to dawn earlier than usual as Rhiannon and Flath dressed and prepared to go down to the waiting ships. Rhiannon's thoughts were filled with sorrow at leaving Flath behind. She also felt a feeling of failure, as though they were being chased from Sona Tuath with their tails between their legs. The official statement was that the queen wanted to be on her own soil to give birth and that the journey had been planned for a long time. She was not sure if anyone really believed it.

Rhiannon was dressed in a roomy, soft, leather tunic and trousers. She wrapped her thick wool cloak around her and let Tyla (standing on a chair since should could not comfortably bend down any longer) place the heavy, ornate, jewel-encrusted Beaynidian Queen's Crown upon her dark head. She was feeling bitter and petty and wanted the people of Sona Tuath to see her legitimacy and authority as she boarded the Siren's Bane to leave their evil city—her city?

She, Flath and Kyia, along with Luna and Jo Jo all climbed into a carriage—Poeso perched on top—and somberly rode down to the docks. Their precession was heavily armed as it made its way down the hill and around the curvy streets of Sona Tuath. Even though the red interior was plush and carefully tufted she was very uncomfortable with her bulk. Large red tassels hung from the corners and swayed as they rolled over the cobbles. She looked out of the large, oval glass windows but saw only horses as her warriors surrounded them. The morning was cloudy and grey like everyone's mood. She was glad for the cover since the opulent carriage was overlaid in gold and would have been a beacon coming down from the castle. The terribly gaudy carriage had been a wedding gift from a rich merchant from Tel 'Rhia, and it had been her first time riding in it. If she had not been swimming in sadness, she would have laughed. She held tight to Flath's hand knowing it would be a long while before she felt his touch again.

Finally, they made it to the docks and, with much effort, Rhiannon carefully climbed out. They walked to the boarding area, and Kyia walked a little way away to give them some privacy. Many people had gathered to see the Archigos off on their journey home, but they were kept at a distance this time. Flath took Rhiannon in his arms as she fought not to cry but ultimately lost that battle. She grew angry at herself for crying in front of these people; for looking weak.

She looked up at Flath through wet lashes and smiled trying to burn the memory of what he looked like into her memory to carry with her through what could be months ahead without him. His mismatched eyes were warm; his pale hair ruffled in the salty breeze. Even though the sun hid behind grey clouds, Flath's golden snake earring sparkled in the fall of his hair. His lips curled into a broad smile, and she ran her hand over his smooth cheek and strong jaw. His touch made her tingle, and she swiped her tears away irritated at herself. "I will always love you, Greannmhor," he breathed and kissed her deeply.

When they parted, she said, "Someday you will have to tell me what that means." He laughed. "I love you." With that she turned away, took Kyia's hand, and, with her crowned head held high, waddled up the ramp to the Siren's Bane with Jo Jo, Luna and Poeso following behind them. Gripping Astrid's gift in the warm palm of her hand, Rhiannon watched Flath sadly standing alone on the docks as they slowly made their way out of the Bay of Gods.

The dreary, grey weather seemed to follow them up the wild eastern coast of Beaynid and into Ventra. As summer ended the already turbulent red waters of the Carnaid churned with even more froth and anger. A cold, soft rain soaked them for the whole five days it took to sail up to Eastern Fort. The Siren's Bane and the larger Willow's Whisper, carrying all of their horses and most of their baggage, carefully sailed up to the docks that had been constructed a few years earlier. Nothing near the sizes of the busy shipping ports down south, these docks were sufficient enough for both ships to dock at the same time. The hulls of four almost completed ships poked out of the landscape in the distance near the Osen Inlet. They should be ready to sail very soon. Ventra will finally have her own ships!

That night they feasted in the large hall and rested in the soft beds of the fort. Rhiannon could not get comfortable and tossed and turned all night. She was not looking forward to the long journey upon Zellan's back. She had not ridden him in months since she got so ungainly. She was not even sure if she could mount him. She sighed and stared at the ceiling which was lost in the darkness. They had wagons here in case she could not get up on his back and felt her face burn at the embarrassment of it all. She dearly hoped this baby was a girl for she was not sure if she could go through this indignity and discomfort again—Beaynid would just have to find another heir!

As the honey-colored sunrise painted the eastern sky over the red Carnaid Sea, Rhiannon and her warriors prepared to start their journey home to Màrrach. The rain had thankfully finally stopped, and it looked like it was going to be a nice, September day. One of her warriors kindly placed a box next to Zellan so she could mount the stallion. In her first attempt, she almost fell over when her enormous belly prevented her leg from swinging across Zellan's back. She heard a few gasps, but when she turned around, everyone seemed to be busy with their own preparations. She could feel the nervous energy in the air, however. The second attempt was successful. She felt Zellan sway a little, damn him, and he stretched his long neck back to look at her as if to check for an additional rider.

She sighed loudly; it would be over soon, and she would have her body back, finally! The baby had stopped its incessant rolling and kicking about a week before, and she tried to push her concern away but was glad she would soon be with Tess. She stared down at her swollen belly and placed her hand on top as if to feel for any signs of life. She knew it was silly, but she had seen much, much stranger things in this world since leaving that ranch in Montana. "It won't be long, little one, and Ventra will finally have her heir," she whispered.

Rhiannon tried to keep up a brisk pace, but the monotonous jostling left shooting pains up her spine and sent her head throbbing. They stopped every day well before nightfall, and Rhiannon sucked down cups of willow bark tea. At night her dreams were full of vivid colors and lurid images of battle and a strange woman with hair the color of the moon and matching eyes. Every time she was close to identifying the woman she woke up. During the day she played back the images in her mind, but they were fuzzy, disjointed, and did not make sense. She suspected the tea might be causing the dreams, but she was in too much pain to care.

Finally, seven days after they had left Eastern Fort their group rode into Màrrach. Rhiannon almost fell from Zellan's back and had to be helped up to her suite of rooms in the Royal Palace. Etâhpe'o-poeso had flown off, presumably to hunt, but Luna worriedly followed after her, whining and running circles around her and the warriors that were aiding her. Jo Jo, apparently forgetting about Rhiannon all together, happily scampered off into the solarium: evidently, the little golden monkey was as glad to be home as Rhiannon was.

At the base of the enormous marble staircase, Rhiannon let out a sigh and almost cried when she thought about the climb all the way up to her rooms. She would have cursed herself for being so weak if she had not been so exhausted. So, with a warrior under each arm, they started up the cool stone stairway.

Finally reaching her rooms, she eased herself down upon her feather bed, her back sending shooting pains up to her neck and making her head pound. She dismissed Tyla and the rest of her personal servants, so they could recover from their journey as well, so other Oread took their places, and she was brought a steaming cup of willow bark tea. Kyia came in after she had bathed and changed her clothing and softly lay down next to Rhiannon. They did not speak, for nothing needed to be said and, as the brilliant sun melted into a red sunset across the land of Ventra, they both drifted off to sleep.

In the morning Rhiannon felt more refreshed than she had a right to be. She soaked in a long, hot bath, then dressed and ordered a wagon be made ready to take her and Kyia to Tess's infirmary in the forest; she would birth her baby there. No one even questioned her decision as she and Kyia left

Màrrach with four war parties, three wagons full of Oread servants, and a cage with a handful of Sona Tuath's birds that would inform the king when the baby arrived.

Three days later, as afternoon rested amongst the trees in the forest, Rhiannon, Kyia, and Tess were gathering herbs when Rhiannon felt wetness gush down the insides of her legs. She gasped at its suddenness and its finality—her pregnancy would soon be over! She looked up from the stains on her damp breeches at Kyia who laughed. "It's time!" she announced happily.

Tess had rushed over to her and took her arm. "Kyia is right; we will soon have a babe!"

As trepidation washed over Rhiannon at what she would soon be forced to endure, she looked at both of them incredulously. "There's no we involved. This will be all me..." Her voice trailed off as it sunk in that she would soon be a mother. She thought of Flath and almost started to cry. She wished he were here with her now. It had only been weeks, but she missed him so profoundly.

Kyia squeezed her arm and Rhiannon looked up at her. "You think of Flath." It was not a question, but Rhiannon nodded. "He will be so proud to hear he is a father." Rhiannon's treacherous mind turned to Jocelyn and her stillborn child. He would have already been a father if it were not for the wasting sickness that took them. Kyia squeezed her arm again and brought her out of her morose thoughts. "It will be fine, Rhiannon." She smiled tenderly up at her cousin.

Suddenly Luna burst from the bushes, back from her exploration, and sniffed the wetness soaking Rhiannon's breeches. The she-wolf sat and looked up into Rhiannon's eyes, and she was sure she knew just what was happening to Rhiannon. Journey-Of-The-Moon had said she had sent Luna and Zellan to protect Rhiannon while she was in her world, she wondered if Luna had some sort of extra sense or intelligence apart from a typical wolf. It sure seemed like it most of the time.

As a cold night blanketed the forest blacking out everything but the winking of the stars in the clear night, Rhiannon's labor intensified sending her to a large comfortable bed. Tess gave her a bitter tasting tea to drink, which she did quickly between contractions. If it had been for pain, however, it did not work, Rhiannon thought with disappointment. A handful of Oread servants kept busy doing what, she cared not at this point. Her warriors nervously milled about outside waiting for their empress to bring forth the heir. Word had been sent earlier to Màrrach that Rhiannon's time had come. She cried out as another pain wracked her body, the shell gripped tightly in her hand.

The night grew old, and Rhiannon suffered on, her plaintive cries carried out over the tall pines. Tess had a fire burning in the large room, and she was bathed in sweat. Her mind was numb with pain and exhaustion. It was like she was living in a dream, a painful, horrible nightmare. She wished Flath was at her side, but he was far away in his own land. She was not aware of anything but her tattered breathing and the next flaring shock of pain as it seared through her body—blood and bone alike.

Finally, just when she thought she was too weak to continue and this child would end up killing her, she became overwhelmed with the need to push. Tentatively she pushed, afraid of more pain. Tess appeared at her side wiping her brow with a cool cloth. "Good, Rhiannon, push. Push harder." Her voice was gentle but firm. Really, though, there was nothing else she could do but push as hard as she could; her body had taken over.

It seemed a long time had passed, and Rhiannon was beyond weary as she pushed with all her waning strength. "I see it! I see the baby's head!" Kyia called out, and she was remotely aware of the relief in her cousin's voice. Then she was gripped by another need to bear down. Time seemed to completely stop as Rhiannon pushed and was brought to her limit. In the back of her mind, she thought the baby must be too large since she had grown so huge. Perhaps she had given voice to her concern because Tess reassured her that she would be able to birth the child.

Eventually, Rhiannon felt the babe start to slip from her womb, and she pushed with the last of her might. Tess carefully took the infant into her wrinkled hands, the umbilical cord still connecting it to its mother, and held it up to the wavering candlelight. "A boy!" Tess announced.

"Noooo!" Rhiannon's scream was hard and alien to her ears as it tore through the cabin in its viciousness. Vaguely she was aware of a couple of her warriors sticking their heads into the room in alarm. "No," she whispered as she began to sob. "I can't do this again!" She saw Tess and Kyia looking at her with sympathy. She could see they did not know how to answer her anguish. In the back of her mind, she thought of her great aunts, Tammrah and Juji, and their tragic story of trying to birth an heir for Ventra and wondered if she were doomed to repeat their sad story—over and over again.

Suddenly her body was squeezed again, and she gasped and doubled over. Through her hazy mind, she became aware of Kyia's hands gently rubbing her back and arm. Her body screamed at her to push, and she had to answer even though she had no strength to do so. She gritted her teeth and bore down again. Rhiannon quickly looked up to her grandmother in concern, the old woman's mouth was round with surprise as she handed Rhiannon's son to an Oread midwife. Rhiannon closed her eyes again, gritted her teeth and pushed with what vigor she had left, which was minimal at best. Over and over again she pushed as she felt her might leaving her body. When she was sure, she could not push one more time she felt another child slip from her body.

Rhiannon crumpled down upon the bed not even having the energy to look at her child. She took in ragged breaths trying to calm herself—it had to finally be over. She heard her grandmother's wavering voice lifted over the crackle of the fire and the crying of two infants. She could tell the old woman was crying, so Rhiannon cracked her tired eyes open and saw Tess holding another child up to the light. "A girl! Ventra has her heir!" She turned the baby toward Rhiannon, and she could clearly see the diamond shaped, blood-colored birthmark upon her tiny breast. Rhiannon started to sob with relief and sheer exhaustion.

After Rhiannon had been cleaned up and she had a few moments to recover from her labor the infants were given to her. She held one in each arm and wondered at their perfectness. They were both darker skinned like the Archigos and had shocks of midnight black hair. Tess opened the drapes that had been covering the windows letting the cheerful golden sunlight into the room. Somewhere in the back of her mind, she realized that today was the fall equinox. It had been exactly two years ago that Kyia had stopped Rhiannon from returning to Montana through the Tree of Jur. She grew contemplative when she thought of that tree sending out its light and mist today to an empty forest. She hoped she never laid eyes on it again!

She looked at Kyia—her savior—and smiled. As if feeling Rhiannon's eyes on her, Kyia turned, walked over, and sat on the bed next to her stroking the hair of each babe. "What will you call them?" She smiled down at them like they were her own children.

Rhiannon had not given it much thought and felt a sting of guilt for not being a more involved mother. Then she looked down at her son and daughter and smiled as a warm feeling settled in her heart. She knew then that she would fight to the death to protect these tiny beings of hers. Nothing would ever separate her from her children. She felt an invisible bond running from each of her children directly to her soul. Things were going to be just fine.

She looked up at Kyia with a smile. "Send the birds to Sona Tuath and tell their father that Princess Fianna and Prince Tristan have arrived."

CHAPTER
FIFTEEN

One day Taylor the Traveling Minstrel rode into town
His voice so smooth, his music so lovely none could frown
So talented he was everyone came to hear him from all around
One day a rumor spread, all tongues wagged unbound
They said Taylor was a king without a crown

—Taylor the Traveling Minstrel; author unknown

Flath sat at a polished table at the Sudsy Dog Inn in Misty Peaks talking to Xavier and Hurr over beers. It was still early, so they were the only ones in the empty hall. A large fire crackled in the fire pit warming the room. The weather had turned cold overnight, even for fall. High up in the Elk Mountains it was cooler than down in Sona Tuath.

Only listening to the conversation with half an ear, Flath watched Alex sitting next to him at the table and playing with the little wooden figurines he had given him. It had been almost a year and a half since he had seen the boy and Alex had grown to twice the size he was before. He was now two and a half and jabbered up a storm, even though only Hurr could understand what he was saying. His thick, brown hair sprung up all over his head in shiny curls. As if feeling Flath's gaze Alex looked up at him with familiar eyes, said something Flath could not decipher and giggled. Flath could not help but laugh as he watched Alex go back to playing with the toys.

All he could feel was pride and love for the little boy.

As he watched Alex play his mind wondered to Rhiannon. It had been almost a month since she had left, and he had heard nothing from Màrrach. A familiar knot of worry tightened around his belly. He had stuck around Sona Tuath for weeks, increasing patrols and making sure there were no signs of the so-called Anti Archigos Movement, or the AAM Warriors—as they called themselves—that they had caught since Rhiannon's disastrous coronation had swiftly been hanged. The graffiti and the attacks on innocent citizens had stopped months ago. With things back to normal in Sona Tuath he planned on leaving for Ventra as soon as he got back. He had not wanted to leave, however, before he saw Alex.

"Taylor." Flath realized someone was calling him and he was brought out of his trance. Hurr was looking at him with concern in his blue eyes. "Let us go down to the cottage, and you can meet my wife, Danja. She is working in her little garden today."

Hurr had told Flath earlier about what had happened to Tonnah. He was saddened at the young woman's death and worried about Alex's care. But then Hurr told him he had almost immediately remarried. Flath thought that odd but Hurr assured him, Danja was a wonderful mother to little Alex. Flath was skeptical and vowed to pay more attention to Alex's care.

"Sure. My legs could use some stretching." Flath stood, quickly put Alex's little coat on and scooped him up before Hurr could. With both fists around his new toys, Alex threw his chubby arms around Flath's neck and squeezed. Flath laughed, but it came out more like a cough. Hurr chuckled nervously, but then Flath could see that he just decided to accept Flath's unexplained obsession with Alex.

As they walked down the wide road that led through town and eventually to the path that would take them to Hurr's cottage, the man told Flath that Danja had just shown up in town one day—matter of fact, right after the last time Flath had left Misty Peaks—and was looking for a place to open her herb and healing business. Flath was skeptical and perhaps even a little wary. It was not as if Misty Peaks were on the King's Road. Most would not even know it was here.

Hurr went on to tell Flath that they had quickly fallen in love after Tonnah's death and what a huge help Danja was with raising Alex. Flath knew Hurr was leaving something out— like the fact they were probably having an affair even before Tonnah had been killed by a bear. Something just did not feel right about the whole situation, but Flath did not know what it was. Or even what he could actually do about it. As he held Alex tightly in his arms and looked deeply into his huge eyes, he felt an emptiness and regret that threatened to swallow him. Flath had given up his rights to have any say so in the boy's life years ago.

After a while, they turned down a smaller path leading back through the trees. Flath had seen Hurr's field before. Hurr's grandfather and father had cleared a huge section of the forest a generation ago, and this is where Misty Peak got much of its vegetables. Flath had never seen the man's home before, however. Finally, they got to the modest cottage in the woods. Grey smoke floated from the chimney of a well-kept log home with two stories and lots of large windows with bright green shudders.

Alex kicked and squealed so Flath put the boy down, and he ran around the back of the house. "Danja will be in the back in her garden planting her fall bulbs and roots." Flath nodded and followed the man to the back and stopped beside Alex who looked confused. Several trees had been cleared to let in sunlight. Standing there, in a shaft of light in the middle of a sizable kitchen garden was a small deer looking back at them. There was a pair of gloves and a spade lying forgotten at its shiny black hooves. "Strange. She should be back here," Hurr said, and Flath could hear the concern in his voice. The man had already lost one wife to wild animals. Hurr called out for

Danja, his deep voice bouncing off of the tall pine trees.

Flath, however, could not keep his eyes from the deer that still stood in the garden looking at him. As he studied the doe, he had an uncanny feeling he knew the animal. The feeling was so extraordinary it almost took his breath away. He was getting the distinct feeling that the animal wished him harm. Reflexively he stooped down and took Alex in his arms without letting the doe out of his sight. The air was suddenly charged with foreboding and danger. Out of the corner of his eye, he saw Hurr look at him and then follow his gaze to the doe. Flath tore his eyes away from the animal and looked at Hurr. "I shall just take Alex back to the inn while you look for your wife. If you need help searching come back and we shall form a search party." He prayed Hurr would let him take the boy.

A strange look came over Hurr's face as he watched the doe. "All right. I will come to the inn if I cannot find her," he said, almost absentmindedly.

Flath's heart was pounding in his ears as he slowly started backing away. He had no idea why he was in such a state of alarm, but all he could think about was protecting Alex. He wished he had his sword with him when recalled the small dagger in his boot. Not an effective enough weapon in relation to the threat he felt, no matter how unreasonable.

Finally, he got to the front of the house and turned and hurried back to the Sudsy Dog. He had already made up his mind that if something were to happen to Hurr, Flath would take the boy back to Sona Tuath with him—rumors be damned! He was not sure how he would explain Alex to Rhiannon, though. Suddenly he was torn between wishing something would or would not happen to Hurr.

The journey back to the inn was a blur since he had been lost in thought. When he got inside he felt reluctant to put Alex down, but the boy was kicking and squirming so Flath relented. Alex put his toys down, threw off his coat and sat on the floor and started to play. A warm feeling took over Flath as he watched the young boy.

"That was quick. Did you find Danja?" Lady Khi walked out of the kitchen carrying her young daughter, Pauii, who was almost two years old now. She sat the girl in front of Alex, who did not want to share his new toys and started crying as soon as Pauii swiped one of his figurines.

"We could not find her, but Hurr stayed behind to look. He was sure she would turn up, so he asked me to look after Alex." It was sort of a lie. He fished around in one his tunic pockets looking for another bauble to quiet Alex's cries and cursed himself for having too much in his pockets. His fingers finally grabbed something he thought might quiet Alex and as he pulled it from his pocket something else fell on the floor with a loud clump.

Flath heard Lady Khi gasp and looked up at her. Her dark eyes were wide, and sudden recognition washed over her face. Fear gripped the pit of his stomach as he looked down at what had fallen out of his pocket: his signet ring! Alex stopped crying and reached over and grabbed it before Pauii could. Flath looked back up at Lady Khi. He knew she had finally remembered where she had seen him before.

"Your Majesty," she breathed and went into a deep curtsy.

Oh no! Flath stood and quickly pulled her back up. "Please, do not say anything to anyone." Her eyes were huge, and she wore a look of confusion on her face, but she nodded. He took a deep breath and let it out slowly. "Thank you. 'Tis hard to explain." Her eyes slowly fell to Alex and then went back up to him and he could see she understood everything. Damn! "No one knows." He tried to explain as he took the ring from Alex and stuffed it in his pocket. The boy started to wail again. Flath did not want to mention Laura for he did not want to implicate her in case all of this became public knowledge.

Suddenly the inn's large door opened, and a cold wind blew in. Alex stopped crying as he eyed the door. Flath hoped it was Hurr. He turned around and was shocked to see Jewel Jass shut the door and walk over to him. "Lady Jewel, you are well come." Lady Khi gave Jewel a slight bow—they were of the same station. Flath sighed. Of course, she would recognize Teo's daughter, Jewel, for the girl danced the entire night at Earl Jade McVail's celebration. Things are getting worse and worse. He turned to Lady Khi again. "Please do not speak of this to anyone; even Xavier." He gave her a pointed look and hoped he hit the right balance between begging and ordering.

"Aye, Your Majesty, as you wish." Lady Khi bowed her head.

"Oh no..." He heard Jewel sigh.

Now that he had taken care of Lady Khi, he turned to Jewel, who was serving as his squire, and took her by the arm and let her away. "Is there an emergency? Has something happened?" Jewel was the only one in the castle that knew of Flath's whereabouts and was instructed to only contact him in an emergency.

A broad smile curved her lips, and her freckled face lit up. "You are a father, sire," she said in a whisper, barely containing her excitement. For a second his traitorous mind went to Alex who was quietly playing with Pauii now. No, she does not know! Then he thought of Teo and how the older man would feel if he knew Flath's secret. "The queen has given birth," breathed Jewel when Flath did not respond.

Suddenly understanding bloomed, and he felt like he was drowning in joy! Rhiannon—how he missed her so. "A boy or a girl?" He was almost afraid to ask. He knew Rhiannon wanted—needed—to give Ventra an heir. He should be there with her.

"Both!" Jewel said a little too loudly.

Flath stared at her dumbly as he tried to comprehend what she was saying. "Twins..." It was a statement rather than a question, but Jewel nodded in excitement. "Both lands have their heirs," he whispered in awe as he stared at the floor. Then his eyes shot up to Jewel. "We must leave immediately."

"Aye, Your Majesty. Viceroy Hodge is already preparing a ship for your journey."

"Bless that man. I am going to have to kiss him when we get back." Lady Jewel let out a very unladylike snort.

It was three days later that Flath and Jewel rode back into Sona Tuath. Flath had quickly stashed Taylor's piebald mount, Peighinneach, in a stable outside of town and picked up his own royal steed, Jax. Jewel had patiently waited for him to change back into something a king would wear and stash his traveling bard clothes into his bag. He debated telling Jewel his secret but eventually realized that someone needed to know where he was in case he was urgently needed. Being Teo's daughter, she was fiercely loyal to him, and he knew she would keep his secret. It turned out it had been a good decision.

Flath stayed in the castle only long enough to talk to Viceroy Hodge informing him it could be months before he returned, he did, however, refrain from kissing the man. Soon he and Jewel were aboard Siren's Bane and heading north to Rhiannon and his son and daughter. The words sounded foreign in his mind, and he repeated them over and over during their week's journey to Eastern Fort. He was loathed to spend the night at the fort wanting to start the trek to Màrrach right away, but he could tell Jewel was ill and fatigued from the sail north.

The next morning, as the yellow sun peeked above the red, watery horizon Flath, Jewel, and a handful of Sona Tuathian Royal Guardsmen that Viceroy Hodge insisted he bring along, left Eastern Fort. The weather had turned frigid, and he pulled his thick cloak tighter as they made their way into the Venturian countryside so much colder than Beaynid. They made excellent time, and three days later they rode into Màrrach. He had not even dismounted before he was met by Gen 'Lon and was told Rhiannon was at Tess'—so they had been expecting him, good.

A brilliant red sun was just setting behind the massive trees ringing Tess' large cabin and stables when Flath and his party arrived. He looked over and watched Jewel wearily lower herself from the back of her tired horse. As if they too had been anticipating his arrival a handful of Oread grooms came to take their horses. When he got to the front door, Kyia was standing in a pool of yellow light coming from inside the cabin. She looked strong and healthy, her dark skin was glowing, and those cinnamon colored eyes were shining. She was actually smiling at him! He was moved. He knew she had been close to Shih 'Ni.

"Greetings, Flath. We've been waiting for you." It was the first time he had heard her actually use his name.

He smiled at her. "You look well, Lady Kyia."

"Thank you. I wish I could say the same for you," she laughed. "Come." She led him into the cabin that was toasty warm and smelled of food and herbs. His stomach growled, but all he could think of was Rhiannon and the babies—his babies. She led him into one of the back rooms. A fire burned in the hearth, and the room smelled like herbs and something else that was not quite so pleasant. Several sconces and candles were burning giving the room a warm, yellow glow.

There, next to the hearth, was Rhiannon sitting in a rocking chair holding their infants in her arms. She looked up when he came in and smiled at him. He quickly rushed to her side and knelt down next to her. Her dark eyes looked like they were sparkling in the wavering light. "I've missed you," she whispered. He reached out and touched her face. It was warm under his fingers; he had missed her even more.

A small noise came from one of the blankets, and Flath looked down. One of the babies was starting to stir. He carefully took the bundle into his arms afraid he would crush the tiny being. He sat on the floor, opened the blanket and stared at the perfect little babe in his lap. He tenderly ran his fingers over a clump of raven colored hair and down a tiny arm, so very soft. There upon her breast was the red diamond birthmark that Ventra had been awaiting. Flath looked up to Rhiannon, tears spilling from his mismatched eyes. "Flath, meet your daughter, Fianna Kossi, the next Empress of Ventra."

CHAPTER SIXTEEN

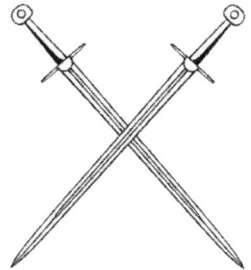

"A man can love his wife and his children, in fact, Ak demands it. However, when a man loves them too much, or shows them too much affection, this can weaken him and impede upon his masculinity and his ability to show discernment and good judgment."

—*A Man's Good Sense; Fif Lincor*

Rhiannon looked over at Flath as they sat in the solarium. He had Fianna in his lap playing with her. Rhiannon had to laugh at the silly look on his face as he blabbered to his daughter. She had just put Tristan down on a soft doeskin blanket, and he was currently rocking back and forth on his hands and plump knees trying to master crawling. Jo Jo was sitting next to him trying to encourage him by patting his back and making small chirping noises. Poeso was napping in the sunlight coming from the massive glass dome, and Luna sat next to Flath, every once in a while, licking Fianna's arm.

A little way away Lady Jewel sat on a bench under a tree with a young warrior. Her long, curly bright red mane stood out amongst all the dark headed Archigos. The young man, Shankee's second oldest son, looked quite smitten but Jewel looked reserved. They had become friends over the winter. However, it was clear he wanted more—she did not. Rhiannon smiled. She was fond of Teo's daughter and respected her for her decision to become Flath's squire and to be trained in combat. In fact, she had been training with her warriors since she and Flath had arrived last fall. Jewel had actually become pretty proficient. The girl was now nobility, she could have found a rich husband or even could have asked Rhiannon to become one of her ladies-in-waiting (if she actually had ladies-in-waiting) but she wanted to go the warrior route. Jewel was a girl after her own heart.

Rhiannon looked back over to her husband and daughter. Her chest filled with warmth and emotion. Her children were beautiful and healthy, she was married to the man she loved, and her kingdom was prosperous and at peace. Her world had been perfect over these past seven months. But that was about to change.

Flath had been putting pressure on her to leave for Sona Tuath as soon as the Carnaid would be safe enough for the babies to sail upon. A scout had returned last week with news that the great red sea had calmed and the last remaining snow had melted days ago leaving only small patches here and there. It was as if Verna herself was giving Rhiannon permission to take her children south.

She looked over to her husband as he held their daughter. His simple golden circlet shown in the sunlight as it sat on his pale hair, as did the golden torc at his neck; both symbols of his position as tjaty. The first few buttons on his shirt were undone so she could see the blue tattoos of his rank scrolling away across this chest. He seemed happy here with his family, and the Archigos had been surprisingly accommodating to him. Even Kyia had warmed to him, finally. But Rhiannon knew he had been away from his kingdom for far too long and needed to get back to Beaynid. She also knew that Beaynid awaited their heir: High Prince Tristan Basilias of Beaynid.

Flath must have felt her watching him because he looked up and smiled at her with his lopsided grin. "You are thinking about our journey in the morning?"

"I am," she said with apprehension. The

longest "journey" they had taken since the infants had been born was the two-hour wagon ride they had taken from her grandmother's cabin to Màrrach when they were eight weeks old.

"'Twill be fine, Greannmhor. You have barely spent five months in Sona Tuath since becoming queen. Your subjects need to see you. They need to know who you are."

Rhiannon snorted. "Oh, they know who I am. The last time I was in their city I hung four of their citizens from poles in the market square."

She heard Flath sigh. "Aye, but you had cause, and I think since those ridiculous AAM Warriors started harming their own neighbors and almost burned down their kirk you have more supporters than you think." Tristan had scooted across the blanket to his father. Flath gently set Fianna down and picked up his son. Tristan smiled showing two tiny lower teeth, his chubby chin shiny with drool. Rhiannon's stomach clenched at the thought of keeping her children safe in Sona Tuath. Mindlessly she took Astrid's gift into the palm of her hand where it grew warm and washed over her with a sense of peace. For what seemed like the millionth time she silently thanked the Selkie Queen for her priceless gift.

"Besides, you are bringing along ten war parties. With that many warriors, you could easily take Sona Tuath. I should not be worried, should I, Greannmhor?" He laughed and turned back to his daughter.

Rhiannon sighed. He was right. With five hundred Archigos Warriors she could probably protect the whole kingdom let alone two infants.

From off in the distance she could see Kyia making her way towards them. She smiled at her cousin. Over the past year, she had put down her books and started training on the practice grounds with Lumah almost every day. She was now quite lethal. Her face had lost some of that roundness, her muscles were taut, and she moved like a predator. Rhiannon knew her new found interest in combat training was a direct result of what had happened to her in Sona Tuath. However, she seemed happier and less afraid now, so Rhiannon was happy that her cousin had found something to quiet her demons.

Kyia walked up and gave her head a slight bow to Flath. "Well, I think I shall take my children and go check on the travel preparations and let you two women talk." Still holding Fianna, he effortlessly scooped up Tristan and walked out towards the entrance of the Royal Palace, Luna following them closely. Jewel had gotten up and followed Flath as well.

Kyia sat on the blanket and looked at her cousin and smiled. "What?" Rhiannon asked, smiling back at her.

"You just look so content with your family."

"I am content." Rhiannon followed Flath with her eyes until he disappeared behind some trees and then she looked back at Kyia. "I have a perfect life." Jo Jo jumped on her lap and stuck her tiny head under Rhiannon's hand so she could pet her.

Kyia pinned her with a look. "I know you don't want to go back there."

Rhiannon snorted. "No, I do not, especially without you. But I understand why you don't want to go back, either."

Kyia looked down, a hollow look washing over her face for a moment, then it was gone, and she looked back up at Rhiannon. "Well, someone's got to keep the place running. Shankee is too busy enjoying her grandchildren to be bothered by matters of state."

Rhiannon gave her a sober look. "Are you just making an observation or are you asking for the responsibility?"

"We both know that Shankee never wanted the position and grew weary of it long before you had even returned to our world. Who knows how long you will be gone and she doesn't want the duty of ruling while you're gone."

Rhiannon leaned back on her hands and stretched out her legs. "You are serious."

"I am. And I'm next in line anyway. The

council won't have anything to say about it."

Rhiannon laughed. "I can see that even if they did have something to say about it, it wouldn't matter." She smiled proudly at her cousin. "You are ready."

"I wasn't chosen before for Proxy Empress because I wasn't bloodthirsty enough, not good enough with a sword." Kyia looked away over the stream that ran through the solarium. "But things have changed."

Rhiannon was chilled at her words and knew from watching her cousin on the training fields; she was very deadly now. Rhiannon sat up and touched Kyia's arm, and she felt her jump. Kyia looked back over at her and smiled warmly. "I know you went through some unspeakable things that night. I haven't pushed you to talk about it, but I've tried to always be here in case you did want to talk."

Kyia sighed. "I know. I just don't see any purpose in bringing it back up. I'm all right now and will never let myself be put in that position again. If someone comes at me again, they will not be walking away."

Rhiannon was sure of the truth in that statement. "If you ever do want to talk I will always be here to listen. Though my advice might not always—or even often—be sage, it will always be given with love." Rhiannon squeezed Kyia's arm and let her hand drop away. "I guess we will need to call a council meeting about your new responsibilities while I'm away." Brightness shined in Kyia's cinnamon colored eyes, and she smiled widely. She hoped her cousin would someday find a man that would be good to her. "So, are you ever going to tell me why you and Shih 'Ni never married?" Rhiannon tilted her head and lifted her brows.

Kyia laughed. "Not that again!" Kyia looked over at Poeso who had started to stir after Jo Jo climbed up on top of her when Rhiannon dared to not show her enough attention. Kyia took a deep breath and let it out slowly. "He could never get over you."

"Me? We hadn't seen each other since we were six!" Rhiannon was incredulous!

Kyia nodded her head. "I know, but he said

he felt in his bones that you would someday return and you two would be together. He said he had tried to be happy with me, but your memory was always there." She could see that Kyia noticed the guilt on Rhiannon's face. "It's all right, Rhiannon, after all, he was right. You did return and take him as your mate."

"Well, you know, we have many fine warriors for you to choose from now." Rhiannon gave her a sideways look and smiled.

Kyia tilted her head back and laughed loudly. "Maybe, someday."

After awhile Rhiannon stood. "Let's get the council together and inform them you are the new Proxy Empress while I am away." Kyia stood, and Rhiannon took up the blanket, and they hooked arms and walked out of the solarium. Poeso hoisted herself up and followed behind them, Jo Jo riding on her back between her huge folded wings.

In the morning the massive group left Màrrach. Flath and Rhiannon rode next to the wagon that carried their children, the nursemaids, and Rhiannon's personal servants. Rhiannon turned one last time and watched as Kyia stood on the huge, pink sandstone steps waving to her cousin in the gentle spring breeze. Kyia now wore the circlet that Shankee had worn for so long. Shankee had been relieved to relinquish her usual duties while Rhiannon was away and the council had been in agreement. She sighed as she watched her home become smaller in the distance as Zellan carried her way.

Five days later they arrived at Eastern Fort and boarded her newly completed ship, Astrid's Gift; her three warships full of her warriors followed them out into the red waters of the Carnaid Sea and down the rocky coast. A week later they sailed into the Bay of Gods and up to the docks of Sona Tuath. There was a huge crowd all wanting to get a glimpse of their new prince and princess. The Royal Guardsmen were struggling to keep the people back. My warriors will take care of that, Rhiannon thought coldly. She hated the sight of the city, and she wondered if she would ever get over her feelings of dread for Sona Tuath.

Rhiannon's warriors disembarked first and filled the docks. If the citizens thought they were going to get a peek at anyone besides Archigos Warriors, they were disappointed. Flath held Tristan tightly in his arms and Rhiannon carried Fianna, her shell desperately gripped in her hand. They were surrounded by warriors and quickly escorted to that garish carriage and whisked up to the castle. Rhiannon sighed with relief when they reached their suites in the Tower of the King.

Exhausted, she flopped onto their bed and looked at her daughter as she held her in her arms. Fianna looked up at her mother with her black eyes and smiled showing slobbery gums and two little lower teeth. Rhiannon was awash in a deep feeling of fierce protectiveness. She felt open and exposed in Sona Tuath. Perhaps it was because of what had happened at her coronation, but in any case, she was already looking forward to getting back to Ventra though she knew it would not be anytime soon.

Two nights later there was a huge celebration for the introduction of High Prince Tristan and Princess Fianna. Teo, Shawna, Adam, and his new wife, and Jade McVail from Tel 'Rhia were in attendance, and even Ryman Toliver and his daughter Abla had sailed up from Cargh to be at the festivities and lavish the children with sparkly gifts. Jewel was happy to see her parents and brothers and sisters again. At sixteen Rhiannon thought the girl was young to be away from home for so long, but children here grew up fast apparently. She was a young girl from Perth no longer; she was becoming a pretty deadly warrior in her own right.

Rhiannon had been feeling surly and defiant, so when they brought out another elaborate costume for her wear to the feast, she sent her Beaynidian servants away with a laugh. She did not care if she offended anyone. Tyla and her army of tiny, pale Oread servants attended their Empress and dressed her accordingly.

Rhiannon wore a deep red, strapless choli

and matching lehanga with golden embroidery hemmed with tiny little bells. Rubies hung from her earlobes, the Necklace of Verna sparkled as it lay, with the emissary beads, across her long neck. Rubies and diamonds circled her wrists and ankles, and a large ruby was put in her navel. Her long, raven hair was twisted into tiny braids and pinned up in an elaborate design with tiny gems winking in the firelight. She wore the Crown of Ventra upon her head—she would not wear the jewel-encrusted Beaynidian Queen's Crown Flath had made for her—that crown would be for Tristan's wife someday.

After she made sure Fianna and Tristan were content and guarded by two of her war parities Rhiannon finally left their suites to meet Flath. She could see the surprise on his face when she emerged from their rooms and perhaps a bit of concern, but then it was gone, and he was smiling at her warmly.

"You look stunning, Greannmhor!"

She laughed, "So do you." He wore a crisp, white long sleeve shirt with frills at the cuffs, tan breeches and shiny black boots up to his knees. Attached to his right shoulder was a long sash; half of it was yellow, and the other half was blue. In the middle was his crest: a white castle on a cliff overlooking a red ocean. He was freshly shaved, his blond hair had been tied back with a blue ribbon, and his crown proudly sat atop his head.

"Well, our guests are going to get a treat. They are going to witness a legend up close: an Empress of Ventra." He tenderly took her arm and led her down from the King's Tower and into the banquet hall.

The festivities lasted many days, and by the time the last visitors left Sona Tuath, Rhiannon was beyond exhausted. The city seemed peaceful and happy to have their king returned to them and quite curious about the new prince and princess, who apparently (according to town gossip) are half hairy giants with dark skin and claws. Rhiannon had to laugh at that one! Whatever keeps people away—let them think my children are monsters that will eat their faces off if they get too close, Rhiannon thought.

As spring blooms gave way to the heat of summer Flath announced that he would be away for a few weeks for he had to see to some important business about the King's Road as it was being constructed on the other side of the Elk Mountains. Rhiannon thought it odd that he did not take any guardsmen and even Jewel stayed behind. She got an uneasy feeling in the pit of her stomach, but she had not been in Sona Tuath for very long, and apparently, he did take frequent trips into the countryside to see how things fared in his kingdom. She was disappointed that he had not asked her to come along—not that she would have left the children behind—but he had not even asked.

When Flath returned, he seemed more relaxed and happy, but he was vague about where he had been and avoided her questions. She was concerned but then felt silly for even thinking something was awry. As they sat out in the Royal Garden in the warm sunshine, she studied him. The twins had just learned how to walk and toddled around on unsteady, pudgy legs.

"What eats at you, Greannmhor? You looked like you had taken a bite out of a lemon." Flath held his arms out for Fianna to toddle into. "That is my big girl!" he laughed, forgetting about Rhiannon altogether.

As the weeks went by Rhiannon got braver, and they started to take rides into the countryside. Fianna loved to ride upon Zellan's back with her mother and Tristan was fascinated by the birds flying amongst the branches of the trees as they passed under. Rhiannon felt safe; her warriors were always nearby.

As the summer finally started to cool and there was a hint of fall in the air Flath announced again that he would be leaving Sona Tuath for a few weeks. Rhiannon pushed him for more information, but he dodged her questions or gave her opaque answers that did not really seem to make sense. Again, she got an uneasy feeling in the pit of her stomach. He did not invite her to come, and this time she would have packed up the children and followed him. They were almost a year old, and she had ten Archigos War Parties protecting them.

Frustrated, she offered to come along. She saw surprise and maybe a little fear cross his face before he became unreadable. "The weather is about to turn, Greannmhor. We cannot have the children out in such weather. Beaynid's storms are much more unpredictable then Ventra's." And that was that. He left as the sun rose in the morning.

From the balcony high up in the King's Tower she watched him marching out towards the royal stables. She noticed he still had a slight limp from the injury he took in the war—the injury that he had almost died from and that she had used her mother's stone to heal him. Her heart was heavy as insecurities filled her mind. She searched her memories for any clue that he had been pulling away from her, but she found none.

A few days later Tristan started to sneeze, and she summonsed Laura Felden. She had not seen the woman since she had been back in Sona Tuath. Laura had been kind to her when she had first been brought to Flath's camp. That memory had seemed like a lifetime ago, but in reality, it had only been five and half years past. So much had happened in that time!

Laura sat on the floor of one the rooms Rhiannon was using as a play area for the twins. Sunlight spilled in from huge windows. The mornings had turned cold, so there was a fire crackling in a large hearth. Rhiannon sat down next to Laura, and Jo Jo immediately jumped into her lap.

Laura had turned Tristan on his belly and squirmed under her practiced hands. She was using some contraption that looked like a crude version of a stethoscope. Rhiannon was very impressed. Finally, she took the little hearing devices from her ears and let the boy go. He jumped up and ran over to his sister who was playing with a doll. "His lungs sound clear. Mayhap the boy just got into some dust which made him sneeze. Or perhaps he is catching a cold. Either way, I will have a potion made up. Tell his nurse to make him drink it twice daily. He will not want it, but tell her 'tis all right to mix it with some sugar."

"Thank you, Laura." The Royal First Physician started putting her things back into her leather bag. "Tell me about Jocelyn." Rhiannon had no idea why she asked that question. She was suddenly curious.

Laura looked over at her with apprehension in her eyes. "What would you like to know, Your Majesty?"

Rhiannon looked over at her twins as they played. "What kind of queen was she?"

"She was...difficult."

Rhiannon looked back over to the physician. "Really?" She smiled, almost in relief.

"I am guessing things were different for her in Yellow Island and she never really got used to Sona Tuath."

"How did she get along with the king?" Rhiannon knew she should not be asking Laura such a question, but who else could she ask?

Laura took a deep breath and looked at Rhiannon with her green eyes. "You must know he disliked the girl very much—and the feeling was mutual."

Rhiannon fought hard not to smile and seem petty, but Flath's unexplained trips out into the country had left her feeling insecure. "The baby..." She did not even know what to say about it.

"Your Majesty ?"

"Was it a boy or a girl?"

"A boy."

"Did Jocelyn name him?"

"Jocelyn had been sick for weeks before the birth, and she was incoherent for her labor, so no, she did not name him."

"Flath did not give the boy a name, even in death?" Rhiannon was surprised.

"The king was less than interested in the whole affair."

Rhiannon could tell Laura was supremely uncomfortable talking about Jocelyn and her baby, but she pressed on anyway. "I heard the child was not buried or taken back to Yellow

Island with Jocelyn."

"Aye. Perhaps you should be asking the king about this, my Queen." Laura turned her eyes to the children. Rhiannon could tell she wanted to leave.

"I would, but the king is away on one of his mysterious trips into the countryside." Laura quickly looked up at her. Is that guilt? The older woman turned her eyes back down to the twins.

Over the next few days, Rhiannon's insecurities and unease grew until she could not contain her worry and anger any longer. She would find the one person who would probably know where Flath had really gone: Lady Jewel.

That afternoon she cornered Jewel coming back from her sword training. Jewel looked like a trapped mouse as she watched Rhiannon quickly approaching. "Your Majesty." She dipped into a curtsy that seemed to last a little too long. Is she guilty or just trying to put off talking to me?

When she finally brought her eyes up to

meet Rhiannon, she saw pure fear in her eyes. Rhiannon felt a measure of sorrow for making the girl feel that way about her, but she had to know where Flath was. "I know you know where he is so don't try to deny it. Viceroy Hodge doesn't even know where he is, but someone has to. And I think that someone is you."

"Y—your Majesty, I uh—" the girl stumbled over her words and her eyes pleaded with Rhiannon to let her be. Damn Flath for making me do this!

Rhiannon reached over and grabbed Jewel's calloused hands. She softened her look and gave her a small smile. "Please, Jewel, I need to know where my husband is."

Jewel let out a large sigh, and she looked down at her booted feet. "He is in Misty Peaks, my Queen." Her words were soft and full of regret.

"Why is the king in Misty Peaks?" Rhiannon thought she might be ill. Why would he be secretly visiting someone in a little mountain town?

Jewel's eyes shot back up to Rhiannon. "I honestly do not ken, Your Majesty. He has never told me why he visits there."

"How long has been going up there?"

"I have only been his squire for a year, milady, but he has been visiting Misty Peaks since you left Sona Tuath to birth your bairns."

Rhiannon's stomach rolled, and she felt like she was going to vomit. She squeezed Jewel's hands so she would not shake. "Thank you, Lady Jewel. Please do not tell anyone we've had this conversation." Rhiannon smiled and quickly left before she got sick.

She swatted at tears rolling down her cheeks as she quickly walked through the halls of Castle Sona Tuath and ran up the stairs to the tower she shared with her husband. She threw herself upon the giant bed and sobbed. She wished Kyia had come with her to this awful place—she felt so utterly alone. She took Astrid's shell in her hand and felt it start to warm. She wondered where the Selkie Queen was at that moment and wished she could just walk into the sea and swim with her, forgetting all her worries.

She must have fallen asleep because when she opened her eyes, the bands of sunshine coming from the windows had moved and changed colors slightly. Suddenly she knew what she was going to do. She jumped up, checked on the twins with their nurses and Archigos guards, and ran downstairs looking for Viceroy Penn Hodge. She found him in the courtyard inspecting some shipments of something or other.

"Viceroy, I need you to ready my carriage—that golden one—and get supplies ready for me to go on a little tip to Misty Peaks." She pinned him with a sharp look, but if he was aware of anything going on in Misty Peaks, he was very good at hiding it.

"Of course, Your Majesty. Um—why are you going to Misty Peaks, if I am permitted to ask..."

Rhiannon smiled at him; no he was not hiding anything, good man. "I think it is time that I start visiting the people of my kingdom and I thought I'd start with Misty Peaks. I've heard it's charming."

In the morning she kissed her children goodbye, left strict instructions for their nurses and the war party leaders that would be protecting them, and then she and a large traveling party left Sona Tuath. It was late afternoon three days later when they arrived at the Sudsy Dog Inn (she thought that was a quite colorful name for an inn and hoped it did not smell like a wet dog inside) and her attendants helped her from the ornate carriage as it shone brightly in the fingers of sunlight peeking through the trees. A man and woman stood on the large, wide porch and watched her approach. When she reached the top step, they both went into a low bow.

"You are well come, my Queen. My name is Xavier McVail, and this is my wife Lady Kih from Caltronia." Rhiannon realized that this young man must be Earl Jade's younger brother and wondered why he had settled in Misty Peaks. Kih, his wife looked nervous, and she kept looking down the wide gravel road that ran through the small town. Rhiannon glanced down the road but saw no one.

"It is nice to meet both of you. I hope I can find room at your inn; I know you weren't excepting me." Rhiannon smiled warmly at them and wondered where Flath was.

"Your Majesty, 'tis a great honor to have you visit Misty Peaks. Please come in and warm yourself by our fire. We have plenty of rooms for you." Xavier looked over at all the people who arrived with Rhiannon and concern washed over his face. "Perhaps not for everyone, though. We are truly sorry, milady."

"That's fine, kind sir, accommodate who you can, and the others can find a place to camp." Xavier opened the door to the inn, and Rhiannon walked in. The hall was very large and unbelievably clean. A huge fire warmed the empty room.

"You are in luck, You Majesty, Taylor the traveling minstrel happens to be in town. Everyone will be here tonight to hear him sing. He is quite good!" Xavier said.

"Really? Well, I'll look forward to hearing this wonderful bard." Could Flath be masquerading as a bard? She could only hope that was what drew him to this little mountain town.

"Come, let me show you to your room. I am sure you are exhausted from your journey." Lady Kih motioned for Rhiannon to follow her up the stairs still wearing a wary look on her pretty face.

"I will have dinner sent up to you. We still have a few hours before Taylor starts singing," Xavier called up to her.

Rhiannon suddenly stopped on the stairs and turned around. "Where is this magnificent minstrel, anyway? I would like to meet him before I leave."

Xavier smiled. "He is helping one of our citizens, Hurr Kemp, harvest one of his fields today. But he will be back soon."

"What a thoughtful bard." Rhiannon chuckled and continued up the stairs.

Rhiannon was shown to the best room the Sudsy Dog Inn had to offer. This room was complete with a bathroom and an adjacent room for servants. Rhiannon had Tyla run a hot bath and then she dismissed all her servants so she could soak and think for a while. She dipped under the hot water letting her long, black hair fan out on the water's surface above her. When her lungs screamed for breath again, she surfaced, closed her eyes and tried to think of a reason why Flath would be here. Could it be that he found being a king too overwhelming and all he really wanted to do was sing and harvest food? Rhiannon was almost incredulous at that idea, and, in fact, she did not know if this bard was really Flath anyway.

She had instructed her people to leave the carriage where it was out of the way and not readily visible and asked them all to keep a low profile. She did not tell them why, of course, but she did not want to scare Flath away. Her Suen servants were oblivious, but she could tell her warriors knew something was not right. Rhiannon took a deep breath and tried to relax. She would have answers tonight.

The sun slowly slid behind the pointy tips of the trees and night fell on Misty Peaks. Tyla and the rest of her servants worked their magic on Rhiannon. She wore a deep blue choli and lehanga, her hair was braided and studded with jewels, and she wore the crown of Ventra on her head. She would give Misty Peaks quite a show in her traditional Venturian dress and jewels.

Finally, she was told that Taylor was downstairs and ready to begin singing. She was nervous that this Taylor was not Flath—then again, she worried that it was him. She took a deep breath and blew it out slowly. It was time to find out.

With a few warriors following behind, she slowly descended the stairs. The room that had been boisterous and full of merriment suddenly fell silent, only the crackling of the fire could be heard. When she got to the bottom of the stairs, Lady Kih met her and led her to a large, comfortable chair closer to the fire. The crowd parted and quietly watched her pass. Rhiannon took a deep breath and held her head up high; she was an Archigos Warrioress and Empress. She would not be cowed by Flath's antics.

Finally, they reached the small clearing where the chair sat conspicuously alone like an island in a sea of people. Rhiannon looked over to Lady Kih, and the woman looked almost terrified. Rhiannon wondered why and sat on the upholstered chair as her warriors took their places next to her.

"Your Majesty, may I present to you Taylor, the traveling minstrel!" Xavier called out proudly. Rhiannon followed his extended arm pointing to the little stage and there, standing amongst the people of Misty Peaks stood her husband, the Kind of Beaynid holding a lute and looking like he was going to be ill. He bowed to her then sat and started playing a tune.

Rhiannon's eyes slid to her warriors standing on each side of her. She could feel their tension, but their faces were completely unreadable, as any good Archigos Warrior. She sighed and gripped the shell in her hand, but even Astrid's magic was not enough to calm the turbulent waters of her heart. She listened to the deep, smooth sound of Flath's poetic voice as it floated over the hall filled with enthralled people, but all she wanted to do was crumble in her seat. She knew her warriors must be wondering what was happening but they were far too disciplined to react. Shih 'Ni would have tried to kill him, she thought offhandedly.

Flath belted out song after song, all ending in thunderous applause. She wondered if that was the reason for this charade. Could he need the accolations from performing? She was indignant that he would leave her and their children so he could get applause for singing! Did he miss his life as a gypsy that horribly?

Suddenly Rhiannon was brought out of her treacherous thoughts by an overwhelming feeling that she was being watched. Of course, I'm being watched. I'm the Queen/Empress sitting in a little inn in the middle of nowhere... She tried to put it out of her mind, but it was like an itch that needed to be scratched. She turned to her right and up on a table was a grey cat staring at her. Foreboding filled her stomach, and she was overwhelmed with the feeling the cat wanted to do her harm! For reasons she did not understand, her hand went to the Necklace of Ventra, and she felt the stones start to warm under her fingers. The cat's eyes grew wide, and it quickly ran away disappearing into the crowd.

Rhiannon took her hand from her necklace, and she tried to calm her racing heart. She wondered if her warriors had felt alarmed also, but they just stoically stared at Flath as if nothing had happened at all. She was trying to tell herself that all was well when the song ended and Flath sat down on a tall stool, taking a small break. She stared at him, but he would not even look at her! A tall blond man holding a small boy walked up to Flath and started talking to him. She could not hear his words, but she looked at the boy. He looked oddly familiar as he struggled in the man's arms wanting to be put down. The man finally put the boy down and continued his conversation, Flath. The boy ran around in a few circles as people moved out of his way then he noticed Rhiannon sitting there in all her sparkling glory and ran straight towards her. Just before he reached Rhiannon, the boy tripped, and she reflexively reached out and grabbed him.

He laughed, and Rhiannon smiled as she brought the boy up to her lap. She heard a gasp, and she looked over at Lady Kih who had her hands covering her mouth. Suddenly Rhiannon was filled with unexplainable dread, as if she were the butt of some horrible joke that she was about to be made aware of. Hesitantly she looked down at the little boy with thick brown curls who was smiling exuberantly back up at her with his large, mismatched eyes! Eyes so familiar and yet so rare... Rhiannon's eyes slowly lifted to Flath who was standing and looking at her with such pleading sorrow it took her breath away. He ever so slightly shook his head as if to apologize and then sat his lute down as if he were going to try and come to her.

She started shaking and then carefully sat the little boy—Flath's son—back down upon the floor. Bile started to burn the back of her throat, and she felt she was about to be ill. Quickly she shot up out of the chair and almost blacked out, but two of her warriors grabbed her arms and pulled her back to her feet. "Please take me upstairs," she whispered weakly, and they quickly left the room.

CHAPTER
SEVENTEEN

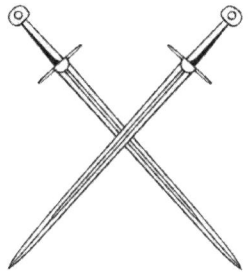

Shining disparate eyes below chestnut curls
Inquisitive spirit and skin the color of pearls
Ten fat fingers and toes
Where he came from no one knows
There is a protection around that boy
Perhaps a spell someone cast in their joy

—Strange Boy; author unknown

Rhiannon sat in a pale finger of moonlight as it shone through the huge windows in the nursery. She sat in a rocking chair mindlessly rocking back and forth holding Tristan in her arms. It was late, and the twins were both fast asleep, but Rhiannon did not want to leave them. Her traitorous mind kept reliving that disastrous night at the Sudsy Dog Inn. She kept seeing that little boy's shining face looking up at her with Flath's eyes.

They had left in haste that night without even an explanation. Let Flath and Lady Kih find excuses, for it was not her mess to clean up. She felt Flath's betrayal with Jocelyn all over again. Tears ran down her face as she was consumed with sorrow and resentment. As soon as they had returned from Misty Peaks, Laura had tried to see her, but she had her turned away. Laura had to have known. She was yet another conspirator. Rhiannon wondered how many others knew of his secret child. They had been back for two days, and still, Flath had not come home. She wondered if he even would return.

And then she felt him in the room. She continued slowly rocking her sleeping son, not reacting, until finally, she could not hold it in any longer. "Why didn't you tell me?" She spoke softly but knew he was close enough to hear.

Flath came near and knelt down beside her chair; the only sound was the crackle of the fire until finally, he spoke. "I did not know how to tell you, Rhiannon."

If he tried to garner sympathy by using her given name, it did not work. "How about, 'Wife, I have a child with another woman that I'm hiding up in the mountains somewhere where no one will find him.' That would have been a start." She did not even try to hide the bitterness in her voice.

Flath sighed, a sad and pitiful sound. "I made a rash and very wrong decision when Alex was born." Rhiannon flinched when he used the child's name. "Laura tried to talk me out of sending him away, but at that time I was certain the boy was not mine."

Rhiannon turned to face him, her eyes burning with anger. "Well, I guess we can put that quandary to rest." She spoke too loudly, and Tristan started to fuss. Flath stood and took him from her arms and gently rocked him back to sleep.

After a while Rhiannon spoke again, her voice wavering with emotion as tears spilled down her face again. "I will not have him here with my children." Flath looked up at her with what looked like surprise. "My son is your heir, not Jocelyn's."

"Of course, Rhiannon. I would never have claimed Alex as my heir over Tristan." He sounded incredulous—good!

Rhiannon looked back over to the fire and angrily wiped at her tear-stained face. "Will you continue to leave your family to sneak off to see him?" Her words were sharp, and she hoped they cut him like a knife.

Flath gently put Tristan in his crib and tucked his blankets up around his son. He walked over to Rhiannon and sat on the carpeted floor next to her. "I think that bird has flown. I am pretty sure several people are wondering at Taylor's authenticity now."

Rhiannon had to fight not to laugh at that.

Whether it was from true mirth or just more bitterness she did not know. She took a long breath and let it out. "How many other people know?"

"Laura was the only one that knew, but Lady Kih figured it out, and as far as I know she has told no one."

She turned to him. "Teo doesn't know?"

He looked at her and smiled. "Are you kidding? That man would have killed me."

Rhiannon snorted. "You would have deserved it."

"Aye. I have made a right mess and do not know how to fix it."

"He looks well taken care of. Are his adopted parents good people?"

"Aye. Hurr is a good man; a hard worker. His wife died but he has remarried, and I have not met his new wife. Alex is healthy and happy, so she must be a good mother."

They stayed silent for a long time then Rhiannon asked again, "So will you continue to visit him?"

"No. My life is here with you and our

children. I know Alex is taken care of. He is a part of my past."

"God help us if he ever finds out who he really is."

"He will be furious, and I doubt that even Ak could save me from his wrath."

"Then let's hope he never finds out who he is."

Flath stood then and took Rhiannon's hand in his and gently pulled her from the chair. "Let us go to bed, Greannmhor, I need to lie with you in my arms, 'tis been too long." As angry as she was with her husband, his touch was what she craved, so she let him lead her out of the nursery and into their bed.

***

Baobh watched the exchange between Flath and Rhiannon and wanted to laugh. Alex would most definitely know he was the heir to the throne of Beaynid and she would once again be living within the white walls of Castle Sona Tuath.

She watched them walk out and listened for anyone else. She knew the next room was filled with warriors, but all she needed was to get out one of the windows. As a tiny mouse, it was quite easy to slip into the nursery unseen. They still thought she had died that night in the Carnaid Sea, so they had no idea to keep an eye out for suspicious animals. If a mouse could smile, she would have.

Sure that no one else would be coming in to check the royal children for a while, Baobh melted back into her natural form. She was the color of the moon and almost seemed to glisten in the pale beams of light as they spilled through the windows. Quickly she went to the windows and pulled them open wide. They would offer an expedient way out of Sona Tuath after her mission was complete.

With her heart pounding in her chest expecting Rhiannon's warriors to burst through the door at any moment, Baobh turn to the cribs and located Rhiannon's heir—it would be no good to get rid of the wrong child! Finding the little girl, Baobh pulled a knife from her cloak and was ready to finally put an end to the prophecy when she heard someone coming!

Blood rushed in her ears as she tried to decide what to do. As the handle on the door turned Baobh stuffed the knife back into her cloak and slipped into the sleek figure of a massive eagle. Hastily she grabbed the girl who let out a squeak and flew out of the window. She could hear someone yelling from the nursery as she disappeared over the sea, the girl's cries lost on the howl of the scouring wind.

As the child squirmed and cried out in anguish, Baobh flew on into the Alba Forest. She should have just let the child go and be lost to the sea, but she just could not bring herself to do it. So, she searched for a clearing in the forest big enough for her to land in and finally found one. She dropped the little girl on the ground then quickly took her natural form. The tiny future empress looked up at Baobh with fear, huge tears running down her chubby cheeks. She took the knife once again from her cloak and knelt down in front of the girl, her almond-shaped black eyes looking to

Baobh for comfort.

Baobh swallowed, her throat was tight as she thought of her own son, Kaat, who would now be four years old. Tears threatened to spill as she held the knife up ready to strike, the blade glinting in the light of the full moon. The girl started babbling to Baobh, and she faltered. Her chest hurt as she clutched the knife tightly trying to bring it down upon the child and end the prophecy. Finally, she took a deep breath, closed her eyes and started to bring the knife down.

A twig snapped, and Baobh turned around. Recognizing the man who melted out of the forest she jumped to her feet. "What are you doing here?" Her heart was beating so fast it was hard for her to catch her breath.

"I am here to stop you." He walked up to her and stood in front of her, crossing his arms across his broad chest.

"You know the prophecy as well as I do. You know I have to do this!" Baobh sounded desperate, and she cursed herself for not being stronger. She knew, however, she did not have the power or might to fight him.

"Mayhap this is why I do this...for the prophecy," he said

Why? Why are you are betraying me!" Baobh howled, her shrill voice floating over the opening and then dying in the thick forest.

"Ah Baobh, you betray your own kind," he laughed.

Trying to use her speed to her advantage, Baobh quickly spun and slashed the knife towards the small child however his grip was solid and unmoving as he clasped her wrist. "Leave now, and I shall allow you to live," he whispered into her ear.

Baobh's scream of frustration was cut short and died on her lips as she whirled into the form of a raven that took flight and screeched her anger down at the man before she disappeared into the night—her chance was lost to her.

CHAPTER
EIGHTEEN

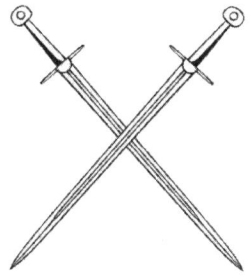

Beauty no words can flatter
Her darkness was bleached pale as the moon

A bird's wing or a tiger's paw
Even a dragon's form she can entertain

Her heart is bleak though
Divided and hollow
She mourns the child she has lost

Upon a bluff, she was raised alone
Her mother's mind shifted like the sand
Sweet child, she was turned

Now she lives only to destroy
Vindication and revenge her only words

—*Pale Woman; Rubi Jep*

At the sound of shouting Rhiannon and Flath rushed into the nursery, Flath carrying his panther-headed sword. He hardly had time to pull on his breeches, and he was bare-chested, his blue Venturian tjaty tattoos lending him an air of dangerousness. In her haste, Rhiannon had thrown on a crinkled shift that hung on her crookedly. She stood in the doorway and looked at the open window, drapery dancing in the salty breeze. Then she heard Tristan crying and rushed to the boy and scooped him up. She followed Flath to the opened window. Warriors and the children's night nurses were looking out into the darkness.

Fianna's night nurse turned to Rhiannon, fear, and sorrow in her eyes as tears rolled down her cheeks. "I'm sorry, You Majesty! I came in, and the window was open, and she was gone!"

Rhiannon felt the blood drain from her face, why wasn't Fianna crying too? Slowly she looked around to find Fianna's crib only to find it empty! Rhiannon began to shake with fear and then it was replaced with that familiar bloodlust, and she lifted her head and let out a half scream half war cry that reverberated through the room and floated out of the window into the night.

Flath turned to a servant that had stumbled sleepily into the room. "Bring Viceroy Hodge up here now!" The boy turned and ran from the room suddenly awake.

Rhiannon found one of her war party leaders and waved her over then and handed Tristan to his night nurse who had been nervously hovering behind her. "I need you to bring your war party in here and guard the prince. Do not let him out of your sight."

The older woman bowed her head, "Yes, of course, Empress."

Rhiannon walked over to the window where Flath was discussing the kidnapping with one of her warriors. She found it hard to concentrate because her body was calling for blood, but she had to figure some things out first—like who to kill first. Her hand clenched and unclenched—not for her shell this time—for her sword.

"There is no rope. I cannot see how anyone could have repelled down the tower."

"Maybe they went up?" her warrior offered.

"This is something Baobh would have done if her bones weren't laying at the bottom of the Carnaid," Rhiannon whispered, and both men looked at her in concern. She looked at her warrior. "Please wake the rest of the war parties and bring Ian up here." She tried to keep her voice calm and smooth, but she thought she sounded desperate and on the verge of doing something very terrible.

"Yes, Empress." He bowed and was gone quickly on his errands.

The castle and the rest of Sona Tuath were searched for three days without even a hint of what had happened to Princess Fianna. Everyone was in great turmoil just waiting for a deadly pronouncement from their violent Archigos Queen. Until one day a group of travelers arrived, and when they heard the Princess was missing, they told of meeting one of the Forest Folk on the road who seemed to be carrying a bundled-up child.

Flath had the group brought up to the castle where they interrogated them. It seemed they had passed one of the Forest Folk as he traveled south along the Elk Mountains. He said he was on his way to Loch Mór. They had not actually seen the child, but he said that the child was ill and needed to be kept bundled up. They also told the king and queen that the Forest Folk was not of the Goyor but of a light-skinned race.

After the group had left, Rhiannon questioned Flath if there were another race of Forest Folk living in Beaynid and he told her there were none that he knew of. However, he had heard of a race of Forest Folk called the Ynny' dagh living in Dar' Ven, a land far to the south.

Rhiannon jumped up and started barking

orders. Her warriors were to take Prince Tristan back to Màrrach upon Astrid's Gift that still sat in the Bay of the Gods. Flath did not fight her, for he knew it would not matter, his heir would be spirited back up to Ventra no matter what he said. Their horses and provisions were made ready, and without delay or fanfare, the King and Queen of Beaynid left Sona Tuath to track down this Ynny' dagh and their daughter. With Jo Jo hanging on and screeching her protests bouncing on Zellan's rump, Luna running alongside them and the great pax flying overhead they headed towards Loch Mór.

Four days later they arrived at the massive inland sea, its placid waters disappearing on the horizon. Dozens of fishing boats lazily floated on top of the shimmering water. They hurried along the shore to the fishing village and inquired if anyone had seen the Ynny' dagh and a child. It seemed the man was not trying to hide at all for many people saw him. He stood out with his fair skin amongst all the tanned people of Tempu (as the fishing village was called). Several people said that he had a bundled-up child with him and that they had spent the night, camping under the stars and in the morning had left with a caravan headed for Cargh, but that had been three days ago.

Flath and Rhiannon bought a pack horse and loaded up with as many supplies and as much water as they could carry, crossed over the surprisingly well-built bridge over the brackish Leth-Shàl River and headed out into the great Katlom Desert. The people of Tempu urged them to wait for a caravan to help them navigate the shifting, deadly desert, but Rhiannon would not listen to reason and urged Zellan out into the soft terrain.

The day was already old, so after a few hours they made camp and lay under the myriad of twinkling stars in a perfectly clear night. They hobbled the pack horse since they did not know if it would wander back to Tempu in the night but let Jax and Zellan go where they may. Luna had curled up on the sand, and Jo Jo happily snuggled up to her; Etâhpe'o-poeso had flown off under the setting sun to find her dinner. The desert night was cold, and Rhiannon lay closer to Flath. They had not talked much on their mad dash to Loch Mór. Rhiannon had been lost in a pool of morose thought, and she assumed Flath had been also.

"Do you think she's all right?" Rhiannon could tell Flath had not fallen asleep yet.

"I believe so, Aye. Why would the Goddess Verna give us an heir just to take her away from us?"

Rhiannon rolled onto her side and grabbed his arm, so solid under his tunic. "Why do you think the Ynny' dagh want our daughter?"

Flath turned to look at her and even under the waning moon she could see concern on his face. "That I do not know, Greannmhor." He leaned over and kissed the top of her head. "We will get Fianna back."

"And what if they won't just hand her over?" Rhiannon had not thought of that until that moment and grew afraid.

"Then we shall return with the combined

armies of Ventra and Beaynid. Then they shall listen to reason."

Rhiannon fell asleep that night on the sand dreaming of a bloody war in a foreign land. The next day a white-hot sun beat down upon them, and Zellan and Jax labored to get through the strangely pink sand. Finally, Flath and Rhiannon dismounted and led their exhausted horses on towards Cargh. Rhiannon looked from Jo Jo, unhappily riding on Zellan's back, to Luna struggling to get over the sand dunes, her diamond collar sparkling in the hot light. It seemed the only one who was not toiling under the relentless heat and stirring sand was Poeso who was leisurely gliding upon the warm air above them.

As the long days passed in an unchanging sea of pink sand and sun Flath's pale skin became alarmingly red. He tried to cover it the best he could, but the sun's mighty rays were insidious. Rhiannon grew concerned when his skin started to blister, and she wished they had asked more questions about the desert crossing. The only information that they received before they left Tempu was that Cargh was a two-week journey due south. Rhiannon was now beginning to think that her hasty decision to not travel back up to Perth and just take a ship down to Cargh was not the right choice. The sand was deceptively hard to travel through, and she had a strong suspicion that they would run out of water before they made it to Cargh. She cast a worried look back at the packhorse carrying all their water as it determinedly plodded along in the pink sand.

The days seemed to melt together as they traveled further and further into the Katlom Desert. They tried to travel as much as they could during the night hours, but it was still too hot during the day even to sleep, so they pushed on with little sleep forcing their legs to move despite sheer exhaustion, even Jo Jo was too lethargic to complain, for once. Luna limped along beside them, and Rhiannon's heart ached. She should have left them behind, though she was sure Luna and Poeso would have followed anyway. Poeso had been gone for almost three days, and she was starting to wonder if her great winged cat had met her demise upon the merciless undulating waves of the desert sand.

The days seemed to pass in an unrelenting stream of heat and thirst. Flath and Rhiannon talked very little to conserve energy and because their throats were just too dry. Rhiannon looked around her, but all she could see was the pink sand dunes undulating into the distance, waves of heat shimmering on their peaks as if to mock her. They had run out of water the day before, and Rhiannon knew they could not go much further. They had expected to reach Cargh days ago, and she worried they were lost.

At dawn, they lay down to rest, but Rhiannon could not find sleep, as weary as she was, for her only thought was of water and of how terribly thirsty she was. Even thoughts of her missing daughter were in the foggy background to her immediate need for water. Her throat was so dry it ached, and her mouth constantly felt like it was full of sand. Her lips were split and sore.

She huddled close to Flath and pulled her cloak tightly around her—she was so cold. She started shivering, and Flath wrapped his solid arms around her. "'T'will be all right, Greannmhor," he whispered in a dry, hoarse voice. She looked at him for what seemed like the first time in days. The blisters on his red skin had popped and reformed, and his lips were cracked and bloody. Her heart went out to him, and she gave him a weak smile for she could not muster up enough energy even to speak.

After a few hours they struggled to their feet and led their poor horses on; Luna still limped along beside them as well. When they were walking along in a valley of tall, pink dunes, Rhiannon thought she heard a strange noise but kept walking fearing her mind was finally leaving her. Suddenly, as if they had appeared out of the sand, they were surrounded by men with large curved swords shining in the unyielding sun. She thought she saw camels in the background, but her eyes would not focus. She heard Luna's low growl, and Flath drew his sword however she did not even have the energy to pull hers from behind her shoulder.

The men, who were covered from head to toe in light-colored cloth, with only their dark eyes exposed, said something in a language that she did not understand and when neither she nor Flath responded they closed in on them. She heard Luna snarl and then her world went blank.

***

Rhiannon slowly became aware of a cool, moist breeze caressing her skin. She heard the music of dancing wind chimes and could smell some kind of ointment. Eventually, she realized she was not laying on the sand but a soft bed. Curiosity finally bade her to open her eyes. She was lying on a low bed in a large room that looked like it was made out of marble. Bright artwork and tapestries hung from the wall, and light-colored carpets covered the floor. Suddenly, she remembered the men in the desert as fear for what had happened to Flath gripped her stomach.

"I see you are awake."

Rhiannon snapped her head around and saw Flath sitting next to her on the large bed casually feeding Jo Jo peanuts.

"You're alive!" Luna had been laying at the foot of the bed but got up and moved to Rhiannon's side when she saw she was awake.

Flath gave her a wry smile. "Do you think ten highly armed Buni warriors could best me? Please!" He blew air out of his cracked lips, and Rhiannon had to laugh despite herself.

"Really, what happened?" she asked while methodically running her fingers through Luna's thick coat.

"So, you do not believe that I single-handedly defeated all those men with my battle prowess?"

Rhiannon smirked. "No."

"All right then, I guess I shall have to give you the truth of the matter. Your crazy pax had flown into Cargh days ago, and apparently, she is the only pax with a diamond collar, so Abla, being the astute person that she is, recognized it as your cat and sent out some of her father's warriors to look for us. They were not sure at first who we were, and that is why they drew their weapons. I guess we appeared pretty scraggily—very unroyal-like."

"Well, you look much better." She reached up and touched his clean-shaven jaw. He had some kind of fragrant ointment on all his blisters.

"Ryman and Abla are wonderful hosts. You have been sleeping for two days. You must have been beyond exhausted because somehow you even slept through their healer giving you water."

Rhiannon lay back and took a deep breath. "I feel much better." She turned back towards Flath. "Did anyone say they saw a man of the Forest Folk with a child?" The desperation came back into Rhiannon's voice as she recalled their mission. Jo Jo cautiously crawled up onto Rhiannon's belly and patted her chest as if trying to calm her.

"Aye," Flath said hesitantly. "He apparently left aboard a ship four days ago."

"We've got to go!" Rhiannon quickly sat

up. Apparently hearing the ruckus, Poeso came into the room and jumped up onto the bed which just got a lot smaller.

Flath laid his hand upon her lap to quiet her. "The port in Cargh is not quite as large as even our port in Sona Tuath. There is not always a ship in port."

"Oh no." Rhiannon felt defeated, and she wanted to cry.

"A ship did come into port yesterday, though."

Rhiannon could tell there was something Flath was leaving out. "But...?"

"Abla says this captain and his crew are not trustworthy and we should wait a few days for a different ship to arrive."

Rhiannon grew indignant. "I am an Archigos Warrioress and the Empress of Ventra, and you are the King of Beaynid. Who would dare to act maliciously against us?"

Flath sighed. "Pirates."

***

That night they dined with Earl Ryman and his independent, shrewd daughter, Abla, in their grand and very ornate hall. They were entertained by those enchanting female dancers and then by male poets that spoke with such beauty and poignancy it almost made Rhiannon weep though she did not know the language.

This ostentatious palace that sat on the edge of the Katlom Desert on the shore of the Desert Sea was so lavish it even outshined Màrrach in its opulent luxury. Rhiannon could easily see why Ryman considered himself the King of the Buni. Abla told Rhiannon that her people had once been nomadic desert dwellers but generations ago they settled on the eastern shore of the Kuori Inlet, named for the famed Kuori Shells that washed up from the sea. Apparently, those shells, when ground into a powder and ingested, were a powerful aphrodisiac and so highly sought after that the Buni made their fortune from them. The bright pink Kuori Shells were only found on the shoreline of the Katlom Desert making them extremely rare.

Rhiannon distractedly nodded to things

Abla was saying, only half listening. Her mind was thinking about getting on that ship and heading towards Dar' Ven as soon as possible.

Abla must have realized Rhiannon was not interested in a lesson in Buni history and she stopped talking. Rhiannon finally noticed she had gone silent and brought her attention back to her lovely host. "I'm sorry, Abla. I'm just so worried about getting to my daughter."

The younger woman smiled at Rhiannon and compassion shown in her dark eyes. "I realize you want to be away after your child as quickly as you can, but I urge you not to go with Captain Tomas. He and his crew have a less than dubious reputation. He buys our Kuori powder and pays an excellent price for it, but I would not sail with him."

"He would be a fool to do anything to Flath or I. Both our kingdoms have warships, and even if my people aren't good sailors yet, they are excellent warriors."

"Tomas is an opportunist, like any pirate worth anything. If he sees an opportunity, he will take it—no matter how suicidal it may seem."

Rhiannon could see the concern on Abla's beautiful face, but she did not care how dangerous it was. "I also have the Necklace of Verna. I doubt he'll want to pick a fight with that."

Abla laid a dainty hand on Rhiannon's arm. "Just be careful, my Queen." The woman smiled warmly up at Rhiannon.

"Please, call me Rhiannon. You saved our lives."

"The Katlom gobbles up many a weary traveler. You were lucky your pax made it here."

Rhiannon looked past Abla to a massive fire burning in a hearth near where Etâhpe'o-poeso lay lazily grooming herself, her diamond studded collar winking in the firelight. "I hope my luck doesn't run out before we find Fianna."

In the morning she and Flath accompanied Abla and a few of her father's warriors down to the dock. Captain Tomas had already agreed to take Rhiannon and Flath to

Dar' Venn, a two-weeks journey south. Rhiannon was filled with trepidation because of Abla's repeated warnings, but she had to get to her daughter no matter the cost.

The captain was standing on the dock near the gangplank. He removed his stout, broad-brimmed hat and bent into a deep bow as Flath and Rhiannon approached. "Your Highnesses, I am honored to be of assistance to you. I hope you will find comfort on my humble vessel," he said as he popped his hat back on his head. He was smiling widely, but the smile did not reach his blue eyes. Rhiannon's stomach dropped, *something isn't right.* She looked over to Flath who was giving the man a stern look. She could tell he did not trust the man either.

Rhiannon took a deep breath; *we don't have time to wait for another ship to come into port.* "All right, Captain, I believe this is the amount we agreed on." Rhiannon tossed him a leather pouch full of gold coins. The price he had asked for was exorbitant, but what was money when their daughter's life was in jeopardy?

"Right this way, Your Majesties. Welcome aboard *The Gypsy's Curse*." He extended a long arm inviting them to board. At the name of the ship Rhiannon looked at Flath and he was wearing a dubious expression but boarded the ship none the less.

Rhiannon and Flath were given a comfortable cabin, if not large. Luna and Poeso were long-suffering about being confined upon a bobbing ship—Jo Jo was not (as usual). Zellan and Jax were kept below decks and were well taken care of, though they were both a bit nervous. Rhiannon spent most of her time up on the deck staring out at the blue water, its vastness stretching out in every direction. Flath stayed by her side always.

The weeks sluggishly drug by, one endlessly sunny day into the next. The wind was always in their favor, and Rhiannon gave many silent prayers to Verna just in case she might be listening. As they crept closer to Dar' Ven, she became increasingly agitated and wanted to be off the ship and looking for

Fianna. Most of Rhiannon's days passed with her desperately gripping Astrid's shell in her hand feeling the calm and serenity radiating from the Selkie Queen's gift.

Finally, Captain Tomas announced they were but two days away from Dar' Ven. He stood at the helm of his ship, his large hands on the wheel and gave them that same disingenuous smile. She would be glad to be off this ship as soon as possible. She watched him out of the corner of her eye. His sandy blond hair hung below his shoulders in tiny little braids. His beard was long and unkempt. He definitely looked like a pirate. He had been nothing but extremely polite and accommodating, she wished she could trust the man, but he radiated a feeling of maliciousness.

Later that evening Flath and Rhiannon and Captain Tomas and his first mate all dinned together, as usual, in the captains' cabin. The food was always excellent and the wine of good quality. Luna and Poeso sat on the floor not far away, each eating from their own bowls of food. Jo Jo was contentedly eating fruit from the table. If Captain Tomas minded, he did not show it.

Shortly after starting to eat Rhiannon began to feel an overwhelming need to sleep. Fatigue laid on her like a heavy blanket. She became alarmed and looked over at Flath who was barely keeping his eyes opened.

Suddenly Jo Jo started screeching and jumping up and down. Her voice grating on Rhiannon's nerves, but she was unable to comfort the excited monkey. Luna started to whimper, and a knot of fear formed in her stomach as she looked over at her friends. Poeso was already lying upon the floor and so was Luna, though she was fighting to regain her feet. Her heart broke, and she tried to call out but could not.

Confused she looked back over at Flath and reached out and put her hand on his arm. He looked at her as if he did not know who she was! "Flath," she whispered and then fell into a deep sleep.

***

Rhiannon's head pounded with every beat of her heart, and she felt stiff. She tried to move her hand up to rub her temples, but they would not move. Slowly she opened her eyes and was thankful she was not lying in the potent southern sunlight. She drug her eyes around the floor and realized she was laying in their cabin. She tried to move her hands again and discovered her hands were tied.

"Rhiannon, are you all right?" Flath's voice was peppered with alarm.

"I don't know," she crooked. Her throat was dry, and her eyes felt like they were filled with sand. With much effort, and as her head painfully pounded between her ears, she forced herself to sit up. She looked over to Flath who was sitting next to her. He looked much like she felt. "Are you all right?"

"Aye, except for this blasted headache."

"He drugged us," Rhiannon cried as a sick realization set in. "Luna and Poeso?"

"I think they are all right. I've heard them. It sounds like they are below decks with the horses. And I've heard that blasted monkey crying, too." Flath pinned Rhiannon with a very serious and direct look, and her stomach clenched. "Rhiannon, he took your necklace."

Just then the door banged open, and Jo Jo ran in and jumped onto Rhiannon's lap. Rhiannon looked from her monkey up to Captain Tomas who stood proudly in the doorway.

"I see you have awoken." He laughed a maniacal desperate sound and Rhiannon frowned wondering at his sanity. His blue eyes were filled with hate.

"You are making a terrible decision, Tomas. You are declaring war on two nations with powerful standing armies." Flath sounded quite sure of himself, but Rhiannon knew he was worried.

Captain Tomas threw his head back and laughed hysterically. "No one will know what happened to you. I will simply tell anyone that comes looking that I dropped you off in Narrwin as agreed. Dar' Ven is a jungle, my fine royals, and many disappear within its borders every year."

His words chilled Rhiannon to the bone because she knew he was right. With her dead and Fianna gone, she had left Ventra with no ruler. She did not know how Kyia would handle being the Proxy Empress long term and she knew Shankee did not want the position any longer—if she ever did.

Rhiannon pinned him with a sharp look. "Why are you doing this? You could ask for a ransom that would make you rich?"

"Let me tell you a story, lass. My brother's story. He was also a pirate, like me. He frequented the eastern shore of Beaynid capturing every ship he could. Especially around Perth since the waters, there were calmer." Rhiannon started to get an uneasy feeling about this story.

"After a while, he began to be plagued by a local that did not take kindly to him absconding with their goods. They called him Red Man. Anyway, he made so much trouble for my brother that he hired a mercenary to kill this Red Man. However, this mercenary betrayed my brother, and he and Red Man captured him." Rhiannon's veins turned to ice, and she looked over at Flath who was wearing a look of shock on his face.

Captain Tomas quickly drew his sword, walked over to Flath and pointed its tip to his chest drawing a small dot of blood. Rhiannon's heart started to pound, and she found it hard to breathe. "You killed my brother, sire." His words dripped from his mouth like venom.

Flath stuck out his chin in defiance and narrowed his mismatched eyes at the pirate. "You are mistaken, Captain, I did not kill your brother."

"Aye, you did! You turned him over to the authorities in Perth. What did you think they would do with a pirate?" Captain Tomas smiled, "For that, you will die. But not before I take you to Falaich òb, our humble pirate city, and have some fun with your queen." He looked over at Rhiannon and leered at her.

"I will kill you if you touch her," Flath breathed. Captain Tomas just laughed and left the room slamming the door behind him.

Jo Jo jumped onto Rhiannon's shoulder

and gently started to pat her head. She looked down to the wooden floor in defeat. "We're screwed." Rhiannon grabbed the shell, and it instantly warmed in her grip. Silently she pleaded with Astrid to help if she could. Rhiannon had no hope that the shell was some kind of conduit between her and the Selkie Queen, but she had seen far stranger things in this world.

They eventually made their way over to the bed, and that night Flath and Rhiannon fell into a fitful sleep next to each other, their hands still bound behind their backs— Rhiannon never letting go of her shell.

At the sound of someone yelling above deck, Flath and Rhiannon both jerked awake and struggled to sit up. Jo Jo started to jump up and down and made a funny howling noise. The sounds of people running back and forth and the grunts of fighting floated down to them. Rhiannon looked at Flath. "What do you think is going on?"

"Hopefully a rescue."

"But how? No one knows we're even here."

The door to their cabin opened, and Rhiannon's head snapped around. There in the shallow light of a dawning morning stood Astrid holding a glowing bone knife. Relief instantly washed over Rhiannon, and she cried out, "Astrid! You heard me!"

"Of course I did, Rhiannon." Astrid quickly made her way to Rhiannon, and the small woman cut her wrists free from the ropes then did the same for Flath. She took Rhiannon's arms and helped her stand. "That shell I gave you does more than just calm nerves." She smiled up at Rhiannon looking at her with those strange black, pupilless eyes. The bioluminescent spots on her face and body were glowing gently; her long, dark hair was dripping water onto the floor, she was still wet from the sea.

"Thank you, Queen Astrid. Rhiannon has often spoken of you." Flath smiled down at the Selkie woman who was quite a bit shorter than both of them.

Astrid inclined her head to Flath. "I am glad she has finally found happiness. But what are you doing on a pirate ship off the coast of Dar' Ven?" She looked back over to Rhiannon.

"Our daughter has been kidnapped, and we are following a man we suspect has taken her."

Astrid's face grew serious. "I am sorry, Rhiannon."

"We think the man is of the Ynny' dagh. Do you know of them?"

Astrid nodded her head slowly. "They used to be a noble and honorable race, but their leaders of late have led them down a different path. They are haughty and seek riches now."

"Why would they take our child?"

"I do not know." Astrid squeezed Rhiannon's hands as if to apologize. "Come, we must get you to Narrwin." Astrid led Rhiannon and Flath up to the deck where Selkie men and women had subdued the pirate crew; all held those large, glowing bone knives.

The sun had just broken from the watery horizon, and Rhiannon was able to see Captain Tomas looking dejected standing at the bow of his ship. She quickly walked up to him, and he visibly flinched. "Where is my necklace?" she asked through gritted teeth.

Slowly he put his hand in his pocket, pulled it out and handed it to her. She swiped it from his hand and fastened it around her neck. She stroked the red stones and felt them warm under her hand. She had never used the stones for anything but healing and did not even know if she knew how to use them as Baobh did.

She was tired, angry and completely frustrated that they had not found Fianna yet. She felt a need for revenge, but the man who stood before her was not the one who took her daughter. He would have to do though!

Rhiannon closed her eyes and brushed her fingers across the stones at her neck again. She felt them quickly answer her touch. A surge of raw power shot through her, and she was suddenly afraid as she was consumed with this desire to lash out. A dark and angry purple glowed behind her eyes as she tried to concentrate.

Rhiannon finally opened her eyes and looked at Captain Tomas and saw the blood drain from his face. She could feel herself glowing with the energy of the necklace. Her mind was screaming at her that this was too much power for her to wield and she should pull her hand away from the stones, but her heart was stronger and pushed out her feelings of alarm. She could feel the stones drawing away her energy; something she had not experienced when she used the stones for healing. If she was going to do something, she had better do it now before she became too weak.

She smiled at Captain Tomas and then she heard him gasp and start to crouch as if under some tremendous weight. It was then Rhiannon remembered how it felt when the stones had been used against her by Baobh. She had a second of doubt but knew that she would have been tortured and killed if Astrid hadn't rescued them.

Captain Tomas cried out as he buckled under the unseen weight of the necklace, then went down to his knees. He tried to speak but was unable. Rhiannon just watched as if in a trance. Half of her was horrified, the other half calling for revenge. Suddenly he landed flat on the deck of his ship, and the sickening sound of bones snapping carried out over the crowd and Rhiannon heard them gasp. Finally, Captain Tomas stopped struggling and went still, blood dripping from his nose, mouth, and ears.

Rhiannon pulled her hand away from the necklace and took in deep breathes as she swayed in the cool breeze. She was vaguely aware of Flath grabbing her arm to steady her. Determined she turned around to face what was left of Captain Tomas' crew.

"Let this be a lesson to all of you! Ventra's might is strong, and her allies are many. Think twice before you come against us!" She turned to the two closest pirates who looked at her with fear and awe. "Throw him overboard!" she barked and walked away.

CHAPTER NINETEEN

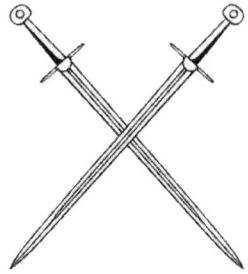

"In the western part of the continent of Dar' Ven, just over the mighty Ceò-Draoidh River, carved into the face of Mount Lonnyh is the stunning Ynny' dagh city of Kyell. The Ynny' dagh are an ancient race, like the Goyor of Beaynid and have lived in Dar' Ven for thousands of years. It is said that long ago the race split in two and half of them left for other parts of the world. Unlike the Goyor who hold the power of plants and animals, the Ynny' dagh hold power over rocks, gems, and metals. These parts of the earth yield under their tender touch and allow them to create great things of power."

—*The Ynny' dagh; Lyall Awinn*

Astrid and her Selkie Warriors stayed with Rhiannon and Flath, keeping the pirate crew under their control for the two days it took them to correct their course and pull into the giant curve of Narrwin Bay.

As *The Gypsy's Curse* pulled up to one of the empty docks the Selkie Warriors quietly jumped overboard, their human forms disappearing under the water only to have the dark eyes of a seal looking back at the ship.

"Thank you, Astrid." Rhiannon hugged the woman tightly. She had long since gotten used to her and her people's nakedness.

"Keep the shell close, and anytime you need me and are near the sea, I will answer your call." Astrid tenderly kissed Rhiannon's cheek and then gracefully dived from the ship—her lithe human body changing mid-dive into that of a sleek, silvery-black seal.

Once the ship was safely docked, Rhiannon and Flath led their horses down the gangplank followed by Luna and Etâhpe'o-poeso, Jo Jo sat happily upon Rhiannon's shoulder. After they calmed the Harbor Master down (he objected strenuously to a pirate ship mooring at his dock), they learned that a Ynny' dagh man had indeed come through four days earlier and he thought the man might have had a child but was not sure.

As the sun tracked across a November sky—much warmer than in either Beaynid or Ventra—Flath and Rhiannon wearily went from inn to inn and tavern to tavern inquiring as to who this mysterious Ynny' dagh man was or where he was next headed. Rhiannon was getting more desperate and lost in morose thought as no one had seen the man or their daughter. She was miserable, angry, tired and hungry. All she wanted to do was hold her little girl again. She thought about Tristan safe at home in Ventra a thousand miles away. Her heart yearned to see her child again. She hoped he would even remember her when they all returned. If they all returned. She angrily swiped at tears that silently fell down her cheeks as they tied their horses to a post and entered the last establishment in Narrwin.

The tavern was filled with acrid pipe smoke and the scent of tallow candles and unwashed bodies. She wanted to gag. The room was loud with drunken or happy boisterous voices, and no one even noticed them enter, even when a wolf and pax followed them in the door.

Suddenly, Rhiannon heard a familiar voice and the blood drained from her face. Even with all the noise and activity in the room, she was sure she heard his voice. She held her breath and searched the room. At first, she did not see him for the tavern was packed, but then she heard his laughter and narrowed in on him. Her mouth went dry, and her stomach clenched—she feared she would be sick, but she had not eaten. She could not breathe, and she started to shake.

As if he felt someone's gaze upon him, Shih 'Ni looked up from his gaming table and stared right at Rhiannon. His usually stoic face wore an expression of morbid shock. Dimly Rhiannon was aware of Flath putting a hand on her shoulder and whispering her name, but none of that mattered.

With speed she did not know she possessed, Rhiannon crossed the packed room. Jo Jo squealing her dismay and jumping from her shoulder, landed on a nearby table knocking over someone's drink. She was vaguely aware of Flath quickly following behind her and all the shrieks and gasps at what must be from Luna and Poeso making their way into the room as well.

When Rhiannon reached Shih 'Ni she was filled with so much fury she could not contain it. She gripped the heavy wooden table and threw it over, sending drinks, game pieces, and coin flying. Shih 'Ni shot up but still did not say a word; he just stared at her with such heartbreaking sorrow.

"W—we went looking for you," she stuttered, barely able to form words. "We found your ship—or what was left of it. I buried Santu's body on a beach littered with bodies!" Rhiannon cried.

Still, Shih 'Ni said nothing, he just studied her face. It looked like he was fighting the urge to take her in his arms and comfort her. As he stood being accused, before all these witnesses, his heartbreak was clear for everyone to see upon his handsome face.

"How could you leave me to think you were dead?"

He took a small step towards her. "I was told by the Goddess Verna that I was not your rightful tjaty," Shih 'Ni answered bitterly, his eyes slipping to Flath. "I made the only choice I could, and I see you wasted no time in making yours." He looked back at Rhiannon.

"What you have done is unforgivable!" Rhiannon's deep voice echoed across the tavern that had suddenly become silent, caught up in the drama that was unfolding before them. "You left your land; your people...you left me!" Her voice cracked with emotion, and she cursed herself.

"What I did was for you," he said quietly.

"You didn't even ask me what I wanted, how can you say that?" Rhiannon did not try to stem the warm tears that rolled down her face.

Shih 'Ni looked to Flath again. "I didn't

have to ask," he said venomously. Rhiannon could say nothing as her rage turned to sorrow. Sorrow for a lost friendship ruined by a union that should never have been in the first place.

Shih 'Ni did not speak for what seemed like a long time, but then, "How did you find me?" he asked, as an afterthought.

"We didn't find you—we weren't looking for you. Everyone believes you're dead." Rhiannon wiped the tears from her face trying to recover her composure.

"Then why are you here?" Shih 'Ni's voice was genuinely surprised.

"Our daughter was taken by one of the Ynny' dagh. We're trying to get her back. Our being here has nothing to do with you." She wanted to hurt him with her words just as he had crushed her the day he had walked away from Ventra.

The expression on Shih 'Ni's face faltered, and she could see surprise and then what looked like a deep pain. "I'm sorry," he said quietly in Venn.

"I'm sorry too," she said, then turned and

left.

***

Flath and Rhiannon slowly walked out of Narrwin with the supplies they had bought earlier while canvassing the town. Flath did not say anything to her, and she did not speak—for she did not know what to say. The city of Narrwin had basically been carved out of a jungle, so the landscape soon turned into a massive crush of vegetation. There was a broad, well-kept road leading off into the jungle, but they had no idea where they were going.

When they found a clearing, they stopped and made camp. They spoke little, and Rhiannon just mindlessly went through the motions. Flath kissed Rhiannon on the top of her head and disappeared into the greenery to hunt. Apparently, he wanted to save their travel rations. Some fresh meat would be nice—if he could find anything in this dense jungle. Rhiannon looked around at her surroundings and as if for the first time realizing where they were. She carefully made her way around the clearing and gathered up anything that looked like it would actually burn, then made a pile and sat and waited for Flath to return with something to cook.

Rhiannon kept playing the scene over and over in her head seeing the pain and betrayal in Shih 'Ni's dark eyes when he saw her walk in with Flath. But he had decided to leave her. What did he think was going to happen? Didn't he admit that he left so I could be with Flath? She put her head in her hands as her temples started to ache. Luna sat next to her and gently licked her arm and Jo Jo, on the other side, had a tight hold of Rhiannon's leg. She guessed Poeso was out hunting. She was not a very emotional cat, but she was there when they needed her.

As the sun set, Flath finally came back with a couple of fat creatures that looked similar to rabbits and got the fire started. Rhiannon set a kettle of water on the fire with the meat, she desperately needed something to make her relax, and she hoped the expensive tea they had bought in Narrwin would do the trick. As the meat roasted—the aroma wafting away on the slight breeze—Rhiannon looked over to Flath. He smiled encouragingly at her.

"So...that was unexpected," she said almost matter-of-factly. She had been so wrapped up in her own feelings she wondered how Flath felt to know that Rhiannon's husband was still, in fact, alive. Offhandedly she wondered if that made her a polyandrist...

"You have quite the talent for making an understatement, Greannmhor." He chuckled when Rhiannon smiled.

"I really thought—we all thought—he was dead. I can't believe he let us think he was dead." Rhiannon shook her head at the outrageousness of the whole situation.

Flath reached over and took her hand and gently rubbed her knuckles with his thumb. "Mayhap he thought it would be easier for you and everyone else to believe he was dead instead of that he just walked away."

"I grieved him, Flath." Tears started to spill over her lashes again.

"Your goddess told him he was not the

right husband for you. What do you think he was going to do? Shih 'Ni and I have not been in agreement on much, but he is a noble, proud man who loves Ventra. He did what he thought was best."

Rhiannon sighed. She knew he spoke the truth and she wiped away her tears.

"Besides, Verna blessed our union right away with not one heir, but two."

"If we can ever find our little Fianna." She started to cry again, and Flath took her into his arms. His chest was solid and warm, and she felt safe.

Suddenly, Luna jumped up and started to growl. Flath and Rhiannon parted, and both jumped up. Rhiannon had laid her scabbard down, and she looked around until she found it. From out of the darkness a small figure came into the firelight. A little girl with brown skin, thick black hair and shockingly bright green eyes stood just on the inside of the arc of light. Rhiannon heard Flath let out his breath and Luna, realizing there was no threat, sat back down quietly. Rhiannon set her scabbard back down and tried to calm her thumping heart.

"Come on over." Flath waved his arm motioning the girl over to their camp. "Share our supper with us."

The common tongue here was apparently also Ska, like in Beaynid, so Rhiannon was sure the tiny girl understood. After a short hesitation, she came over and flopped down on the ground next to the fire and watched the meat cook.

"My name is Flath, and this is my wife, Rhiannon. What is your name, little one?"

Her haunting green eyes slipped from the cooking food up to Flath and then to Rhiannon as if she was trying to decide whether or not to stay. Finally, she stuck out her chin. "My name is Terran."

"'Tis nice to meet you, Terran. Supper should be ready in a minute. Would you like some tea?" She nodded her head, and Rhiannon quickly started to make her a cup. "Where are your parents, Terran? You are not out here by yourself, are you?" Suddenly there was apprehension in the little girl's eyes. She glanced out at the jungle like she was about to bolt. "I am sure you can take care of yourself, though. You probably know this place very well and could warn us of dangers." Flath quickly added with a smile. Terran relaxed a bit, and Rhiannon handed the girl a cup of tea. They had bought an extra cup in case one got broken, and now Rhiannon was glad for it.

After they all ate to their full and the night was getting old. Flath handed Terran a blanket, and the girl rolled up in it—the weather was warm, so it was mostly to keep bugs away. They watched Terran sleep for a while then they, too, lay down to sleep. Rhiannon thought about her own daughter and wondered where she was and if she was safe and happy. Tears stained her face as she fell off to a deep sleep.

The next morning Rhiannon awoke with a strange, thick dew all over her exposed skin. She wiped it away with her blanket and sat up. She was surprised to find Terran tucked up tightly to Poeso's side; the huge cat had curled up around the small child. Rhiannon was stung with a feeling of jealousy and then laughed at her pettiness. At the sound, Poeso cracked open one abnormally large, duel-pupiled eye and looked at her, and then slowly closed it again.

Rhiannon started making their breakfast of oats, fresh fruit and tea and Flath started to pack up the camp. She had no idea where they were going, but they had to find out where this Ynny' dagh man could have taken Fianna. Luna had left to hunt up her breakfast, and Jo Jo happily hopped from tree to tree screeching out in glee.

As they sat around eating their oats and fruit, Flath casually asked, "Terran, do you happen to know of the Ynny' dagh?" The little girl looked up, and there was fear in her green eyes. She slowly nodded her head. "Did you mayhap see a Ynny' dagh man with a small child?"

Rhiannon could see the girl was thinking and there was a kind of worldly wisdom in her young eyes. She wondered if perhaps Terran was older than she appeared. "Terran, if you've seen this man it is essential that we find him," Rhiannon said softly.

Terran's eyes turned down to her bowl, and she stayed silent.

"Please, tell us if you have seen him. We think this man may have our daughter," Flath implored the girl.

At that, she did look up, and an expression crossed her face like she had made up her mind. "I did see that man in Narrwin days ago."

"Did he have a child with him?" Terran jumped, and Rhiannon regretted her over-enthusiastic question.

"I could not tell. His people were here also, and they put him in a carriage and quickly left." Rhiannon let out a mournful sound, and she put her head in her hands fighting to hold the tears back. "I know where Lord Rull went." Terran's words were soft and hesitant as if she wanted to comfort Rhiannon but was afraid.

At that name, Rhiannon and Flath looked up at each other in shock. "Did you say, Lord Rull?" Rhiannon was suddenly overcome with fear. This is the man who apparently helped Baobh take Sona Tuath so long ago. This was the evil monster Suen's whispered about? Rhiannon could clearly see alarm on Flath's face then they both looked back at the little girl.

"Lord Karha Rull. The King's brother."

"Do you know where he is?" Rhiannon forced her words to be calm and slow.

"Aye. I can take you to Kyell." Terran started eating again then stopped and looked up one more time. "But 'tis dangerous." Then she continued to shove the oats into her mouth.

They traveled east for almost two weeks. The road was broad and well maintained yet they saw no one on the road at all. Terran had taken to riding on Poeso's back as she padded down the jungle road. She thought the cat could probably take off into the air with Terran on her back—the girl was so slight. Rhiannon thought it odd that Poeso took to her so quickly and completely, but she seemed to make the girl happy.

At night they would find a place not visible from the road and Flath would go out to hunt the tasty little rabbit-like creatures that seemed to be abundant in the jungle. As the sun set, when other monkeys would come to investigate, Jo Jo would timidly hide behind Rhiannon's back making a weird crying noise she had never heard the little monkey make before.

One night, as Terran sat on the ground, her back propped up against Poeso, she quietly told Flath and Rhiannon that her parents used to harvest guna fruit way up in the trees. They are very hard to reach as they grow high up in the canopy, so they sell for a good price. There were not may guna harvesters. One day her parents were caught harvesting the guna too close to Kyell, and Lord Rull had them put to death. That explains why she's afraid of Rull, Rhiannon thought. She also told them she was in her tenth year, which surprised Rhiannon because the girl was so small. She wondered if it was because of malnutrition or if her parents had been small as well.

Finally, as the sun slipped behind the thick canopy of vegetation, they reached the enchanted city of Kyell. Its impressive castle was made out of stone and glass and looked like it was carved right out of Mount Lonnyh.

"Castle Luisnich," Terran whispered in awe.

As the night got darker the castle began to glow in an eerie white color casting a gentle light upon the flowing waterfall that bisected the castle and fell into a great river: the Ceò-Draoidh. It too seemed to glow, as mist floated up from its water covering the sandy banks.

They left Zellan and Jax—and much to her distress, Jo Jo—in a hidden spot in the jungle not far from a large bridge across the misty river. Then under cover of darkness Terran lead Flath and Rhiannon across the stone bridge that was now covered in mist. Apparently, the girl crept around Kyell a lot in the years since her parents were killed, so she knew it well and knew how to stay out of sight.

Man, woman, child, pax and wolf carefully made their way up to Castle Luisnich and climbed a forgotten stone stairway, barely wide enough for one person, up to the balcony that led to a room Terran assured them would take them to the Rulls. Rhiannon was thankful that the castle stones glowed giving them enough light to ascend the dangerous ancient stairway. The air was thick with humidity, and even though it was a clear December night, the air was still hot and unmoving. As she moved over the ancient glowing stones, the stones of her necklace seemed to warm. She touched them, and they were definitely warmer than her skin. She wondered if they were somehow answering the enchanted stones of the castle.

Finally, they reached the top and climbed over the balcony wall. Luna followed Rhiannon and Flath over the wall, but Terran did not want to come. She stayed behind the wall silently shaking her head, her large green eyes sharp with fear. Etâhpe'o-poeso stayed with the child, protectively wrapping her long tail around the girls thin, dirty legs. "We shall be back," Flath whispered to the girl who nodded.

Flath and Rhiannon carefully went from room to room looking for their child—or any sign that there was even a child in residence. They found nothing. The sound of two men talking floated down a hallway. Rhiannon and Flath both drew their swords and silently made their way towards the voices. They were speaking in Venn! A coldness gripped Rhiannon's spine.

"I'm telling you, they will be here."

"You should have stayed in Narrwin to make sure that they arrived. They could be dead at the bottom of the sea for all we know!"

Rhiannon could barely make out what they were saying, for the roar of the waterfall was so loud now; the water must be under the room! She peeked around the corner and saw two well-dressed men talking. They looked so similar that they had to have been relatives. The room was being used as some kind of office or something. There were a few desks, and hundreds of books lined the walls and racks full of scrolls were everywhere. It was not quite messy, but obviously, a lot of work was done here. On the west wall was a huge opening that led to a large balcony: this was where the noise from the waterfall was coming from.

"My Sgàth has returned and told me they were in Narrwin."

"That was weeks ago. Perhaps you didn't leave enough clues for them to follow." The man was clearly agitated.

Rhiannon had heard enough. She rushed into the room, her Venturian sword gleaming in the lamplight. Her heart pounded in her ears, and her sight took on that familiar red tinge. "Where is my daughter?" she hissed. Both men looked up at her with shock on their faces. She was vaguely aware of Flath standing beside her, and she heard Luna growling from somewhere behind her.

"Empress Kossi, we've been expecting you," the taller of the two men said, and they both bent into a deep bow.

"Where is my daughter?" she demanded again. The shorter man, who looked younger, had the good sense to look a little alarmed at the sharpness in her voice. The other one did not look worried at all, and that made Rhiannon even more livid.

"Let me introduce myself. I am Ooilley Rull, King of Dar' Ven. And this is my brother, Lord Karha Rull." He stretched out his arm to indicate the younger man standing next to him. "You are well come to Kyell." His bearded face crinkled into a smile, his green eyes twinkling. Rhiannon thought he must be insane.

"I do not care who you are. Where is our daughter?" Flath's voice was low and dangerous. If these men did not have the good sense to be afraid of her, they should take pause in the face of Flath's measured rage.

"My brother never had your daughter. It was a ploy to get you to Kyell."

Rhiannon crinkled her brow in confusion. "What? Tell me where my daughter is!" she demanded through clenched teeth.

"I have no knowledge of where your daughter is. Baobh took the child and what she did with her is none of my concern."

"Baobh?" Flath and Rhiannon both asked at the same time.

"Oh, yes. She lived. My brother's Sgàth pulled the woman from the Carnaid as she was about to expire. He nursed her back to health in our compound in the Sangron Oasis. This was our plan all along: to get you here."

The tip of Rhiannon's sword started to droop as she was overtaken by a feeling of utter defeat. "But why?" she asked, completely dumbfounded.

"Because, my dear, we are going to make a new race of warrior and Forest Folk. You see, a millennia ago our races were once one. For reasons no one remembers, we branched off: one group became fierce warriors, one group became powerful alchemists. But now it's time for us to come together. We are going to once again reunite our races into one ultimate race that will rule the world. You are here to have my children, Rhiannon, to be the mother of a new race."

All thought went out of her mind except to spill Rull's blood. She howled a battle cry, gripped her sword with fury and started towards the man. He quickly held out his hand to the side, and a sword that she had not even noticed until then shot up from its hiding place and into his hand. That's new.

Their swords clashed, and she could tell he was on the defense. He did not want to hurt her. "Listen to me, Rhiannon, I have read the ancient scrolls they tell of our races coming back together. The time is now!" She yelled again and brought her sword down upon him, but he blocked her easily and threw her blade aside. She wondered at his skill because he clearly was not a warrior. His blade must hold some power.

She heard others rush in the room, presumably guards and the sound of swords clashing and Luna attacking filled the room even louder than the waterfall. Flath grabbed hold of her tunic and was pulling her towards the balcony. They cut through several guards on the way. She was so busy fighting she did not even have time to activate her necklace that she knew now would answer her call.

She heard Rull yell out, "Do not hurt her!"

They backed up all the way to the wall of the balcony and Rhiannon peered over the side. All she could see was the water dripping down into the mist of the river. She doubted they could survive the fall. There had to be another way out. Suddenly a guard made it through Flath's block and stuck his sword halfway down the hilt through Flath's side. He grunted in pain and Rhiannon cried out in anguish. She felt something bite into her neck and brought her hand up to a dart that she quickly pulled free.

Flath turned to Rhiannon and mouthed her name just as he slipped and fell backward over the wall and disappeared into the mist below. "Flath!" Rhiannon cried! She peered down into the thick, white mist and could not see Flath at all. She bent her head back and gave a long, mournful wail of death that rang out over Castle Luisnich and all of Kyell. Then her world went dark.

CHAPTER
TWENTY

*"Under the utter darkness of the new moon and the
stifling heat of the jungle, we crept into the Ynny'
dagh castle of Kyell. My winged cat, Etâhpe'o-
poeso stayed by my side. She was my protector, my
love. We sprinted over the misty bridge and
crawled up the tiny glowing stone stairway hidden
across a sheltered wall. I was so afraid, but I knew
I must help this couple find their daughter, no
matter if it took my life."*

—*Diaries of a Lost Girl; Terran K-B.*

Terran had heard the sounds of fighting and could not contain her curiosity any further. If Flath and Rhiannon were able to kill King Rull, she wanted to see it. Carefully she climbed over the wall, Poeso following closely, and made her way to the room where she heard the fighting. But she was too late. By the time she got there Flath had been run through, and she saw him slip into the waterfall, and then Rhiannon gave her death cry and she too, fell to the ground. Distraught, Terran made her way back to the balcony where she climbed upon Poeso's back, and the giant cat took flight.

They flew over the foot of the waterfall but did not see Flath, so they continued on down the Ceò-Draoidh River. She could hardly see anything with all the mist, but finally, she spotted something. It was Luna! She wondered how the wolf had gotten out of Castle Luisnich. When they circled closer she could see Flath's body on the sandy bank of the river; Luna was still pulling him out of the water. They landed, and Terran jumped down and ran over to the man who had been so kind to her. It took all her effort, but she turned him on his side and was shocked to find him still breathing, though he was bleeding badly from a wound in his side. Terran touched his face, and it was cold and clammy. She knew just where to take him.

She looked up to Poeso who was wearing a concerned look on her feline face. "Take me to the horses, all right?" She jumped back onto the pax, and they leapt into the darkness. Terran was confident that Poeso understood her, so she was not surprised when they landed in the clearing where the horses stood giving her dubious looks. Jo Jo jumped up and down upon Zellan's rump and made a hideous screeching noise. Quickly she untied the horses, jumped on Jax's back (Zellan scared her) and they galloped back down the long path to where Flath lay dying. Jo Jo hung on to Zellan's saddle for her life and was silent for once.

Eventually, they reached the bank where Flath still laid motionless. Luna was loyally lying by his side licking his face. Terran tried for what seemed like forever to get Jax to lie down so that she, Poeso, and Luna could drag the man onto the back of his horse, but he just would not do as she asked.

Finally, with an uncanny sound of exasperation, Zellan shoved Jax out of the way and lay down next to Flath. Terran's big green eyes grew wide when the Archigos Warhorse turned his enormous head around to look at her as if to say, all right, I am ready.

It seemed to take the rest of the night, but after about twenty minutes of struggling, and with the help of the pax and the wolf, Terran finally got Flath's lifeless body onto the back of Rhiannon's horse. Exhausted, Terran crawled up onto Jax, and they were quickly away, following the river south. It took about an hour, but as the sun rose above the thick, steaming vegetation, they crossed a small bridge at the narrowest point of the Ceò-Draoidh River and rode up to a little house tucked up against Mouth Lonnyh. Terran gave a loud whooping call and slid off the horse.

"Is that you, Terran?" A woman of middle years opened the front door to her house and stepped out, her sightless eyes gazing about yet seeing nothing.

"Yes, Lady Stone. And I have brought you a customer!" Terran led Zellan to the front door. "Unfortunately, he is unconscious and upon the back of this horse..."

Lady Stone let out a gush of air. "Oh, that does sound serious." She thought for a moment. "Well, lead the horse inside to the bed, and I suppose we could drag him off onto the bed."

Terran nodded her dark head, "All right." She slowly led Zellan into Lady Stone's house, and toward the large bed, she kept for the sick. Zellan obligingly laid down next to the bed, and his back was surprisingly level with the bed so without much effort Terran, and Lady Stone were able to drag Flath onto the bed. He did not even make a sound. Jo Jo jumped onto the bed next to Flath and refused to leave. Luna lay at the foot of the bed and whimpered.

"Goodness, did this man come with all

manner of animals?" Terran laughed and then told the healer about the great winged cat called a pax. She went on to tell Lady Stone the whole story of what had transpired at Castle Luisnich and of the demise of Flath's wife, Rhiannon. The healer shook her head in sorrow and disbelief that anyone would come against King Rull.

"And they never did find their daughter. She must be dead, too, then," Terran said in a sad, small voice.

Terran hung around the house and did chores for Lady Stone and even helped care for Flath as he lay unresponsive for a month. Every morning when she woke up she was sure that Flath would be dead, but he lived on. His wound started to heal, and his fever eventually died away. Finally, one day in January he woke just long enough to drink and call out to his dead wife, and then he fell back to sleep. He continued on like that for a few more days, and then he was suddenly awake.

Flath started mumbling and pushing the blankets aside. Terran grew afraid that he would injure himself again. "Everything is going to be alright. You are healing in my cabin. You are safe now." Lady Stone's words were soft and soothing, but they seemed to have no effect on the man!

"I must get to Rhiannon. I must save her." His voice trembled, whether from emotion or from sickness Terran did not know. The young girl looked up at Lady Stone's face, a wrinkle of concern formed between her sightless eyes.

"Sir, I am very sorry to tell you, but your wife is dead." Terran sucked in a breath waiting for Flath's reaction. Lady Stone patted his shoulder as Flath looked up at her as if realizing she was there for the first time.

Terran jumped when he howled, "No!" With much effort, he pushed himself up and ever so slowly drug his legs off the side of the bed. "She cannot be dead. Rull did not want her harmed. She is alive, I know it!" He looked delirious with illness and grief.

"Please, Flath, lay back down. You will open your wound. You need heal." Flath smacked her hands away, and Terran backed away in fear. She knew the man was not strong enough to make it out of the house let alone back to Kyell. "Young Terran saw your wife expire. Please, get back into bed before you join her!"

Flath pierced Terran with his strangely mismatched eyes. "I can feel in my heart that she still lives," he declared as he slowly rose from the bed, his legs trembling under him. Luna started to whimper nervously as she watched him. Slowly he started to shuffle his feet towards the door. Etâhpe'o-poeso passed back and forth, and Terran could feel the cat's unease.

Lady Stone let out a sound of alarm as he moved away from her. "I must get to my wife...I must save my wife...," he mumbled over and over as he made a slow, shaky track to the door not caring that he only wore a dirty, stained tunic.

"Please, Flath, you must return to bed, or you will re-injure yourself. You were so close to death I was barely able to snatch you away from the darkness!" Lady Stone pleaded with him as she grabbed his solid arm. He pulled away from her hands with more strength than Terran thought he had.

Finally, as he neared the door Terran knew she must do something, so she dashed in front of him and held up her little arms to stop him. His trance seemed to shatter as he looked down at her as if he were just now recognizing her. "Terran," he whispered in confusion although he had just been looking at her moments before.

"Flath, it is true that Rhiannon is dead. If the king did not want her harmed, then something went terribly wrong because I saw her scream and fall to her death." Tears started to stream down the little girl's face as she was griped in the horrifying memories of that night—Rhiannon's death scream echoing through her mind. "I am sorry, Flath, but Rhiannon is dead. I saw it with my own eyes," she cried.

"No!" he yelled again. His hands were shaking, as were his legs. He put one trembling hand upon his chest. "I feel her in my heart. She cannot be gone," he sobbed. He turned his face up to the ceiling and let out a mournful bellow that broke her heart. From outside she could hear Zellan's answering scream. Luna lifted her huge head and howled making Terran break out in gooseflesh all over her body.

Suddenly Flath crumbled to the floor; Luna whined and licked the tears from his face. His whole body convulsed as his sobs rolled through the still room. Lady Stone quickly walked over to her cabinets and started putting different herbs into the special stone cup Terran had seen before. Then she ladled steaming water over the herbs and took a silver spoon and mixed it all up. She could hear the woman chanting a spell under her breath as she slowly waved her hands over the cup. Terran watched as a purple light started to flow from her hands and danced around the brew and then was suddenly gone. Terran had seen her do this before, but every time she saw it, it left her breathless.

Carefully Lady Stone brought the cup over to Flath and he put up no fuss as he drank it down quickly. Finally, she and Lady Stone were able to help him up from the floor and back to the bed where he fell into a deep sleep and stayed that way for weeks, only waking to take some broth now and then.

Terran knew her job was over, so she quietly climbed upon Poeso's back, and they took to the mild winter sky and disappeared.

***

Flath felt like he had been sleeping for an eternity, though he was exhausted to his bones. His side burned and was sore and gave him a stab of white-hot pain every time he moved. When he had opened his eyes, he found a kindly woman, her pretty face barely starting to fade into age, and Terran standing over him with worry, the fringe of her black hair brushing her small shoulders. The monkey, the wolf, and the pax were all there also—but his beautiful wife was gone!

Lady Stone relayed to him the story

Terran had told her about watching him fall from the balcony and seeing Rhiannon drop to the floor in death. He had felt like he was being crushed under an enormous weight. His heart cracked with every beat. At first, he did not believe it, but as the weeks went by and Rhiannon did not appear by his side, he became sure she was, in fact, dead. He had not thought Rull had wanted to hurt her, but she would have gotten away from him by now if she were still alive. He cried himself to sleep every night and sometimes during the day, too.

Jo Jo and Luna did their best to comfort him, and Lady Stone stayed out of his way, letting him grieve. He had not only lost his beloved wife but his precious daughter, also. If his battle wound did not kill him, his grief surely would.

His physical recuperation was taking a very long time, but his heart would never heal. He thought of his son in Ventra and wondered how he would tell him when he got older about how his father could not protect his sister or his mother—if he went back home at all. The thought of resuming his life as the King of Beaynid and raising his son alone was overwhelming. Mayhap he would just molder his life away in this jungle. Terran had flown off on that pax as soon as Flath had woken up. She had the right idea—just disappear into the jungle.

Winter came to a close and spring took over, not that you could tell in this jungle. There were no seasons here. Lady Stone pushed him hard to walk and exercise as much as possible. As she was blind, she had a man bring her supplies every few weeks, including fresh meat and the herbs she used for healing. He was surprised that she was of the Ynny' dagh and wondered why she did not live in Kyell. She did not offer the information, and so he did not ask.

After what seemed like a very long time sitting around Lady Stone's house or yard, he started to take walks in the jungle. Luna was always at his side and Jo Jo on his shoulder, as she used to perch on Rhiannon's shoulder. At first, the walks were short, for he got very winded and his side ached. As the months progressed, however, he would stay gone for most of the day, sometimes even bring back dinner for he and Lady Stone.

Eventually, he felt fit again, and his wound only pinched if he moved quickly in a certain way. He had lost his panther-headed sword in the battle, so he had no sword to practice with. However, he did not know why he even needed to practice. He still had not made up his mind whether he would bother to return home. Mayhap he would just take up drinking, and gaming in a tavern like Shih 'Ni had, and everyone would think him dead, also. Flath sighed, but Shih 'Ni was not a king. Flath had many responsibilities, and one of them was to raise his heir. He had no choice but to go back to his son.

One sunny May afternoon Flath and Lady Stone were relaxing in her yard under the shade of a broad-leafed tree. Jo Jo sat on his lap watching the older woman, and Luna lay napping at his feet, her diamond collar winking in the stray sunlight that poked through the leaves above them. Both of the animals had been grieving right beside him but still gave him their loyalty and support, for that he was enormously thankful. Even Zellan tried to cheer him up though he could see the great warhorse missed Rhiannon sorely.

As they sat on a gentle rise in Lady Stone's yard, Flath told her about what Màrrach was like and the great Archigos Warriors. He studied her as she sat and listened to his deep voice talk about his wife's people. He had long suspected her to be a relative of the Rulls— though he did not ask. Her similarity to the king and his brother were unmistakable. Her sightless, almond-shaped eyes were green; her pale skin was barely lined with age. Long, dark brown hair lightly veined with gray was kept pulled back with a red ribbon. Her dresses were always fastidiously clean and neat—as was her house.

"Your wife must have been a great warrioress to have been the Empress."

"She was! She almost killed me once."

"Oh!"

Flath laughed nervously at the shock on her face. "It was not on purpose...at least I think not. Anyway, she married me after that."

"Well, then it turned out for the best." Lady Stone looked at him and smiled kindly.

Finally feeling bold enough, he inquired: "I hope you do not mind me asking this, but I cannot help but see the resemblance between you and the king. Are you two related?"

Lady Stone turned her face down as if looking at her tightly clasped hands. Flath was immediately sorry that he was being nosey. "I am sorry. I should not have asked."

She looked up and smiled at him again. "I am the king's older sister."

"Oh." Flath had to contemplate that for a moment.

"I was to be queen, you see, after our father died. However, I did not want to rule in the same way that Ooilley did. He was obsessed with your wife's people and bringing them back to Dar' Ven. He considered it his mission. Eventually, he had our father killed and almost killed me, too. I lost my sight in the fight, but some sympathetic subjects hid me and then snuck me out of Kyell."

"Does he know you still live?" Flath was incredulous. How could a man try and kill his own sister...but did he not do the same?

"Oh, he knows. However, I am not a threat to him any longer. I would not want the rule anyway. I am too old to adapt to that life anymore."

It was then that Flath heard the sound of large beating wings and they both looked over to a sunny clearing where Poeso landed softly in the grass with Terran clinging to her thick, tawny fir, the great cat's diamond collar glinting in the powerful rays of the southern sun. It had been five months since he had seen the girl or the pax. He assumed that he would never see them again. She smoothly slid off the back of the pax and quickly ran up the rise to Flath and Lady Stone, Poeso padding behind her. She was wearing a ridiculously fancy dress to be flying around the jungle in. By the time she reached them, she was out of breath. Luna went up and rubbed up against the great cat who licked the wolf's head. Jo Jo jumped up onto Poeso's back and hugged her.

"Terran, is that you?"

"Aye, Lady Stone." She took deep breaths. "I have some wonderful news!" Flath could see the girl was so excited she was shaking.

"Oh? Tell us then, Terran." Lady Stone encouraged her.

"Rhiannon yet lives!"

Flath heard the words as they fell out of the girl's mouth, but it was as if he did not understand them. He blinked a few times, and both Terran and Lady Stone were looking at him with trepidation.

"What did you say?" he asked slowly trying to get his brain to work.

Terran grabbed Flath's arms. "Your wife is alive! I have just come from Kyell, and I saw her!"

Flath jumped up so fast he was dizzy. He sent Terran back, and she tripped and fell on her rear. "Where? Where did you see her?" Flath demanded and then realized he was too forceful. He tenderly picked Terran up from the ground and sat down with her on his lap. "Please, Terran, tell me everything."

"I like to sneak around Kyell sometimes. I can find nice clothes there. I heard something, and I looked up, and I saw Rhiannon standing on a balcony looking at the river. I could not believe what I saw, so I climbed up a tree, and I saw her again. She is in Kyell!"

Flath felt like he was going to be ill. He hugged the girl and sat her back down next to the pax. She had been waiting there for him to rescue her! Or mayhap she though him dead. Either way, she has been languishing in Rull's custody for almost half a year! "I must go to her right away."

"You cannot!" Terran pleaded. "For the king will kill you...again!"

Flath stood up, this time much slower. "I must go to my wife."

Lady Stone was already on her feet. "Come, I must show you something before you leave." She led him into the house and to her bedroom where she opened an ancient looking chest and took something from it. It was very long and wrapped up in cloth. She carried it back out of her bedroom and placed it on the table where they took their meals and carefully unwrapped it. It was a long sword made of polished stone. She lovingly ran her fingers down its dull blade. The thing should have been far too heavy for the woman to pick up, let alone carry around her house!

"A sword of stone?" Flath asked, confused. He looked at Terran, and the girl just shrugged her shoulders.

"This is a special sword." Lady Stone looked up at Flath, her sightless eyes wandering. "I created this sword to beat my brother. 'Tis stronger than his and has been blessed by our Goddess, Movue. I created it with Yun—our power as Ynny' dagh—along with my skill in metallurgy, alchemy, and geology. Why do you think they call me "Lady Stone"?" She laughed. "This sword is made of gems that will cancel my brother power. With this, you can defeat him."

Flath picked it up surprised that it was not

very heavy at all. Before his eyes, it turned from dull stone to a shining, lethal blade! He felt the hilt warm in his hand, and it gave off a very low hum that he had to concentrate to hear.

"I see it answers to you. Good. Now take it and kill my brother."

Flath was taken aback by this kind healer's words. Had she been waiting all this time for someone to come along that would rid her of her brother? Flath gripped the sword tighter, feeling it answer to the anger in his heart. He laughed, but it was full of danger, was devoid of any humor. "I will not only kill one of your brothers; I will kill them both."

***

It took Flath and Terran almost two weeks to make it back to Narrwin. Flath knew, even with his enchanted stone sword he would need help—the help of an Archigos Warrior. And Flath found this warrior in the exact same place they had left him six months before. Flath walked into the noisy, smoke-filled tavern (Terran had stayed outside with the animals) and his eyes roved around until he found Shih 'Ni sitting in a corner playing a game of chance, drinking ale.

Always the warrior, he sensed someone approaching him and Shih 'Ni's black eyes slid up to Flath. He could see apprehension in the Archigos expression when he did not spot Rhiannon. Shih 'Ni stood up and moved away from the table and wordlessly followed Flath to a relatively quiet corner. "Where is she?" His voice was low and calm, but Flath knew he was holding in much.

"Rull has her."

"You could not even protect her in the jungle?" he shouted, and a few people around them looked up but soon went back to what they were doing—getting drunk. Flath thought they were going to come to blows, but Shih 'Ni finally calmed down slightly and pinned him with a sharp look of dread. "How?" he demanded.

"We thought he took our daughter, so we confronted him, and he almost killed me, and I thought he had killed Rhiannon. All this time

I have been recuperating Rull has been holding her prisoner."

Shih 'Ni punched a wooden beam and said some choice words in Venn. "How could you take her to that demon, Rull?" The warrior balled his huge hands into solid fists. "Why did you not protect her?" he asked again, through clenched teeth.

Flath sighed for he did not have an answer for him—he had been asking himself the same thing for the past six months. However, he thought Rhiannon had not needed protecting...perhaps better reinforcements, though.

"What does he want with Rhiannon?" He finally spoke again, his voice more level— more lethal.

Flath blew out his breath. "He wants to create some kind of super race of Archigos and Ynny' dagh."

Shih 'Ni's dark eyes widened, and he saw fear on his usually reserved face. "Then we must go at once."

Even with the child—for she spent most of

her time in the air on the back of the pax, they made good time and arrived in Kyell a little over a week later. Just like before, they waited until the cover of night and then crossed over the mist covered Ceò-Draoidh River to the glowing Castle Luisnich as it sat at the food at Mount Lonnyh. Terran told them that she saw Rhiannon in the very rooms that they had met and fought Rull in seven months before. They left all three horses tied in the same spot and just as before, Jo Jo angrily protested being left behind.

Silently the three climbed the hidden stairway and climbed onto the balcony. Luna and Peso right behind them. One dark, one light: both men were here for the same woman they loved, and they would not fail to bring her home. Shih 'Ni's deadly Venturian sword glinted in the firelight and Flath's new sword of stone glowed lightly like the rest of the castle. It warmed in his hand once again as if to say it was ready to spill Rull's blood.

Motioning for Terran to stay behind them, they crept through the room. Flath vaguely noticed it filled with expensive looking furniture, paintings, and brightly colored rugs. Rull lived an opulent life here in the middle of Dar' Ven. In the back of his mind, he had been wondering why he would keep a prisoner in his personal apartments but quickly shoved the thought aside.

They were about to leave the room and search another one when they heard a woman's startled voice. "What are you doing in here?" she demanded.

Both men knew that voice intimately and turned around quickly. Rhiannon had been lying on a couch, but its back was toward them, so they had not seen her. Her head stuck up over the rim of the couch; her hand grabbed the plush fabric along the back with long nails painted blood red. Instantly Flath knew something was very, very wrong.

"You need to leave! My husband will have you both killed!" With effort, Rhiannon hoisted herself off of the couch and came around to face them. Flath heard a gasp and then realized it came from him. He looked at

Rhiannon's angry face then his eyes slid down to her swollen belly. Rage started to simmer at his spine, and he knew that it would soon be so bright and so hot that it might consume everyone in Castle Luisnich.

Shih 'Ni bravely strode forward and took her arm. "Rhiannon, we must go now. We must hurry." He pleaded with her urgently. She violently ripped her arm out of his grip and looked at him like she had never seen him before.

It was then that he noticed how she was dressed: she wore gauzy cloth of gold robes with sparkling anklets and toe rings, her toenails painted the same dark red. Her wrists were filled with golden bangles almost all the way up to her elbows. He was shocked to see the shell still hanging amidst all the bracelets. Her robes, flowing everywhere else were tight-fitting across her chest and very low cut showing her diamond-shaped birthmark and Archigos tattoos. Her neck still held Verna's Necklace and the emissary beads but was also home to a dozen or more golden necklaces.

Her diamond-studded nose ring had been replaced with a large golden hoop, and several rings of gold pierced Rhiannon's ears. Upon her head was a relatively dull circlet with a stone resting right on her forehead. The stone was glowing.

"Guards!" Rhiannon screamed out, and Flath jumped.

Beside him, he heard Terran, "Oh no!" The little girl yanked on Flath's arm until he looked down at her. "'Tis the circlet on her forehead. You must get it off of her!"

Flath nodded but before he could get to Rhiannon a handful of guards rushed into the room. Flath and Shih 'Ni fought them off with ease, especially with the wolf and pax helping.

As the last guard fell a woman ran into the room, her sword held ready. She was dressed like the other guards, and upon finding them dead, she started yelling out for more guards. Her long auburn hair was caught up in a tight pony-tale. She looked young, but that may have been a Ynny 'dagh trait. Her uniform had more decorations than the others, so she must have been the Head of the Guard.

In poured a dozen or more guards, both women and men. In the midst of battling Flath spared a second to look at his wife, she stood in the corner with her hand at her mouth. She really did not recognize him! Fury burned inside of him causing him to strike down any who come before him. It even dulled the tenderness of his almost fatal wound that he had suffered here but seven months earlier.

Finally, the last guard fell and heaving for air he turned to look at Rhiannon who now held a large dagger in one hand, and the other was placed protectively over her belly. "My husband will see you dead for this," she shouted with such venom Flath flinched. Standing next to her was Rull holding a sword almost identical to Flath's. Both held an eerie glow.

Flath looked over at Shih 'Ni who held the Head of the Guard at the point of his sword; her sword was on the floor. He looked around but did not see Terran. He figured the little girl had run off again. King Rull's brother's body lay not far from Shih 'Ni. That 'tis one Rull down, one to go, he thought viciously and started toward Rull.

It felt like fire burned in his veins, and both men's swords glow increased to a brightness neither seemed to even notice, for they were intent upon each other. Flath, being taller than Rull brought his sword down upon the man who came up and met him with a solid block. The swords almost screamed when they met, their humming increasing to an irritating level.

"I see my sister has finally finished crafting her sword. Too bad she did not try to come here and use it herself."

Flath took another swipe at Rull, and he quickly blocked it again. "You are in the habit of cutting down defenseless women?"

The sound of enchanted swords clashing in a fierce battle filled the room. Rull laughed, he was genuinely amused. "My sister is in no way defenseless, even as blind as she may be," he hissed as Flath came down on his blade.

Their blades clashed again and slid down

the shaft until Flath and Rull were face to face. "Not like your wife, however, who is very defenseless—and as you can see, going to be the mother of my child."

Flath shoved Rull so hard that he flew back and slammed against a table sending crystal vases and cups smashing to the floor. Flath was on him before he could recover and brought his blade down upon his arm almost cutting it off. Rull's enchanted sword fell to the floor and stopped glowing. Flath held Rull at the point of his blade as the man bent backward over the small table.

He heard a gasp, and he looked over at Rhiannon who had a desperate look on her face. But then, behind her, silently crawling up on to the couch was Terran. The little girl got right up to Rhiannon without her even noticing and as quick as the strike of a snake Terran ripped the enchanted circlet off of Rhiannon's brow.

Rhiannon blinked a few times and looked around the room, but it seemed like nothing was registering. Her apprehensive eyes went from Shih 'Ni to Flath to Rull and down to her protruding belly. A hard expression of rage came over her beautiful face, and Flath knew she was back. She tilted her head back and gave out a loud war cry, then, like a bolt of lightning, ran up to Rull who Flath still had pinned across the table.

Flath saw the anger and shame burning in her eyes, and he lowered his sword and backed away. This was her revenge to seek. She screamed again and plunged the dagger she had been holding into Rull's chest up to the hilt. His eyes sprung open wider, and then he crumpled to the floor.

Rhiannon began to shake and then sob. Flath took her gently into his arms. Shih 'Ni walked up to them with concern in his eyes. "We need to get her out of here," Flath said. Shih 'Ni nodded, and they started walking toward the door.

"Show us the way out," Shih 'Ni demanded of the auburn-haired woman that he had been fighting with, her sword now sheathed. She stood with her arms folded across her chest looking at Shih 'Ni.

Her shrewd hazel eyes slid down to Rull's body then up to Rhiannon. Flath could see shame on her pretty face. "I suppose with that degenerate Rull dead; she is our queen."

"I am going to take my wife back to Ventra, and you had better hope she does not return with both of our armies and wipe every single one of you vile creatures off this miserable continent." Flath's voice was low, and he spoke through gritted teeth.

A look of fear quickly passed over her face, but she did not move right away. "The council did not support the king and his brother's actions. We fought hard to control them, but they were...insistent," she sighed. She looked back over to Shih 'Ni as if she was searching his eyes to see if he believed her. Vaguely he wondered why she cared what Shih 'Ni thought of her.

"As a member of the council and Head of the Guard, I hold very little power and no sway over the Rull brothers." She tore her big eyes from Shih 'Ni back over to Flath. "If you chose to retaliate against us, know all of the rest of us are innocent." She lifted her chin in defiance. "I was always kind to your wife, and I was the one that informed Terran of what had become of her, so she could warn someone." She looked back over to Shih 'Ni, and this time Flath could see the warrior's face soften a little.

"Show us the way out, now!" Flath repeated Shih 'Ni's words. Her eyes shifted from Shih 'Ni to Flath with a look of defeat on her face.

Rhiannon did not speak or even acknowledge any of them as they left Castle Luisnich behind. Once back at the horses Flath made the decision to take Rhiannon to Lady Stone. Terran and Poeso had made it there well before their weary party, so Lady Stone had been told all about what had transpired and in what condition Rhiannon was in.

Flath and Shih 'Ni hovered over Rhiannon as Lady Stone examined her and laid her down to rest after she had given her some tea. "Physically she is fine, and 'tis obvious what has happened to her since she is with child, but emotionally this will take a very long time to come out of." Lady Stone gently explained to the men.

After two weeks Shih 'Ni announced that he would be leaving. He was going to go back to Kyell to find out what was happening there and report back to Lady Stone, for despite her earlier declarations, she was interested in what was to become of the rule of Dar' Ven, for it was her responsibility now.

Rhiannon had taken to sitting outside every day, watching the various animals scurry about in the jungle. Jo Jo always on her lap or at her shoulder. Luna and Poeso also refused to leave her. As Shih 'Ni was leaving he bent down and kissed Rhiannon on the top of her head, then he bent lower and whispered something into her ear. She looked up and stared at him for a long time but said nothing—she still had not spoken a word. Shih 'Ni tenderly touched her belly then kissed her on the cheek. Shih 'Ni then walked over to Flath and they clasped forearms, comrades finally.

"Take care of her. She will need you now more than ever."

"I shall. She will not leave my sight again—and before doing anything even mildly absurd, we will make sure to have our armies with us." Shih 'Ni shorted and nodded his head. The men smiled at each other and then Shih 'Ni climbed onto the back of his horse and rode away. Flath wondered if he would ever see the man again.

Over the next two weeks, the weather turned even warmer than it had been. Lady Stone and Rhiannon had gotten into the habit of taking long walks in the jungle as Flath had when he was recovering. They would be gone for hours and had the pax and the wolf not gone with them, he would have worried—and of course, he followed along close enough that if they yelled he would hear them. He knew Rhiannon needed her space. Every night they lay together, and every time Flath tried to touch Rhiannon to offer comfort she would stiffen until he took his hand away. He felt powerless and ineffectual. He was thankful she had finally started talking to Lady Stone, however.

Finally, one morning she turned to him in bed and smiled. "I'm ready to go home now."

Joy and relief flooded over him and he took her into his arms. "Let us go home, then."

It took a while for them to hire a reputable ship and crew to take them to Sona Tuath. Rhiannon did not want to dally there but was determined to visit Ghroc and find out from Journey-Of-The-Moon exactly what had happened to their daughter—for she was sure the Goyor would know. They did not have time to delay, for Rhiannon's belly grew more every day, and soon it would be unsafe for her to travel by horseback.

While they were waiting in Narrwin, Rhiannon called the Selkie Queen, and she came. They met on an isolated beach just east of the city. Rhiannon and Astrid sat and talked for most of the day. Flath wondered what a Warrior Empress and Selkie Queen would have to talk about but figured it was none of his business. He tried to strike up a conversation with one of the queen's guards who stood naked on the beach, but the man was not very conversational, so he wandered off and talked with Terran who had decided she wanted to see the world. She had gotten very excited when she had learned Rhiannon was actually the Empress of Ventra and they were also the King and Queen of Beaynid. The small girl had an affinity for fancy dresses, and she would soon have too many to choose from.

As the sun dipped under the blue horizon, the women finally stood, and Astrid gave Rhiannon a soft kiss on her lips then she disappeared under the waves. Flath walked up to his wife and took her into his arms. She cried. A long time later they walked back into Narrwin, and in the morning they left for Sona Tuath.

Almost a year after they had ridden out of Sona Tuath looking for their daughter they returned—without the princess. They rested for a few days, Flath met with the Viceroy and his advisors and apologetically explained they would soon be leaving again and that he would be in Ventra for a while. A message was sent to Teo down in Perth for him to come up and stay until Flath could return.

In the morning they left Sona Tuath with a handful of guards on their way to the hidden village of Ghroc deep within the Alba Forest. Flath could tell Rhiannon's righteous anger was simmering and would be unleashed upon the Goyor if they did not tell her where their daughter was. He hoped she was even still alive.

CHAPTER
TWENTY-ONE

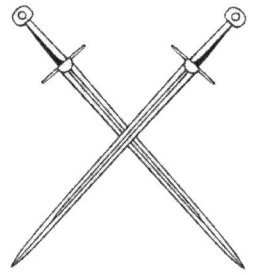

A little dragon she was given
Another voice
This little thing she will love
Only death will separate
Pink scales in the sun
This child will love
Are you here
Yes, I am

—Diaries of a Lost Girl; Terran K-B.

As they rode out of Sona Tuath, Rhiannon was not sure her relief came from getting out of that dreaded city or thankfulness for finally being on the way to Ghroc. Her baby moved and kicked all the time, and it was uncomfortable to stay astride a horse, even Zellan, for very long. Thank Verna that Ghroc was halfway to her ultimate destination: Ventra. She hoped she would not give birth on the side of the Vel 'Kur Mountains. They could have taken a ship and been in Ventra under a week, but she had to visit Ghroc first.

They traveled as fast as Rhiannon was able; They traveled northwest for a week and a half, then found a relatively narrow spot and traversed the brown waters of the Huntsman's River. On their left, they spotted the ancient clearing where the Tree of Jurr proudly stood with its ghoulish white bones dancing in the summer wind. Rhiannon looked over at Flath who was explaining what the tree was to Terran as she rode upon her horse, her eyes wide with wonder and awe.

A week north of the Tree of Jurr they arrived in the dense tangle of shrubbery that would lead them to Ghroc. With help, Rhiannon slid off of Zellan's back and, leaving the guardsman behind, she, Flath, Terran and the animals walked into Ghroc.

As if they had been waiting for her, Singing Brook, her younger brother Fox, and Bear Paw and his cousin Kaat were all standing in a shaft of warm sun. Rhiannon smiled at the children who had left toddlerhood and were now small children. They ran up to her all clamoring for her attention, but she kindly told them she had an important matter to talk to Journey-Of-The-Moon about. Rhiannon looked over at Terran who had gasped. "Their skin is so dark! They are so beautiful..." she whispered, mesmerized by the Goyor children.

When Rhiannon looked up the children were gone, and Journey-Of-The-Moon stood before her with a grim look on her elegant face.

"You know why I am here." She did not even try and soften her tone. Flath walked up beside her and took her hand.

"You seek information about your daughter."

"Where is she, Journey-Of-The-Moon? Rull told me that not only is Baobh still alive but she is the one that took our daughter."

Journey-Of-The-Moon sighed, and her face turned sad. "Did he tell you why Baobh sought to kill your daughter?"

Rhiannon's grip on Flath's had tightened. "No."

"The prophecy is not about you, my dear, it is about your daughter. She will be the one to end Baobh's wickedness."

"Where is she? Where is our daughter?" Flath demanded.

"I shall show you." Journey-Of-The-Moon bent down and started petting the top of Poeso's head. "My Lady, you have done so much already but can you show the king and queen the fate of their daughter." She then stood and held her hand out for Flath and Rhiannon to sit before the great winged cat.

Flath helped Rhiannon down to the

ground, and then he sat next to her. Poeso blinked those huge, uncanny eyes a few times and then she started to glow an amber color. Terran quietly sat down next to Rhiannon tightly holding on to Jo Jo. Poeso's shining got to be so bright all three had to shield their eyes, and then everything went dark. Rhiannon dropped her hand and gasped when she saw she was in a clearing with Baobh—or at least who she thought was Baobh, for the woman was pale like the moon. Fianna sat on a large rock, and Baobh brought her dagger down to run the small child through. Rhiannon cried out, but her voice was lost in the abyss. Suddenly Fire-Caller was there, and they struggled. He easily overpowered Baobh who fled. He tenderly picked up her daughter and then they were running through the forest. A clearing was up ahead, and Rhiannon saw his destination: The Tree of Jurr!

Fire-Caller did not even have to wait for the tree to open its portal since it had been the fall equinox when the child was taken. He entered the tree with Fianna in his arms. Huge tears ran down Rhiannon's face as she, too, was sucked back through the tree. She saw him run through forest and meadow and finally up to Daniel and Matthew's ranch house. He sat Fianna down, who was sleeping soundly and rang the doorbell several times. He hid in the bushes, and soon the door opened.

Rhiannon started to shake and sob when she saw Rosa open the door and take Fianna up into her arms. It was then Rhiannon noticed a strange amulet around her neck. Rosa gently took Fianna in her arms, kissed the top of her head and shut the door. Rhiannon buried her face in her hands and sobbed.

She felt both Flath's arms around her and Terran's little ones. When she opened her eyes again, they were all back in Ghroc, and Poeso was looking at her with concern. As quick as she could, Rhiannon got back up to her feet. She pointed an accusatory finger at Journey-Of-The-Moon. "How could you let him take my child away?"

"Rhiannon, we had to keep her safe. She has to fulfill the prophecy."

"I don't care about the prophecy! She is my daughter! She's just a baby!"

Rhiannon turned to Flath. "The tree is about ready to open again. We'll just go and get her." She was almost hysterical.

Rhiannon heard Journey-Of-The-Moon sigh, and she looked over to the Goyor. "The tree has been sealed, dear one."

"What? What does that mean?" Rhiannon's voice was carried through Ghroc, but she did not care that she sounded like she was crazy.

"That amulet you saw? It was given to her by us, and it is the only thing that will reopen the portal. When she is ready, she will use it to come home and fulfill the prophecy."

Rhiannon screamed as loud as she could: a sound of pure anguish. She ripped the emissary beads from her neck. "You are dead to me!" she screamed and threw the beads at Journey-Of-The-Moon's feet. The woman looked saddened and then she and the rest of Ghroc simply disappeared. Gone from Rhiannon forever.

Two weeks later they rode up to Tess's

large cabin in the woods. Rhiannon could tell that the Guardsman that had accompanied them all the way from Sona Tuath were disappointed they were not stopping in Màrrach—Terran was also grumbling about it. A step was produced, and Flath helped Rhiannon slide from the back of her warhorse. Stiff and sore she waddled up to Tess who was standing at her door with a wide smile on her kind face.

"Another royal baby on the way!" Tess clapped her hands together in delight. She must have seen the dejected looks on her and Flath's faces because her smile faded into worry.

"In a manner of speaking, I guess," Rhiannon replied and then turned to one of the Oread who was standing near ready for orders. "Please go to Màrrach and ask Kyia to bring my son here." The Oread bowed and was gone in an instant.

Rhiannon and her grandmother sat on her comfortable couch while an Oread made them some tea. Flath stayed outside with his guardsmen. She told her grandmother of everything that happened since they left Sona Tuath looking for Fianna. She recounted exactly what had befallen her at the hands of King Rull in Kyell—as that enchanted circlet took away her will but did not take away her memories. Rhiannon was overcome with shame and was happy that Flath had left him for her to take his worthless life.

Rhiannon looked through wet lashes as tears streamed down her face at her grandmother's kind eyes. The woman put her wrinkled, calloused hand on top of Rhiannon's hand; it felt warm and full of love.

"You will overcome this, Rhiannon, just as Kyia did. My granddaughters have strong spirits and wills. You girls could easily conquer the world."

Rhiannon laughed and wiped her tears. "Well, I don't know about the whole world, Grandma." Just then her baby kicked so hard it made Rhiannon jump. She took her grandmother's hand and placed it upon her belly.

Tess' eyes grew wide, and she laughed a hardy sound. "It won't be long now, and you'll be holding your little baby in your arms." Rhiannon smiled sadly. Did she even want to hold the baby in her arms? "Don't worry, my daughter, as soon as you see that babe you will know it is yours and it will lay claim to your heart just as the first two have."

Kyia and Tristan arrived just before supper. Kyia looked from her swollen belly up to Rhiannon's eyes and knew immediately that something was not right. However, she did not mention it. Tristan's little Oread nurse hurried behind the little boy as he rushed up to Kyia and immediately threw his arms around her legs almost knocking Kyia over.

Rhiannon was overcome with emotion at seeing Tristan again for the first time in a year. He had grown from a baby to a little boy! His skin was red-dark like all Archigos, as were his black eyes and straight black hair which had grown long enough to be pulled back into a queue. She wanted to squat down next to him, but in her current condition, she could not manage it. So she bent over and touched his soft, shiny hair. He looked up at her with his huge eyes, and she could tell he did not know who she was. Tears started to drip from her eyelashes, and she saw it was upsetting Tristan, so she walked into the next room where she flopped on the bed and sobbed. She heard Flath come in and softly shut the door behind him.

It took him a few days, but the boy finally started to warm up to Rhiannon and Flath. At night Flath held him in a rocking chair and sung to him the same songs he used to sing to the twins every night. Tristian stared up at his father with a contented, relaxed smile; it was as if he almost remembered the tune— perhaps he did. Rhiannon's heart ached for Fianna, and she knew Flath's did as well, but he was trying to be strong for her.

At some point, Tess must have told Kyia what had happened in Dar' Ven because her cousin never asked her to explain. It was going to be hard enough to explain to her Council (not to mention Beaynid) why their empress/queen has given birth to an elf child. She would leave that concern for another day. Perhaps her Archigos DNA would overpower the baby's Ynny' dagh blood like it does with other races, then she would not even have to mention what took place in Dar' Ven. She could only hope.

A few weeks later, Rhiannon felt that familiar twinge in her belly that soon grew to pain, which progressed to cussing Rull and feeling sure she was going to die. She labored all through the day, Flath holding her hand and tenderly encouraging her, Oread midwives ran in and out of the room and her grandmother kindly reassured her that everything was going smoothly.

Finally, as the sun was setting on a late September evening, the delicate child slipped from Rhiannon's womb. Just like before, Tess held this child up to the room in the dying sunlight that was streaming through the windows. "You have another daughter, Rhiannon! And Beaynid has another princess!" Tess announced then handed Rhiannon, her daughter.

Rhiannon looked down at the tiny, pale skinned baby with her brown hair and pointed ears and started to cry. Not because she was Rull's daughter, but because she was hers. All hers—she had killed Rull, after all. Flath tenderly kissed his wife's brow and affectionately caressed the top of the baby's head.

"What shall we call her—our daughter?" Flath asked as he smiled down at the baby.

That, of course, made Rhiannon cry even more. When she was finally able to catch her breath, she replied, "Lilly."

"Ah, Princess Lilly it 'tis then! 'Tis perfect, Greannmhor."

EPILOGUE

A fall sun slowly melted into the western horizon turning the sky over Màrrach a brilliant pink. The leaves had already fallen from all the trees in Ventra—except those in the solarium, of course. The air was cold, the wind blustery. Rhiannon stood on the steps of Màrrach in her thick, fur-lined leather tunic and breeches. She watched as the group approached from the east. They had landed at the Eastern Fort (which had become a pretty busy shipping and fishing port of late)

almost two weeks ago, so she knew they were coming—but why?

Flath was in Sona Tuath with Tristan, and she and Lilly were supposed to have followed them and then she heard her visitors were on their way. Now that the season was too late to take her ship across the Carnaid, she would have to book passage out of Turr' ah and then travel east on the King's Road all the way from Tel 'Rhia to Sona Tuath. Which would normally be an enjoyable journey, but with a four-year-old it was going to be hard.

Finally, the Ynny' dagh reached the courtyard and slid off their horses. Their strange flying creatures all started lighting on the ground all around them. They were something between enormous lizards or small dragons. Each one was a different color that sparkled in the dying sunlight. They were definitely not the strangest things Rhiannon had seen in the years since she was pulled through that tree from Montana into this new world. Jo Jo shifted nervously on her shoulder eyeing the little dragons.

Rhiannon looked at Kyia who was standing next to her. The younger woman smiled up at her trying to give her some confidence. Terran and Poeso stood next Kyia. The little girl had grown into a pretty young woman now, but she still had an affinity for those colorful fancy dresses from Sona Tuath like the one she wore now. Luna was standing at Rhiannon's other side, and she was glad for it. She had an irrational fear of these people—for she was surrounded by the mighty nation of Archigos, what could a handful of Ynny' dagh do to her—or more to the point, her daughter?

Finally, a woman approached Rhiannon and bowed low. "Empress Kossi, it is wonderful to meet you."

Rhiannon had to curb the insanely undiplomatic action of kicking her down the steps. Lilly, who had been standing behind her peeking around Rhiannon's hip stepped fully out from behind her mother and looked up at the woman in shock—someone who looked like her!

The woman looked down at Rhiannon's daughter and smiled brightly. "This must be Lilly. My, she has retained all of our features, remarkable!" the woman breathed.

Rhiannon scooped up her daughter and took a step back. Jo Jo squeaked and jumped down, and Luna started growling. "Why are you here?"

"I am sorry, Empress. Please let me introduce myself," the woman said, giving no attention to the wolf. "I am Pau Chib, and we are delegates from Dar' Ven." She motioned with her arm for the others to approach. As if they did not want to be there, the two women and two men hesitantly climbed the steps up to Rhiannon. "These are my associates, Kemul Tu, Bri, Omera Gyuum, and Fah Numl."

In the back of her mind, Rhiannon wondered why she left out poor Bri's sir name. She took a deep breath. "Now that we all know each other, why are you here?" Rhiannon did not even try to keep the frost from her hard words. It had been four years

528 † MELISSA E. BECKWITH

since she had been raped by that monster. She pinned them under her dark gaze and to their credit, even Pau started to look nervous. It had taken her years to recover!

Trying to compose herself—not a little offense crossed over Pau's delicate face—she took a step closer to Rhiannon and smiled at little Lilly in her mother's arms. "We are going to be the little queen's teachers and instruct her in the Ynny' dagh culture and our ways for when she reaches her majority and takes the throne." The woman's blue eyes slipped from Lilly up to Rhiannon as if to challenge her.

"What of Lady Stone? Is she not your queen?"

"Queen Omily, Lady Stone, as you call her, had no children, so she has named Lilly as her heir. Lilly will be our new Queen of Dar 'Ven." Rhiannon had to resist the urge to start screaming at the pompous woman. Goosebumps formed on her arms, and she felt chilled at the thought of sending her daughter to Dar 'Ven. She yearned for the feel of her sword in her hand.

Rhiannon took a deep breath. She knew this day was coming. She had word that lady Stone had, in fact, gone back to Kyell to rule until Lilly was old enough to take the throne of Dar' Ven, but she had put the thought out of her mind. She had hoped Lady Stone would have had an heir, so Rhiannon would not have to give up her child. Lilly was her daughter!

"It would be a much kinder thing for Lilly to be educated in our ways while she is still young than to just expect her to learn everything while trying to rule at the same time." Pau tried to give Rhiannon a friendly smile, but she looked more like she had just bitten into a lemon. "Oh, I almost forgot!" She turned around and made some funny noise, and one of those little dragons jumped into flight and landed softly in her arms. This was one was a bright, iridescent rose color and a quarter of the size of the others. "This young Sgàth is not much older than our little queen."

Rhiannon drew her brows together trying to consider whether or not the animal was dangerous and then it suddenly said, "Greetings, Lilly! I am Tuii, your Sgàth." Lilly squealed and threw her arms around its brilliantly colored neck, and Rhiannon let out a long sigh of defeat.

About the Author

Melissa has been writing books since before she had learned to read, in the form of picture books, and planned to be an author at age 4. She spent her youth penning short stories, poems and writing in her diary. At nineteen she married her high school sweetheart and started her family. She has spent her adult life raising her three children and teaching herself the business and craft of writing. Born and raised in beautiful Southern California she and her husband now live along the Ohio River in Indiana to be near their beloved grandson, Bryar.

Melissa enjoys the outdoors and nature, especially camping. She has an interest in the natural world, particularly the wonder of birds and bugs. She can't grow plants to save her life, though she likes to try. She loves art and paints a little herself. She has a great interest in history and plans on trying her hand at historical fiction in the future. Someday she hopes to travel the world starting with Scotland, Ireland, Africa and Australia.

Melissa loves to listen to heavy metal, Irish rock, and Celtic music...well, anything Celtic really. She loves dangly earrings, big rings, bright clothes, the color red, yellow roses, orange cats, and little dogs, like her fuzzy Shih Tzu, Abby.

Most days you will find her tapping away at her

keyboard, doing research for her next great novel, or catch her with her nose stuck in an epic fantasy or historical fiction story.

Melissa E. Beckwith

Fantasy Author

melissaebeckwith.com

Acknowledgments

This third book of the Sword of Rhiannon series was much more fun to write. I felt like I had a little more confidence and the words flowed a little easier. I want to thank all of you that have stuck with me through the first three books of this series. Thank you for believing in me and thank you for your continued interest in my stories.

A huge thank you to my beloved sister, Amy Marshall-Waddell for not only encouraging me and some wonderful ideas but also painstakingly proofreading all 72,000 plus words in this story.

I want to extend a hearty thank you to my hard-working editor, Courtney Cannon, from http://fiction-atlas.com/ who is also responsible for my beautiful cover design and making this book look fabulous with her formatting skills.

Thank you to my talented cover artist, Jackie Felix for bringing my visions of Rhiannon and Flath to life! You can find more of her breathtaking art here: https://jackiefelixart.deviantart.com/

I'd also like to thank Cornelia Yoder for my magnificent map of Ventra and Beaynid and her seas. It was so exciting to see my world take shape! You can find her at: http://www.corneliayoder.com/

A big thank you to the fun and accomplished Charles Renne from Under Production Multimedia at http://underproduction.tv/ for making me look so good in my professional headshot.

Thank you, Annie Beatty, from Mirrors and Chairs Salon for doing a terrific job of taming my tresses and making me look so spectacular for my photo! You can find her here:
http://www.facebook.com/annieatmandc

Please be on the lookout for the fourth book in The Sword of Rhiannon series, Daughter of the Forgotten Tree which should be out this winter.
Come explore my website at
www.melissaebeckwith.com.

While you're there, you can check out my calendar for book signings and release dates and read some of my short stories and poetry.
Don't forget to sign up to get updates!

You can also find me on these social media sites:

Facebook: https://facebook.com/caliprincess.beckwith

Twitter:
https://twitter.com/M_E_Beckwith

Instagram:
http://instagram.com/author_Melissa_E_Beckwith

Printed in Great Britain
by Amazon